# THE RISING TIDE

LIMINAL SKY: THE ARIADNE CYCLE BOOK 2

## J. SCOTT COATSWORTH

Published by
**Other Worlds Ink**
PO Box 19341, Sacramento, CA 95819

*This one is dedicated first of all to my Mom, who hooked me on sci fi and fantasy when I was a kid. It's all your fault, Mom, and I love you for it.*

*It's also dedicated to Mark, my husband of twenty-eight years, for always believing in me, even when I don't believe in myself.*

# CONTENTS

PART III
## FLIGHT

# ACKNOWLEDGMENTS

I WANT to thank my beta readers for the book—Daniel Mitton, John Michael Lander, LV Lloyd, Mary Newman, Amy Leibowitz Mitchell, and most of all Pat Henshaw, who captured what a couple others were feeling and gave it shape and form and helped me fix a glaring issue with the story and the ending.

Thanks also to Rory Ni Coileain for making my first ace character more authentic. Santi wouldn't be Santi without you.

I also owe a debt of gratitude to Ben Brock, Ryane Chatman, and Angel Martinez, who help run Queer Sci Fi and make the market for this kind of work stronger.

# ARIADNE

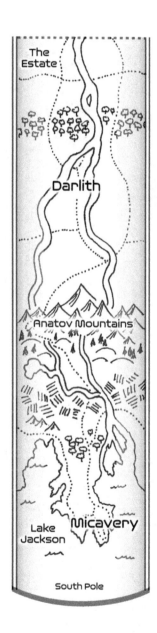

# PRINCIPAL CHARACTERS

**Aaron Hammond:** Oldest son of Jackson and Glory Hammond; Director of Forever Project 2160

**AnaLex:** The combined minds of Ana and Lex; see also Lanya

**Anastasia Anatov:** Crew on the *Dressler*, doctor/geneticist

**Andrissa "Andy" Hammond:** Daughter of Aaron Hammond

**Bella:** Andy and Shandra's daughter

**Colin Dale:** Son of Marissa and Matt (Matthew)

**Colin McAvery:** Captain of the Dressler, later Director of Transfer Station; retired 2160

**Davian "Dav" Forrester**: Eddy's ex and a systems specialist

**Eddy Tremaine:** Former military (NAU Marine Corps).

**Gordy:** Kid who worked for the Red Badge in New York City

**Gunner:** Another empath who has similar powers over the world as Andy and her family

**Jackson Hammond:** Engineer aboard the Dressler, later part of the world mind

**Jayson Hammond:** Younger son of Glory and Jackson Hammond

**Lex:** Ship-mind of the Dressler, later the World mind of Forever

**Lilith Lott:** Head of the Red Badge in New York, later was transferred into a bio mind

**Marissa:** One of the oldest of the Liminal kids
**Santiago Ortiz (aka Santi):** Sheriff's deputy in Micavery, son of Dana Ortiz
**Sean Hammond:** Aaron and Keera's second child and Andy's brother
**Shandra Clarke:** Traxx driver, later Andy's girlfriend

# FOREWORD

This is the second edition of "The Rising Tide," book two in the Ariadne Cycle *and* the Liminal Sky series. There are nine planned books in this series: books 1-3 will be rereleased in quick order, followed by books 7-9—the Oberon Cycle. Next year I'll start working on the middle three books in the series, the Forever Cycle, and I also have an offshoot series in the works.

I wrote "The Rising Tide" in late 2017 and early 2018, and it's either my fourth or fifth novel. See, I did this crazy thing where I wrote two trilogies at once, alternating between them *and* "The River City Chronicles," which I wrote as a blog serial before finally publishing it in book form. So it all gets kind of fuzzy timeline-wise.

"The Rising Tide" has a secret history of its own. My regular readers know I wrote my first novel, "On a Shoreless Sea," back in the mid nineties. It took place in the timeframe of what will eventually be the Forever Cycle, though the new books will bear only a passing resemblance to the plot of original book from the nineties.

There was a throwaway line in that book about a character named Davian the Betrayer, who had done something horrible to the world which I didn't bother to specify at the time. Still, that line stuck with me, and when I went back to write Forever's origin story, I made sure to include a shifty character named Davian who slips away into the crowd at the end of the book.

"The Rising Tide" is basically his story, though we never see it from his point of view. It's defined as much by his malign absence as anything—the way he warps the world around him—and his plans set off a series of events that change everything.

This isn't the only time a minor character in one of my books has popped up again later. These things happen to me with disturbing regularity.

In fact, keep your eye out for a throwaway character in Part One of this one who will become a major part of book three—"The Shoreless Sea."

So read on—and I hope you enjoy "The Rising Tide."

# PART I

## RENDEZVOUS

2171 AD

# PROLOGUE

ANA CLOSED her eyes, visualizing the seed ship's current trajectory. They'd rendezvous with 42 Isis in five days, their last stop in the solar system that had birthed mankind. Five years past, it had nearly been the location of its destruction.

The asteroid contained a high percentage of olivine, a mineral high in useful elements like oxygen, iron, magnesium, and silicon—a veritable feast.

Around Ana, the clean white laboratory that was her personal vee space domain was in perfect order, every surface spotless. A swipe of her virtual hand brought up an image of Forever, the long cylindrical generation ship hanging in the dark void of space between Mars and Jupiter.

The world sails had been pulled in, and Ana was in the process of nudging Forever into alignment with the asteroid, firing off excess bits of waste material to bring her into the proper trajectory. If all went well, Forever would end up with enough mass to finish build-out, along with a shield to help absorb space radiation on the journey to their new home.

*Thank God.*

Ana shook her head. *That* was clearly one of Jackson's thoughts. She even picked up some of Lex's thoughts at times. The original world mind veered off into philosophical territory to a degree that often surprised Ana—how an AI had become a philosopher poet.

The three Immortals, as they had jokingly taken to calling one another, were bleeding into each other more and more. It worried her.

This new second life was a gift beyond measure, certainly nothing she had ever expected. A chance to go with her creation across the stark divide, between the stars. But if the ultimate price was her own individuality, was it worth it?

She made a minor adjustment in the world trajectory, then shut off that part of her awareness. If she were needed, the system would let her know.

She slipped off through the conduits of the world mind to find Jackson.

The three Immortals had created a number of virtual worlds in vee space to pass the time when their skills weren't needed. While it was possible to create AI personalities to populate each of their various worlds, these constructs took a lot of processing power, and the Immortals had quickly grown tired of that game.

The worlds they built now were usually empty except for the three of them.

She found Jackson in Frontier Station, sitting all alone in the gardens. The blue-green ball of Earth, as it once had been, stretched out below him.

"You're bleeding into me again." Ana took a seat on the bench next to him.

He glanced up, his face drawn, his nose red and puffy. He concentrated, and the tears and puffiness went away. "Was I? Sorry. I was just thinking of Glory."

*Even in vee space, we emulate our old human selves.*

His wife, Gloria, had just passed away a few days before, after a protracted battle with cancer that the new world's facilities weren't set up to treat. So much had been lost in the flight from Earth.

They had agonized over whether to bring Glory into the world mind.

Jackson had requested it, but Ana and Lex, the other two Immortals, had both been against it. Their little team worked well enough together, and adding additional human minds was likely to muddy the waters. Besides, the mind only had so much capacity. It couldn't hold everyone within its confines. It hadn't been created for that purpose.

Ana sighed. She wasn't blind to the human cost of that decision. "She liked it here." She squeezed his shoulder. Jackson's vee space *was* beautiful, though it broke her heart to see Earth once again as it had looked before the Collapse.

Jackson nodded. "This is where we first met."

He must have been just as annoyed at her bleed-through thoughts. She was being insensitive again, considering all he was dealing with.

Being effectively immortal was turning out to be harder than she'd ever imagined. She put an arm around his shoulders and hugged him. "I am so sorry about Glory."

He regarded her in surprise. "Thank you. That means a lot."

"Ours is a lonely path. We must make sure they get where they are going. Nothing else matters."

He nodded. "I know. But it's hard. Good Lord, guide me."

Although she didn't believe in a higher power, she squeezed his arm gently. "I hope *he* does."

# 1

## A FOUL WIND

EDDY TREMAYNE rode his horse, Cassiopeia, along the edge of the pastures that were the last official human habitations before the Anatov Mountains. Several ranchers along the Verge—the zone between the ranches and the foothills—had reported losses of sheep and cattle in the last few weeks.

As the elected sheriff of First District, which ran from Micavery and the South Pole to the mountains, it was Eddy's responsibility to find out what was going on.

He had his crossbow strapped to his back and his long knife in a leather sheath at his waist. He'd been carrying them for long enough now—three years?—that they had started to feel natural, but the first time he'd worn the crossbow, he'd felt like a poor man's Robin Hood.

He doubted he'd need them out here, but sheriffs were supposed to be armed.

He'd checked with Lex in the world mind via the South Pole terminal, but she'd reported nothing amiss. In the last few years, she had begun to deploy biodrones to keep an eye on the far-flung parts of the world, but they provided less than optimal coverage. One flyover of this part of the Verge had shown a peaceful flock of thirty sheep. The next showed eight.

The rancher, a former neurosurgeon from New Zealand named Gia Rand, waited for him on the top of a grassy hill. The grass and trees shone with bioluminescent light, and the afternoon sky lit the surrounding countryside with a golden glow. The spindle—the aggregation of energy and glowing pollen that stretched from pole to pole—sparkled in the middle of the sky.

The rancher pulled on her gray braid, staring angrily at something in the valley below. "Took you long enough to get here."

"Sorry. The train was out of service again." Technology was slowly failing them, and they had yet to come up with good replacements.

She snorted. "One helluva spaceship we have here."

He grinned. "Preaching to the choir." Forever didn't have the manufacturing base yet to support anything close to the technology its inhabitants had grown used to on Earth. Which wasn't necessarily a bad thing, if you asked him. With technology came new and better ways to kill. He'd seen it often enough in the NAU Marines. "What did you find?"

"Look." Her voice was almost a growl.

Eddy looked down where she was pointing. "Oh shit." Her missing sheep were no longer missing. They had been slaughtered.

He urged Cassiopeia down the hillside to the rocky clearing. A small stream trickled down out of the mountains there. He counted ten carcasses, as near as he could tell from the skulls left behind. Someone had sheared a couple of them and given up. It looked like they had skinned and cut the rest up for meat, the skin and bones and extra bits discarded.

Gia rode down the hillside behind him.

"Didn't you report twelve sheep missing?"

She nodded. "Bastards took the two lambs. Probably for breeding."

"That actually might help us."

"How's that?"

He dismounted to take a closer look at the crime scene. "They'll have to pasture them somewhere. May make it easier to track them down."

"Maybe so." She dismounted and joined him. "This was brutal work. Look here." She picked up a bone. "Whatever cut this was sharp but uneven. It left scratch marks across the bone."

"So not a metal knife."

"I don't think so. Maybe a stone knife?"

He laughed harshly. "Are we back to caveman days, then?" It wasn't an unreasonable question.

She was silent for a moment, staring at the mountains. "Do you think they live up there?"

"Who?" He followed her gaze. Their highest peaks were wreathed in wisps of cloud.

"The Ghosts."

The Ghosts had been a persistent myth on Forever since their abrupt departure from Earth. Some of the refugees had vanished right after the Collapse, and every now and then something would end up missing. Clothes off a line, food stocks, and the like.

People talked. The rumors had taken on a life of their own, and now whenever something went missing, people whispered, "It's the Ghosts."

Eddy didn't believe in ghosts. He personally knew at least one refugee who had disappeared, his shipmate Davian. He guessed there must be others, though the record keeping from that time had been slipshod at best. He shrugged and looked at the sky. "Who knows?" It was likely to rain in the next day or so. Whoever had done this had left a trail, trampled into the grass. If he didn't follow it now, it might be gone by the time he got back here with more resources.

Gia knelt by one of the ewes, staring at the remnants of the slaughter. "Could you get me some more breeding stock? This... incident put a big dent in my herd."

"I'll see what I can do." He took one last look around the site. It had to have taken an hour or two to commit this crime, and yet the thieves had apparently done it in broad daylight. Why weren't they afraid of being caught? "I'm going to follow the trail, see where it leads."

Gia nodded. "Thanks. We're taking the rest of the herd back to the barn until you get this all figured out."

"Sounds prudent. I'll let you know."

Slipping on his hat, he climbed back up on Cassie and followed the trail across the stream toward the Anatov Mountains.


ANDY STEPPED BACK to look at her handiwork.

The wooden trellis climbed about forty feet, interlacing with three others high above, each "arm" as thick around as her leg. She'd been working on this monument for weeks, crafting each part by hand, her mind *reaching* deep into Forever to touch the world mind and its latent routines. Each of the trellises was shaped as one of the six continents back on Old Earth, a memorial to where they had come from. Though she had never been there, she had seen it often enough, and one of her friends at the South Pole station had printed out a map for her to work with.

The Darlith Town Council had commissioned her to do the work, transforming a sparse square into a work of art and a gathering place for the town. She had two more pieces of the sculpture to grow, but she was about done for the day. The work took a lot out of her.

Once it was done, she'd apply a sealant and polisher to help preserve it against Forever's limited elements.

Around her, the city bustled. The All Faiths Church had just let out, and congregants were on their way home or out to lunch in one of the cafes that dotted the riverside.

"It's beautiful," one of the women said, stopping to stare up at it.

Others frowned and hurried on. Not everyone wanted to be reminded of what they had lost.

There was a pile of waste she'd trimmed from the sculpture and would have to haul over to one of the town dissolution pits when she was done, where it would be dissolved and repurposed. Nothing went to waste in a closed ecosystem like Forever.

Andy wiped her brow with the back of her hand and took a sip of water from her canteen. It was standard-issue, made from metal extruded by the world mind and stamped into shape. Forever's production had taken on a decidedly utilitarian cast since the Collapse, as the colonists had suddenly had to do without any supplies from Earth. The world was not ready to be self-sufficient, and yet here they were. Andy saw it as her duty to bring a little beauty into a world that was basically operating at a subsistence level.

*Call from Colin,* the world mind whispered in her head.

"I'll take it." She tapped her temple to accept the call and wondered what Lex, Ana, and Jackson thought of her little art project. "Hey, kiddo." Colin's jovial voice through the loop connection made her smile.

"Hey. Where are you?"

"We're coming down to Darlith today to sell some produce at the market. I heard you were in town."

Her father, Aaron, asking Colin to check up on her. Andy grinned. "Yeah, working on the art thing." It had been a hard sell with the Darlith town council, until she'd offered to do it in exchange for room and board. "It's coming along nicely. Here, take a look." She sent him a capture of her own vision.

"Oooh, that's beautiful. Pretty good for a girl who never made it down to Earth."

"Thanks. I have a good map. When are you arriving?"

"In the morning. Want to meet us there? Stall 72."

"Of course. Tomorrow's perfect. Gives me a chance to clean up. I'm a mess now. This is sweaty work."

He laughed. "Can't be nearly as difficult as building latrines for a tent city."

"Maybe not, but this takes a lot more concentration." She wanted it to be right so future generations would be able to look at it and remember the world their ancestors had come from.

"Is Delia with you?"

"No, she stayed back at Micavery." It was weird sleeping alone, but she'd be home soon enough. "The fabrication center keeps her busy."

"It's amazing what they're doing over there. Have they cracked a new loop yet?"

Andy shook her head. "No, that's fiendishly difficult with the materials and tech level we have right now. Most of their time is spent on new plant and animal hybrids and on medicines to combat the viral and bacterial bugs the refugees brought up with them."

She could hear his mental sigh. "Yeah, I'd hoped we were free of the common cold forever."

She laughed. "'Fraid not. See you tomorrow?"

"Sounds good, kiddo. I'll bring you some berries from the estate." There was a double click in her head as he signed off.

She grinned. McAvery-Trip red berries were the sweetest in Forever.

Andy checked the time. She had just enough to get back to the house where she was staying before the ceremony began.

She missed her grandmother. Glory had been a beautiful woman, inside and out, even in her final year. Andy had been with her that last night, holding one hand while her father held on tightly to his mother's other one.

Today they would honor her memory.

DAVIAN WATCHED as Gunner sealed up the rock wall behind his little raiding party, "growing" the rock via tiny capillaries that the human eye could barely see. The man was a marvel, able to manipulate the world in ways that would have made him a god, if he weren't so badly damaged. As to his real name, Davian hadn't a clue, but Gunner had been his dog when he was a kid, and the name seemed oddly appropriate.

"Good boy." Davian tousled the man's hair.

Gunner smiled weakly.

Davian fished in his pocket for one of the fungus "candies" they'd started growing back at camp, with Gunner's help. The man took it eagerly and put it in his mouth, chewing on it contentedly.

Gunner rarely spoke. Who knew what kinds of thoughts, simple or otherwise, went on beneath that bland exterior?

It had taken a stroke of luck for Davian to figure out that the refugee had such a connection to Forever. He'd caught Gunner playing around with his power, using it to make little twisted men out of extensions of the roots that grew far under the world's surface. Like that Andy girl and her father. He'd known then that the man was something special.

The others of the hunting party stood in silence, awaiting the orders of the Preacher.

Davian grinned. Being called the Preacher suited him. He wasn't quite ready to claim godhead status. Not yet. "Come on. I want to make camp within the hour." He'd taken his men on a raid to sharpen their skills and to get some red meat. It was good to feed killers on red meat. It made them stronger.

The wool was a secondary benefit, as was the fear and uncertainty his little raid would sow in the above-grounders. They had no idea how to run a long-term, functioning society. They didn't have the skills to keep control of the human impulse for centuries at a time until the ship reached its destination.

"Come on, Gunner." Over time and hundreds of brief conversations with the man, he'd worked out that Gunner had been sent up there as a weapon by the Sino-African Syndicate to bring down the project by destroying Transfer Station.

It still made Davian whistle whenever he thought about it. He'd been one of the few human witnesses to the catastrophic destruction.

Gunner had inserted the virus into the station-mind, the one that had killed it and then blown the station's core. That Gunner had done it, mentally handicapped as he was… he was a powerful weapon.

Gunner had been picked up on the streets of Spokane by the Sino-African intelligence and pressed into service as the war was heating up.

Davian knew firsthand some of the methods that the Chafs would have used. He still woke up some nights screaming, thinking he was in the hotbox.

No matter now. The Chafs were gone to blood and dust, and they'd unwittingly left him the key to taking over this new world.

Now he just had to figure out the best way to use it.

AARON STARED out the window of his office at the gently waving, glowing branches of the Mallowood trees.

Today was the day. His mother was gone, and they would celebrate that fact with some kind of ceremony that Keera had whipped up. It rubbed him wrong, somehow, to think about *celebrating* Glory's death.

His office was a far cry from the white, pristine office he'd had on Transfer Station. Here almost everything was made of native wood and other local materials, lending the office a warm, almost golden radiance.

Of course, it was aided by the glow from the plants and the sky outside. At this distance, the spindle—a stream of windswept pollen that provided a diffuse glow over the whole world, augmenting the plant light—was almost uniform. It obscured the view of about a third of the world above his head.

It had taken him the better part of six months on the ground to get used to that strange and wonderful vista—the sight of the world curving up around him like a great multicolored patchwork wall, cresting like a wave far above his head. Now he rarely noticed it, though some deep animal part of his brain still grumbled about it from time to time.

Once he'd relied on his AI for data. Now, his reports were mostly on paper. Sure, the colony still had technology—the world mind itself was a supreme achievement of Earth's high-tech society—but they no longer had the infrastructure to build so many things they had come to rely upon on Earth and at Transfer Station.

His train to Darlith, for instance, that would likely never go any farther.

The Collapse of the Earth had come on too quickly for neat planning and careful stocking of equipment and supplies. It was left to the survivors to figure out a way to make it all work.

Some reports did come in over the network. Most people still had loops in their temples, though those that malfunctioned couldn't be replaced. He took this information down on paper, by hand, using graphite pencils made at the fabrication center. At least they could manage that much.

There were more reports of Ghost activity all along the Verge. From the sheep slaughter that Eddy was out investigating to petty larceny—clothing stolen off the line, crops raided, etc.—things were getting tense. There'd even been a fire along the foothills of the Anatovs, which the world mind had quickly put out with some well-timed rainfall.

*The Anatovs.* Aaron shook his head. That had been a hard name to get used to. He could still see Ana's face when he closed his eyes. She had let herself be subsumed into the world mind as he held her in his arms, deep in the bowels of the world.

She was still alive, in a sense, and his mother, Glory, was dead.

He spoke to Ana from time to time about matters important to the colony, such as the upcoming asteroid rendezvous, and she was still the same cantankerous genius she'd always been.

He turned his attention back to the reports on his desk. There was something going on out there, and it bugged the hell out of him that he didn't know what it was. A rising tide of strangeness.

There had been personnel disappearances, too, over the last six years, in addition to the surprising undercounts at the refugee camp after the Collapse. Aaron was sure it all added up to nothing good. He needed more data.

Aaron sighed. He was putting it off. He knew it, but he had to get going.

"Hey, Dad." Andy's voice came through his loop. "You ready?"

"Yeah. I suppose so." He'd spent the last month fighting with the world mind—with his own father even—begging for them to take Glory in. She didn't have to die, not forever. His father was proof of that.

But Jackson had been steadfastly against it. "It's not fair," his father had said. "We can't save Glory because we can't save them all. And she would never have it."

They'd kept the knowledge of Jackson's existence in the world mind from his wife. From just about everyone, actually. Few people knew about any of the Immortals. Now Aaron wondered if that hadn't been a mistake. In the end, he and Andy had been there for her as she departed this mortal plane, although Jackson had stolen the last few moments from him.

Jayson, Aaron's younger brother, had been the first of his nuclear family they'd lost—God rest his soul—in the War on Earth. Now it was just him and his immortal father.

Andy pinged him. "Can I *ride* along?"

"Of course." He felt her slip in alongside him in his mind as he opened his senses to her so she could see what he saw and hear what he heard.

Feel what he felt.

It wasn't true telepathy, but it was as close as he'd ever experienced, a product of Jackson Hammond's gift to his children and grandchildren.

He put the papers away in a folder in his desk and left the room, glancing out the window once more at the serene scene outside. Jayson would have liked it here.

Andy agreed.

He closed the door softly behind him, and they went out to find Glory's friends.

# 2

## LIGHTS IN THE WIND

LEX SOARED over his world, his golden eagle wings extended to ride the trade winds. He had taken his male form, exulting in it. Some days he discarded gender altogether, flowing through the day without worry for which side of himself he was presenting.

Far below, Earthsea stretched out for hundreds and hundreds of miles, smaller and larger islands dotting the azure blue.

He'd taken inspiration for it from an Old Earth sci-fi series, one that spoke to him even if it was just bits of ones and zeroes representing the printed characters of mankind. These humans, some of them at least, were adept at painting pictures using only words, stretching a twenty-six-character alphabet and some assorted punctuation across canvasses as wide as a world. Or larger.

He liked to go there when he was feeling stressed. To soar, to swim, or just to bask in the sunlight for a few moments. It helped him clear his head.

Only part of him was here, of course. The rest was still grounded in the world mind, running its processes, responding to its needs.

Lex shifted his perception. He had no eyes, per se, but he could see through the eyes of the humans he carried, those with loops and those with augmented abilities. Those who allowed it, anyhow.

He also had a small army of biodrones.

Lex could see the universe outside as well, through the sensors embedded on the flanks of the world. The universe mankind could no longer see and might one day forget altogether.

The sun was just a small ball of light from here. Five years of travel had brought them out to the asteroid belt, to their last stop before leaving Sol and her planets behind. The seed ship had been in slowdown mode for weeks as they matched velocity with Isis.

Lex went back to his sanctuary, settling down on a small island whose volcanic cone towered above a black sand beach. His wings disappeared, and his feet crunched on the sand, the waves lapping over them to leave a foamy rime on his toes.

"Who… who are you?"

Lex turned to see a woman standing on his beach, staring at him, her eyes wide open. The woman had black-and-silver hair and copper-colored skin. Lex would have guessed her age to be in her late sixties or early seventies.

He was as startled to see her as she was to see him.

"Are you an angel?" Her mouth was wide open.

Whoever or whatever she was, she *couldn't* be here. It was impossible. Lex checked his subroutines. There were no AI personality files running in his Earthsea sim. And yet… "I'm Lex. And… who are you?"

"Glory." The woman stood up taller, as if uttering her own name had given her back some of her confidence. "Glory Hammond."

Lex didn't pay much attention to the goings-on in the human world, but he knew who Glory was. "You're—"

"He's gone. Jackson. I can't find him."

*How are you here?* "I don't understand—"

Glory vanished. A wave washed over the sand where she had been standing, wiping away her footprints.

*How strange.* Jackson would know what was going on. Or maybe Glory was one of his memory figments, bleeding through.

Lex slipped off to look for him, checking all his usual haunts.

There were telltale signs in the system that would usually lead Lex to him, even when he had shut himself off to work on something. Or to mourn, a human emotion he had only truly come to understand when Ronan, the Transfer Station mind, had died.

Lex searched for Jackson with growing concern.

He couldn't find the other immortal anywhere. Lex felt a rising sense of panic, something he wasn't used to and frankly didn't like much.

Ana. He had to tell Ana. Then they could figure out what to do.

CASSIE CLIMBED the foothills at the edge of the Verge, carrying Eddy up toward the Anatov Mountains. The horse seemed to enjoy being out there in the wilds. As wild as they could be on a man-made world.

Eddy stared up at the vast peaks that towered above them. Even after six years, Forever still had the capacity to surprise him. It was hard to accept that the world—built on such a grand scale—was the work of the hands of man. Or woman. *The* Anatov—Ana Anatov—who had gifted her name to these peaks.

The foothills were sparsely planted, mostly a crabgrass variant that spread on its own, and occasional wildflowers—though to call anything on Forever "wild" was a stretch.

There were only scattered trees up there. The glowing grass had been beaten down along the path of the marauders, creating a dark and ugly stain across the hills.

It was hard for Eddy to imagine anyone doing something like this on Forever. He'd seen enough of the crimes of humanity when he'd fought in the wars that had consumed Earth in her last decade. But his world was *supposed* to be different.

The world was like an island among the stars. Where was there to hide?

He checked his loop for the time. It was close to nightfall. His circadian rhythms had adapted, aligning themselves with Forever's days and nights, but he missed things like *cold* and *hot*. On Forever, it was always temperate, a side effect of the seed ship's living architecture. It never snowed, and it was most certainly never hot.

He climbed to the top of one of the rolling foothills and turned to look at the world behind him. From here, he could almost see the South Pole, the wall that marked the end of Forever. Around him, the walls of the world curled up to meet high above, their point of merger hidden by the sky glow.

Micavery was too small to see at this distance.

He'd come all this way on horseback, while traveling inside a ship floating in the void. It was surreal. He supposed future generations would come to see it as normal, everyday even—but he was still an Earth boy at heart.

The grasses around him went dark, as did the glow that emanated from the middle of the sky. Nightfall swept toward Lake Jackson far below, passing the Verge, the ranches and farmlands, and the orchards where so much of the world's food came from.

At last, the shores of the lake winked out, and he could finally see Micavery Port, the lights of it, anyhow, as they shone in the newly come darkness.

Above, the golden glow of the spindle had diminished to a silver gleam.

He sighed. It was such a beautiful world, but it seemed it still harbored some of Old Earth's evil. Wherever mankind went....

Eddy dismounted, lit a lantern full of luthiel, and set about making camp.

IT WAS time for Glory's ceremony. Aaron had been avoiding thinking about it all day, but his mother kept creeping into his thoughts.

He followed the path that wound through Micavery Port down toward Lake Jackson. The town had doubled in size after the influx of refugees during the Collapse, as everyone was pressed into work gangs to build housing for the new and unexpected population.

Two little girls ran past him, shrieking.

Aaron laughed. It was good to have so many new children in the colony. Though he supposed they were a colony no more.

People were doing what people did when there was space to be filled. They'd managed to keep up with growth on the food-supply end—barely—but at some point they'd have to look at some kind of population control. Another one of the long-term plans that had to be sped up to stabilize this new world.

Keera met him at the village green, under the tall antenna that supported the colony's communications. They'd need more of them, eventually—another pressing problem that was put off until another day, when they could find the time to build the infrastructure they needed to manufacture that kind of tech.

"Hey." He kissed her on the forehead.

"Hey there. Rough day?" She massaged her belly unconsciously. She was five months pregnant with their second child.

Even the director wasn't immune to the pressures of his base humanity.

Keera had insisted on keeping up her work responsibilities running the fabrication center, and Aaron knew better than to push.

"Yeah, a bit. More Ghosts." He was sick of Ghosts.

Hand in hand, they walked down to the wharf.

"That again? Half of those are just folks forgetting what they did with their stuff. Or not wanting to admit how they screwed up and lost it."

Aaron nodded. "But if even half of the rest are real?"

"The marauders?"

"Yes." Aaron was worried about the growing lawlessness. They were only two steps away from chaos.

"Enough time to worry about them tomorrow. Tonight, we're honoring your mother." She squeezed his arm and leaned her head on his shoulder.

"I still don't understand."

"Why your father wouldn't take Glory into the world mind?"

"Yes. It's been a great comfort to me knowing he's there. Talking to him when I'm lost. When I don't know what to do."

"He has his reasons." She sighed. "I know that doesn't make it any easier."

"No, it doesn't." It was hard enough knowing Glory's body had been reclaimed in one of the dissolution pits. They had to come up with a better name for those. Her constituent parts were now a part of the world around them. There was no room to bury the dead. She was truly lost to him now.

He hadn't spoken to Jackson since his mother had died, and every time he thought of it, it made him angry. Even Ana had been accepted into the mind —the woman whose actions had taken away Aaron's father so many years before. So why not Glory?

"Let it go. Just for tonight." Keera kissed him on the cheek.

He nodded. She was right. Keera was almost always right, but that didn't make it any easier.

"Aaron, look!" She let go of his hand to run down toward the dock.

Hundreds of people were waiting by the water of Lake Jackson, each one holding one of the new candles Keera had made, the ones that burned clean without any smoke. The crowd parted as he approached, clearing a space for him along the wooden pier that jutted out into the lake. "Are you seeing this?" he whispered to Andy. His daughter had been riding his mind in respectful silence.

"It's beautiful." He could hear her tears.

He wiped his own eyes with the back of his hand. "It is." His mother would have loved this.

People touched his arms and shoulders as he passed, whispering condolences.

"So sorry for your loss."

"She was such a sweet woman."

"You okay?"

"I will be," he said to the last.

Aaron reached the end of the pier and turned to survey all the waiting faces. He checked his loop—he had about three minutes.

"I am happy to see all of you here. To realize how many of you my mother touched in her time at Transfer, and later on Forever."

Keera handed him a candle. Aaron held it while she lit the wick with her own.

He held it up in the air. "Like her name, she was a bright light in the world. Mama, I miss you. God is waiting in heaven for you." The last bit trailed off in a sob, but he didn't care. He'd not been as religious as his parents, but right now he could use a little old-fashioned faith that she was in a better place.

Keera squeezed his arm. "May I?"

He nodded and stepped to the side.

"Later on, we'll tell each other about our memories of Glory." She held her candle high. "But nightfall is upon us. Each of your candles has an apparatus attached to a hinge. Please rotate the hinge like this." She demonstrated. "This will make an air sail."

Aaron looked down at his own candle in wonder and smiled gratefully. When had she had time to arrange this? He raised his own candle's sail.

"Here comes nightfall!"

The light of the world dimmed all around them, the trees and grasses and cattails fading, and within thirty seconds it was dark. The jetty was lit only by a few lanterns and by more than a hundred candles.

Keera's face shone with a golden glow. She lifted her candle again. "Love you, Glory," she whispered so softly that only Jackson could hear.

Then she let the candle go. It floated into the air over the lake, drifting up into the darkness. Soon it was followed by another and another, then tens, hundreds of them.

Aaron held his up. "May God find you." He let his go and looked up into the sky. It was filled with lights.

He pulled Keera close. "It's so beautiful. How did you—"

She put a finger over his lips. "Leave me a few secrets."

One of the lights flared, an incandescent supernova in the night, and then it was gone.

"What the heck?"

"Watch."

There was another, then another, and suddenly the sky was full of flares.

Glory really would have loved this.

Aaron closed his eyes, remembering the last time he had seen her:

Glory held his hand.

"I'm here, Mama."

"Jackson?"

A strange surge had run through him, and suddenly he was a bystander in his own body.

"Yes, Glory, I'm here."

Aaron looked on as if over his own shoulder, feeling paralyzed and angry. How had Jackson done it? And why? This was *his* time with his mother.

"I knew you'd come back to me." Glory cupped his face with her hand.

"I wouldn't let you go into the night alone."

Jackson squeezed Glory's hand and kissed her forehead. "I'll see you soon." Then everything had gone black.

When Aaron had come back to consciousness again, Jackson was gone from his head, leaving a bad taste in his mouth.

When Aaron looked down at his mother, he saw she had gone too.

His father had taken that final moment from him and then had vanished from his mind without a word.

Keera was right. He would let that go, for the night.

Tomorrow he was going to find his father and give him hell for it.


ANDY SAT BACK in her chair at the River Bend Café looking over the Rhyl, sipping a cup of morning brew, or embrew, as the locals had taken to calling it. Some folks still yearned for the days of coffee, but Andy had tried it once and thought the whole thing was wildly overrated.

She stared out over the river, visible in the darkness by the lanterns hung along the Riverwalk. People passed by in couples and small groups.

Glory's ceremony had been beautiful, but she was uneasy about her father's mental state.

Few people knew about this thing they could do, riding on each other's perceptions. They'd discovered it by accident, about a year after the Collapse, when they'd been rock climbing in the Anatov Mountains.

Her father had been right below her.

She'd slipped on a rough footing, sliding past him, and he had reached for her....

And then he'd been in her head, grasping at a handhold and bringing her slide to a stop.

She'd never known if she would have survived without his help—but in that moment, they'd discovered a new way to connect with each other.

Her father was so upset by her grandmother's death, and by her grandfather's response to it. Normally he didn't let her see what was going on *behind the curtain* when she rode with him. But he'd clearly been distracted and had forgotten she was there.

When the ceremony had ended, she'd backed out of his mind quietly.

Why wouldn't Jackson want Glory to be part of the world mind?

It puzzled her. Her father hadn't spoken a word about it to her over the last few weeks, but clearly it was something that had been eating at him.

She closed her eyes and sought a connection. *Jackson?*

She never really called him Grandpa. He'd only been a ghost to her, an online companion, and his name had always seemed a more natural way to address him.

There was no answer. Maybe he needed his space too.

Andy resolved to talk with her father about the whole mess when she got back to Micavery.

She finished her embrew and sandwich and made her way back to the little house where she was staying while she worked on her art project.

The McHenrys, her hosts, were a nice couple who had come up as refugees and now ran a small laundromat out of their home on the outskirts of Darlith.

She had promised to improve the place in exchange for lodging and breakfast, but she had her work cut out for her. It was gonna be a long night.

# 3

# GHOSTS AND MARAUDERS

ANA WAS deep in consultation with Keera about improvements to be made to some of the feed crops in the next release when she felt someone else's presence in her lab.

"Those are all great ideas." She wrapped up her notes and flicked them back into her archive, and they popped and vanished. "We're in rendezvous mode, so things are hectic now. But I'll see what I can do when I have a moment." Keeping an ecosystem in balance—especially a small closed one like Forever—required constant small changes to keep the trend line running straight down the middle. If things got too far out of whack, they could rapidly spiral out of control.

"Thanks. Will we feel the effects of the rendezvous here?" Keera's disembodied voice floated through the air.

"Maybe a slight bump. If all goes smoothly, the disruption will be minimal, but there are always risks when you bring together two large objects in space. We'll do the best we can to warn you ahead of time."

"Thanks."

Ana paused. "It was a beautiful ceremony."

"You saw it?"

"Yes. Through one of the other colonist's eyes."

"Did Jackson see it?"

"I don't know." Keera was one of the few people who knew about the split identity of the world mind.

"Tell him hello for me." Keera was a peacemaker, always trying to bridge the gap when the people in her life were at odds. Ana admired that about her.

"Will do." Ana cut the connection. "You're lurking," she said without looking up.

Lex emerged from the shadows at the edge of the lab. "I didn't want to intrude."

"Appreciated. What do you need?" She turned to give Lex her full attention.

"He's gone." Her face looked tired and drawn. After the first year, Ana had long since stopped wondering at how well the virtual world mirrored the real one.

"Who?"

"Jackson." Lex created a chair for herself out of the white floor and sat down, worry lines at the edges of her lips giving away her anxiety. "There was a ghost in the system."

Ana frowned. "What kind of ghost?" Lex wasn't prone to superstition or error.

"Glory."

"Ah." Probably a memory slip. Of late, there'd been an increasing amount of bleed-through between the three of them. One of the consequences of sharing a mind. "Maybe Jackson's?"

"Maybe." Lex looked up, her eyes bright. "She said she couldn't find Jackson, and then she was gone. I checked everywhere. I can't find him either."

Ana covered her mouth with her hand. "Do you think he…?" She couldn't say it. Self-deleted, they called it. An option they had become aware of a few years before—the ultimate death for those who otherwise could live for centuries.

"I don't know. He's still drawing processing power, but I can't find him anywhere." She looked dejected. Lex and Jackson had grown close—big brother–little sister close. AIs really were human, in their own way.

Ana pulled Lex in for a hug, aware of the absurdity of what she was doing, offering a virtual hug to an artificial life-form. But somehow that didn't matter. "We'll find him."

Lex nodded. "I hope so."

. . .

EDDY WOKE to a perfect Forever morning. The air was comfortable on his skin, and the morning light had already crept by, brightening up every blade of grass and every "wild" flower that dotted the meadow where he'd stopped for the night.

Cassie grazed contentedly off to one side of the camp.

He climbed out of his sleeping bag and wandered over to the creek that ran alongside the campsite. The watercourse brought fresh, clean water out of the mountains whose foothills he was climbing. The water was warm, having run down from the heights where the rising heat provided an almost tropical atmosphere. It would cool as it ran down toward Lake Jackson.

Eddy knelt beside a shallow pool in his underwear, dipping his hands into the water to splash some on his face and over his arms, giving himself a rudimentary cleaning.

Then he sat back, looking around at the paradise he'd struggled so hard to reach six years before. That crazy ride in the Moonjumper in the last days of Earth seemed simultaneously so fresh and so long ago.

He wondered for the hundredth time what had become of Davian, his partner on the long, hot, claustrophobic trip up from Earth.

Eddy splashed some water over his hair and massaged it into shape with his fingers, smiling as he remembered how much time he used to put into his appearance when he'd been Evelyne. He caressed his flat, firm chest absently, comfortable in his current form. That had been a long time ago too.

He returned to the camp, shaking out his shirt and pants and pulling them on. Some of the estates outside Darlith were growing a new hybrid cotton, and Forever was finally gaining its first homemade fashion—if you could call lumpy shirts and baggy pants *fashion*.

Eddy packed up the camp and put Cassie's saddle on her. He turned to stare up at the sky. It would rain later in the day—he could feel it in the air.

Eddy ate a roll and some cave cheese, along with a bit of dried fruit. Some entrepreneurial spirit had discovered the curdling powers of the glowing mold that filled Forever's caverns. It made a tart, light-bodied cheese that was delicious despite the off-putting bright green marbling the fungus left behind.

He fed Cassie a couple of sugar cubes, patting her neck gently. Then he tied down his pack and his sleeping bag and climbed onto the saddle, guiding her to follow the path of trampled grass. It was already starting to recover—another day and the way would be almost impossible to see amid the general glow of the hillsides.

Ahead, the Anatov Mountains were arrayed around the circle of the world like a gap-toothed dragon's grin, the inspiration for their original name. Legend said that Ana Anatov had died there, but it had happened twenty years before Eddy had arrived on Forever.

He followed the trail up and over the rolling hills, crowned with glowing copses. Whoever had slaughtered the sheep didn't seem to have made any attempt to conceal their trail. It made a straight path through the grassy hills toward the mountains. If anything, it was as if they *wanted* it to be followed.

That thought gave Eddy pause. He could be walking into a trap.

The land ahead had many places where marauders could hide, hills and folds and stands of trees, hedges of wild red berry bushes that might conceal three or ten or more.

His old instincts from his dark time in the Hong Kong battle zone kicked in.


EDDY BACKED up against the smooth wall of the old temple, a two-story building in the heart of a land of superscrapers. He beckoned his squad to come up behind him. One by one, they crossed the street and slipped up against the same wall.

A carved green dragon with a red tongue stared at him from the corner of the temple roof.

Crap, he missed the NAU.

It was quiet on the street. Too quiet. In Eddy's war experience, quiet was almost always bad.

When all his men were with him, he poked his head around the corner. The street seemed empty, but two-hundred-story buildings lined both sides of it, with lots of windows and a fair share of gaping holes staring down on the street.

It could be a death trap.

This mission stank to high heaven—sneaking through the edge of Hong Kong to find some Chinese dissident who supposedly had information critical to the war effort.

Eddy was a soldier. Soldiers followed orders.

He signaled his men to follow and slipped around the corner.

That's when all hell broke loose.

. . .

EDDY GRIMACED. He'd witnessed the best and the worst of behavior during the war—the depths of human depravity and the reactions of decent people in the face of it.

In the end, of course, depravity had won. The world he'd known was gone.

Eddy slowed down, taking care to search out each potential hiding spot as he followed the trail. He fingered the leather whip at his waist uneasily.

Toward midafternoon, the sky started to darken as clouds slipped along the spindle. He pulled Cassie to a halt and stared at the storm clouds for a few minutes, still fascinated at how tempests formed in Forever.

It started as a thin gray line, which threaded its way along the spindle, following the world's trade winds. The line expanded into a series of billowing clouds, darkening as they spread out toward the ground.

Eddy continued on, hurrying to beat the storm. He crested another hill, and the trail he was following went... *strange*. It led down to a dry gully that ran along a gray rock wall. All the grass at the base of the hill was trampled, as if the party had stopped there for a few minutes to rest. Then the trail just ended.

Eddy pulled Cassie to a halt, slipping off her saddle and tying her to an alifir tree on the hillside.

His instincts told him to stop. Something was wrong here. Something bad was about to happen, like that day in Hong Kong when he'd lost half of his men.

He slipped down the hill cautiously, looking for any sign of where the bandits might have gone. On the hillside above, Cassie neighed nervously.

The rain started, just a few drops at first. The storm had reduced the light by half.

Eddy reached the base of the hill, scrambling to review the scene before the rain washed any evidence away. There had been at least five or six people here, from the various shoe treads he found. They seemed to all lead up to the rock face.

It made no sense.

Eddy ran his hand along the rock. It was rough for a stretch, and then it smoothed out. He traced the smooth patch. It was about six feet high and four feet wide. He stood back, unsure what to make of it.

The rain grew stronger, pelting the disturbed earth.

Eddy turned to head back up the hill and stepped on something hard. He knelt to pull it out of the mud.

It was a knife. A black stone knife, beautifully crafted as if it had been molded instead of chiseled. He touched the edge. It was wickedly sharp and stained with blood.

Eddy guessed the world mind could have made it, but he hadn't seen its like before.

He tucked it into his belt next to his long knife and decided he needed to get out of the gully before the water from the storm started flowing down the watercourse.

Eddy turned to go, but his left leg wouldn't lift. He looked down to see that he'd gotten stuck under a root. He tried to pull his foot out, but another one curled up around his ankle. "What the hell?"

A third root wrapped itself up his right leg, and when he tried to grab it to break it off, it snaked around his arm as well.

Eddy pulled out the knife and tried to cut it off, but the effort was like trying to slice through iron.

He shoved the knife into his belt and tried his own. The sharp metal fared no better than the sharpened stone.

He tapped his loop. The rain was pelting his back now, and he was trapped in an awkward position as the roots continued to wrap their way up and around him.

"Get me, Andy," Eddy gasped over the connection.

Agonizing seconds passed while the world mind tried to connect him.

Water was flowing down the gully now, running over his feet, and the roots continued to pull him inexorably toward the ground. He would drown if he couldn't get free.

"Hey, Eddy, what's up?" Andy's voice sounded cheery as always.

"Andy, you have to help me!"


"IT'S BEAUTIFUL." Colin rubbed the silver beard on his chin, staring up at the partially completed sculpture.

Trip nodded. The other former starship captain was still wildly handsome in his senior years, with his silver hair, blue eyes, and booming deep voice. "You have a lot of talent, young lady."

Andy beamed. The afternoon rains had just passed, the clouds threading their way past the ring of the Anatovs toward Micavery and the South Pole. Her sculpture glistened in the afternoon light.

"It's really quite impressive. It's funny how things seem—smaller?—when you ride on someone else's shoulders." Colin stepped up to touch the wood. "Feels quite sturdy too."

Andy laughed. "The town council insisted on it being able to bear a lot of weight. They think it's a big jungle gym."

Colin laughed. "I could see that."

Andy traced the edge of South America. "I got the inspiration from one of our talks that time I came to your house." She closed her eyes. "You told me what a shame it was that I'd never see the skies of Earth." She remembered that day like it was yesterday. She opened her eyes and walked around the sculpture, picturing the last bits that still needed to be grown. "There's so much we won't remember in another fifty or a hundred years."

Colin nodded. "The world mind will remember for us, but I know what you mean." He looked up again at the sculpture. "It's a good thing you're doing. Someday our descendants will have no memory of Earth at all." He laughed ruefully. "It's thoughts like that which make me feel old."

"You're not *that* old."

He looked up at her with a twinkle in his eyes. "I *am* that old. But it's kind of you to say so."

"I'm—" Something was coming through on her loop. "Oh *fuck Ariadne!*"

"What's wrong?" Colin frowned.

"I'm sorry. It's Eddy. He's in trouble." She knelt and touched the wood at the base of one of the parts of the sculpture, making a strong connection to the world mind. She closed her eyes and *dipped* into it, leaving Colin behind. She followed Eddy's signal out of Darlith, past the mountains, and down into a gully where he was trapped as the runoff rose. He was thrashing about in panic.

"It's okay, Eddy. I'm here," she said in his head through the loop.

"Andy?"

"It's me." Something was holding him down. "Look, I can't help you unless you let me in."

"I can't… the water is rising…."

"Eddy, listen to me." She marshaled as reassuring a tone as she could manage. "Close your eyes. It's gonna be okay. Let me in."

"Okay."

She felt Eddy's mental resistance drop away and slipped in through his connection to the world mind. Then she was riding his perceptions like she'd done with her father the day before.

She opened his eyes.

The rain was heavy, and the runoff from the mountains was quickly rising in the narrow gully. She didn't have much time.

Eddy dipped down into the ground below him.

Roots, like those she had summoned for the sculpture, had wrapped themselves around his legs and arms. They weren't from a tree or bush. These were part of the world itself. Something or someone had trapped him.

She concentrated on the one around his left arm, urging it to withdraw. It loosened its grip, but then it stopped moving, resisting her efforts.

Andy had never seen that happen before. The world was always responsive to her.

She had loosened it enough to pull out Eddy's arm with a bit of wiggling, and it didn't reengage. That was something.

She touched the root that wrapped his other arm, and it too loosened. Then it stopped too.

The water was up to his chest now, and she could feel Eddy starting to panic again.

"Hang in there. You're going to be okay," she said with more confidence than she felt. If she couldn't get it to withdraw....

She gripped the root tightly and commanded it to break.

This time she succeeded. It fell into a handful of pieces that were immediately washed away by the rushing waters.

Emboldened now, with both of Eddy's arms free, she grasped the roots that held his legs with his hands. In seconds, both of them crumbled to bits too.

She let go of Eddy's mind and shouted, "Run!"

Eddy wasted no time, scrambling out of the water and up the hill, while she rode his senses. He collapsed on the wet grass above the water line, gasping for breath. "Holy hell, what was that?"

"I don't know. I'd get farther away from it, though, just in case." The world mind didn't attack people. This felt intentional, though how someone could have done it, she had no idea. In fact, only she and her father and the world mind itself had the capability, as far as she knew.

Was there someone else on Forever who could manipulate the world's subroutines like she could? Or maybe better than she did?

Andy shivered. She remembered the day Ronan, the Transfer Station mind, had died. Someone from Earth had broken into the mind to infect him with a virus that had destroyed the Station and killed him, and had almost resulted in the deaths of hundreds of station personnel.

She and her father had discussed the possibility that there was another *talent* on Forever. Someone who could connect to and manipulate biominds directly with their own mind.

If that were true, though, how had they stayed hidden for so long without anyone noticing? Were they there still?

"Eddy, did you see anyone here when you arrived?" she asked through the loop.

"No. The place was abandoned. I'm chasing a band of Ghosts who slaughtered a dozen sheep on the Verge."

"Some Ghosts, if they can manage something like that."

"My thoughts exactly."

"Look, I have to go. Colin is with me, and they'll be getting worried. I need to see what you have there. Can you wait for me? I'll come as quickly as I can."

"Where are you?"

"In Darlith. I can be there in the morning."

"Okay. I'll pull back a little. I don't want to get trapped again."

"Good idea. I'll see you soon."

"Andy?"

"Yeah?"

"Thanks for saving my ass."

"Hey, what are friends for?" She let him go and slipped back to herself. She opened her eyes to find Colin by her side, staring at her anxiously.

"Everything okay?" Colin helped her up.

She shook her head. "Something—someone like me, I think—attacked Eddy." She explained what had happened. "I'm worried."

Colin whistled. "You think there are more people like you and Aaron?"

"I don't know." The thought made her head hurt. "I need to go see what Eddy found. Damn."

"What?"

"I didn't bring anything with me. My backpack, my hiking boots—everything's at home. All I brought was some clothes and my hunting knife." She patted the sheath that held the short, wicked blade, made by an artisan in Micavery. "I'll have to go back there first."

Colin sighed. "Never thought we'd need weapons up here. Hey, I have a little pull in Darlith. Why don't you let us help you get what you need?"

Trip nodded. "We're happy to help."

"I used to be someone, you know." Colin grinned.

Andy laughed. "Yeah, so I heard. That would be great—save me a trip. Is the train running again?"

"As of a couple hours ago." Colin rubbed his chin.

Andy frowned. "The town council will be upset if I don't finish this—"

Colin put his arm around her shoulder. "You can complete your sculpture later. This sounds like it's much more important."

"I'm worried about Eddy." Since he'd arrived on the scene six years before, they'd become like brother and sister. Anything that threatened him, threatened her.

"I'm sure you'll figure it out. Now come on. Let's go get you what you need for your journey."


AARON WAS MEETING with Dania Thorpe, the city manager, when the call came through.

He tapped his temple. "Hey, Eddy, can you hold just a sec?"

"Sure, boss."

"Are we about done here?" he asked Dania.

"I think so. I'll get those figures for you on farm production in a couple days. It feels like we're starting to turn the corner, doesn't it?"

"Finally." Resources had been tight since the refugee influx had strained the ship's resources six years earlier. "I want to try that new corn hybrid I've been hearing about. Keera says it's delicious."

"I'll bring some in next time." Dania shook his hand.

"Say hi to Margene for me!"

"Will do. Same to Keera." She gathered her notes and left the office. Aaron took Eddy off hold. "Hey, what's up?"

"Remember that sheep thing I've been chasing down out here on the Verge?"

"Yeah. Where are you?"

"Near the Anatovs. Things have gone from strange to dangerous out here." Eddy sounded worried.

"What happened?" Aaron stood and went to look out his window. He could see the peaks of the mountains in the distance. Eddy was out there somewhere.

"I think there's someone else who knows how to dip into the world mind."

Aaron stiffened. He'd considered the possibility, six years before, during the crisis, but he had never found the culprit behind the destruction of Transfer Station. Aaron had hoped whoever it was had died in the blast. "So, what happened, exactly?"

"How about strange roots coming out of the ground to tie me down in a gully in the middle of a thunderstorm?"

"Yeah. That's not right." He scratched his neck absently. "You should talk to Andy—"

"She's already on her way. Saved my bacon too."

Aaron chuckled. "Sounds about right. You two be careful, and let me know what you find."

"Will do. Let me know if anything else… weird gets reported?"

"Of course." Aaron cut the connection.

Ghosts and marauders, and now this? What was coming next?

His loop buzzed again.

"Yes?"

"Aaron, it's Ana."

"Hi, Ana… everything going to plan for the rendezvous?" He was worried about that as well. Too many things going on this week.

"Yes. That's not why I called." She sounded worried too. What, was the whole world going to hell at once?

Aaron sighed. "Lay it on me."

"It's about your father—"

"Sorry, Ana. We're not talking." After what Jackson had done? He'd planned to confront his father, but then he'd decided he was still too angry.

He could almost see her nod. "I know. I'm so sorry about what happened with Glory. But that's not why I called."

Aaron sighed. "What has he done now?"

"Aaron, Jackson's gone missing. We want you to help us find him."

# 4

---

# PUZZLES

"You have a message."

Andy rubbed her eyes, feeling groggy, and stared up at the wooden ceiling.

She'd worked half the night to finish the upgrades for the McHenrys before she left in the morning. A deal was a deal, but the work had wiped her out.

Jon and Candra now had a waste disposal system that fed back into a dissolution pit and ultimately into Forever's processing systems, and she'd grown them some nice wooden counters and seats for their customers as well. "Who is it from?"

"Delia."

"Put it through." Andy closed her eyes, and she could see Delia's face in her mind's eye.

"Hi, Andy. Sorry. I know this is a bad time. It's always a bad time, I suppose…."

What was she talking about? "Hey—is everything okay? I'll be home in a few days."

"I…. No. No, it's not." There was silence for a moment.

"Delia—"

"I don't want to see you anymore, Andy. It's not… I mean, I don't hate you or anything. It's just… I met someone else. I hope you understand." Delia cut the connection.

"Delia? I don't understand...." What had just happened? Andy blinked, stunned. They'd been together for three years. Sure, she was gone a lot to Darlith and the farms out on the Verge. But she'd never felt like Delia resented her absences.

Maybe this was why.

She got out of bed and stumbled over to the washbasin in the corner. She splashed some water on her face and looked at herself in the mirror. Her face was drawn and tired. *What did I do wrong?*

She'd thought everything was going well.

*I met someone else.*

"Goddammit." She covered her mouth. Glory wouldn't like her cursing like that, taking the Lord's name in vain.

Then again, Glory wasn't there anymore.

She tapped her loop. "Call Delia back."

"Acknowledged."

Andy brushed her teeth while she waited for the call to go through. They would talk it out. She would set things straight, or at least get a better explanation.

"Sorry, Andy. She's not responding."

Andy sank down on the bed, closing her eyes. "Dammit." How many months had they spent together? It wasn't easy to find someone who matched so well, especially on Forever, with its limited slice of humanity. *What did I do wrong?*

She wanted to throw something, to break it into a million little pieces.

This wasn't her place. These weren't her things.

Instead, she stuffed it down inside. She would deal with her grief later. There was nothing for her to do about it now.

She had more important things to worry about. She had to go find Eddy to try to figure out this whole Ghost thing. She'd talk to Delia when this was over.

Andy got dressed and packed her belongings, along with the new supplies Colin had purchased for her. He and Trip were so kind. She made a mental note to head out to the estate to see them next time she had a few days free, and maybe help them spruce things up.

"Thank you, Andy." Candra gave her a hug. "You did an amazing job. It's so much more than we expected."

Andy was surprised to see them up so early. In the few days she'd been there, they'd never been up before first light. "You're welcome. I'm just sorry I have to leave in such a hurry. Something came up, and I have to head back toward Micavery." That much was true, anyhow.

John shook her hand. "Good luck. You're always welcome here."

Andy waved and set off toward the train station.

It was quiet this early in the morning. It was still dark out. Luthiel lanterns lit her way, casting a golden glow on the cobblestone streets that ran throughout central Darlith.

Darlith felt *safe*. Andy had never lived in a place that wasn't, but she'd seen the dark side of humanity during the Last War and the Collapse. Hordes of unauthorized refugees had been shipped up to Forever in the last months of the war, and many had died in transit, including small children. All so someone could make a profit that would be meaningless when the world finally annihilated itself.

Forever was different, or so she hoped. But she'd also heard whispers of Ghosts and strange incidents along the edges of civilization. And the sheep slaughter that Eddy was investigating sent shivers down her spine.

Colin was waiting for her at the station.

"Hey, I didn't expect you to see me off!" Andy gave Colin a big hug. "Where's Trip? And why are you carrying a backpack?"

Colin grinned. "Trip's sleeping, but I was hoping you wouldn't mind if an old guy tagged along with you."

Andy laughed. "Mind? I'd be delighted. But are you sure you're... um... in shape?"

Colin grinned. "Nicely put. Yes, I can manage. We do work all day out on the estate, you know."

Andy blushed. "Sorry."

"And there's another benefit to me coming along. I commandeered a traxx, so we can make good time across country to where Eddy's waiting."

That was excellent news. "Who's bringing it out?" It would be nice to have his company on the way.

"I asked Shandra to do it."

"Oh." She barely knew the woman. She seemed nice enough. "When will the train depart?"

"About fifteen minutes. Should we get a seat?"

"After you. Age before beauty, and all that."

Colin snorted. "This is gonna be a long trek, isn't it?"

·  ·  ·

KEERA LOOKED WORRIED. "What do I do if you don't come back out?"

Aaron shook his head. "It doesn't work like that. I'll be inside the world mind for a long stretch, sure. But I should still be home in time for dinner." He kissed her cheek. "Ana and Lex will be there to keep an eye on me." He plugged his dipping interface into a jack in the wall by his bedside. It would provide a more secure link into the world mind than his own direct connection, and he could lie on his own bed so his body didn't cramp while he was busy elsewhere.

They'd decided to tell everyone that he was sick, and to do this at home to avoid awkward questions. He figured the job owed him a little sick time, as he'd worked almost every day since the Collapse.

There were some practical issues to worry about.

"Ready for this?" Keera held up a smooth plas catheter.

Aaron shuddered. "Sorry, not so thrilled about that part."

"You said you didn't want to be interrupted in the middle of your little quest, just to get up and go to the bathroom."

"You sure you're good at this?" He eyed the catheter suspiciously.

"Yes. I've been volunteering at the clinic, remember? The nurses have been giving me training courses. I've done this at least ten times."

"Ten times," he grumbled. "All right, let's get this over with." He pushed back the covers and pulled off his pants.

Keera whistled.

"Hey, enough of that. It's bad enough that I have to be subjected to this indignity, but the derision of a beautiful woman too?"

She grinned. "You've been so busy lately. It's been a long time—"

"When this is over, we'll take a nice vacation, go out sailing on Lake Jackson." He lay down on the bed, getting comfortable.

"Promise?" She pulled on gloves and disinfected him.

It was cold. "Yes. You sure you're good at this?"

"Hey, don't squirm." She coated the catheter with lubricant. "Here it goes. It's worse coming out."

What followed wasn't exactly pleasant, but he managed.

"All done." She kissed him on the cheek. "But humor me. If you don't wake up, what should I do?" She stripped off her rubber gloves and pulled the sheet up over him. She sat down on the bed next to him, taking his hand.

"Find Andy. Or talk to the world mind." He squeezed her hand. "And don't worry. It's vee space. It's not real. Nothing can hurt me in there."

"Okay. I'll see you tonight for dinner?"

He grinned. "Any chance of some apple pie for dessert?"

"If you make yourself a *virtual* one."

Aaron laughed. "Love you."

She pecked him on the lips. "You too. Travel safely."

He put his hand on the cross that hung around his neck, the one Ana had given him. The one that had been his father's. *I'm coming for you, Dad.*

He closed his eyes and put his hand on the interface.

The world shifted, and he was standing in a wide valley in front of a stone tower. Around him, a breeze blew through the grass, which didn't glow.

Lex was waiting for him. He was in his masculine form. "Welcome to Earthsea."

ANDY AND COLIN disembarked in the foothills on the far side of the Anatov Mountains from Darlith.

The train departed, sliding down the rails toward Micavery far below. It was a lovely day, the air fresh and clean after the previous day's rainfall. Everything looked shiny and new.

The land there rolled down in stages toward the settled part of the Verge. It was still growing, as more families moved out of Micavery and took up a farming and ranching life.

Shandra was waiting for them with the traxx, as promised.

"You must have left pretty early this morning to make it out here by now." Andy loaded her things on the back of the low, sturdy transport vehicle.

Shandra nodded. "I left about three this morning. Colin said it was urgent. I'm so sorry about your grandmother. It was a lovely ceremony." Her hazel eyes were a startling contrast to her brown skin.

"Thanks. I miss her." It was sweet of Shandra to think about Glory.

Shandra shrugged and turned back to the traxx. Shandra always had been on the shy/serious side. She checked to be sure everything was properly tied down.

The traxx had been fitted with several extra seats. *Good, we won't have to sit on our luggage.*

"Any trouble on the way up?" Colin asked, taking his seat and buckling himself in.

"Not at all. It was well before the commute hour."

Andy looked to see if she was smiling, but the woman's face was as serious as ever. Shandra was two years older than she was, if she remembered correctly. She had a hard time imagining the woman giggling.

Shandra helped Andy up onto her seat, her hand lingering for just a minute on Andy's. Or had Andy imagined it?

It reminded her of Delia. In truth, she hadn't been able to get her girl-friend out of her mind all morning. *Three fucking years. What the hell was that?*

Shandra climbed over the treads and up into the driver's seat of the heavy-duty hauler. "Everyone ready to go?"

"Yup." Andy managed a smile, pushing her anger at Delia down deep inside. This time Andy got the slightest grin back. It transformed Shandra's somewhat average features into something beautiful. Then it was gone like a cloud shadow. "Here we go." Shandra put the traxx in gear, and the vehicle lurched forward, making its way across the foothills.

The vehicle rumbled under their feet. Andy hadn't ridden on one for years. It was kind of fun. "My father said he rode a traxx through here once."

"Yes, he did." Colin laughed ruefully. "Against my direct orders, if I remember correctly. He was off on a mission to rescue Dr. Anatov."

"Did he succeed?" Shandra glanced back at him.

Colin and Andy shared a gaze. Shandra didn't know about her and her father's abilities, or about the world mind's split personality. Very few did. "He made it there in time to be with her when she died," Andy said carefully, and Colin nodded. "It's really beautiful up here."

It was a wide-open country, with few trees to block the view. Ahead, the sweep of the world bent toward the sky, and to her left, the Anatov Mountains provided a stark backdrop that climbed to the sky like a dragon's maw.

"This area was a barren wasteland then." Colin's vision was unfocused. "I remember when we found him and his companions—your mother and Devon. That was the week they met, if I remember correctly."

Andy tried to imagine her father at seventeen—three years younger than she was now. She failed miserably. "Did you know my uncle?"

"Jayson?" He shook his head. "I met him once, when your grandmother brought him and your father to see Jackson off on one of our supply runs on the Dressler. What made you think of him?"

"My dad said he was thinking about him at Glory's funeral." She glanced at Shandra.

"Death tends to remind us of others we've lost." He lapsed into silence.

Andy wondered who he was thinking of.

They made steady progress. Andy closed her eyes and hopped into vee space, working on her studies. She was taking a course in astrophysics from Ana, and she had a set of exam questions to complete that were proving hard for her to solve.

Someone touched her shoulder.

She opened her eyes and looked around. The traxx had stopped. They were perched on the top of a large hill that looked strangely familiar. "What…?"

"We're here." Shandra offered to help her down. "You kinda zoned out there." Her hand was warm in Andy's.

"Sorry. I was just… thinking about some homework that's overdue."

"Hey, you made it!" Eddy appeared and gave her a big hug as she stepped down from the traxx. He looked good. The whole Nottingham Sherriff thing worked for him. She missed tri dee, sometimes.

"I wouldn't have missed it. Anything new?"

Eddy shook his head. "Just waiting for you." He let her go. "Hey, Colin. Good to have you along! Come on. I'll show you where it happened."


EDDY WAS glad to have company. He loved the outdoors, but being so close to the place of his near-demise was making him extremely uncomfortable. If *things* could come out of the ground *over there* and attack you for no good reason, who was to say it couldn't happen *over here*?

Andy was staring at the gully below, her brow furrowed.

"Good to see you, Eddy." Colin gave him a bear hug, halfway crushing the wind out of him. "This is Shandra, our traxx driver."

Eddy shook Shandra's hand.

Andy strode down the hillside toward the gully.

"Careful," Eddy called after her, then shut his mouth. She was far better equipped for world mind weirdness than he was, but still….

"Got it." She strode right into the midst of the battlefield from the day before.

Nothing happened.

She knelt, touching the earth and closing her eyes.

"What happened here?" Colin asked while they waited.

"I was following the trail of a group of people who had slaughtered almost a dozen sheep on one of the ranches. The trail dead-ends there." He pointed to the rock face. "Damned strange, as if they'd walked right through the rocks themselves."

Colin frowned but didn't say anything.

"Then something... roots, I think? They attacked me, winding around my arms and legs and pulling me down to the ground. Andy saved me."

Shandra was looking at him, her eyes narrowed. "Andy was here yesterday?"

"Not exactly...." He looked at Colin to help him. Here he wasn't in Andy's company more than five minutes, and he was already blurting out her secrets.

"WHAT HE MEANS IS that I was inside his head." Andy strode up the hillside, frowning.

Colin frowned. "Andy, are you sure...?"

"She may as well know, if she's going to be spending time with us. Save us a lot of dancing around the fact." She turned to address Shandra directly. "You probably know I can manipulate parts of the world, like my father."

Shandra nodded. "I've heard rumors."

Andy laughed. "I'm guessing not all good?"

Shandra shrugged. "People are idiots. So what's the big secret?"

*I think I like you.* She grinned. "I can ride inside people's heads if they are connected to the world mind. And if they let me."

"Oooh, the possibilities." Shandra's eyes twinkled. "Maybe you could show me sometime."

Andy laughed. "Not the reaction I expected." *She's definitely hitting on me.* Andy wasn't sure how she felt about that. She was still entangled with Delia, after all.

She imagined Delia in the arms of another woman, or maybe a man, and growled.

Shandra frowned. "You *do* have to have permission, right?"

"Yeah." *Damn you, Delia, for messing with my head.*

"So you jumped into Eddy's head and helped him? That's cool."

"Thanks." She pushed Delia out of her head again. She had more immediate things to worry about.

"So, what did you find?" Eddy asked. "You don't look happy."

"It's hard to explain. As near as I can describe it, that area where the attack happened—it's dead."

"Dead? Like... how do you mean?"

"Inert, maybe? I tried dipping there, reaching down to touch the world mind. I can do it here." She knelt, closed her eyes, and touched the ground. She opened them again and looked toward the gully. "But back there? Nothing. It's almost like the trap that caught you was set to self-destruct." She shook her head. She'd never seen anything like it before.

"What does it mean?" Colin asked, scratching his beard thoughtfully.

Andy frowned. "Either the world mind has it in for Eddy personally, or there's someone on Forever who is better at manipulating the world mind's subroutines than I am. I had no idea there was a way to leave a delayed command like that. It was probably triggered when you walked over the spot by the rock wall."

"This all sounds like something I've seen before but hoped we'd never have to deal with again." Colin stared at the gully.

Eddy nodded. "They meant to cause fear."

"We've long suspected there were some people living up here in the mountains, pulling off the occasional petty crime. But this feels different. That sheep slaughter was meant to have an impact."

Eddy looked toward Micavery. "I thought it was strange how clear a path they left across the hills."

Colin snorted. "They wanted to lure someone here. To kill them, if possible. Up the ante."

"Why?" Andy was puzzled by the whole thing. Why would someone act that way?

"To stoke people's fears." Colin shook his head. "But where are they hiding?" He looked up at the mountains, as if they would reveal their secrets to him if he glared at them.

"Come look at this." Andy led them all down to the gully. Eddy was a little gun-shy. "The rock here. It looks different than the rock around it."

"I saw that." Eddy ran his hand along it. "It's smoother than the rest."

"Almost like it was melted and then reformed." Andy had never seen that either. The bones of the world—the "roots" and the other living parts of Forever—responded to her coaxing. But not the rocks.

"So you think they went through a rock wall?" Colin looked incredulous.

"I do. Look."

He knelt to see what she was pointing at.

She'd seen it when she completed her inspection earlier. "It's sheep's wool. Embedded in the rock."

"Well I'll be damned."

"I found this too." Eddy held out the knife.

Andy looked it over. "Nice workmanship. Not as polished as what Zach makes at the Knife's Edge, but still."

"I thought so too. So, can you get us inside?" Eddy asked, frowning at the wall.

"Yes. It'll be messy, but I think I can." She looked at her three companions. "Should we? Or should we head back to Micavery for reinforcements?"

"They already have a day's lead on us," Colin said.

"Let me send Cassie home, then." Eddy climbed the hill to where his horse was contentedly chewing up the glowing grass. He untied her and gave her a good slap on the hindquarters, and she took off toward Micavery.

"Do you think you can follow their trail?" Colin asked Andy.

Not if what was in there was as dead feeling as it was out here. "I can try."


AARON LOOKED around at the beautiful valley. "What is this place?"

"It's something I created a long time ago." Lex spun around, dancing through the tall grasses. "It's an island. Beyond the forest, there are many more."

Aaron grinned. Such playfulness wasn't something he expected from the world mind.

"I come here when I need to relax or work something through."

He glanced at the stone tower in the middle of the valley. "Is this where my father met you?"

Lex nodded. "When he saved me from the wreck of the Dressler. He was my knight in shining armor."

"He always spoke highly of you." It was weird, talking about Jackson Hammond as though he were dead. Which Aaron supposed, in a way, he was. "So how do we find him?"

Lex took his hand. "Each of us has our own worlds in here. Places we can go to escape the claustrophobia. I don't feel it so much. This world is natural to me. But the other Immortals… sometimes they need wide-open spaces."

Immortals. *Jackson and Ana.* He nodded. "I get that. Humans like to wander."

"Jackson built himself a series of interconnected worlds. I have access to certain 'public' parts of his creations. But to reach the others, we have to follow his rules."

"Rules?"

"Each of our worlds has its own internal sets of rules. We'll start in Frontier Station where he first met Glory. But from there, we'll have to find our way to him on our own."

"Got it." He was still a little confused. He'd had a lot of experience dipping into biominds of various types, but this was sure to be a qualitatively different experience. "I'm glad to have you along as a guide."

"This is only an avatar of me. It will stay connected to me, and I can offer you suggestions as we go. But you have to make the decisions."

"Ah."

"Ready?"

He nodded. "Ready as I'm going to be."

He took Aaron's hand, and they slipped through into the gleaming halls of Frontier Station.

# 5

## INTO THE MOUNTAIN

ANDY SUMMONED up roots like the ones that had almost killed Eddy. He stood back, giving her a wide berth.

She'd had to work off to the side of the dead zone, as she called it.

The roots crawled up the rock face, sinking into it as if it were made of butter. They traveled across the surface in the shape of an arched doorway, and the rock groaned like a living thing.

"Stand back." Andy took a step or two away from the wall.

With a sharp crack, the wall disintegrated, showering the immediate vicinity with pebbles and dust.

The roots withdrew into the ground.

"Nicely done," Eddy said as the open doorway emerged from the dust. He coughed a little as the dust spread and settled.

"Just so we're clear, we go in and see what we can find. Then we go back and report to Aaron, *right*?" Colin glared at Eddy and Andy.

"All right, all right." Poor guy must have had some issues with people flouting his authority before.

Andy nodded. "I should tell my dad what we're doing, before we go on." She closed her eyes and then opened them wide in surprise. "He's not responding."

Colin frowned. "Try your mom."

After a moment, a look of relief passed across Andy's face. "He's holed up with the world mind. Something about Jackson. I'm not to tell anyone but you three."

"That's odd." Eddy glanced in the direction of Micavery, invisible behind the hill. "He didn't mention anything when we spoke yesterday."

"It's a long story." Colin brushed dust off his shirt. "His mother's funeral was the day before yesterday."

"It was beautiful." Eddy looked wistful.

"Who's Jackson?" Shandra asked, frowning.

"I'll tell you later," Andy said. "Let's see where this leads, shall we?"

The rock wall had hidden a dry cavern. Eddy looked around the place. It was about fifteen meters wide and half that deep, with a low ceiling just a meter above his head.

He had to remind himself that all this had been built by the world mind. So much detail in this artificial world!

Andy was touching one of the walls and frowning.

"What?" Anything that made her uneasy made him uneasy too.

"I can't sense anything." She looked around, her eyes narrowed. "It's like we're not even on Forever."

"What does that mean?" He tried his loop. There was no answer.

"I don't know. Something's blocking the world mind here? It's like the dead zone outside. I don't know how to guide us."

"Um, guys?" Shandra pointed to a dark corner of the cavern.

A perfectly round doorway opened from the cavern into a long tunnel. The tunnel itself was rough, natural-looking. But the precision of the doorway left no doubt about its human origins.

Andy touched the smooth curve and jerked her hand away as if she had been burned. "Holy crap! It's like it's seething with energy."

Eddy touched it. "I don't feel anything."

"It's underneath. There's something keeping this doorway open. Like the trap they set for you. Whoever did this knows how to leave commands in the system, like an application that keeps running after they leave."

"Are you two sure we shouldn't go back and tell someone?" Colin asked.

Andy shook her head. "I'll go out and send Dad a message, but this guy might disappear again if we don't stay on his trail now."

Eddy nodded. "I agree with Andy. Aaron knows where to find us. We should go after these guys now. Once we know more, we can call in the posse."

"All right. But no one barges into anything. We take it slow and steady." Colin glared at each of them again.

"Deal." Andy put out her hand.

Eddy had a bad feeling about all this.


AARON LOOKED AROUND. It *was* Frontier Station, down to the last detail. He could even smell the subtle lavender scent they used to keep the air fresh. The floor was hard under his feet, as centrifugal force created an artificial gravity. He could see it down to the minutest detail.

And yet it was absolutely empty.

"What do we do now?"

Lex shrugged. "We look around. Did your father ever tell you about his past? Any of it?"

Aaron thought back. They'd had long conversations in vee space these last few years, filling out the portions of each other's lives they'd missed after Jackson had died. "Some of it. A lot of it, actually. When I was a kid, he used to tell me how he met my mother, here on Frontier Station." He looked around. "She was a waitress at the Blue Moon Café."

"That place?" Lex pointed behind them.

*Sure enough.* It was a long retail space that followed the curve of the station, filled with tables and chairs, with a bar along the back, fronting the runway of Frontier. "Yeah, that's it." The blue neon sign overhead said "The Blue Moon."

"It seems like as good a starting place as any."

Aaron nodded.

*I used to walk by the place every day, trying to work up the courage to go talk to her.*

Jackson's voice echoed in his mind. So this was where it had all happened. And one day, his father had gotten up the nerve to sit in her section.

Aaron entered the café and looked around. The place, like the rest of this virtual version of the station, was deserted.

He looked down in time to see the green-and-blue ball of Earth roll by against a field of stars. He gasped.

Stars, shining against the empty blackness of the void, spun past beneath his feet. And there was Earth, before the Collapse. The place of his childhood, of humanity's childhood, that was no more.

Lex steadied him. "You okay?"

Aaron nodded. "Didn't expect that." He looked around. "He used to sit in one of these booths with the stars at his feet, but he only had eyes for Glory."

What had changed between them? Why had his father denied Glory her passage into this virtual heaven?

Aaron paced by the booths, finding a table at last that felt *right*. "I think this is the one." He couldn't say how he knew. "Should I sit?"

"Sure. We're trying to find any traces he might have left behind—clues as to where he went."

"Got it." Aaron slid into the booth, setting his hands down on the cool plas table.

The station exploded into chaos.

Busboys wiped down tables and carried away piles of plas dishware. A hundred patrons sat around the place, chatting, eating, and taking in the view, dressed in the fashions of at least thirty countries.

"Shuttle to the Fargo Skyhook departs in fifteen minutes from Hangar Seven." The AI's voice was dry and loud.

*What the hell?* He must have triggered something in the simulation when he sat down. None of this was real. His companion was gone. "Lex?" he called. There was no response.

"No one named Lex here, sunshine." A blonde waitress gave him a broad smile. "I'm Andra. Can I get you something to drink to start off?"

Aaron closed his eyes and tried to contact the world mind.

Nothing happened.

He opened his eyes to find the waitress still staring at him. "All right, I'll give you a couple minutes. If you need anything, just give me a holler." She winked and moved on to the next table.

"Thanks," he muttered, acutely aware he was talking to a simulation.

Where had Lex had gone?

*No worries. I can just wake up and then reconnect. Must be a glitch.* He tried to back out of the system to wake himself up, but nothing happened.

He closed his eyes and tried the manual protocol. "Disengage."

Still nothing.

Aaron was starting to panic, his virtual heartbeat racing. He jumped out of his seat. "Hello? Can anyone hear me?" He looked around wildly—he was stuck all alone in this simulated space station. Surely Lex would come for him.

A hundred heads turned to stare at him and then went back to their meals.

"Hey there, calm down. You're okay." A beautiful woman with long black hair, tied behind her neck, guided him back to his seat. "Space gets to some of us after a while. They call it Spacer Sickness."

He allowed himself to be seated and looked up into the eyes of his benefactor. "You... you're Glory."

She smiled. "Yes, I am. You been stalking me or something?"

She was a lot younger, more like she had been when he was a child. But it was *her*. She was beautiful. Aaron could see how she had stolen his father's heart.

Aaron's own heart started beating faster. He closed his eyes and slowed his breathing. *You can figure this out.* He tried to remember the stories his father had told him about this place.

"You okay?"

Aaron opened his eyes again to see her looking down at him with concern. "Yeah. I think so. I will be." He looked around the restaurant. "Just a little dizzy. It'll pass."

"Good. Hey, you're that guy that works in hydroponics, right? Jimson? Jason?"

"Um... Jackson?"

"That's it. Andra said you'd been staking out the place." She winked at him. "I'll get you some water."

"Got anything stronger?"

"How about some Moonbeam? Got a fresh batch up from Luna Colony today."

"That's perfect."

"Be right back."

"Okay." He knew where he was now, and what had happened. If not how or why.

He'd dipped into his father's memories.

DAVIAN STOOD on the wide balcony Gunner had constructed for him, surveying his domain, the broad cavern he'd named Agartha. He loved the dark beauty of that name, the history. He was the master of his own little world within a world.

He'd built his own little empire under the mountains, after the chance discovery that the mountains were hollow inside. The world mind had needed to be thrifty with its materials, apparently, both to conserve them for other uses and not to create such a great weight along the world's girth that it would present a danger of throwing the whole world off-balance, or even collapse it entirely.

That much he'd surmised.

Davian was proud of what he had accomplished here. What had been a vast, dark space lit only by tiny veins of cave moss was now a small world unto itself. Judicious harvesting of plants from the outside world yielded light during the day, and luthiel lanterns burned smoke-free at night.

The new lambs grazed contentedly on a patch of grass along one edge of the small town where his people lived in perfect harmony. There was no crime in Agartha.

His people were the dregs of this new society, drawn from the refugees who had arrived just before the Collapse of Old Earth. Young and old, rich or poor, none of them had the skills to fit into the new egalitarian society being built by the fools outside.

Here everyone had a purpose. He assessed them and gave their lives meaning, creating in the process his own great society.

Soon it would be time to impose it on the larger world outside.

## 6

# ZOMBIE MOUNTAIN

DEVON POWELL stared up at the arc of the world. "Might be the last time I see it." He'd come a long way in Forever, from showing Aaron Hammond around on his initial visit to the new world to his planned extra-Forever sojourn now.

Rafe laughed. "You'll be fine. Just think, you might be mankind's last astronaut."

Devon rolled his eyes. Why he'd decided to take on this mission, he had no idea. Sure, it seemed simple enough—out to the new asteroid, Isis, place a few charges to stabilize her rotation, and then come home. In reality nothing in space was simple.

"You ready to go?" Ana asked through his loop. "We're on a tight schedule."

"Is she bugging you again?" Rafe grinned.

"Yeah, gotta go."

Rafe hugged him and then gave him a big kiss, one of those only-in-the-movies, passionate, over-the-top ones where he leaned Devon down with a theatrical flair. "Wherever you are, whenever you're lost, I'll always come for you," he whispered.

"Devon...." Ana sounded impatient.

"Promise?"

For his answer, Rafe kissed him again.

"Okay, I really have to run. Love you, Romeo."

"You too, Puck."

They parted.

Devon climbed aboard the shuttle and took his seat in the pilot's chair.

Technically Ana was the pilot. He was only a passenger.

Still, he would see the stars.

He waved to Rafe as the shuttle ascended, until he could no longer see him below.

Then he closed his eyes to rest, as much as he could manage, on the ride out to the asteroid.

ANDY RAN her hand along the smooth side of the tunnel, wondering why she felt absolutely nothing but the cool touch of stone. It was disconcerting.

All her life, she'd been just a touch away from another world. On Transfer Station, that was Ronan's world, the station mind. He'd created hundreds of lands for her to explore and had been both her playmate and confidant.

Even now, six years later, his death still stung. Sometimes she wished she had faith, like her grandmother. It would make things easier.

Here on Forever, she'd been able to access the world mind, in small ways by playing with its subroutines and in larger ones by talking with Lex, Ana, and Jackson themselves and exploring their worlds.

But now, for the first time in her life, she was cut off. Like one of her arms was missing.

She sighed. If she couldn't divine things from her extra senses, she'd have to make do with the five she had.

The three of them had decided to proceed as silently as possible, since their voices would carry a long way in the confined tunnel. Everything was done with hand signals—a hand on the shoulder for stop, a tap on the back for go.

Andy pulled Eddy to a stop.

The moss that usually grew in Forever's rainwater tunnels grew there too, casting a green glow and looking anemic and sad. These tunnels had been created by the world mind as it built out Forever and were used to carry runoff into the reprocessing systems, or stomachs, as her dad liked to call them.

Eddy shot her a questioning look.

She knelt and touched the ground. It was bone-dry, which was probably good for them, as it meant less risk of a flash flood sweeping them down into the bowels of the world.

It meant something else too.

It had rained the day before, rather heavily. The stone should at least have been damp and the moss thriving.

Someone had rerouted the plumbing under the mountains. Surely it was the same someone who had left a trap for Eddy or whomever would be foolish enough to follow this trail. Somehow they had created a dead zone here, around their camp, where the normal rules of Forever didn't apply.

They were more than just a small group of outlaws or marauders.

Andy gestured for a halt and placed her palms flat against the side of the tunnel. She closed her eyes. She was in absolute darkness. She felt around for something. Anything. Any bit of connection to the world mind. There was *nothing*.

Andy shivered.

"What is it?" Eddy whispered into her ear.

"This whole thing is bigger than we thought."

He nodded, looking suspiciously down the tunnel ahead of them.

On the plus side, if she couldn't access the world mind down here, her unknown adversary probably couldn't either.

"Do we go on?" That was Colin.

"We have to." This was too important to let go. Andy shivered. Something bad was coming. She could feel it. If she had a chance to stop it, she'd have to find out what it was.


AARON SAT in the middle of Jackson's quarters on Frontier Station. He'd found his way back there after his encounter with Glory at the diner.

The room was cramped, a square cubicle maybe two by two meters. On one side, there was a small utilitarian cot, on the other, a tiny white plas desk with a few knickknacks.

Aaron looked around the room, wondering what his father's life had been like here. Aaron had spent a chunk of his own life on a space station. It was a strange place for a human being to spend time. *We were made to live under a blue sky. Not in a tin can.*

Aaron picked up the photoplas from the neat, uncluttered desk. It brightened as he lifted it, showing a picture of his father in an AmSplor uniform, with Luna Base in the background.

He flipped the photo, and this time it showed Jackson standing in front of a garden—probably the Frontier Station garden he was charged with maintaining. Jackson had often spoken about it and how he had loved taking care of the plants. How Glory would come and spend time with him there, almost like a real date.

Aaron flipped it again, and it showed a scene from New York. The drowned city was beautiful in its own postapocalyptic way, the old skyscrapers covered in ivy. He reached out to touch it, and the colors of the world swirled around him.

Aaron's stomach lurched, and he fell to his knees, throwing up on the rough gray ground. His virtual stomach emptied itself, leaving a foul taste in his mouth.

He stayed there, one hand half-buried in gravel, until the nausea passed.

Aaron got up on his knees and looked around for something to wipe his mouth.

*What the hell?* He was on a rooftop covered in plants, a virtual jungle in the heart of a city. A cloth lay on the ground next to him. He picked it up and sniffed it. It was greasy, but it would have to do. Carefully he wiped the sides of his mouth.

He threw it aside and stood to survey his environs.

The roof was about twenty meters square, and it was covered by makeshift pots and garden beds. Black irrigation lines snaked through the man-made jungle, all running to a water tank at one corner, hooked to a condenser unit. The condenser was old, patched into working order with an impressive array of scrounged parts, including part of a trombone, some flexible plas piping, and loads of duct tape.

The water tank looked far older, and with all the rust at the edges, it was a minor miracle that it held water at all.

He turned to look the other way and gasped.

It was New York City. The Big Apple. Hundreds of superscrapers reached for the sky around him, and below, the waters of the Atlantic roamed the city unchallenged.

What a glorious place it must have been in its heyday, before it was drowned by the rising tide. Even now it was stunning, rows upon rows of feats of human engineering that would never be repeated in his lifetime, or likely even the lifetimes of his great-grandchildren.

Though she was a sodden mess now, the city retained some of her former glory, like an elderly Hollywood actress pulling her green shawl around her shoulders in defiance of those who were ready to pronounce her dead.

There was still life here, of both the vegetable and human kinds. Rope bridges crossed the canyons between many of the buildings, a primitive answer to the new challenges imposed on the population by Mother Nature.

Boats plied the canals below, both "real" ones and rafts and craft lashed together out of urban debris.

One of the rope bridges connected to his building was swaying.

"Jackson!" A boy in his late teens bounded across the rickety structure as if it were made of concrete.

Aaron's heart lurched to see the way it swayed.

"Yeah?" May as well play along and see where this led.

"The Boss wants you."

Who the hell was the Boss? "Where is he?"

The boy smirked at him. He could have been Huck Finn from the tri dee —barefoot, his pants rolled up, and a straw hat on his head. "Very funny. Come with me, I'll take you to *her*."

Aaron could hear the capital letter in the kid's voice. "I'm not in trouble, am I?"

The boy squinted at him. "Not unless you turn her down."

*That* made Aaron nervous. *Turn her down for what?*

This was only a memory. *It can't really hurt me, right?* In normal vee space, he'd have said no, but so far this experience had been anything but normal.

"Come on!" The boy turned and ran back across the bridge.

Aaron frowned. He climbed onto the bridge and looked down. His virtual stomach churned again, threatening to bring up whatever virtual things might be left inside. It was a long way down to the water below—at least ten stories.

*It's just a memory.* He wrenched his gaze away from the water to look across to the other building.

"Come on!"

He forced himself out onto the bridge. It swayed and then stopped again. His knuckles were white on the rope rails.

"You okay?" the kid called.

"Yeah. Just a little sick—the flu, I think."

Something zipped by his ear.

The boy whipped out a small gun and shot at it. It burst into smoke and flames and spiraled down to the water below. "Damned Hexers, always trying to squick our business."

Aaron nodded. He remembered. The Hex was the gang that had controlled the northern part of the drowned city.

He willed his feet to take him forward. Maybe if he closed his eyes....

"Come on!"

Damn, the kid was insistent. Aaron opened his eyes and found he was on the far side of the bridge. He hoped to God he never had to do *that* again. "Hey, what's your name?"

"Gordy." The kid looked at him as if he'd lost his mind. "You been smoking *terfies again*?"

Again? What, had Jackson been a terfhead? "No. Sorry. Being sick has my head all scrambled up."

"Well, you better get it on straight before you see Her." Gordy led him inside the building. They clambered down the access stairs a couple floors before coming out into a wide space. It must have been an office space at one point, but all the cubicles had been cleared out. In the center of the room was a platform that held a giant plas tank filled with blue fluid. Something huge sat inside, moving slowly in the murky darkness. It was like an aquarium.

Aaron stared at it, trying to work out what it was. Feeder tubes ran back and forth from the tank, and a small Sipson generator sat nearby.

"Well, go on." Gordy pushed him toward the platform. A short flight of stairs led up to an open space in front of the aquarium.

Aaron climbed the steps, wondering what the hell was going on here. His father had never mentioned anything like this.

He stood in front of the aquarium looking at the thing inside.

It was a mind. A biomind, like they had used on Transfer Station. Like the world mind. Only he'd never seen one so huge back on Earth.

It shifted in the fluid, and a voice issued from a speaker at his side. "Hello, Aaron."

EDDY LED them down the tunnel toward the enemy's lair. Or at least that's how he pictured it—like something from an old superhero tri dee. The mountain they were walking under would have a huge cavern entrance in the shape of a skeletal maw, jagged teeth above and below dripping with water—or maybe blood—threatening anyone who dared enter. Dead eye sockets peering out at the world.

That's how one always knew it was the villain's lair.

The reality seemed a lot more mundane. There were no markers, other than the subtle bits of world crafting they had found when they entered the tunnel.

He was a little worried, though. This cavern had no side branches either. While that was good for them, assuming the marauders hadn't sealed them off after they passed like they'd done at the cavern entrance, it also made them easy targets. There was nowhere to hide if they should run into enemy forces coming from the other direction.

The weight of the rock above them weighed heavily on him, as did the oppressive silence.

Something shifted.

It took him a moment to figure out what it was. Eddy pulled the others to a halt and pointed to his ear. There it was again. A definite *clang clang clang.*

They moved more slowly.

Soon the tunnel brightened. A soft glow came from up ahead, lighting their way. After another three or four minutes, he could see the end of the tunnel at last, but his eyes hadn't adjusted to the new light yet.

They edged up to it. As they got close, he gestured for them to get on the ground and crawl the last bit of the way.

Colin grimaced.

Eddy mouthed, "Sorry." It was probably hard on the old man.

He moved forward on his hands and knees and peered over the edge. "Holy shit."

The inside of the mountain was hollow, or had been hollowed out. Someone had filled it with glowing plants, creating a virtual Vernian jungle underground.

Huge stone columns reached up from earth to sky—or in this case, from Forever to cavern ceiling. Above, the vault of it glowed in bright blue patches… moss? Or something else?

In the middle of the jungle stood several enormous trees and a wide lake.

Eddy halfway expected to see a brontosaurus lift its head from the water, or to look up and see pterodactyls flying overhead. There *were* some birds—

seagulls, like the ones they'd recently introduced over Lake Jackson a couple years ago. *Strange.*

In the middle of it all, near the lake, was a village, if you could call it that, made up of primitive wooden huts with thatched roofs.

There were several hundred people down there in the cavern too—adults and children—each one working industriously and silently, harvesting fruit, trimming plants, building dwellings.

"There's something wrong," Andy whispered.

"You mean besides there being an entire hidden world under this mountain?"

She nodded. "Look closely at the people."

He watched them for a while. Sure, they were industrious. There was nothing wrong with that.

"No one's talking." It was Shandra, who had edged up on his other side.

He looked around. She was right. Not a word was said by any of the people he could see close by. Not only that, but they hardly interacted at all.

Eddy shivered, and his hand slipped unconsciously to the hilt of his long knife. "It's Zombie Mountain." The weekly tri dee serial had run for almost a decade and was eerily similar to the scene in front of him now. Except the zombies hadn't been particularly good builders or gardeners. "What the hell's going on?"

# 7

# CROSSINGS

A PIECE of Ana's consciousness soared across the void, guiding the shuttlecraft toward its rendezvous with 42 Isis. She'd spent the last few months observing it through the scopes mounted on the outside of the world, checking and cross-checking her own calculations to be sure she had this right.

The last rendezvous had been accomplished with the help of a fleet of Earth ships, towing 41 Daphne to Forever and then aligning it for docking.

Ana had replayed the memories of that event from the world mind's core. She'd gone over the impact as the new source of resources collided gently with what was left of 43 Ariadne, Forever's original asteroid. She'd seen how Forever's roots had immediately dug into the new food source, lashing it to the existing world and starting to feed off its rock and ice.

Forever created gravity via centrifugal force, spinning constantly so that everything remained on the ground and didn't float up into the sky.

Each asteroid had its own spin and had to be aligned with Forever's before docking, lest the two collide and tear each other apart.

With Keera's help, Ana had designed a series of charges that she would deliver to the asteroid. When set off at the right time and in the right order, they would bring the asteroid's spin in line with their own at the moment of rendezvous.

It was a project years in the making.

Now, as she flew the shuttle toward their target, self-doubt stirred in her gut. What if her calculations were bad? What if she had failed to take into account something critical? The results could be catastrophic.

And yet, they had to do this. Under the original plan, the rest of the world building would have been done in near-Earth space, under carefully controlled circumstances. But Earth didn't exist anymore. Not in any meaningful sense.

The project managers had long before calculated the necessary size for a generation ship like this, one that would hold enough resources for the journey if they were carefully recycled, and that would allow enough room for the inevitable population growth.

They were only about halfway there.

Though she flew the shuttle remotely, it felt good to be out in wide-open space again. If she carried the weight of humanity's survival on her shoulders, why shouldn't she relax and enjoy the view until it was time for action?

*Let there be lights in the expanse of the heavens to separate the day from the night, and let them be for signs and for seasons and for days and years; and let them be for lights in the expanse of the heavens to give light on the Earth.*

*Genesis.* "Jackson," she whispered. "Where are you?" For all that she was an atheist, his worldview had changed her. He saw good in things where she saw only cold logic and hard science. Maybe a little bleed-through, now and then, wasn't the worst thing.

She checked her clock. Two hours until she reached Isis.

Devon Powell slept inside the ship she piloted, so he'd be ready to help her set the charges when the small shuttlecraft reached Isis. Not exactly by the book, but they'd burned the book when the world had ended.

Ana settled in to wait and watch the stars.

AARON LOOKED AROUND, confused. The mind had just called him by his own name. This was his father's *memory*. How was that even possible? Though he'd been skirting the outer edges of possibility ever since he'd dipped into this virtual world. "How... what are you?"

The mind chuckled. "That's a good question. I'm one of Jackson's memory constructs. So I suppose I'm the sum total of what he knew about the original me all those years ago."

"That's... bizarre." Aaron looked at Gordy, who seemed just as mystified as he was.

"You're telling me."

"Are you sentient?"

He could almost feel the mind shrug. "Who can know? Maybe I'm just a big Turing test. Do I *seem* sentient to you?"

"I don't know. I mean, yes. But it would take a lot more time for me to decide."

Her voice lowered an octave into the silky range. "I'm not going anywhere."

Aaron laughed harshly. "Good point." He was at a loss on how to proceed. This wasn't anything like what he'd expected, although if pressed, he would have had a hard time explaining exactly what he had expected. Still, he had to press on if he was to find Jackson. "Can I ask you some questions?"

"Of course."

"What were you. I mean, in real life? When Jackson knew you?"

"Ah, that's a hard question to answer. Once upon a time, I was a woman. Her name was Lilith Lott."

"You were human?"

"She was, yes. She was the commander of the Red Badge."

"Ah." Aaron considered the mind in front of him. There was nothing feminine about it except for the voice. He wondered what Lilith Lott had looked like, how she had lived her life. "And how—"

"Did Lilith become the stunning creature you see before you today?"

He nodded. "Yeah. Sure." She still had a sense of humor.

"She was diagnosed with a fast-moving lung cancer and given two months to live." He could hear the echo of that pain even in this copy, twice removed from the original woman. "She was resourceful, though, and she'd heard of this new experimental procedure to upload a human consciousness into a biomind."

Aaron nodded. So it *had* happened before. "Did Jackson know Lilith, before...?"

"Yes. He helped her transition into her new form when her body was dying. He volunteered to be loaded with special blackware to help him accomplish the task."

Aaron staggered, catching the railing to stop his fall. This explained so much.

Why they had this strange ability in their family.

Why Jackson had been so ready to accept the consciousness of Lex, the Hammond's ship-mind.

Why Aaron could do what he could do.

"Were you... like her? Like the original Lilith?"

The mind stirred in its container, sending liquid sloshing about over the edge. "No. The technology was imperfect back then. Some days, I was calm, serene, logical. Others I was quite mad."

Aaron laughed nervously. "Are you mad today?"

"No," she purred. "You caught me on a good day."

Given that she was a simulation of a memory of a biomind running in vee space inside another biomind, he had no idea how to take that.

"You're from *outside*, aren't you?" Gordy had climbed onto the platform and was staring at him in awe.

"Yeah, I guess so." Did the denizens of these memories know they weren't real?

"Take me with you! Nothing ever changes in here. It's so boring."

Aaron laughed. "You have a whole world to explore." If only the kid realized how lucky he was.

"Nah, I can't ever leave New York." The boy looked crestfallen.

*Of course.* Jackson's memories were of Gordy only in this one location. The boy had no existence outside of this place.

Aaron felt a deep sense of sadness, even if Gordy was really just an advanced collection of ones and zeroes. *In the end, aren't we all?* "I wish I could. But I don't even know where I'm going next. Or how." He looked around the room, filled with tubes and machinery and dark corners, and wondered what it was like to be trapped inside someone else's head.

The mind rumbled in its container. "You're looking for Jackson." It wasn't a question.

"Yes."

A tentacle lifted out of the blue water, holding something small and sparkling. "Take this."

He held out his hand, and the sparkly thing dropped into his palm. "What is it?"

"It's a bit of code dressed up in a pretty bauble." She seemed pleased with herself. "Isn't it shiny?"

"Yes, it's beautiful." She seemed to be tipping over to the mad side of things. Time to leave before things got even weirder. "What does it do?" he asked.

"Squeeze it tight and think of him, and the stars will crash down, the stars crash down, the galaxies fade, and the angels will play...." The last was in a singsong voice. The thing in the tank bounced around, sloshing more of the liquid out over the top. "I used to be beautiful, with the most wonderful hands to grab things. I was the Queen of the City. Now I'm a hideous beast that sings and wishes she had wings...."

Aaron looked down at Gordy, who looked frightened.

"What's wrong with her?"

"She had bad days. Really bad days." He was shaking now.

*Fuck it.* Code or no, the boy shouldn't be left to suffer through the depravations of a mad mind. He grabbed the boy with his left hand and closed his eyes, squeezing the bauble with his right, thinking about his father.

"Don't go, don't go, oh beautiful man...," the mind warbled, reaching for him with her tentacles, but she faded away before she could reach him. Her calls were replaced by silence.

Aaron watched in horror as the boy faded too, his hand dissolving in Aaron's grasp. The anguished look on Gordy's face as he vanished tugged at Aaron's heart.

He opened his mind to see his mother, Glory, standing there staring at him, her mouth hanging open.

"WE SHOULD GO BACK and tell Aaron." Colin was adamant.

"Tell him what?" Andy stared at the zombies below, trying to work out what was going on down there, in the strange cavern in the bowels of the mountains. "That we followed a trail and found a bunch of narced-out people harvesting fruit under a mountain?"

"Well, basically—"

"We need to find out more first." Drugs. It had to be drugs. Someone was dosing these poor people with something. Yet they didn't walk like they were drugged. Their movements were crisp, clean, efficient even.

Maybe some kind of designer drug, then, tailored to suppress the personality? But where would you find something like that up here?

"Andy's right." Eddy was staring out across the wide space, his brow furrowed. "We need to find out more. We were lucky to get in here without running into anyone, and with the number Andy did on their front door… they're going to know someone was here. Look!" He pointed to a green patch about halfway around the cavern. "Two fluffy white specks."

"Our lost sheep?" Colin stared across the intervening distance.

Andy nodded. "Looks like it. So are we agreed?"

Colin looked at her, respect warring with concern on his face. "I suppose so. Though I'd feel better if we sent someone back to report what we've found so far."

They all looked at him.

"All right. The old guy should go." He laughed softly. "I guess that makes sense."

Andy grinned. "Age before beauty."

"Or wisdom before inexperience." He kissed her forehead. "You be careful. All of you." Then he backed away into the dim light of the tunnel.

Andy glanced back after him. He stood, waved, and then disappeared into the darkness.

She was glad Colin was out of harm's way. He was in good shape for a guy his age, but she was worried what would happen if things got violent. She'd grown fond of him. He was the uncle she'd never had.

She turned her attention to the task at hand. "Where will we find some answers?" She pulled out her knife and tested its edge thoughtfully.

Shandra pointed across the wide cavern. "There's an entrance to something —maybe another cavern?—over there." Their shoulders touched.

Andy decided she didn't mind.

She squinted across the distance. Shandra was right. She could see a dark opening in the cavern wall and above it several more. And maybe a balcony or two? At this distance it was hard to tell what it was, but it was something. "Sounds good to me. How do we get there?"

"There are pathways through the jungle, but we might be better off making our way around the perimeter." Eddy pointed. "Less chance that we run into anyone, and more cover."

Andy nodded, slipping the knife back into its sheath.

Stairs led down from the tunnel to the floor of the cavern below. They were exposed to view, but if they slipped off the side, they could drop to the jungle about two meters below the tunnel mouth, hopefully unnoticed. "How close are we to nightfall?"

Eddy pointed. "I'd say pretty close." As one, all the workers they could see had set down their tools and were making their way back to a cluster of huts near the center of the cavern.

Not a word was spoken between them. They walked in silence, side by side, until they reached the huts. Each one entered a separate hut, and then the strange little world under the mountain was completely still.

"This place is kinda freaking me out," Shandra said softly, reaching out to clasp Andy's hand.

"Yeah, me too." Nightfall came, plunging the cavern into darkness as the wave passed through the plants that lit the space.

"Damn." Andy had gotten used to the coming of night in the bigger world above, but under the mountain, it had a kind of frightening finality.

It wasn't completely dark, though. A row of lanterns lit the main street that ran through the cavern, and some plants still glowed—red ferns in many of the trees gave off a pale pink glow, and night ivy shone silver on the walls of many of the huts.

"We should go find one of those people."

Andy looked at Eddy's silhouette in the darkness. "What?"

"The zombies. Maybe we can snap one of them out of whatever is making them… like *that*."

"What if they sound the alarm?" Andy wasn't sure about this plan, but then again, she didn't really have anything better to offer.

"How else are we going to find out what's going on here? I don't like it either, but we have to do something." Eddy turned to look at her. "Plus there's three of us. We can always knock them out if things go off the rails."

Andy could barely make out his features.

"He's right. We need to do something, and the darkness will make it a lot easier than the morning light." Shandra squeezed her hand.

Andy tried to ignore the shiver that touch sent through her. "Okay." She put her free hand on the ground below her, palm down, searching for a connection, a spark of recognition. Still nothing. "I'd feel a lot better if I could connect to the world mind."

"I know." Eddy understood better than most, having spent so much time with her. "So?"

"I'm game if you two are." She glanced across the cavern in darkness. "Whoever runs this place probably lives up there, in the caverns."

Eddy nodded. "Let's see if we can get in and out before they know we're here."

# 8

## XANADU

ANA CHECKED her stats. "Five minutes to first landing."

Devon nodded inside his suit. "No pressure, right?"

Ana laughed. "A little pressure, maybe. But you'll be great. We practiced this a hundred times on Forever, remember?" She liked this guy. He was easy to work with.

"Yeah, but that didn't involve a space suit, a tumbling asteroid, and live explosives."

"You okay?" She tried to use her most soothing voice.

"I'll manage. I still don't know why you picked me for this." He was shaking.

"Because you have steady hands. And a steady mind." Ana nudged the shuttle closer to the asteroid, adjusting course so the little ship would come down flat at the first diversion point.

They'd christened the little shuttle *Puddle Hopper*, or *Hopper*, for short.

Watching it roll by as she synched *Hopper*'s motion, she couldn't help but remember that wild ride down to Ariadne that had started off this whole mad adventure. That voyage, some forty years before, had changed her life in such a fundamental way that she didn't even recognize her younger self.

That flight, from the deteriorating *Dressler* down to the asteroid's surface, had been much hairier than this one. Here she had direct control of the shuttle's attitude jets, along with the capability to instantly recalculate vectors and force an angle of approach with each minute change. She was, in some ways, a calculus goddess.

Ana grinned at the image. Nothing like taking oneself too seriously. The universe was always ready to knock a person down a peg.

The organic fuel they'd engineered to fill the shuttle tanks seemed to be doing the job. The three shuttles from Transfer Station had been mothballed after the mad dash to evacuate the station six years before, and they'd been all but out of fuel after the overstuffed runs they'd made to get everyone out before the station blew.

"Three minutes." She nudged *Hopper* a little closer, taking into account a spur of rock that could smash the ship to pieces if she wasn't careful.

Devon was a good kid. Aaron had recommended him when she'd asked for a volunteer to help her with this mission. "How's Rafe?"

Devon's shaking subsided a little. "He's good. He's a bit nervous for me—"

"I'll take good care of you. If I had hands...."

He laughed. "Hands are overrated."

"Says the man with two of them. Two minutes." *Hopper* drifted closer to the asteroid. "But don't worry. It's a simple process. You've done it in the practice runs a hundred times. Just take the charge out onto the surface of Isis. It will flash slower and slower until you find the right spot. Then set it down, and it will lock onto the asteroid magnetically."

"Yeah. Easy as pie." He shook his head. "What if it goes off when I put it down?"

"Then you won't have anything to worry about, will you?" she said dryly.

Devon looked up at the camera, a deep frown creasing his face. "Very funny."

"Seriously, the charges can't go off until I trigger them." They were another thing she'd been working on these last few months with Keera.

"Easy for you to say. This thing blows, and you're still safe back home."

"Fair point." She tried to make her voice sound comforting. It wasn't a part of her normal skillset. "Really, you'll be fine. We'll do the first one, and you'll see how easy it is."

"Fine."

"One minute."

Devon nodded without words and unlatched his seat belt, spinning around in the weightless environment to make his way to the hatch. Each of the seats had one of the charges strapped in, deadly passengers on a one-way trip.

The first landing spot was directly below them now, and Ana had matched the spin of the huge chunk of rock and gas and ice. She nudged *Hopper* downward.

"Landing in ten, nine, eight...."

"Yeah, I got it." Devon had freed up the first charge, and he waited, braced against the back of one of the seats.

The shuttle settled down roughly on the asteroid surface, throwing Devon on his ass. "Hey!"

"Sorry about that. I'll do better next time." She didn't tell him it had been intentional, to shake him out of his headspace.

"Save it. I gotta get this thing placed." He punched the release. The air evacuated into the holding tanks, and the shuttle door opened.

He clambered to the ground, held the charge up, and then started off to put it where it needed to be.

*You're still safe back home.*

Forever was their home now. At some point, it had gone from being something new and amazing and alien to the place where they belonged, out in the blackness of the void. A little piece of Earth they were carrying to the stars.

Ana would never get to walk on the soil of an alien world. Her corporeal days were long behind her. She would never know the feeling of an alien sun on her skin or the smell of the air on a new world.

She had been given far more than she had asked for in this life, far more than she'd ever dared to hope.

Somehow that was enough.


COLIN WENT along the tunnel as quickly as he could manage.

It was dark and claustrophobic, even for someone used to the tight confines of a spaceship. He wondered if this was how Ana had felt all those years before. There were no side tunnels and nothing other than patches of glowing moss to relieve the monotonous sameness of the way before him.

On the other hand, it would be hard to get lost.

The mountains were hollow. Who knew?

Actually, the world mind must know. She had built them, after all. There must be many secrets she kept, out of necessity or simply because she had such a vast store of information.

In any case, he would be glad to breathe fresh air again, to look into the wide sky. The liminal sky.

It was a concept he'd played around with over the years. Liminal was one of those strange little words he'd run across once, and it had intrigued him enough to want to look it up. It had two primary meanings—a transitional stage of something, and being at or on both sides of a threshold.

They were certainly on the threshold of history, living in a place the likes of which mankind had never conceived, outside the pages of science fiction. It was also a time of great danger for the species, a moment when the story of mankind had squeezed down from the vastness of the Earth to a relative handful of souls in this generation ship. And maybe the other two ships, if they'd been lucky.

He wondered if anyone had survived on Luna Base or, God help them, on the blasted surface of the Earth itself.

He didn't remember it having taken so long to get to that strange cavern on the way in.

*What the hell was that back there, anyway?* He was uneasy leaving Andy and the others behind, but they were right. Someone had to get the word to Aaron and the folks in Micavery. They had no real organized police force or military, but maybe it was time to create one.

Colin almost fell when he finally reached the edge of the tunnel, it was so abrupt. He found his footing and looked around at the cavern where they'd first entered the mountain.

He tapped his loop. There was still no signal.

Undeterred, he stepped outside into the fresh air.

*God this feels good.* He drew in a deep lungful of the clean air and tried his loop again. "Good evening, Colin." That voice had accompanied him through the last thirty-five or forty years of his life, first as the ship-mind on the *Dressler* and now as the world mind for this grand venture.

"Hi, Lex. I need to speak with Aaron. You, Jackson, and Ana should be a part of this too."

There was a long pause.

"Lex?"

"Ana, Jackson, and Aaron are unavailable at the moment."

"What the hell?"

"Ana is busy with preparations for Rendezvous with 42 Iris."

"Ah, that makes sense. And the others?"

"Jackson disappeared after Glory's ceremony." She sounded uncharacteristically sad.

He'd heard from Aaron about the debate—whether to allow Glory to become a part of the world mind. For his own part, he was ready to go into the great beyond when his time came, but the fight had all but torn poor Aaron apart. "And Aaron?"

"He went to find Jackson."

Now *that* was news. "Went where?"

"I don't know. We thought we would explore Jackson's virtual worlds. Maybe Aaron would have a better sense of where his father might have hidden himself. But then Aaron vanished too—"

"Vanished? How?" This was getting into stranger and stranger territory. "He's gone missing?"

"Not exactly. His body is still in Micavery. But his virtual self... we think he went into Jackson's memories."

"You think?"

"It's the only thing that makes sense. He and Jackson are still here. But we can't reach them."

"What happens if Aaron can't find his way out?"

Another long silence. "I don't know," Lex admitted at last.

*Damn.* "Get me Keera."

"One moment."

Colin shook his head. What had Aaron been thinking? And where the hell was Jackson?

"Hello? Colin?"

"Yes, it's me. Lex's here too. She was just filling me in on the harebrained thing Aaron is doing."

"Have you heard from him? He was supposed to come out of it for dinner. That was an hour ago. I'm starting to get worried."

"He's fine," he lied smoothly. "Look, he's going after his father, and that's just taking longer than he planned."

"That's good." Her relief flooded through the connection between them. "When will he be back?"

"We don't know yet. But I'm with Andy. I'll let her know too."

"Okay."

"Not so fast. We have a problem." He relayed what had happened that afternoon to both of them, ending with the strange scene in the cavern.

"That explains the Ghosts," Keera said when he was done.

"Some of them, anyway. Lex, do you know anything about this place under the mountain?"

"Not really. I know those places exist, of course, but I didn't know anyone was living there. They're waste-processing facilities."

"You mean stomachs?"

"If that metaphor helps, yes. Someone must have found a way to draw out the digestive fluid from one of them." He could almost hear her frown. "That's odd. There's an unusual resource draw in that part of the world, but it didn't trigger any alarms. It's almost as if my senses are deadened there."

"That's what Andy said. Like something had cut that part of Forever off from the rest of the world." He stared up through the darkness at the silver light of the spindle. He missed the stars.

"Let me see what else I can find out," Lex's voice growled. "Now that I'm aware of it, it's really annoying."

"Like having something stuck between your teeth."

"What?" Lex sounded perplexed. "Oh. I see. Yes. Like that."

He had to remind himself Lex wasn't human. "Andy thinks there's someone else on Forever who can manipulate things the way she can."

"Aaron always thought that one of the refugees had inserted the virus that killed Ronan and destroyed Transfer Station," Keera told him.

"Could whoever it is be a danger to you, Lex?"

"Possibly. You should proceed with caution, but in all haste," Lex said. "Whoever it is could cause a lot of damage if we don't contain them. I'll try to break through the bubble."

"Keera, can you roust up a security force and send them my way? Lex can give you the location."

"I'll see what we can do." Her voice sounded strained over the connection.

"Don't worry about Aaron. He can take care of himself."

"I know." She sighed. "I just wish he'd be a little more careful."

Colin laughed. "You knew what you were getting into when you married him. He'll come back to us. I'm going in. When your people get here, send them after us."

"Will do."

He cut the connection and took one last look at the beautiful liminal sky above him.

Then he shrugged and went back inside the cavern. Hopefully Andy and crew hadn't gotten themselves in any trouble.

"I THOUGHT YOU'D ALREADY LEFT." Aaron's mother was frowning at him.

"Left for what?" He looked around. The duffel bag was sitting by the front door. The house was just as he'd remembered it—simple and clean. The warm artificial wood floors gleamed with polish. The walls glowed with radiant paint, the soft shade of gold his mother had chosen when he and Jayson had gone with her to the hardware store. And she wore the same floral-print dress he remembered from the day he'd left.

"Don't give me that. I know you're hell-bent on going to find out what happened to your father." She took his hand and pulled him down to sit on the couch. "And I know I can't stop you. Much as I wish I could."

Aaron was suffering from an intense feeling of déjà vu. He *remembered* this scene, exactly as it was playing out here. His father had been long dead by then.

Was this *his own* memory?

"I have to find him." The same words, separated by twenty-six years but as true today as they were then. Maybe... maybe she could help him now. "Where did Dad love to go more than anywhere else?"

She placed her hands in her lap, squeezing them nervously. "I don't know what you mean."

He'd gone off script. Maybe that made her nervous. Nevertheless, he pushed on. "Where were you happiest together?"

She looked away, as if seeing it in the distance. "There's a little park not far from here, along the banks of the Red River." She got up and made her way to the fireplace mantel. She picked up a photograph in a wooden frame and brought it over to him. "It used to be a golf course, back in the day. Now it's a wild park. Your father liked to take me there when we first came down to Earth. We would walk along the path that fronted the riverbank and try to imagine what the world had been like when it was new."

Aaron took the photo. It showed the two of them on a bench with a bunch of greenery behind them. The sky was a deep blue, without a single cloud. They looked so young. "I think he took me there once, when he was home for a few weeks."

She sat down next to him. "Are you sure you have to go?"

Aaron closed his eyes. He wanted to tell her no. Tell her that he had all the time in the world to spend with her. That he would never leave her side again. She was alive here, as alive as he was.

It wasn't *real*. But did that matter?

He pulled her close. "I love you, Mamma," he whispered, aware of the tears that ran down his cheeks. He looked around at the house, blurry through his wet eyes, and wished he could turn back time.

"Jayson's gone, too, you know. Off to fight the war. They sent him to Seattle for his training."

He stiffened in her arms. That had happened after he left. His memories were getting all jumbled up. "I'm sure he'll be okay," he lied, and let her go, kissing her cheek. "Can I take this?" He held up the framed photo.

"Go ahead. He would like for you to have it."

Aaron nodded and put it inside the duffel.

"Call me when you get to Frontier Station." She rubbed his arm and then turned away.

Aaron pulled out the bauble Lilith had given him and opened the door.

He squeezed it and the world changed.


ANDY EASED herself over the lip of the tunnel, dropping to the ground into the space on one side of the stairs.

It was dark down there, covered by a variety of tropical foliage, huge green leaves black with night shielding her from view.

Shandra and Eddy followed, landing softly next to her.

They'd decided to stop and eat before they went into the strange little village in the middle of the cavern. Who knew if the food was safe to eat, or if it was what kept the villagers drugged?

"We should call it Xanadu," Eddy whispered as Andy pulled out something for them to eat from her pack.

"Xanadu?" Andy knew the old tri dee update—something or other about roller-skating, if she remembered right.

"From 'Kubla Khan.' The old Samuel Taylor Coleridge poem."

· · ·

*In Xanadu did Kubla Khan*
  *A stately pleasure dome decree:*
  *Where Alph, the sacred river, ran*
  *Through caverns measureless to man*
  *Down to a sunless sea.*
  *So twice five miles of fertile ground*
  *With walls and towers were girdled round:*
  *And there were gardens bright with sinuous rills,*
  *Where blossomed many an incense-bearing tree;*
  *And here were forests ancient as the hills,*
  *Enfolding sunny spots of greenery.*

"Oooh, that's beautiful." She wasn't familiar with it, but it had a lovely rhythm.

Eddy nodded. "The story is that Coleridge was high on an opium trip. He had this amazing dream and woke up to write it down, but he only managed a couple pages before he was interrupted by a visitor. When he returned to it, the rest of the poem was gone from his head." Eddy took a sip of water from his canteen.

They shared a quick meal of dried meats and fruit that Andy had brought with her from Darlith. "That's amazing. And a little sad."

"It is. I always wonder what the rest of the poem would have been like. My mother used to read it to me to put me to sleep. She had this old pop-up book that had been her grandmother's." Even in the darkness, Andy could see the faraway look in his eyes.

"I still miss Earth too, sometimes." Shandra's voice was soft, distant.

As she chewed on a piece of dried apple, Andy stared out into the darkness. It wasn't pitch-black. A red fern not far from their hiding place gave off a soft pink glow, enough for her to see the edges of things.

The place was eerie, though. Nothing moved. There was no breeze inside the mountain, and the temperature was a little warmer than she was used to.

She wiped sweat off her brow with the back of her arm.

Shandra pulled something out of her pack and sprinkled it with water. "Here."

It was a clean cloth. "Thanks. Not sure I'd want to live down here. It's a bit...."

"Claustrophobic?"

"Yeah." She wiped her face. The cool water felt really good. "Where did you come from, Shandra?" She'd met the woman before, but they'd never spent much time together.

"Detroit. My mother met a man who was paying for a spot on one of the refugee ships in the final days. She… convinced him to bring her and me along." Her eyes were bright in the partial light, but her dark skin faded into the night.

Andy reached up and touched her cheek. It was wet. "What happened to her?"

Shandra looked away. "Both of them died in the coyote run. The ship was old, falling apart. One of the seals broke, and everyone in that hold died."

"Holy fuck." Eddy shook his head.

"I was in the bathroom, which stayed sealed. It was two more days before we reached Forever and they found me."

Andy took Shandra's hand and squeezed it. "I remember those ships. My father took me to one of them in the middle of the refugee crisis. It was the most horrible thing I've seen in my life."

Shandra nodded. "I still have nightmares. I remember you, though." Shandra kept hold of her hand. "You were a couple of years younger than me. When they brought me onto Transfer Station, you saw me, and you ran to me and gave me the biggest hug. You wouldn't let go for five minutes."

Andy shook her head. "I don't remember that. Those were awful days."

"They were." Eddy closed his pack. "We barely made it here before the end."

"You and…?"

"Davian. He disappeared soon after." He stared out at the cavern. "I wonder if he's here? One of the zombies of Xanadu?" It was probably intended as a joke, but it came out wistful.

"He's the only one here who you knew before, right?"

Eddy nodded. "We had a complicated relationship. He was my lover once, before I transitioned."

"I wonder sometimes what trans folk will do here, where we can't offer them genetic reprofiling anymore." It was a question that had bothered her before. So many skills had been lost in the mad rush to escape the Earth. Treatments for cancer and other deadly diseases. Technology to build, to create, to communicate. They were having to learn a whole new way of life.

"I don't know." He was quiet for a moment. "I guess we'll do what they always have—adapt the best we can."

Andy thought about it for a moment. "I suppose that's all we *can* do. So, shall we go?"

"We should leave our packs here." Eddy looked around. "There's a dark place by the stairs where we can cover them in dead leaves. Take only what we need."

"Good idea." Andy took out a flashlight and her knife and closed her own pack. She tucked it into the hollow in the cavern rock that he'd indicated.

When the others had stashed theirs too, she covered all three with enough debris to hide them from casual inspection.

Eddy, with a nervous glance at the darkness, pulled his crossbow off his back and cocked it.

Then they set off through the jungle, paralleling the pathway toward Xanadu.

# 9

## IN THE HUT

Devon collapsed in the pilot's chair of the shuttle, pulling off his helmet. "Fuck, that feels good." Cool air washed over his face.

"You did a great job." All eight charges had been placed, a process that had taken more than six hours to complete. Though she no longer felt physical fatigue, Ana was tired too. She wanted something distracting to clear her mind. Once she got Devon home—

The shuttle shook, her visuals going jarringly out of focus.

"What happened?" She'd lost control of the shuttle. That shouldn't have happened.

The shaking stopped. She could see Devon's face staring up at the camera, white with fear, but she couldn't hear what he was saying. "Can you hear me?"

Devon was panicking. He looked around wildly and started to unstrap himself.

"Devon, I need you to calm down. If you can hear me, sit down and nod."

He stopped, sank into his chair, and then nodded.

"I can't hear you. I need you to answer me with yes or no answers. Nod for yes, shake your head for no. Is that clear?" He was in danger, and she was *safe back at home.*

Devon nodded.

"Good. Okay, I'm guessing something struck the ship. Is it still holding air?"

He nodded.

"There are no leaks, as far as you can tell?"

He shook his head.

"Good. That's very good." Why couldn't she control the ship? "Okay, I want you to run a diagnostic. Here's what you need to do. I will give you each step, one at a time. Are you ready?" She needed to discover if the ship was still operational. If so, she had a chance to get him home.

He nodded again. "Okay, here's what I want you to do." She walked him through it, step by step. Thank the stars he could still hear her. This would have been next to impossible if her audio channel to the shuttle had been shut down in both directions.

He followed her instructions perfectly. In three minutes, the diagnostic was running.

He sat back and started shaking.

"Listen to me, Devon. We're going to get you home. You hear me?"

"How?" he mouthed.

"We're going to teach you how to fly a shuttle."

AARON STEPPED through the door into the park, and when he turned to look behind him, his mother's house was gone.

It was a cool, cloudy day, like early November, with a breeze blowing up off the river to thread its fingers under his shirt.

Aaron shivered.

The river was brown with silt. A woman ran past him, jogging along the riverside path. A hover boarder zipped by overhead from the other direction, giving him a thumbs-up.

How had all these people faced their last day, when the end had finally come?

A man stood with his back to Aaron, down at the waterside. He wore a checkered flannel shirt. His square shoulders and red hair told Aaron who he was at a glance.

Aaron crossed the pathway, careful to avoid a slide boarder who slipped past him heading north. He came to stand next to the man. "Bit cool today."

"Sure is. Might even get into the fifties this winter…." The man turned to look at him. "Hey, son! What are you doing down here? I thought your mother was watching you this afternoon."

"It's a long story." This was his father at around thirty-five, not long before he'd left them for good. Aaron was familiar with the shirt. His mother had given it to Jackson for Christmas that year. "What are you doing?"

"Just soaking in a little of the Old Lady. I'll be gone for a couple months this next time. I like to have some memories to tide me over while I'm stuck in a tin can."

Aaron nodded. "I remember what it was like when you were gone. Mom took care of us, but it wasn't the same. Then you'd come home and bring us something amazing from Frontier Station, and it was all forgotten." He sighed.

Jackson ruffled his hair. "I always miss you when I'm up there."

"I know you do." Aaron took a deep breath. It was a gorgeous day, the sun warm on his shoulders. He'd almost forgotten what that felt like. A pair of ducks flew over the river, the mallard quacking and chasing after the other.

"What brought you down here to find me? You did tell Glory you were coming."

Aaron nodded. "I was looking for you. Ana and Lex sent me." He was pretty sure this wasn't Jackson, though. Not the current Jackson. Another memory.

"Who?"

"Nothing. Just a couple friends."

"Ah." His father—or the memory of him—knelt to pick up a flat rock. "Did I ever show you how to skip a rock across the river?"

Aaron smiled. "Yeah. But show me again."

Jackson grinned, that wide smile that always made those around him feel good. "You hold it like so." He held up his hand. "Wrap your index finger around the edge. Keep it flat to the ground. Then you pull back, and let it go like this." The white rock flew through the air and skipped across the surface of the river. "One, two, three times!" Jackson picked up another and handed it to Aaron. "Now you try it."

His hand was warm on Aaron's arm as he showed his son how to fling the rock through the air with enough spin and speed to skip across the water.

Aaron picked up a stone, remembering how simple things had been then. He closed his eyes for a moment, squeezing back tears.

Jackson patted him on the shoulder. "Go ahead. Just like I showed you."

Aaron pulled his arm back and then flung the stone across the water.

"One, two, three, four!" Jackson exclaimed, holding up his hands to high-five Aaron. "The student surpasses the master."

Aaron laughed. *This* was the man he missed, the carefree soul who loved to spend time with his sons when he was home. "I wish you were still here."

"I know." Jackson pulled Aaron into his arms.

His father thought he meant the next mission. Not his father. His father's memory.

"I'm sorry I left you and your mother and brother. I'm sorry I didn't come home."

Aaron stiffened under Jackson's embrace. "What?"

Jackson held him out at arm's length. "I'm not him. But I remember what happened to him. To me. We loved you, Aaron Hammond. He still does."

The memories were all flowing together. Time was confused, and so was Aaron. "I don't understand."

"Come with me. I'll show you where he is. They're waiting for you."

"They?"

"Shhhh. Everything will make sense soon." He took Aaron's hand and pulled him up onto the pathway, putting an arm around his shoulders.

Aaron allowed himself to be led down the riverside, hoping he wasn't losing his mind.

EDDY STARED WARILY at the small hut that lay across an open lawn, maybe fifteen meters from where they knelt. The jungle gave them cover, but there was nothing to hide them in the intervening space.

His crossbow lay on the ground next to him, ready for him to take up at a second's notice.

The huts were clustered around a small lake that glimmered in the light from lanterns around its perimeter. The huts themselves were small, no more than two meters square. How they managed to fit anything besides a small bed inside, he had no idea.

It had taken them the better part of an hour to get there from the edge of the cavern. They'd taken their time, working their way through the under-brush. There was no animal life here, at least none they had seen beyond the two sheep and the people who had vanished into their dwellings for the night.

"There's no one here," Andy argued, glancing around the wide green sward.

"You can't know that for sure. Any one of those huts could house a guard or two." He could see at least seven of them nearby, each with a dark window space pointed in their general direction.

"We haven't seen any activity since nightfall. Do we just wait here all night?" She sounded annoyed.

"I didn't say that. Let's just give it some time to see if anything reveals itself." Eddy got it. He was tired too. It had been a long day and a weird one at that.

"All right. Ten more minutes." They sat in silence, watching the cluster of huts.

These must have been mostly refugees, people who had come to Forever hoping for a new start, for an escape from the tyranny, pollution, and decadence of Old Earth. People who had never been officially accounted for, or counted and logged at Transfer Station before it had been destroyed.

And what had they found? Some kind of mass enslavement, cut off from the rest of human society.

Eddy shuddered as he thought about the lives these poor souls led in Xanadu. It was paradise in appearance only.

"I see something." Shandra interrupted his thoughts. She pointed at one of the farther huts.

Eddy picked up his crossbow.

Sure enough, someone was coming out of it. Whoever it was whistled softly in the darkness as he climbed the stairs of the next hut and disappeared inside. "What's he doing?"

Andy shrugged. "Making house calls?"

"Your guess is as good as mine."

By mutual agreement, they waited another ten minutes. Eddy was just about to suggest that they try one of the huts when the man came out again and clambered down the steps to the lawn. He turned and bypassed the next cabin, then entered the one closest to them.

It was hard to make out any details other than his general shape. He was stocky and masculine, with close-cropped hair, its color indeterminate in the dim light.

The door closed, leaving them in doubt again. He eased the crossbow back to the ground.

"I say we go into the hut he skipped." Andy stared across the grassy space at the dark building.

Eddy nodded. "He seems to spend ten minutes or so at each hut. Let's wait and see if he moves on first."

Sure enough, the man emerged like clockwork from the hut and moved along down the line, disappearing from sight.

"Okay, this is our chance. One at a time. Andy, want to go first?"

"Sure—I'll make for the porch. It looks dark up there." She crept out of the jungle and ran across the intervening space to the structure. Night ivy on the side of the house cast a silver light across the ground, throwing the darkness of the porch into sharp relief.

Turning, Andy signaled for them to follow.

Shandra went next.

Soon all three of them were on the little porch. The hut looked like it had been made by hand from mallowood or something like it. It was neat and utilitarian, with no visible decoration. "Ready?" Eddy whispered.

The others nodded.

He pushed open the door a hair with the end of his crossbow. "Hello?" he said softly.

There was no answer.

Eddy opened the door wide and stepped inside. His eyes took a moment to adjust to the darkness, but soon he could make out details in the gloom.

The room was tiny, with space only for a small bed. A woman lay all alone on it, fast asleep. At least, he *hoped* she was asleep.

Andy and Shandra came in to stand next to him.

"I think I know what he was doing in the other huts," Eddy whispered.

The woman was pregnant.

# 10

## DREAMS AND NIGHTMARES

ANA BREATHED a sigh of relief.

It had taken them half an hour, but they'd managed to get the audio online. It was so much easier now that Devon could reply to her directly instead of miming or writing down his responses.

The diagnostic had confirmed what she had feared. Something—probably a stray chunk of Iris following along in her wake—had sheared off the shuttle's navigation and guidance module. They'd been lucky. Half a meter's difference and the shuttle could have taken a direct hit, leading to explosive decompression.

She refrained from mentioning that part to Devon, who was scared enough as it was.

Ana tended to forget the risks of being flesh and blood, safe as she was in the confines of the world mind. It had been twenty-six years since she'd felt the wind on her skin or real danger.

*Twenty-six years since I saw Glory in the real world....*

She shuffled Jackson's thought aside. Even when he was gone, he bled into her mind.

"So, Doc, what now?" Devon stared up at her through the camera.

*Keep it together, Ana.* "Okay, from here on out, it's easy."

Devon snorted.

"Okay, relatively easy. Put your palm on the sensor. You've already been authorized to fly *Hopper*."

"There's a green flashing light."

The shuttle systems were so simple compared to modern ships. Not that there were any more modern ships. "Great. Now speak this command. 'Manual control to pilot.'"

"Manual control to pilot. Hey, something's happening!"

"Yes. The manual controls should have appeared on the dash. There's a joystick and a landing button. The first controls your thrust through space. It's simple. Just point in the direction you want to go. There's just one catch."

"What's that?"

"The diagnostic shows that you are low on fuel. There may have been a leak. We were getting low to begin with, but we were still within operation parameters—"

"Meaning?"

"We had enough to get you home. Now...." She checked the numbers again.

"Don't leave me hanging like that."

"Sorry. It's going to be close."

"How close?"

"Just... close." She had to come up with a backup plan, just in case. She was *not* going to have another death on her conscience.

"Okay. So, what now?"

"Say, 'Target location.'"

"With my hand still on the pad?"

"Yes."

"Target location."

"Then repeat this." She reeled off a string of spatial coordinates.

"Done."

"Okay. Say, 'Lock target.'"

"Hey, I'm not blowing something up, am I?"

Ana grinned. "No, just locking in your destination."

"Got it." He gave her the thumbs-up.

"Now use the joystick. In the cockpit window, you should see a cone of lines."

He pushed forward gently. "I see it."

"Line the ship up with the center of the lines."

A short pause. "Hey, I'm doing it! I'm flying a fricking shuttle!"

"Yes, you are. Let's get you up to about 600 kilometers an hour, then ease off. Can you see Forever from the shuttle?"

He peered out of the window. "No, I don't think... wait, there was a glint there in the middle of the cone."

"That's it. Once you get up to speed, just let it coast. You should be here in six hours."

"Then what?"

*Then we hope you have enough fuel left to slow down.* "Then we bring you home."

FOR JUST A FEW MOMENTS, Aaron was a child again, basking in the warmth of his father's love and approval. Everything else fell away as they walked along the riverside, shaded from the afternoon heat by the ancient oak trees that lined the pathway. They talked about simple things—the weather, the plans for their next vacation, Jackson's hopes for Aaron and his brother Jayson.

Aaron let himself be lulled by the fiction. His father at his side. The feel of the sun beaming down on his face. The return to a time before he had so much responsibility weighing on his shoulders.

For a brief moment, he was simply happy and whole.

The interval came to an end when Jackson took his arm off Aaron's shoulders. "We're here."

"Where?"

"Look."

This part of the park had a short wooden pier that sat over the Red River. At the end of the pier, two figures stood looking out over the water.

Aaron shot a questioning look at his father.

"Go."

Aaron hugged him. Even if he was just a memory, he was a good one, and he'd brought Aaron comfort. Aaron let go, and his "father" smiled, fading into nothing until only his Cheshire grin remained. Then that was gone too.

Aaron turned to approach his father and whoever was with him. He stepped onto the pier, and Jackson turned to smile at him.

*The real Jackson?*

"Hey, Scout. I wondered when you would get here."

Aaron was at a loss for words. He was still angry at Jackson for taking away his last minutes with his mother, but he'd come so far to find him.

Then the other person turned around. It was Glory, looking like she had when she was thirty.

"Mom!" He ran toward her, and she held out her arms to him, squeezing him tightly.

"Hey, *mijo!*" She kissed his cheek. She smelled just like he remembered her, the perfume she had shipped from Mexico City that smelled like citrus and sunshine.

He held her out at arm's length. "Is this really you? Or are you just another memory?"

She laughed. "It's me. I think. Your father brought me here."

Aaron looked at Jackson, who nodded. *When I blacked out....* "But you said you couldn't.... That it wasn't right." *Am I going crazy?*

"I know. I'm so sorry, Scout. I wanted to save her. More than anything. Ana and Lex told me it was a bad idea. We could only accommodate so many of us in here. That it would set a bad precedent."

"So, you did it anyhow."

Jackson nodded. "In the end... how could I not? I knew the others wouldn't agree. I hid her here, and we've been talking ever since."

Glory looked around. "This is an amazing place. I still can't believe you never told me about this. And him."

*She's right.* "I know. We thought.... Jackson thought it would be too hard on you. That you wouldn't understand."

"He told me. Just as he told me why he took his own life, all those years ago." She sat down on a bench that looked out over the water. "Those were hard years, just the three of us. Then we lost Jayson...."

Aaron sat down next to her. "I know, Mamma." He stared at her, hardly able to believe she was there. "I can't tell you how happy I am to see you again."

She took his hand in her lap and squeezed it. "About that...."

"What?"

Glory looked up at Jackson. "We have something to tell you."

Jackson came to sit on his other side. "Your mother and I have talked this out for days, since she... came here."

"Forever—the world itself—is a divine creation, even if it was sculpted by the hands of man. And these virtual worlds...." She shrugged. "We could live in here and explore for years. Create new places. Be together."

Aaron's eyes narrowed. "I don't like where this is going."

"I've always believed I was brought to Forever for a reason. That it was my job to help shepherd humanity from Earth to the stars." Jackson put a hand on Aaron's shoulder. "I've been proud of the part I played and even prouder of you and Andy."

"Don't say it." His voice caught in his throat.

"I think my time here will be over soon."

"Over?" Aaron was confused. He'd just found his mother and father, and they were trying to tell him they were leaving? Now he really did feel like he was fifteen all over again.

"Yes. This isn't real. This marvelous place is all bits and zeroes, and I don't understand the rest. But it's not where we were meant to go, not in the long run. Your father and I—we believe we were put on Earth, put here for a reason, and when our time is up, we will be called home." She touched the cross that hung around his neck. "I remember when the priest gave your father that, to commemorate your confirmation."

"I wear it every day." Aaron had never considered himself a particularly religious man, though he'd gone to church regularly with his parents, and then with his mother. And yet he knew how important her religion was to her, and by extension, to his father. "I don't think.... I'm not ready." He suppressed a sob. "I—"

Jackson pulled him close. "I know. We never are. I wasn't ready to lose you when the time came on the *Dressler*. Glory wasn't ready to go when cancer took her." He squeezed Aaron tightly to his chest. "We love you more than you can know. We'll always be with you, even once we're gone."

Glory put her arms around them, and he could no longer hold it in.

Aaron wasn't ready. They couldn't go. *Oh God, I can't do this.*

He cried for what seemed like an age, the tears running salty into his mouth, until he was exhausted with grief.


ANDY AND the others had searched fifteen of the little huts so far—about half of the huts on this side of the lake. Every one held a single woman, and more than half of them were visibly pregnant. They wore matching gray night-gowns, with gray work clothes hung next to their beds.

They also slept like the dead.

Andy had tried to wake several of them, but nothing would shake them out of their unconscious state.

Andy sank down on the edge of the bed of one of the women, who looked to be at least seven months pregnant by the size of her belly. "I don't understand it. What's going on here? A zombie city, women and men sleeping alone, and all of these women with child. What am I missing?"

"Who was the man we saw? Was he... was he impregnating these women?" Eddy scowled.

Andy agreed. Whatever was happening in this place was monstrous. Something had been done to these women to keep them compliant. They were like brood mares. She shuddered.

They had to find a way to reach one of them, to get some answers.

Shandra sat next to the woman, smoothing her hair back. "She looks so peaceful." Shandra squeezed the woman's hand. "Could you... could you do that thing you do with biominds... with her?"

Andy shook her head. "It doesn't work like that. I can connect with people if they're on the network, just like any of you." She didn't mention how she could ride along with someone's consciousness. "But I don't think I can just reach into a normal mind."

Shandra nodded. "Maybe hers isn't a *normal* mind."

"What do you mean?"

Eddy responded. "Nothing we've seen down here is remotely normal."

"He's right. Look at the trap someone left for Eddy. And the way someone sealed up the cavern entrance with stone." Shandra glanced at the sleeping woman. "Maybe this isn't normal either."

Those things had been bugging Andy too. She'd assumed the women were drugged. That some external substance had been used to make the people docile.

What if she was wrong? What if this was something else? "It couldn't hurt to try. I'll need to touch her."

Shandra switched places with her.

The woman was pretty enough. Probably midtwenties, brown hair cropped short, fine features. Who was she? Where had she come from? Her skin tone said maybe Filipino or some mix of South Pacific and Southeast Asian.

Had she chosen to come here? Or was Xanadu chosen for her?

Either way, had she expected to be treated like this?

The events six years before had been a crash course in the depths of what humanity was capable of. Atrocities as impersonal as the Collapse, when mankind had destroyed its own home, and as personal as the treatment of refugees who'd been left to die from hunger, thirst, sickness, and exposure in the various bits of space junk that had been used to haul them up into orbit and ultimately to Transfer Station.

The cruel death that had been meted out to poor Ronan, the Transfer Station mind who had given his own life to keep her safe.

Even so, this was a new low.

Andy sighed. She supposed she would have to find a way to put a little light into the world to combat the darkness she'd seen.

She closed her eyes and laid her hand on the woman's forehead, expecting nothing.

Static electricity shocked her, and the following flood threatened to overwhelm her senses. A thunderstorm raged inside the woman's mind, fog and thunderclouds, hard rain, lightning and thunder.

That was the best she could manage to describe it, as her own mind struggled to make sense of what she felt and saw. Beneath the calm exterior, the woman's mind was in constant terrible turmoil.

She let go and the shock receded.

"You okay? Your face went white." Shandra put an arm around her shoulder.

"I… I think so." Thunder. Lightning. "You were right. She is different. I made some kind of connection, but it's chaos in there."

"Can you get through it?"

Andy considered. "I don't know if there *is* anything else."

Shandra squeezed her hand.

"I guess I have to try." Someone had done this to these women. She was sure of it, though she didn't know how. "I can try to draw off the noise, the confusion."

Eddy shook his head. "That sounds dangerous. What if you get lost?" He grimaced. "Your father would never forgive me."

"I have to try. Whoever did this… what if they decide to do this to others? What if they start bringing more women here?" She took a deep breath. "What if they plan to do this… out there?"

They all knew what she meant. In their own homes.

She had her answer. "I have to try."

Eddy stared at her for a long moment. At last he nodded. "But you break out at the first sign of danger."

"I'll try." In truth, she'd never confronted anything like this before, so she had no idea what would happen.

They sat next to her, each putting a hand on her shoulder.

Andy reached out and touched the woman's forehead again. She was expecting it, but it was as bad as she remembered.

Wild winds howled, and mist spun through the darkness. A wayward gust caught her, spinning her off into the void.

She clung to her sense of self, visualizing it as a golden cord that led back to her mind. To the real world, and to Shandra and Eddy. She held it tightly, fighting the wind, pulling herself hand over hand toward some sense of control.

When she reached the end of the rope, she turned back, holding on with one hand and stretching the other arm out into the storm.

She closed her eyes and pulled.

The storm responded, streaming into her, rending and ripping as it went.

Her arm shattered, and she screamed, but she kept pulling as she was battered, inside and out, with hail and electricity and hurricane-force winds. Her skin darkened as if she'd been burned, and the storm raged.

It threatened to tear her apart.

Then she felt it, Eddy's touch on her left shoulder and Shandra on her right. They weren't *here*, but they were with her.

She turned toward the storm and redoubled her efforts, dissipating in turn, breaking it apart and taking it into herself piece by piece. Hours went by that lasted just seconds, and time stretched out and snapped into place.

At last, it was gone. There was only white light, and in the middle of it knelt a woman.

Andy's broken arm healed, her skin lightening until she was as she had been before the storm.

She approached the woman, kneeling next to her. "It's okay. The storm is gone. You're safe now."

The woman opened her eyes, looked up, and screamed.

## 11

## JUMP

Lex was stymied. She'd been trying to find a way into the bubble that someone had used to sever the cavern under the mountain from the rest of the world. It was a dead zone, as if someone had cut off one of her limbs. She could still tell it was there, but she couldn't reach it or *feel* it.

*Andy.* The girl was down there, and while she couldn't reach Lex, maybe Lex could reach her, through her loop. It was worth a try.

She was going to have to redirect a few resources to make a signal strong enough to pierce the mountain. In the process, she might blow out some of the other colonists' loops, but it was a risk that had to be taken. If she could direct the signal tightly enough, she could probably avoid collateral damage.

Whoever had taken out Ronan, the Transfer Station mind, could do the same to her as well. To the three Immortals who formed the mental core of Forever. If that happened.... She shivered.

If that ever happened, everyone else was as good as dead.

Devon was sweating. He could feel the drops dotting his forehead inside the visor.

Ana had told him to put his suit back on. He sat at *Hopper's* controls, watching as his whole world approached through the plas window of the shuttle. It was dark now—it must be night inside.

His loop confirmed it—about 4:30 a.m. Forever Time.

"Is this going to work?" he asked nervously across the comm. Why had he agreed to take this mission? Rafe was right. He was an idiot.

Then he remembered. He'd wanted to see the stars again.

Ana's voice came back after a two-second delay. "It should."

He'd hoped for a little more certainty in her voice.

"Okay, commence slowdown now." He did take solace in having her to guide him.

Devon watched the fuel gauge closely. It was perilously low. "Commencing slowdown." He eased the joystick backward and the shuttle's attitude jets fired in reverse. The drag started to slow *Hopper's* forward momentum. "It's working."

"Watch your fuel. When you have just one bar left on the display, ease up on your deceleration."

"Got it." Through the plas window, Forever seemed as close as his hand, and as far away as the sun.

The shuttle's forward motion slowed, but he was still moving forward at a fair clip, according to the readouts. It was hard to tell objectively, without any nearby reference points. Devon decided that he *hated* space.

His fuel was almost out. "Switching to vertical." Ana had shown him how to access some of *Hopper's* basic programming, and they'd set up a shortcut to reorient the shuttle so her belly was facing Forever. He activated it and felt the ship shudder as it began to turn.

There was a sharp crack.

"That doesn't sound good." A whistling sound pierced the thick fabric of his suit. "Dammit, I think we just lost structural integrity." He smiled despite his dire circumstances. His tri dee viewing habits were finally paying off, just in time for him to die. Life really was the shits sometimes.

"Are you okay? Is the shuttle holding?" Ana sounded nervous. Well, it was more that special kind of calm where you knew the person was nervous as hell inside but didn't want you to know it.

He looked around behind him. Loose things in the ship were being sucked to a point near the back of the shuttle. "It's holding together, but there's a bit of a hole."

"Okay, we're going to abort the last part."

"The landing jets?" They had hoped there would be enough fuel to bring *Hopper* to a near standstill as he approached Forever.

"Yes. I'm afraid any more trauma to the hull might... well, let's just say it would be bad for you."

"Fair enough." He'd seen enough videos of explosive decompressions in his lifetime to know what she meant. "So?" His hands were shaking. He forced them into his lap.

"You're approaching Forever. You'll be passing by in about two minutes."

"Shit." He unbuckled himself from the pilot seat.

"I have *Catcher* out here to pick you up. I just have to perform some space gymnastics to pull it off."

"*Catcher?*"

"One of the other shuttles. Just a bit of baseball humor."

Devon frowned. "Are you good at gymnastics?"

"Of course. I'm Russian, darling."

He laughed despite his circumstances. "Okay."

"Get to the exit." Ana remembered that time, decades earlier, when she'd had to make such a leap herself. When only Jackson's calm action had saved her.

"Going."

"I want you to release the door in ten seconds and jump. Ten, nine...."

Was she serious? He was supposed to just leave the admittedly dubious safety of *Hopper* and fling himself out into space?

"... three, two, one... go!"

*Shit oh shit oh fuuuuuuuuck....* The door blasted away from the shuttle. He didn't have to jump. The remaining atmosphere inside pushed him out, knocking the wind out of him.

He gasped, trying to catch his breath, watching helplessly as *Hopper* and he diverged courses, the little shuttle becoming smaller and smaller.

At last the air returned to his lungs in a huge gasp. "Oh fuck." He heaved, trying to get past that horrible feeling of suffocation.

He spun past Forever, seeing it each time his body tumbled over. As he passed, it lit up with morning light, a glorious sight from the outside. *Maybe the last thing I'll ever see.*

He closed his eyes, remembering all the moments that had brought him here. His mother back home in South Africa. His brothers, lost to the wars. His selection as a colonist on Forever.

Meeting Rafe.

Their on-and-off-again thing had become an always kind of thing.

Rafe's face floated in the darkness before him, his brown eyes and ready grin warming Devon's heart. His beautiful Rafe. "I love you," he whispered.

"I love you too," came Rafe's voice over his comm.

Devon tried to turn, to look around, but there was nothing to give him purchase. "Rafe, is that you?"

"Yeah, damn straight it is."

"How in the hell…?"

"We're coming up to get you. I see you now."

Out of the darkness the other shuttle, the one Ana had labeled *Catcher*, appeared like the sweetest bit of heaven Devon had ever seen. It was under him, and he was slowly falling into its embrace.

Ana had matched his speed and trajectory. "You're a helluva gymnast after all." He dropped slowly toward the shuttle.

"Told you so." She sounded just a little proud.

A figure was standing on *Catcher's* roof, anchored to it with magnetic boots. Rafe. He waved.

Devon literally fell into his arms, almost knocking them both off the shuttle, but Rafe caught him, and his magnetic boots held.

He tilted Devon down so his own shoes grasped the metallic surface of the shuttle, and they touched helmets.

"Hey." Devon was still in shock.

"Told you I'd always come for you."

"You did. I could kiss you."

"Later." He took Devon's hand. "Come on. Let's go home."


LEX ASSESSED their hastily cobbled-together apparatus. Keera had helped them with it, scrounging materials from one of the shuttles—an amplifier for Micavery Port's main antenna. With it, they should be able to pierce the mountain where Andy was hidden, and if they could connect, they might be able to find a way to pierce the bubble.

They sent messages to Ana and Jackson. Ana was free and responded immediately. "What's happening?" She appeared next to Lex.

"Something strange has come up." Lex shared all they knew in an info burst, and Ana's brow furrowed. "That shouldn't be possible."

"And yet…."

Ana nodded. "What can I do to help?"

Lex felt the familiar warmth that meant Jackson had joined them too. "Your timing is impeccable. Where have you been?"

"It's a long story, one we can deal with after whatever crisis you've cooked up." He grinned. "You're looking lovely and androgynous today."

"Yeah, thanks." Lex laughed wryly. "And this crisis is not my fault." They shot him the same information they'd sent to Ana.

Jackson frowned as he reviewed it. "That's not good."

"Always a talent for understatement." Ana looked over her transmitter's specs. "You sure this won't burn out anyone's loops?"

Lex shook her head. "I'm sending out a warning now for everyone in range to shut down their loops for an hour. That's the Verge, the Anatovs, and a little way past them toward Darlith."

"Can I help?" Aaron, or his virtual self, stood there next to his father. As did his mother, Glory.

Lex stared at Jackson, frowning. "We'll discuss this later."

"Of that I have no doubt."

"Aaron, let your wife know you're okay. She's been worried sick." Humans were such a jumble of contradictory emotions.

"She wasn't the only one." Aaron closed his eyes. When he reopened them a moment later, he nodded. "Done. Now what are we doing?"

"Sending Andy a lifeline."


INSIDE THE HUT, Andy clamped a hand over the woman's mouth, getting bitten for her trouble. "It's okay," she said softly as Shandra ran to check the door. "You're okay now." The woman's mind was clear, the raging storm gone.

There was only stark-naked fear.

"I'm going to remove my hand now." Andy loosened her grip. "We're not going to hurt you. Do you understand?"

The woman nodded.

Andy let her go.

The woman's whole body was shivering.

Andy pulled the blanket up over her body. "Do we have anything to give her to drink?"

"Water?" Shandra offered her canteen, still looking out the door.

"Something stronger?"

Eddy handed her a metal flask.

She twisted open the cap, smelled inside, and wrinkled her nose. "What is it?"

"Home spirits. One of my friends makes them out on the Verge."

"Good enough." Andy held out the flask to the woman. "Here. It will calm your nerves."

The woman shook her head.

*She doesn't trust me.* No big surprise there. "Here, watch." She took a sip, and her mouth twisted in disgust. "Damn, Eddy, this is some strong stuff."

He grinned. "Just a little takes the edge off."

She handed it to the woman, who looked at it for a moment, then sat up to take a sip. The same grimace crossed her face, but after a minute, she took another and then handed it back, nodding. "Thank you."

Andy gave the flask to Eddy, mouthing a silent *thank-you*. "I'm Andy."

"I'm Sara. Sara Finch." She wiped her mouth with the back of her hand.

Andy had so many questions, but she didn't want to spook the woman. She'd obviously been through a traumatic experience. "Are you... do you feel better?"

Sara laughed harshly. "I don't even know how to answer that."

"Okay." *Try another tack?* "We want to help you. We want to help all the people who are trapped here, but we need to know how you got here and what happened to you. Do you think you can manage that?" She put her hand gently on Sara's, but the woman jerked away.

"I... I can try. I'm sorry. Please don't touch me."

"Okay." *Poor thing.*

Sara wrapped her arms around her knees, pulling them toward her chest. "We came up from Earth the last month before everything ended. Trevor was an electrical engineer. I taught high school kids in Winnipeg."

"My family came from Fargo."

A wistful look crossed Sara's face. "We went to Fargo once, on vacation."

Andy nodded. It was something. "So, what happened next?"

"About half of the people in our cargo ship died from some *Chaf* virus." She spat the word out. "Trevor came through it okay. I got really sick for about a week, but then it passed, and they put us in the refugee camp."

"I remember that place. I was there many times." Andy wanted to take the woman in her arms and hug her, but the poor thing was so frightened of any touch.

"The camp was a terrible place. Living out in the open, with little food or access to personal hygiene supplies. But it was heaven compared to Agartha."

"Agartha?" Andy didn't know that one.

"This place. 'Paradise at the center of the Earth.' That's what the Preacher calls it."

Now they were getting somewhere. "You're doing great, Sara." She noticed that Sara had a scar on her left temple. "Who is the Preacher?"

"No one knows. He showed up at the end, right after we heard about what happened to Earth." She stifled a sob. "So many beautiful places back home. So many people—family, friends. Gone forever."

"I know." Andy had never seen them, not firsthand. She had a hard time imagining the wide-open skies of Earth. But she had seen pictures of so many amazing places, past and present. She wondered if they were still fresh, for Sara—or if whatever the Preacher had done to her had left her in an arrested state. "So... the Preacher?"

"He came to the camp and convinced a bunch of us that we were second-class citizens up here. That we would never get what we deserved, not unless we went off on our own." She shuddered. "If I had known then what I know now...."

"Um, Andy?" Shandra looked nervous.

"Give me a sec. We're getting somewhere here."

"Sorry. We have company." She pointed outside.

"I'll be right back." Andy crept up behind Shandra to look out the doorway.

The villagers had woken up, and at least ten of them stood outside. "What are they doing?"

"Nothing, so far." Shandra and Andy exchanged a worried glance. "Maybe you can hurry this along?"

"I'll try." Andy went back to the bed. "Sorry, Sara, but your... friends are starting to arrive. When we found you, there was this weird... fog? Storm? Static, maybe, in your head."

"How did you know about that?" Sara's eyes went wide.

"I can touch minds, especially biominds...."

Sara's eyes went wide. "*You're* the one who made the bathrooms at the refugee camp. I remember you."

"Yeah, I did. But I would never use my ability to hurt someone. I didn't even know I could touch someone else's mind directly. Not until I tried with you."

"You took away the pain." Her eyes were wide.

"Yes."

Sara launched herself toward Andy. Before Andy could defend herself, Sara had her arms around her. "Thank you, thank you, thank you. Oh God, you don't know how horrible it was."

"You're welcome."

"I was trapped in my own mind. I could see everything. Feel everything. Feel it when Gunner would come here every night to rape me...." She trailed off into silence.

Andy let go of Sara, easing her onto the bed. "Gunner. Is he the one who did this to you? This thing in your head?"

"Yes."

"I'm so sorry." Jesus, how monstrous was this place? Forced labor, mental pain, rape....

"You have to help the others."

"Is your husband still here?"

Sara shook her head. "I don't know. We rarely see the other men."

Andy sighed. "Okay. I'll do what I can." She touched the woman's temple. "You used to have a loop, yes?"

Sara nodded. "Yes. The Preacher cut it out of me."

Andy shuddered. Who was this *Preacher*? "Okay, Shandra, can you stay here with her?"

"What are you going to do?" Shandra looked as angry as Andy felt.

"I'm going to fuck with the Preacher's plans."


IN THE VIRTUAL park beside the Red River, Jackson frowned.

"What is it?" Aaron thought his parents had moved beyond their concern for Earthly—or was it Foreverly?—things.

"Lex needs us. It's Andy."

His father must have reopened communications with the other Immortals. Aaron got up from the park bench. "Let's go." What had she gotten herself into now?

Glory took his hand. "We'll fix it, whatever it is."

He hugged her tightly.

Jackson took their hands, and the river faded away as if it had never been.

## 12

---

# STORMS AND THUNDER

THE VILLAGERS had gathered around the hut. There were maybe a hundred of them in all. Most were adults, but there were at least fifteen children, ages five and under, from the looks of them, and as many or more pregnant women.

"I'm not going to hurt you." Andy held her hands open, palms up, trying to show them she was no threat.

Behind her, Eddy eyed the crowd nervously. "You sure this is a good idea?"

"No, but we have to do something."

The people were like cattle, silent, shuffling back and forth from one foot to another. They needed a leader to tell them what to do.

Andy knelt next to a five-year-old girl clothed in some kind of home-woven brown cloth. Her reddish-blonde hair was trimmed short, and she had the same vacant look in her eyes as the others.

"Hi, sweetie." Andy cradled the girl's cheek in her hand. "I'm gonna make you feel better. I won't hurt you."

The girl stared at her, uncomprehending. Was she like Sara, or did she not know how to communicate at all?

Andy closed her eyes and reached inside the girl's head.

Immediately the fury of the storm slammed into her, and it kindled a corresponding fury in her own heart. How could someone do this to a child? To anyone?

Eddy put a hand on her shoulder again. "You can do this."

She nodded. She was better prepared this time.

She pulled the storm out of the girl, bit by bit, tethered by Eddy's presence. It wracked her mind and heart, but she was stronger now, ready for it.

The little girl's body shook as the last of it was pulled from her mind.

Andy grabbed her and held her tight as the tears started to flow. "It's okay, little one. It's okay."

The girl cried for a long time while the rest of the village watched. Behind each of those eyes, a soul waited for her to set it free.

It was too much. She couldn't possibly help them all, could she?

She had to try.

Shandra had come out of the hut. She knelt next to Andy, and with her permission, she took the girl in her arms. "Sara says she will take her."

Andy nodded. She tried to keep herself calm, to push down the rage at the people who had done this. *To a child.*

Shandra stood and carried her inside.

Andy also stood and took a deep breath before moving on to the next person, a young dark-haired man with beautiful mocha skin.

Eddy anchored her again, and she reached.

The same storm raged inside his head. As she unspooled it, to spin it away through her own consciousness, Andy wondered where it had come from. How had this been done to these poor people?

This time it was a little easier, as if the channel through her mind had become hardened by the passing of the previous storms, beaten down and solidified like dried mud after a tempest.

Bits and pieces of the man's life passed through her mind. On Earth, when he'd worked in a huge tower in a desert country, and later, when he'd come here, to Xanadu. Or Agartha.

Never-ending days of work in this forsaken place, followed by food and forced sleep.

She felt when his eyes focused, that moment when he came back to himself.

"*Astaghfirullah.*" His eyes were wide open.

"Are you okay?" Andy pulled back to look him in the face.

"I... I think so. *Shaytan* took me... how long have I been here?" He looked around as if seeing Agartha for the first time.

"Best guess, six years?"

"*Subhan Allah.*"

Andy figured that must be the Islamic equivalent of "Holy shit." "I'm trying to free everyone, but if you could help?"

He looked shaky, but he nodded. "Of course. What can I do?"

"Gather them as I reach them and tell them what happened. Tell them to follow the trail to the tunnel over there...." She pointed to where they had entered Agartha. "We need to get everyone out of here as quickly as possible."

He nodded. "*Insha'Allah*." He must've seen the look of confusion on her face. "It means God willing."

"Thank you. I'm Andy."

"I'm Asif. You have no idea the hell we've endured here."

She nodded and hugged him tightly and then squeezed his arm. "It's over now."

She moved on to the next person, an older man with gray hair.

Andy worked as quickly as she could, and soon five, then ten, then fifteen people had been freed. Most of them were in shock.

Some screamed—Eddy and Asif helped her with those.

Some collapsed, while others just seemed filled with a soul-crushing sadness.

The rest waited their turns, and suddenly it was morning.

Light flared across the cavern, momentarily blinding her. She let go of the last child she had freed and stood, staggering in the daylight.

"What the hell are you doing?"

Andy shielded her eyes to look at the man who had spoken to her. He was dressed all in black, slender with black hair and dark brown eyes. And he was furious, his face red with anger.

"Davian," Eddy whispered.

"Hello, Eddy. I have to admit, I'm surprised to see you here."

A man with close-cropped red hair, probably in his late thirties, stood next to Davian. He looked at Andy with a weird intensity. He was... familiar somehow. Then it hit her. "You're the one who visited the huts last night."

Davian nodded. "Gunner here helps keep the peace. Looks like you've been undoing some of his best work."

Andy's gaze snapped back to Gunner. *He* was the one who had done this to these poor people. "Asif, get these people out of the way," she said to her new friend through gritted teeth. If Gunner had done this, he was stronger than she, or at least way more practiced.

"Gunner, would you help Ms. Hammond here to see the light?"

Andy started at the mention of her name.

"Yes, I remember you. We saved you and your father out there, in the void." He pointed off to one side. "Should have left you both to die."

"Why are you doing this?" Eddy looked around Agartha and then warily at Gunner.

"You should know the answer to that one better than anyone. If left to themselves, humans will destroy this world, just like they did the last one. You saw it too—the endless war, the stupid strife over things that didn't matter. The endless greed." He shuddered, sweat beading his brow. "The fucking Chinese put me in a hotbox for two goddamned months!" He stopped and took a deep breath. "I'm *not* going to let that happen again."

Eddy started laughing.

"What's so damned funny?" Davian scowled at them.

"What do you think you've done here? Every one of these people is in his own personal hotbox. Because of you."

Davian growled. "That's not true. I've given each one a place, a purpose. I've taken away their distractions and let them focus on their new lives."

"Like the Chafs let you focus on being trapped and tortured?" Eddy hummed with barely controlled rage. Andy could feel it.

Davian snarled. "I'm so *fucking sick* of your sanctimonious attitude. You're not even a real man, you know that? You're just a little *cocksucking bitch*."

"I'd rather be someone's *bitch* than some *fucked-up psychopath* who thinks he's God."

"Enough. Gunner, take the girl. I'll settle with Evelyne here."

Gunner stepped forward, reaching for Andy.

"Leave her alone." Eddy's crossbow was in his hands, and pointed at Davian's throat.

In Davian's hands, a gun was pointed at Eddy.

Andy felt the blood leave her face. *Oh shit.* There weren't guns up here. There weren't *supposed* to be guns up here. "Listen, we don't have to escalate this. You can lay down your weapon, and we'll take you back to Micavery for a fair hearing." She kept her voice calm.

Davian laughed, a bitter sound. "You don't even have a courthouse."

Eddy nodded. "She's right. I promise, you will get a hearing. In front of Aaron and myself."

"Not interested. Why don't you three turn around and walk out of here—"

Something barreled into Davian from the cover of the trees with a scream, knocking him to the ground and sending him flying.

Eddy dropped his crossbow and leapt after the man.

Davian was beating on someone. Sara. The woman from the hut.

Eddy pulled Davian off her, sending the two of them rolling across the grass.

Gunner advanced on Andy, with madness in his eyes. He grinned at her, the side of his mouth twitching.

Andy shuddered. If he locked her inside of herself, she might never find a way out.

There was really no choice. She was the last line of defense for these people.

She pulled out her knife and drew up her anger like a hammer to throw herself at him.


COLIN REACHED the end of the tunnel and stopped, bending over and holding his side, breathing heavily. He was no longer a young man, and all those years had taken a toll on him, farm work or no.

Colin struggled to calm himself, one deep breath at a time. His racing heartbeat subsided, and his breathing slowed at last.

He stood and looked out across the cavern.

Something was happening. There was a large crowd gathered out on the lawn in front of the village of huts they'd observed the evening before, and people were streaming from there toward the steps where he stood.

It looked like some kind of fight.

What had Andy and the others gotten themselves into while he'd been gone? At least there was no need for stealth now.

He clambered down the steps and set off toward the little village as quickly as he could. As he made his way down the path, he encountered a small group of people going the other way—a couple of kids, two alert adults, and many others with glazed looks in their eyes.

"What's going on down there?" Colin pointed toward the village.

"Are you with the outsiders?" the man asked. He looked Middle Eastern.

"Yes. We came to find out what was going on down here."

The man shook his hand. "The girl… Andy?"

Colin nodded.

"She was freeing us from the Preacher when he found her and your friends. They told us to run while we could."

That sounded like Andy. He didn't ask about the zombies. "Micavery is sending help. Follow the tunnel out and wait for them if they're not yet there."

"Thank you." Asif gave him an impromptu hug as the others filed by. "You don't know what life down here has been like."

"I can't imagine." Colin shuddered. "Go! Get out of here!"

Asif led his contingent on toward escape, and Colin set off again toward the village, hoping he wasn't too late.

EDDY AND DAVIAN rolled one over the other across the lawn, coming to rest with a thunk against the thick trunk of a mallowood tree.

Davian tried to get up, but Eddy pulled him down, punching his ribs hard.

Davian got in a good blow across Eddy's jaw, sending Eddy's head spinning as Davian got to his feet and tried to stagger away.

Eddy got up and shook his head to clear it. He leapt after the man who had once been his lover and friend, and he knocked Davian to the ground. "What the hell is wrong with you?"

Davian tried to twist out of his grip. "What the hell's wrong with *you*?" his old friend retorted. "With all fucking humankind?" He got his knee under Eddy's chest and pushed him away with a sharp crack.

"Fucking hell!" Eddy fell backward onto the grass, grabbing his ribs.

"Look what a goddamned mess they made of Earth. Those greedy men who sent you and me into battle? For what? For a little bigger slice of the pie."

Eddy breathed heavily, getting up again. "Look at this place. How are you any different?"

They circled each other warily. Eddy glanced over at Andy. She was locked in mental combat with Gunner, Davian's pet psychic, or whatever he was.

"I give these people peace. Agartha is a paradise."

Eddy glanced around. It *was* beautiful. Like a bright red apple that was rotten to its core. He remembered Sarah's scream when Andy had taken away the mental storm that had kept her trapped. "What happened to you? How did you get like this?"

"People need a strong leader. Someone who will lay down the rules and give them something meaningful to do with their lives. There's no crime here.

Everything is clean and safe and efficient. People raise families here, unafraid of what their neighbor might do to them."

Eddy shook his head. Davian really believed it. "That's bullshit." He lunged at Davian.

The man dodged him, and as Eddy fell, screaming out in pain as his ribs connected with the ground, Davian leapt on top of him and crushed the air out of his lungs. "You could join me. Show this pathetic chattel that you're a real man."

Eddy struggled to catch his breath, gasping raggedly as he tried to get air into his lungs. "Never," he croaked, shaking his head.

"Fair enough." Something snaked around Eddy's neck and pulled tight against his windpipe. "It was nice to see you again, old friend."

LEX JOINED hands with the others—Jackson, Ana, Glory, and Aaron—as they prepared to try to reach Andy. Such contact was unnecessary, strictly speaking. Lex was weaving them together under the surface of vee space. But symbolism was important to humans and would facilitate their sense of shared effort.

"Are we ready?"

"Yes," Jackson answered for them all.

"Keera?"

"Yes, the transmitter is ready to activate."

Aaron's face was grim and determined. "Let's go help my little girl."

ANDY AND GUNNER were locked in combat.

She'd lost her knife in the initial assault, when he'd knocked it out of her hands to send it skittering across the glowing grass. She'd grazed his left cheek first, though, and a trail of blood dripped down his face.

They held each other's arms like a couple engaged in a strange dance or maybe a wrestling match, their arms rigid, as they punched and jabbed at each other's mental defenses.

Gunner was strong. Fearsomely strong.

Andy was already tired. Keeping him at bay while trying to breach his walls was rapidly wearing her down, but she had seen the price of failure.

She barely noticed Shandra coming up behind Gunner with a big stick in her hands.

Gunner's right hand let go of hers and snaked out to touch Shandra, who went down in a heap.

That broke through to her. She lost concentration for just a moment, staring at her friend as Shandra fell. Andy's mouth fell open to shout "Nooooooooooo...." as if in slow motion, and she let her guard down.

It was all Gunner needed. He pushed forward in that instant and forced her hard onto her back, his hands at her throat.

She struggled to push him off, but his grip was firm on her. He started to close off her airway, his gaze as vacant as any of the zombies. *That* was what scared her the most. There was no humanity left in those eyes, only the determined gaze of a killing machine.

She struggled against him. He might be older, but he was also physically stronger.

*This is it. This is the end.* Her vision started to fade.

*Andy.*

"Dad?" It was impossible. He was in Micavery, and there was no way for him to reach her. Not here.

*Andy, we're here with you.* His voice was warm and reassuring.

*How?*

*Your loop. You have to let us in.*

Her mind was foggy, but she understood on some level what he wanted. It was dangerous. Opening her mind could let Gunner in too.

What did she have to lose? *Okay.* She let down her walls.

Gunner was taken by surprise, loosening his grip for just a second. She opened her eyes to see his, wide open. So he *could* still feel emotion.

Her mind blurred and spun, and she felt the presence of her father, of Lex and Ana. Of Jackson. And Glory.

They fell together and became one, and her power increased fivefold.

Their hand shot up as if of its own accord to grab Gunner's throat. Their other hand reached the soil, and they dipped deep into the earth, ripping through the bubble Gunner had made to cut this place off as if it were tissue paper. Through it and past it to find the roots of the world.

They called the roots. Ten of them, a hundred, up toward Agartha. Toward them.

Shandra stood and was staggering toward her again.

"Shandra, take everyone else and run." The earth was shaking beneath them.

Shandra stared at them and shook her head. "I don't want to leave you!"

"We'll be okay, but you *have to run*! You're the only one who can get them all out."

Shandra looked at the rest of the villagers and nodded. "I'm coming back for you!"

Andy was too busy to reply. They turned their attention to Gunner.

This time, there was real fear in his eyes.


EDDY STRUGGLED against the rope that was stealing his life. Tears slipped from the corners of his eyes, and he whispered a soft apology to Andy and Shandra for letting them down.

The world around him was shaking, or was he just imagining it? It was going dim too.

Weird little pieces of his life flickered by in his head. Not the neat scroll they always showed in the tri dees, but broken, jagged images that pushed each other out of the way.

His mother holding his hand as they walked the seawall.

Davian fucking him before his transition, in the middle of the Manila campaign.

Staring out at the rain in Sugarloaf Mountain, Florida.

The hiss of air from the pinhole in the Moonjumper.

That had been Davian. He was sure of it now.

Suddenly the pressure on his neck was gone.

He rolled over on his side, gasping. The world gradually came into focus.

Colin stood over him, holding a branch in one hand and extending the other to help him get up. "You okay?"

Eddy nodded. "Cracked rib, I think." He winced at the pain in his side.

The world *was* shaking.

He sat up, took Colin's hand, and stood, looking around.

The villagers were gone, and so was Shandra. He hoped she was taking them to safety.

Davian lay off to one side, his head bleeding.

"Good timing. Things were about to go black." Eddy rubbed his neck.

"What the hell is going on here?" Colin looked around as the huts began to collapse.

"This was some kind of mind control experiment. My old friend Davian and the man Andy's fighting were behind it."

"You'll have to tell me more later. Should we help her?"

Eddy shook his head. "I wish we could. There's nothing we *can* do. She's the only one who can do this. Lex says the Immortals are with her."

Colin shook his head. "It's a strange world we find ourselves in out here."

Eddy spat. "No shit."


WITH THE FULL force of their father and the Immortals behind her, Andy *pushed* their way into Gunner's head. It was a maelstrom inside. Now they knew where the madness had come from that had trapped the villagers. They shuddered to think how close it had come to ensnaring Andy.

Maybe they could draw it off, like Andy had done with the others when she had been alone. Together, they were stronger than Gunner.

They pushed him back slowly, bending his mind to their own will, and then they tried to unravel the storm in Gunner's head.

His mind was hopelessly scattered.

As they tried to siphon off some of the madness, random images passed them by.

*Gunner, having sex with one of the villagers, staring down at her empty eyes.*

*The Space Needle in Seattle, before a terrorist attack had brought it down.*

*Cramped in the hold of a cargo ship, being towed with other refugees up to Transfer Station and Forever.*

*Dipping into Ronan's mind to plant the virus that would kill him.*

Andy burned with rage at the last one.

*A little white house on a quiet lane.*

Andy paused. They knew that house.

The part of her that was Jackson whispered, "Jayson?"


COLIN WATCHED THE MIND BATTLE, amazed.

Andrissa Hammond, the fifteen-year-old girl who had come to his estate for help six years before was now a woman, an amazing woman in full control of her abilities. And yet she was compassionate too, kind to others to the point of putting herself in harm's way.

As she bent over Gunner, her expression wasn't one of hatred or anger. Instead it was full of concern.

"Colin!" Eddy pointed.

Colin turned to see Davian sitting up and aiming *something* at Andy. Eddy leapt, but he was too far away.

Colin didn't even think.

He jumped between Davian and Andy.

He took the gun's blow full-on in the chest, sending him tumbling into Andy and Gunner. The shock protected him from the worst of the pain, but he could see the injury was bad. Really bad. His chest was a bloody mess.

He was vaguely aware of Andy looming over him and Gunner scrambling away.

She was truly a credit to the race and an argument that humanity really was ready to inherit the stars. He could live with what he had accomplished if there were people like her to take his stead.

Then there was darkness.

ALL THE VOICES in Andy's head babbled at once.

"Holy crap, it really is him."

"How is this possible?"

"My brother is still alive?"

"Why is he helping Davian?"

Andy was flooded with emotions too. Relief. Anger. Fear. Disgust. Joy. "Quiet, all of you! We can deal with this later. Right now we have to—"

Something knocked them off Gunner, slamming them hard and forcing the breath out of their lungs.

As he scrambled away, Andy opened their eyes and found to their horror that Colin lay beside them, his chest torn apart.

Ten meters away, Eddy was beating the crap out of Davian.

"What happened?" they shouted, kneeling before Colin. He was going too fast, and the wound was too big. There was nothing they could do to save him.

Eddy gave Davian one last savage blow and got up. "Davian shot him with this." He held up a gun.

Andy stared at it. "I thought those weren't allowed up here."

"He must have brought it with him from Earth when we came up." He tucked it in his belt and ran over to help.

*We can help him.*

*But should we?*

*Jackson is going away. We need a strong third.*

*Jackson is going away?*

*No time to explain. Are we agreed?*

No one dissented.

They put Andy's hand on Colin's cheek. His eyes opened, and he tried to say something. All that came out was a croak.

"It's okay. We have you."

He nodded.

They thrust Andy's hand into the ground and connected to the world mind. "Here we go."

Andy had never done this before alone, but a part of *them* had.

The floodgates opened, and Colin's mind, heart, and soul flowed through her, a torrent of thoughts and emotions and memories.

For the first time, Andy saw the skies of Earth as if through her own eyes, the big blue vault of heaven over Colin's father's ranch, and she wept at the sight of it.

The others gathered around her, their hands on her shoulders.

Colin's life flowed through her like an electrical current, pouring into the world mind to become a part of Forever's legacy and its future.

It lasted an eon. From the first breath of life to the last moment of death, it left its touch on her soul.

At last, it was over.

Andy opened her eyes.

"He's gone," she whispered to Eddy. *Gone, just like the others.*

"He's with Ana, Lex, and Jackson now, isn't he?"

She nodded.

"He gave his life to save you."

That was something she'd be carrying with her for the rest of her life. "Where are they?"

Eddy looked around. "Oh shit."

In the midst of the transfer, his once-friend Davian and the man's pet psychic had disappeared.

The shaking had stopped as well.

"Goddammit. We'll find them."

Andy nodded. "It wasn't Jayson's fault." She was still reeling over that revelation. Her uncle, whom everyone had assumed had been lost all those years before, on Forever. And the things he'd done.

"Jayson?"

"The man who did this to them."

Eddy frowned. "I thought his name was Gunner."

"It's a long story." One they'd have to figure out. Why was he helping Davian? Was he even still *in there*? Andy shuddered.

"The shaking—that was you?"

She nodded. "I needed to distract him and to break the bubble."

*Baaaah.*

Andy turned to see the two lambs that had precipitated this long goose chase and ultimate tragedy. They must have been spooked by the shaking and had run toward the village.

"I know someone who will be happy to see you." Eddy scooped them up. "What should we do with Colin? Can we carry him out of here too?"

Andy shook their head. "He's a part of this place. We'll make a suitable tomb for him." They called to the world mind again, and a pair of roots appeared to spin a fine filigree over Colin's body. It covered him entirely like a cocoon, and after a moment, collapsed and withdrew into the soil. He was gone.

"Ashes to ashes," Eddy whispered, his face a little gray. He retrieved his crossbow and slung it over his shoulder.

"Let's go." They stood and took one of the lambs, holding it gently.

They made their way out of Agartha, down the now empty path. At various intervals, great roots had pierced the surface, knocking aside trees and huts and blocking their way.

They detoured around them as best as they were able and eventually came to the stairs that led to the tunnel.

Shandra was waiting for them. "Are you okay?" she asked, running forward to embrace Andy. "I was so worried."

"I will be." Andy was shaking. They handed the lamb to Shandra. "Stand back."

Shandra and Eddy did as they were told.

Andy turned and knelt, touching the ground and dipping into the world mind.

This place had been profaned by what had been done here.

She tapped into another of the mountains and called up the fluids that the world used to dissolve its waste, like those that had ended Ana's life so long before under these very mountains but a hundred times stronger.

She flooded Agartha below, sloshing back and forth, wiping it clean of the vegetation and human habitations that Davian had placed there, making darkness descend on the hollowed-out space. Then she called up the roots to tear down the vault of the mountain.

A flock of seagulls rushed by over her head, forcing her to duck as they shrieked in her ear and fled down the narrow passageway of the tunnel.

The roots wound their way up the inside surface of the cavern roof and up the sides of each of the massive stone columns that supported it, digging into the rock as easily as if it were butter. Up and up they went, and when the roots reached the apex, Andy shouted, "Run!"

They pulled down the walls of the cavern with a terrible crash, as she and Eddy stood and ran down the tunnel.

Behind them, Agartha collapsed into a pit of rubble.

EDDY STARED DOWN NERVOUSLY at Andy. She had collapsed when the cavern had been destroyed, and he'd handed the other lamb to Shandra, who'd scooped her up to carry her to the outside world.

Shandra knelt at Andy's other side. They had lain her on the grassy hillside outside the small cave where they had first entered Davian's own version of hell. "Is she going to be okay?"

"I hope so." There was something budding there between them. *Good.* Delia had been a fool to let Andy go.

"I'm not dead, you know." Andy's voice was soft but still managed to carry her deadpan sense of humor.

"Oh thank God." Shandra squeezed her hand and knelt to kiss her.

Andy's eyes flew open, but she didn't resist.

Eddy chuckled to himself. *Score.*

Shandra helped her sit up.

"Did everyone get away okay?"

Eddy nodded. Typical Andy. Think of everyone else first. "They sent out a bunch of traxx to shuttle the villagers to the train station. Your father will help you *clear* the rest of them, when you've rested a bit."

"Is that what we're calling it now?" She grinned her lopsided smile.

"Yup. Came up with that one myself." He grinned back.

"And Davian and Jayson?"

Eddy shook his head. "No sign of them." He sighed. "Your father explained the Jayson thing to me."

"It's so strange to know he was here all along. That he was the one who took out Transfer Station."

"Was he always evil?"

"I don't think so." Andy tried to remember the things her father had told her about Jayson. "I think someone found out what he could do and broke him. They turned him into a weapon that Davian found and used for his own ends."

Eddy nodded. "We'll find them. It's a small world."

"I hope so." She rubbed her temples.

"Headache?"

She laughed bleakly. "You try sharing your brain with five other people."

Eddy snorted. "You feel up to moving? I want to get you home so you can recuperate."

"Yes, a warm bed and a cup of embrew sounds about perfect at the moment." She let them help her up. "One more thing?"

"Anything."

"Next time you call me for help, it better be for something simple."


DAVIAN STUMBLED ALONG AFTER GUNNER, his whole body aching from the beating Eddy had given him. He cursed himself for getting out of shape.

The cavern rumbled, showering him with dust and knocking him to the floor. He screamed at the pain as his bruises and wounds impacted with the hard stone.

Gunner knelt next to him and lifted him as the shaking stopped.

The tunnel held.

*Always have an escape hatch.* He'd drilled that into himself, and his foresight had proved prudent when that bitch and her friends had destroyed everything he'd built over these last six years.

He should have killed Eddy when he had the chance, when they'd first reached this new world.

But one good thing had come from this whole misadventure.

As he lurched forward, he replayed it in his head, over and over. How the girl had taken the old man in her arms and thrust her hand into the ground. How her head had rolled back and her eyes had gazed, sightless, at the cavern ceiling.

He'd worked out what she had done. She'd sent the man's soul into the world mind.

And if she could do it, then so could Gunner.

He would bide his time and learn more before taking that ultimate step. There were things to prepare, and he wasn't quite ready to let go of the corporeal world.

But his time would come soon enough, and then he'd have all of Forever at his beck and call.

# 13

## PASSING

Jackson squeezed Aaron's hand. "It's time."

Aaron's mother and father had brought him and Andy back "home" to the little white house for one last meal, and for a couple hours, he'd been fifteen again, just a kid at dinner with his parents. He wished Jayson could have been there with them.

In reality, his parents were already dead, his father decades before, and his mother so recently it still stung like a knife in his gut. And so was the Jayson he had known.

Nevertheless, this extra time with Jackson and Glory was an unforeseen and unexpected blessing.

"Are you ready?" His mother took his other hand and took Andy's too. The late-afternoon sun shone through the kitchen window behind her, giving her a glow like an angel.

*Of course I'm not ready.* How in the hell could you be ready to lose both of your parents at once, for good? But she didn't need to hear that. "I will be."

"We're ready, Grandma." Andy squeezed his hand.

"Ana and Lex are waiting for us." Jackson got up. Aaron and Glory followed suit. Aaron's father took one last look around the old house. "I'm going to miss this place," he said gruffly.

Glory wiped her eyes. "Don't get me started."

He kissed her cheek and took both of their hands.

The house shimmered and vanished, leaving them standing in a wide green valley. Aaron recognized it instantly—Lex's world.

Lex and Ana were waiting for them at the top of the hill, next to the stone tower. Lex was looking decidedly feminine, with long black hair and a rich blue silk dress. Like a princess.

Jackson climbed the hill and hugged Lex. "I'm so proud of you."

"Thank you for taking care of Jackson for all these years." Glory was smiling. Mostly.

Lex nodded. "It was my pleasure."

Jackson turned to Ana.

She had an anguished look on her face. "You don't have to do this, you know."

"It will be okay." He pulled her close, and Aaron was surprised to see her start to cry.

"I know you believe that there's something out there waiting for you. But you're here *now*. Both of you are, despite our agreement otherwise." She pulled away and glared at him. "We can make it work."

"I know, I know." He spread his hands. "I'm sorry I went behind your backs. I couldn't let her go. But now...."

"Are you sure?" She searched his eyes. "Why can't this be your heaven?"

"I'm sure." He looked rested. At peace with himself and his decision. "We talked about it for two days. It's the right thing for us. We're ready."

Ana laid a hand on his cheek. "I'll miss you most of all, scarecrow."

Jackson laughed. "I'll leave you everything. My memories, my ideas. All of me but me."

Andy ran forward to hug him. "I'll miss you." She didn't try to hide her tears.

"I know, little one. You take care of your dad and your new little sibling, okay?"

She nodded. "I will." She hugged Glory too.

"I'm so proud of you, my little angel." Glory hugged her fiercely. "You have a bright future, *mija*."

Jackson turned to Aaron. "It's time."

Aaron nodded, though his heart was beating like a machine gun.

Jackson hugged him from one side, and Glory did from the other.

They held him tight. "You have become more than I ever hoped for."

Aaron smiled bleakly. "I had a good role model. Two of them."

"Love you, Scout," Jackson whispered.

"Love you too."

Aaron closed his eyes. He didn't want this to end. He'd gotten used to having his mother nearby and his father on call when he needed him.

To lose them both, and Colin, all at once? It seemed inconceivable.

Although Colin would be back, after a fashion, once he'd managed to integrate himself with the world mind.

When Aaron opened his eyes, they were gone. Andy, Ana, and Lex were embracing him instead.

He let everything out that he'd been holding inside, and they joined him.

When his immediate grief ran its course, he wiped his eyes and flashed a sad smile at Andy.

It was the next generation's turn.


THE WORLD EDGED CLOSER to 42 Iris. Ana smiled. The explosive charges had worked as planned, and the two worlds were now spinning in perfect synch.

The tremor that marked the mating of Forever and her next source of expansion materials would be felt all along the length of the world, but she hoped to make the union as smooth as possible. "You can come out of the shadows." She'd known he was there for a while, but she remembered what it had been like at first, when she'd transitioned from her old life and body.

"Sorry. I'm still a little disoriented." Colin stepped out into the light to stand next to her.

"You're just in time for the big show." She pointed to the virtual screen.

"Then it's off to the stars." His eyes sparkled.

Ana closed her eyes. "Remember that day on Ariadne, when I found you staring up at the heavens?"

"You mean when Jackson died?"

She nodded. That old wound no longer gave her such pain. "I saw the look in your eyes. You wanted to go out there. To see what the universe held in wait for us."

He laughed. "It was that obvious?"

"Let's just say I was familiar with the look." She took his hand. "We're the lucky ones. The chosen. We get to see how it all turns out, while they—" She gestured behind her. "—will live the spans of normal mortal folk."

"Is it a blessing or a curse?"

She smiled wryly. "Yes."

"How are we seeing this?" He pointed at the virtual screen.

"The external cameras still work. Mostly. And I have a shuttle out there giving us eyes on the process."

"Ah."

The distance between the two bodies shrunk slowly, almost imperceptibly, until at last there was a crunch as the masses met. "Bet that spilled someone's embrew in Darlith."

She laughed. "Probably." This was the most critical part. Ana joined with Lex as they reached out to extend themselves into the new asteroid, anchoring it firmly to Forever. World roots dug in and pulled Isis tightly into their grasp. "There. It's done."

As they watched, a thin sheet of organic material spread out from the end of Forever where it met Isis. It floated out into the void like a gossamer umbrella, ready to catch the solar wind.

"All this from that one little seed." Colin whistled. "She's aptly named."

She kissed his cheek. "This is all because of you. Would you like to take the wheel?"

# PART II

## COUP

2181 AD

# 14

## HAPPENINGS

HE WAS hungry.

He stumbled along the stream bed, kicking up water from the little creek to wet his dirty gray trousers.

The world around him was gray, too, as if it were smothered in fog.

*When did I eat last? When did I see another human being? Who am I?* These things were all mysteries to him. He only knew that he was starving and exhausted.

Through the haze that overlay his vision, something new materialized in the distance. It was a....

He struggled to find the word.

A... house. It was a house. A farmhouse.

He clambered up the hill, reaching out toward it, afraid it would vanish in the mist.

There were people there, outside. A man. A woman. A teenager.

He remembered children. There had been children, before. In the other place. The one he could never quite remember. Small children.

He'd been happier there. He'd always been fed, had things to do.

"You okay?" the teen asked. A boy.

"He doesn't look so good." A woman's voice. It soothed him somehow.

"I... hungry...." His voice was raspy and weak, as if he hadn't used it for a long time.

He couldn't remember. Something was missing. Someone. The person he had talked to, sometimes.

Davian.

He nodded.

"What's your name?" The man this time.

"Davian. Yes, that's right. Davian." He tottered and then lost his balance and collapsed on the ground.

"It's okay," the woman said. "We'll take care of you."

"Hungry," he said. Then he fell asleep.


COLIN SLUMPED at his desk in his neat vee space office, staring at the view on the wide screen plastered across one wall.

A biodrone captured the sight of his former estate, where Trip was out minding the red berry bushes that brought in about half the income to the estate.

Colin wore his dress whites, though he could just as easily have lounged around his virtual office in a virtual bathrobe.

Still, old habits died hard.

He wished he could reach out to Trip, tell him he was okay. Even ten years after his death, that still hurt, though he recognized it as the right decision. The colonists couldn't know about the Immortals, as they'd taken to calling themselves, or everyone would want to become a part of the world mind when they died.

They simply didn't have the capacity.

And some people were too unstable to ever get anywhere near the levers of power Lex, Ana, and Colin held over the world. Look at that nasty mess with that fool Davian, which had ended with Colin dead and consigned to the afterlife here.

Not that it was all bad.

He had sent Trip the occasional dream, a love letter to the man he'd been separated from too soon.

He closed the screen and got down to business. Lex and Ana had relegated the day-to-day administrivia to him, not as any kind of punishment, but because he was good at it, and he enjoyed this kind of work. Decades in administration had given him the tools he needed to manage the affairs of Forever.

After the Agartha affair, they'd set up a nascent government. The social scientists who had envisioned a society that would span the void between the stars had hoped for an egalitarian culture with a minimalist socialistic government, but events had outpaced all of their plans.

The society that had evolved after the Collapse was becoming complex enough to need bookkeeping and dispute resolution, and the world mind had the impartial capacity for both.

First up was a boundary dispute on the exact location of the border between two landholders out on the Verge.

Those issues were easy enough. The world mind held detailed property records that made it simple for him to compare the submitted information from the Clancy family and the competing claim from Harry Zimmer. In this case, both were a little bit right. Colin appended notes to the file and returned the results to Lex to provide to the litigants.

The next three issues were new contracts, one to sell a parcel of land in the middle of Darlith—hot property now—to someone who wanted to open a tool shop. The second involved personnel services in Micavery. And the third was a marriage contract between Harold Devener and Maxine Thorpe. He hoped the Devener-Thorpe wedding was all the happy couple hoped it would be.

He rubberstamped them after reviewing them against the Ariadne Legal Code, which had been adapted from NAU law when Transfer Station had first been built.

The code formed the basis of the loose organization that now governed the world—two city councils that governed the surrounding areas and reported to him and the world mind. In time it would take on more responsibility of its own.

The Darlith city council had forwarded him a few zoning requests for final approval. He ran those by the world mind to check for any conflicts.

The next item caught his eye. It was a request for someone to come out and get a man who had wandered into a farmstead out on the Verge. The Olafs had taken the stranger in when he had appeared on their doorstep, dirty and lost.

Probably just one of the homeless who lived away from society on the foothills of the Anatovs, or a camper who had lost his way. But given the location and the circumstances....

They never had found Davian or Jayson.

Colin pinged Eddy. The man was the head of the new sheriff's force they'd created after the Agartha Incident. The department included many former residents of that cursed city.

"Hey, Cap." Eddy's voice was cheery. Too cheery.

"Did I interrupt you at a bad time?"

"No, not really. It's just… nothing. What's up?"

Colin laughed to himself. He had a good idea what Eddy had been up to. "I just ran across something I thought you should check out, if you have a little time."

"Sure. Shoot."

"One of the landholder couples out on the edge of the Verge just reported the appearance of a stranger on their doorstep."

"What did he look like?" Eddy's voice was suddenly sharp.

Colin looked through the data. "It doesn't say. I thought you might want to find out?"

"Of course. Send me the information, and I'll take a team out there."

"Don't scare the locals."

"I won't. It's probably nothing…."

"But that's what you thought the last time you were sent out there?" When they'd found Agartha.

"Yeah. Something like that."

"I can send a biodrone over, if you'd like, get a visual."

"Please. I'll head out in the morning with a couple deputies."

"Thanks, Eddy. Let me know if you need anything."

"Will do."

Colin cut the connection. He sat back and stared at the blank wall in front of him.

What if it was Davian? Would they bring him to justice? If so, how?

Forever had no jails and no real courts beyond the world mind.

It might be time to do something about that.


MARISSA ROLLED HER EYES. "We're learning about *animals* today."

Delancy and Danny, the two other kids from Agartha who were the oldest at about fourteen, stood apart in one corner of the schoolhouse's playground area, shaded by the porch roof of the little red schoolhouse that gave the protected valley its name.

Delancy shrugged. "I like learning about them."

Danny nodded. "I wish we had more than just horses here." He looked really handsome, his dark hair cropped close just the day before by Shandra. His brown eyes had that faraway look he often got when he was daydreaming.

Marissa grinned. They'd been out riding on their last free day, and they'd found a shaded spot in a spur canyon where they'd done a little extracurricular exploration of their own. They weren't supposed to—something about genetics and all that—but who else was there, out alone in the wilderness?

Delancy was oblivious to the interplay between them. She was staring out at other kids, who were engaged in various games of tag and other scrappier games.

There were thirty-eight of them altogether—the kids from Agartha—who ranged from ten to fourteen. Andy and Shandra called them the Liminal kids.

They had been universally rejected by their mothers. Children conceived by force who were constant reminders to the women who had birthed them of that terrible time.

Andy and Shandra had taken them all in to teach and train them.

Marissa's peers were playing in the schoolyard, a mostly idyllic scene, though a couple of the girls had gotten into a scuffle the day before. Andy—their teacher insisted on informality between them—had set them to scrubbing their pants after school.

Marissa looked up at the curve of the world. The schoolhouse was the greenest patch in the Anatov Mountains, inhabiting the crater where Agartha had once stood, before Andy had pulled down the mountain.

They were closest to the South Pole. She could see it, a gray wall in the distance, looming over the world.

Marissa hoped to visit both poles one day, if Andy and Shandra ever let them leave this place.

The whole poles thing had been weird for her at first, having been born under a mountain, but Andy had explained it to them well enough. Stand at Micavery, and you were in the South. Face the other end of Forever, and that was North. Left was West and right was East. Though it was confusing too. If you went far enough west around the curve of the world—about twenty-six kilometers in all—you'd come back around to the east.

Whatever the direction, she felt safe here, if a little confined at times. When Andy had rescued them, the kids had known only the most basic English and little else. Now, they had built a community, learning to use their abilities, and had been taught so much about the world around them and the history of humankind.

Sometimes Marissa wished they could live out *there*, among the others. Andy said it wasn't safe, that people wouldn't understand her kind and their abilities. She and Shandra had trained them all to fight and defend themselves, just in case.

As Andy liked to tell them, the world wasn't ready for them yet. Marissa wasn't sure what that meant, but she wished the world would hurry up and get its act together.

Andy came out of the schoolhouse and whistled. "Come on, kids!"

They flooded into the classroom, all except Chris and Toby, who were engaged in a battle of wits, staring at each other intently.

Shandra grinned. "You get the others settled. I'll go grab those two."

The schoolhouse was full of chatter as the kids tried to get a little more playtime in before class started.

Marissa didn't feel like playing. She rarely had. Even here, far away from Agartha in time if not in space, that dark place had left a mark, especially for those who had lived there the longest.

The children had all chosen their own names when they'd been freed from Agartha. The Preacher hadn't allowed them to be given names, and they'd been kept docile and compliant by Gunner's mind fog.

"Marissa" meant "the sea." She had heard tales of Earth's vast oceans, but they were little more than ghosts to her. Still, one day she hoped to stand on the shores of Lake Hammond, with her toes in the sand, and imagine that it went on forever.

And "Callas" had come from a great opera singer. Ana had played audio from one of her concerts for Marissa once. She had lived so long before, but her voice across the ages had made little Marissa's spirits soar.

Andy squeezed Marissa's arm as she passed by. Marissa smiled shyly in return.

"Okay, everyone, take your places." The room held thirty-nine soft mats, and next to each was a smooth flat wooden touch pad Andy had helped them fashion as part of their training, which connected them to the world mind. As Shandra escorted the two tardy miscreants in the door, everyone lay down on their mats.

"Can we go to the space station today?" Timothy asked, his eyes wide. He loved space.

"Not today. I thought we'd look at some of the animals of Old Earth."

There was a general sigh.

"Why do we have to learn about that?" Alberto asked.

"You guys *love* seeing the animals."

"Earth is dead and gone. They're not real."

Marissa nodded. He was right. Why did they need to learn about a bunch of long-dead animals none of them would ever see in person? They should be learning about the here and now, about the things that would help them get by when they graduated and left for Darlith or Micavery.

Marissa winked at him, and the younger boy blushed.

"That's true, but it's important to know where we came from so we know where we are going."

Alberto frowned. "But I'll be dead before we get there."

"Do you want to be dead *and* stupid?"

The other kids laughed, and Alberto closed his mouth.

"Ready?" Andy asked.

"Ready!" Marissa shouted in unison with the other kids. No matter the lesson, going into vee space was always fun.

She closed her eyes and laid her hand on the wooden touch pad.

The world around her dissolved, and she opened her eyes to find herself under a wide orange-and-white-striped tent. One by one, the others appeared, popping into existence all around her.

Andy lifted the tent flap at the back of the big space, and a host of animals paraded in. There was an elephant, a zebra, a giraffe that had to duck its neck to get through the low entry, and a hippo that trundled across the open space. They were followed by a flurry of furries—a wolf, a mongoose, two otters that splashed into a pool on one end of the tent, a rabbit and a tiger that entered together, and a selection of more slithery creatures.

"These are some of my favorites." Andy picked up the snake. "This is an American rattlesnake, but don't worry, this one can't hurt anyone. Look at the beautiful rattle." She held up the snake. "He used it to warn off strangers. Rattlesnakes rarely bit anyone unless they felt threatened."

"I wish I had a rattle." Alberto mimed it in the air.

"See? I knew you liked animals." Andy turned to the rest of the class. "The Earth was a biodiverse place, with millions of unique species of plants and animals. Some were herbivores, meaning they only ate plants—like our friends the giraffe and the zebra here. Some were carnivores. Anyone know what that means?"

Timothy raised his hand. "That they liked carnivals?"

Marissa stifled a laugh.

Andy smiled. "It means that they ate meat."

"Are we carnivores?" That one came from Giorgio.

"We're omnivores. Omni means everything. We eat a little of both, though we eat a lot less meat than our ancestors did." She held up the rattlesnake. "There are five main classes of animals with vertebrae—mammals, birds, fish, amphibians, and this guy. Anyone know what class this snake falls under?"

Marissa raised her hand. "Reptile?"

"Very good." She frowned. The snake had wrapped itself around her arm tightly, and its rattle was shaking. Maybe they'd programmed it a little too realistically. "We don't have any reptiles here on Forever." The snake's head was weaving back and forth. "What do we know about reptiles?"

"They're cold?" Timothy's brow was furrowed.

"Cold-blooded. They—"

Marissa watched in horror as the rattler sunk its teeth into Andy's arm.

"Holy...." Andy swayed and fell forward as the snake wriggled out of her grasp and slithered away.

Marissa jumped to her aid. "Are you okay, Andy?"

"I... I... I cccccan't...." She reached up toward Marissa, her eyes pleading.

Then they closed, and she fell sideways onto the hard-packed earth.


"SHANDRA!" MARISSA ran out of the schoolhouse calling for Andy's partner. "Shandra!"

Shandra looked up from where she was planting new tomato plants. "Over here!" She stood and dusted herself off, waving to Marissa. "What's wrong?"

Marissa ran the remaining twenty meters. "Andy!" she managed, panting. "Snake!"

A look of disbelief crossed Shandra's face. "Slow down, girl. Tell me what happened."

"We were in class in vee, and a snake bit Andy." She couldn't calm her racing heart. The horror of it kept replaying itself in her head.

Shandra frowned. "It's okay. It's not real."

Marissa shook her head. "Something happened. We were in this big tent, with animals. Andy collapsed in vee, and she won't wake up."

"Oh sh… damn." Shandra dropped her spade and sprinted past Marissa, running toward the schoolhouse.

Marissa ran after her, racing up the steps and into the classroom.

The other kids were gathered around Andy's supine form where she lay on her pad. A couple of the youngest kids were crying.

"Okay, I need everyone to clear away a bit." Shandra knelt next to Andy to check her pulse.

"Is she okay?" Marissa asked, pushing her way in.

"Her pulse is steady." Shandra sighed. "She's going to be okay." She shooed the kids toward the door.

Marissa knelt next to her. "Are you sure?" she whispered.

"I hope so. What happened? You said something about a snake?"

Marissa nodded. "She was showing us a bunch of Earth animals. She had some kind of snake—a rattler?—in her hands, and it bit her." She snorted. "No wonder people killed all the animals."

Shandra shook her head. "Don't say that. Most animals never harmed anyone. Snakes in particular were reclusive. Humans were the true predators." She looked at Andy. "Where did it bite her?"

"Right here, on her left arm." Marissa indicated the spot.

Shandra lifted Andy's arm. The skin was smooth and untouched. "Andy, can you hear me?" She shook Andy's shoulder gently. "Andy, it's Shandra. Can you hear me?"

There was no response.

She tapped her loop. "Lex, get me Aaron." She looked around at the gathered children. "You all have chores to do, right?"

"Not until after class." Timothy looked worried.

"Andy will be all right, but we need to let her rest. Marissa, can you keep an eye on the rest of the herd while I sort this out?" Her eyes went unfocused. "What? Aaron's not available? Find him for me, okay? I need him to take me into vee space." She touched her loop again, cutting the connection.

"I can take you." Marissa pulled her long blonde hair back behind her ear. "Danny can take care of the kids."

Shandra shook her head. "It's too dangerous. If there's really something wrong with vee space—"

"I know vee better than anyone. I can help you find her." She touched Shandra's shoulder. "Please, Shandra. She might be in pain in there."

Shandra regarded her for a long moment, then nodded. "Okay, but at the first sign of trouble, we bail."

"Okay."

Danny and Delancy had shepherded the other kids outside. Shandra poked her head out. "Timothy, you're in charge of cabin cleanup today. Harris, can you check on the livestock?"

"Got it!" Harris sounded a little too cheery, like he was trying to cover his emotions.

Marissa knew how he felt.

When they were gone, Shandra lay down on the mat next to Marissa's.

She was worried. Marissa could tell. Her lips were pursed, and those tell-tale lines had appeared on her forehead again.

Shandra took Andy's hand, squeezing it, and Marissa lay down next to her and took hers.

"Ready for me to ride with you?" Marissa asked.

"Yes."

It must be a weird sensation for the *solos*, the people who didn't have the gift. She closed her eyes and entered Shandra's mind the way Andy had shown her. They hardly ever got to do this, and only the oldest kids had been taught the skill.

She and Shandra were linked, far more intimately than the loop by itself allowed.

*Are you okay?*

*Yes. It's weird. But… yes.*

*Okay, let's touch Andy's forehead.*

They reached out to touch Andy. An electric shock ran up her arm, and then they plunged into her world.

They were standing in the empty tent again, the orange-and-white-striped circus tent that Marissa remembered. It was quiet and still in the dusty space.

They looked around.

*She was here? With you and the other kids?*

*Yes, this is where it happened.*

They knelt, and they reached out her arm to touch something.

It was a slender golden thread. As they touched it, it vibrated and glowed. It extended to the edge of the tent and beyond.

*Come on.*

They followed it to the side of the tent. They ripped open the fabric and climbed through the rift after it.

The golden thread traversed a desolate gray space the color of an empty vee plain, before Andy and Ana painted the details on.

*This is amazing.*

*You've never been here before?*

They followed the line as it plunged into the gray.

*Andy's taken me once or twice. But it's been a long time.*

They gasped as the fog cleared, and they found themselves on Transfer Station. The station was quiet as it spun through space. They went to one of the portholes and could see Forever hanging in the inky blackness outside.

They followed the golden thread down the Runway, halfway around the circle of the station. It veered right, into a cabin whose door was closed. They reached a hand out to palm the door open.

It slid clear quietly.

They stepped into the room and looked around.

Andy sat huddled in a corner, her arms around her knees.

A man sat next to her, holding her hand.

"Get away from her!" Shandra shouted, ready to throw themselves at the man.

*It's okay. That's Ronan. Or a memory of him.*

Andy had introduced the kids to him once, or at least to the *memory* of him that still lived in Andy's mind.

*Ronan?*

*The station mind.*

The man stood and nodded at them. "Marissa, so good to see you again. She's a little shaken up, but she should be okay."

"Thanks, Ronan."

He shrugged. "She needed me. So I came."

*He was a good man.*

"This is her girlfriend?"

"Yes. Shandra and I came to find Andy."

"Nice to finally meet you."

Marissa felt the discomfort through her link with Shandra. This was way outside of her experience. It was a little odd for her too, truth be told.

They knelt next to Andy. She looked up at them, her eyes wide, like she was six years old. "Shandra. You came."

They nodded.

"Who brought you?"

"Marissa is riding with me. Or me with her."

"Doesn't matter." Andy threw herself into their arms.

"We'll take her home. Thanks for looking after her."

"Good to see you again." Ronan squeezed Andy's arm.

*He's just a memory.*

*A memory that deserves our great respect. Because of him, not a single additional life was lost when the station blew.*

Shandra nodded. *I'm just not used to treating memories like people.*

*Me neither. But you get used to some strange things in vee, especially where it runs up against the human mind.*

*I guess so.*

They lifted Andy gently and carried her home.

# 15

# TELLTALE SIGNS

MARISSA RODE with Shandra as she called Aaron. "Aaron? This is Shandra, and Marissa."

"What's going on?" Aaron sounded calm, self-assured.

It made Marissa feel better.

"Something's happened to Andy."

Marissa could feel the steel behind Shandra's words through their bond.

"Is she okay?" Aaron's calm, measured tone cracked, just a little.

"I think so?" Shandra was holding her concern in check.

"What happened?"

"She was in vee space with the class. The kids say she was holding a snake, and it bit her."

"That's impossible. And even if it wasn't, it wouldn't have hurt her. That place isn't real."

"I know. But she wouldn't wake up, so Marissa took me into vee to find her. We brought her back, but she's pretty shaken up."

"Okay. Let's keep everyone out of vee until we figure out what's going on."

"Will do."

"Can I talk to her?" The fatherly concern in his voice was clear. She wished she had a real father, and not for the first time.

"She's sleeping," Shandra said. "I'll have her contact you when she wakes."

· · ·

EDDY MOUNTED UP, glancing at the Sheriff's Headquarters. He'd started to pull together a small informal sheriff's force after the events at Agartha. They'd gotten the blessing of the newly formed city council in Micavery, and the previous year they'd built a new building to house it out of gray block manufactured by the fabrication center. The result was a staid and serious headquarters befitting a police station.

The force was about twenty strong now, and they'd settled into handling mostly local disputes—things the world mind sent them and issues that arose when someone got a little too drunk or a lover's quarrel escalated into a public nuisance.

They'd taken a page from England on Old Earth and had issued all the officers billy clubs. They were also trained in knife play and crossbow use for patrol up on the Verge, but no other projectile weaponry was allowed.

So far there'd been no outright murders on Forever, except for Colin, of course. But their civic infrastructure wasn't growing nearly fast enough to accommodate the increase in the population.

Fifteen years before, the world had been staffed by professionals and their families, but the influx of refugees and the abrupt departure from Earth had changed all of that. Now it was a motley mix of people from all kinds of backgrounds, ethnicities, and religions. There were bound to be issues.

"You sure you've got a handle on everything here?" he asked his lieutenant, Jendra Khan.

"Yes, for the tenth time." She glared at him. "Things are quiet at the moment, but you've trained everyone well enough to handle a two-day absence."

"Sorry! It's just—"

"It's just that 'nobody knows how to do this job like you do,' blah blah blah. Now go! We'll see you on Thursday." With that, she turned and went inside the station, letting the door slam behind her.

Eddy laughed. "Guess I deserved that."

His two deputies, Brad Evers and Santiago Ortiz, grinned.

Santi laughed. "You do need to learn how to let go." He'd lost most of his thick Spanish accent over the last couple years.

"It's just…." Eddy sighed. They were right. He was a control freak. "Yeah. I do. You two ready to ride?" The train to Darlith was down again and had been for weeks. Keera was working on fabricating some replacement parts, but for now, horseback was the fastest way to get around, after glider, and gliders weren't great for arriving at precise destinations or for taking off from ground level.

Someone had been experimenting with travel by balloon too. There had to be a better way.

For this trip, Eddy had opted for his trusty crossbow, while Santi and Brad were carrying throwing knives.

"Let's go." Brad had been part of the informal group that had evolved into the city council to run the day-to-day operations of Micavery, but he'd jumped at the chance to be a sheriff.

They set off toward the hills that separated Micavery from the Verge. Micavery was bustling. It was Market Day, and everyone who wanted to buy or sell something was heading down to the town square.

"Hey, Eddy!" one of them called. It was Jared Smith, the retired traxx driver who now grew luscious tomatoes in his home garden. He was carting a wheelbarrow of them toward the Market.

Eddy waved. "They look beautiful!"

"Thanks. I found a new way to fertilize the plants with more nitrogen."

"Looks like it's working." He gave Jared the thumbs-up.

"You know everyone, don't you?" Brad said drolly.

Eddy laughed. "Don't you? It's a small town."

"Yeah, I know everybody. But you know *everybody*."

They passed through the new Thatch Hill residential district, where the houses were all built with dark red mallowood, a fast-growing lumber that took on a lovely dark sheen as it aged.

They made it out of town with only fifteen or twenty more greetings and soon crossed over the stone bridge that marked the northern end of the city. It was a beautiful day, like pretty much every day on Forever.

Eddy loved the good weather, but sometimes he longed for a really hot day, or a night that would make him shiver and raise goose bumps on his arms.

"So who is this guy?" Santi asked as they climbed into the hills.

The road from there to the Verge had been paved years before, but the horses preferred to trot along the edge over the hard-packed earth.

Eddy had his suspicions. "We're not sure. I should have an image of him soon."

"Who do you *think* he is?"

"We think he was involved in the whole Agartha mess five years before."

They'd kept the details to a minimum, letting the rest of the world know only that there'd been a cult with a separatist camp set up in a cavern under the Anatovs.

Brad whistled. "Big mess, that. Those poor kids born in that place."

Eddy nodded. "Imagine what that would do to your head." He'd been out to the schoolhouse a few times, visiting Andy and Shandra, who were doing a great job with the kids.

As they rode up into the hills, he spotted a stand of alifirs off to the east that had gone dark, their needles sagging. The normally healthy brown of their bark had taken on a gray pallor. "That's odd." Eddy pointed at the trees.

Santi shrugged. "Things die."

Eddy snorted. "True enough. But I'd like to go take a look." He didn't like things he didn't understand. He pulled Cassie to a halt and slipped off her, patting her side gently. She put her head down to graze on glowing blades of grass along the side of the road.

To get a better look at the anomaly, he crossed the open field, leaving dark footprints in the grass in his wake. There were seven trees, each twice as tall as he was. The trunks looked almost burned, although there was no sign of fire in the other plants in the vicinity.

He reached out to touch the needles on one of the branches, running them through his partially closed hand.

They dissolved into a fine ash, which wafted into the air on the breeze.

Puzzled, he pushed on the trunk.

There was a soft crack, and the whole tree fell, knocking over two more.

Brad and Santi had come to stand next to him.

"That's not normal." Brad touched one of the other trees.

Eddy tapped his loop. "Lex, any reports of strange tree deaths this month?"

"Checking…," her voice said in his head. "Some trees up on Tanner Ridge burned last week. Looks like it was a camping fire."

"Yeah, I remember that. Anything else?"

"A mallow tree was replaced in Micavery. It was probably poisoned by industrial activity at the fabrication center nearby. That's all."

"Okay, please let the administrator know I found a stand of dead alifirs a little way outside of Micavery. They look like they were burned, but there's no other signs of fire."

"Will do."

Eddy tapped off his loop. "The administrator" was the code word he used for Colin when in company. He pulled out a sample bag and gently took a few needles off one of the trees, before sealing it tightly. "Brad, can you take this to Keera?"

"You sure?"

"Yeah. Santi and I can manage with the stranger. I don't want to leave this too long. It's probably nothing, but if I'm wrong…." He handed the sample to Brad.

The deputy nodded. "Wouldn't want something like this to spread."

They were all passengers on a small world. Eddy was acutely aware of how quickly damage to the biosystem, which they depended upon, could get out of hand.

"Good luck out on the Verge." Brad mounted his horse and set off toward Micavery.

Eddy climbed back onto Cassie as his loop beeped. "Tremaine."

"Eddy, it's Colin. I got your message from Lex. With what happened out at the schoolhouse, it has me a bit worried."

"What happened?"

Santi shot him a questioning look.

"Just a sec." In his head, Colin filled him in.

"Oh shit," Eddy whispered when Colin got to the snakebite part.

"What?" Santi asked.

"Something happened out at the schoolhouse."

"What is it?"

"I'll tell you in a minute." To Colin, he asked, "Did we get a pic of our lost boy?"

"Yeah. Here you go."

Eddy whistled. "It's Jayson."

"Yes. Taken all together…."

"It makes a nasty picture." He scratched the back of his head. "Where has he been this whole time?"

"Maybe you can ask him."

"I will. I'll let you know what I find out."

"Thanks, Eddy. May you live in interesting times, huh?"

"Indeed." He cut the connection.

"So?" Santi looked a little annoyed at being kept out of the loop.

"Looks like our little quest just got more important."

· · ·

ANA CROSS-CHECKED the seed ship's trajectory, making slight adjustments to the sail that scooped up particles and fed them down into the belly of the world as it harnessed the solar wind to push them out into the void. The ship had crossed the orbits of Jupiter and Saturn now and was still picking up speed.

Their chosen destination, 82 G. Eridani, at twenty light-years distant, was the closest star the project scientists had decided had a good chance to have an inhabitable planet.

At the speed at which Forever was capable of reaching, it was a five-hundred-year one-way trip, and the slightest error in calculations at the beginning of this journey could have huge consequences on the far end.

She recalled when she'd been a little boy in New York, staring up at these same stars when the city was almost dark and wondering if she would ever find her way to them.

Ana smiled at the memory. It was one of Jackson's, not hers, but she had become accustomed to having them by now.

He'd left them behind when he and Glory had passed on, and they had become a part of the mind of the remaining Immortals, along with his hopes and weaknesses, his aspirations and fears.

She'd even caught herself wondering at the possibility of an afterlife once or twice.

*Are we on course?* The thought floated through her consciousness, though she recognized it as Lex's. They were shading into each other more and more, something that had really bothered Ana at first.

Now she was a little more blasé about it. They were engaged in an unprecedented experiment in the fusion of human and artificial minds. Everything evolved, even Immortals.

*I think so. It's sad, leaving our home behind.*

In response a wave of *blue* washed through her mind. *Colin is reporting some strange things.*

Ana sighed. Their newest member was still insisting on keeping his identity confined to himself. He communicated with them only in the old-fashioned way, interface to interface. Ana sent back a wave of greens and blues that meant "I'll go talk to him."

She wrapped up her course corrections and opened a connection to Colin's space.

She stepped through, imagining herself as she had been when they'd been on the *Dressler*. She liked to feel young and vital again. "Lex said you called?"

He nodded, shuffling papers on his virtual desk. She supposed it helped him to keep this semblance of the "real world," but it seemed like a big waste of time. "Andy was attacked this morning."

"Really? What happened?" She could feel Lex's consciousness embedded with her own.

"She was in vee space with her kids, showing them some Earth animals."

"I know. We helped her make them." She smiled weakly. "The hippo was my favorite."

"One of them, a rattlesnake, bit her."

"Not possible." She pulled up the file for the circus they'd constructed. "It's not part of the programming."

"Even so. Andy got lost, and Marissa and Shandra had to go pull her out."

"That's odd." Something must be off somewhere in the system.

Colin grunted. "Then there's this." He handed her a video.

"What is this?" She passed her hand over it and set it in the air between them. It ran, showing her a stand of burned trees. Alifirs, if she was right.

"I sent Eddy out to check on a mysterious stranger's appearance out on the Verge. On his way, he found those."

"Fire?"

He shook his head. "I don't think so. Nothing around them was burned."

"Who's this stranger?"

Colin handed her another file. "Jayson Hammond."

Ana stared at it. The moment they had feared might be coming to pass. "If Jayson Hammond has turned up, where is Davian Forrester?" She shuddered, remembering the abomination the man had visited on the world.

Colin nodded. "Where indeed?"

# 16

## THUNDER

MARISSA SAT next to Andy's bed, carving a piece of wood into the shape of a dolphin, one of her favorite of Old Earth's creatures. She'd grown the wood to the right general shape and was using a small knife to whittle it into the form she wanted. It was one of the things that helped her cope when the blackness from Agartha threatened to swallow her whole.

Andy had suggested she try art as an outlet for her emotions, and she found it gave her a way to channel her anger and fear in a way that added something beautiful to the world.

Next to her, Andy mumbled, turning over on her side and rubbing her temple. Her eyes opened.

Marissa set her carving aside. "How are you feeling?" She was sitting in a beautiful wooden chair that Delancy had made. Her friend had a gift for woodwork, too, both with and without her talent, and she'd started making chairs for each of the people at the schoolhouse.

"I've been better." She sat up, and her face turned a pale shade of green. She reached for the mattress to steady herself. "Was all that real? The snake? Transfer Station? Oh God, tell me you and Shandra didn't have to come and find me."

Marissa came to sit next to her on the bed. "Lie down. Shandra's watching the kids this afternoon." She smoothed Andy's hair away from her face. "And yes, it was real. In vee, but it was real."

"The snake… it bit me." She held her arm up and examined the skin. It was smooth, unblemished. "It felt so real."

Marissa nodded. "Ana is looking into it."

Andy frowned. "What aren't you telling me?"

"Maybe we should wait until you feel better."

"I feel fine." Andy sat up again. She looked dizzy, but she steadied herself and stared at Marissa. "Tell me."

"My father is back." It pained her to call him that. "Your uncle, Jayson."

Andy's hands squeezed the sheets. "Where?"

"Shandra said he wandered into a farmhouse out on the edge of the Verge. He was starving and confused." Marissa looked out the window, wondering where he had been. If he ever thought about the children he had fathered. How he'd been able to do what he did. "The sheriff is on his way to see him."

"Eddy?"

Marissa nodded.

"And Davian?"

Marissa shook her head. "Shandra said there was no sign of him. She told me, but she hasn't told the others."

"She trusts you." Andy sighed. "God, I hope Davian is dead. After what he did to you…."

"Do you think… did my father know what he was doing?" Marissa squeezed her hands in her lap.

Andy looked troubled. "I really don't know."

"Shandra says no more vee, for now." Marissa looked out the window at the schoolyard.

"No more vee. No more dipping. No more using our talents until we know what's going on." She pushed herself up out of bed.

Marissa tried to block her. "Are you sure it's a good idea for you to be up?"

"I have to. The other kids need to hear from me, see that I'm all right."

"But are you?" Marissa laid a hand on her shoulder. She hated to see Andy overextend herself.

"All right. That's enough." Her voice was sharp. "Sorry. I didn't mean to sound so harsh, but I have to do this." Andy reached for her trousers, which sat on another chair. Marissa handed them to her and helped her pull them on.

"Does that hurt?"

Andy managed a grin. "Only a lot."

Marissa handed her a shirt. Andy was the closest thing she had to a mother, and it was hard to see her like this.

"I'll come back and rest right afterward, I promise." She started toward the door.

Marissa pulled her back. "*Right* after."

Andy laughed. "You're quite the task mistress."

Marissa snickered. "I learned from the best."

Andy kissed her forehead. "Love you, Marissa."

They left the small cabin Andy and Shandra shared and stepped out onto the porch. It was starting to rain outside, the air heavy with moisture.

Marissa helped her stay upright as they followed the covered pathway, breathing in the fresh air.

Music floated out of the open windows, and Andy stopped, enchanted.

THE HEART *of the mallow tree,*
  *The needles of the alifir,*
  *The glow on my grass-stained knee*
  *The song in my heart does stir....*

"WHO WROTE THAT?" Andy whispered.

Marissa cocked her ear. "I think that's one of Danny's."

"As long as we still make music, I have hope for humankind." The vocals were accompanied by the strumming of a pantir, a string instrument Rolly had come up with, something like a violin but with a richer, earthier sound.

Marissa squeezed her hand.

When the song ended, Andy mounted the stairs. She took a deep breath to steady herself, put a smile on her face, and entered the schoolhouse building.

"Andy!" Shandra got up and threw herself into Andy's arms. Soon she was surrounded by the kids' happy faces.

"Yes, I'm okay. Please sit down."

They did as they were told, though the youngest, Rain, clung to her leg. Marissa took a seat at the back, watching the scene fondly.

Shandra brought Andy a chair and she sat down carefully, lifting the ten-year-old up into her lap. "You all sang so beautifully. I just had to come hear you. Danny, that was lovely."

Danny beamed. "Thanks, Andy."

Delancy raised her hand.

"Yes?"

"What happened to you? In vee?" Concern creased her brow.

"Probably just a glitch in the system." Andy held up her arm. "I'm fine, see? Just a little headache."

Delancy looked doubtful.

"For now, though, we're going to stay out of vee." There were sighs around the room. "Just until we know what happened."

"It's for the best." Marissa looked around the room at her classmates. "Do you want something like that to happen to Andy again?"

George snickered.

"Do you want it to happen to you?" She glared at him.

He looked down at the ground, his cheeks reddening. "No, Marissa."

"Okay, then." There were some perks to being the oldest, after all.

"Thanks, Mari." Andy flashed her a grateful smile.

"You're really okay?" Andy should be in bed recuperating, not taking a hundred questions.

Andy looked a little queasy. "A good night's rest and I'll be good as new."

Marissa smiled, and so did most of the rest of the kids.

"That means no dipping, no touching the world mind. Do I make myself clear?"

"Yes, ma'am," they answered in unison.

Andy chuckled. "We'll start class again tomorrow. In the meantime, you all have the rest of the day off."

There were cheers at that.

"Okay, ready to go back to bed now." Andy was wobbly on her feet.

"Good girl." Shandra helped her get up, gently disengaging Rain from her leg. "Keep an eye on everyone?" she asked Marissa.

"I will."

Marissa watched them go. She loved them both like they were her own parents, but still, she wondered.

*What's my father really like?*

. . .

EDDY AND SANTI reached the Verge by midafternoon. They'd stopped to pick apples from the orchards that ringed the world on the highlands above Micavery. Eddy loved getting a bite of the fresh fruit, plucked off the tree seconds before.

Things had been bad on Earth in the waning days before the Collapse, and fresh produce had become increasingly hard to come by. Many days, he'd gotten by on old canned goods.

For soldiers, there had always been some kind of food, but most of it was packaged, and half of it was an artificial paste the troops called spackle, though it was really called Standard Produced Artificial Comestible, or SPAC for short. It was flavorless, and although it supposedly contained all the nutrients a human body needed, it always left him unsatisfied.

Plus, it was a little too Soylent Green for his tastes. Who knew what they put in that crap?

Now they rode through the first part of the Verge. A storm was coming, and it looked to be a heavy one. "What do you say we wait out the storm under the trees there? We can string up a tarp." He pointed at a stand of elm trees that had been reengineered for Forever's ecosystem.

"Sounds good." Santi left the roadway and urged his horse into a trot across the open field.

Eddy followed, glancing up at the sky. The storm clouds wound around the spindle, darkening it and dimming the world as they prepared to let loose their moisture.

He urged Cassie up the hill and underneath the glowing branches. He dismounted and unpacked the canvas tarp he'd brought with him.

Santi helped him tie it to four of the trees, creating a slightly angled roof that would keep off the worst of the rain.

They tethered the horses and sat down under the tarp to wait out the tempest.

Eddy pulled out a couple more apples. They'd lost their glow but still looked delicious. He also took out some bread and cheese and his canteen. "We can have a proper picnic, here in the woods."

Santi laughed. "Some woods." He looked around the little copse of trees. "I suppose we can. I brought a little raisin bread, if you want some."

"Oooh, we have raisin bread again?" He accepted a chunk of it happily. "I do miss the supermarket sometimes."

"Oh, don't get me started. Pepsi and those little chocolate Ovango cookies—"

"And pasta. Holy shit, I miss lasagna, and raviolis—"

"And garlic bread." Santi took one of the apples and bit into it, the juice glowing as it ran from one corner of his mouth.

The rain started, setting up a pleasant thrumming on their canvas roof. One of the horses nickered, then went back to eating grass.

"I bet we could still have garlic bread. The world mind carries all the genomes for common plants and animals." Eddy bit into the raisin bread. "Holy crap, this is good."

Santi nodded. "That would be *fucking amazing*. Did you know there's a place in Darlith that makes a half-decent spaghetti?"

"Seriously? That *would* be amazing. I'll have to check it out next time I get into town."

A deep rumble shook their little copse of trees.

"That sounded like thunder." Eddy squinted out at the storm. Thunder and lightning were rare occurrences on Forever. They happened from time to time, but in the last fifteen years, he could only remember a handful of occasions.

"That's weird." Santi grinned.

The rain was heavier now, coming down in thick sheets that cut off the view to fewer than a dozen meters in any direction.

Eddy picked up a chunk of cheese. It was one of the newer varieties, grown in caverns close to Micavery, and had a pleasantly nutty flavor. "You should try this—"

A lightning bolt struck one of the trees, the flash blinding as it knocked Eddy backward into the trunk of one of the other trees in the grove.

Eddy opened his eyes, but the afterimage almost blinded him.

He crawled forward, looking for his companion. "Santi, are you okay?" he shouted over the rain and thunder.

Eddy found him lying flat on his back. Frantically he scrambled up to him and checked his pulse. Santi's heart was still beating.

As his vision returned, he could see that the tree that had been struck by lightning was in flames, though the heavy rain was slowly dousing them.

Santi hadn't responded.

"Santi, can you hear me?"

His eyes were closed, but his chest lifted and fell.

Eddy put his hand under Santi's head. It was sticky. He must have been knocked into something by the bolt too.

Eddy didn't want to move him.

He reached out and captured some of the rain that was dripping off the edge of the tarp and rubbed it gently across his companion's cheek and forehead.

Santi's brown eyes flickered open as he looked up at Eddy. Santi focused on him and stiffened. "What are you doing?"

"Hey, it's okay." Eddy held up his hands to show he was no threat. "I was just checking to see if you were all right. You got knocked around pretty good by the lightning strike."

Santi stared at him for a moment and then nodded. "You weren't trying to…." He seemed to have a hard time saying it.

"No. Not at all. I was scared that you were hurt. That's all."

"Okay. Sorry. It's just that I didn't… I don't want that. Not with you. Not with anyone."

Eddy held his hands out in surrender. "Okay. Look, you don't have anything to worry about with me." He'd always found Santi attractive, but nothing had ever happened between them. Maybe now he knew why. Someone must have hurt him.

Santi laughed ruefully. "Right. I know that. I'm sorry. Just got a bit shaken up."

"I get it."

The air felt *weird*. Santi's hair was rising on his head, making him look like a monster from some tri dee flick. "Get down and cover your ears!"

They fell to the ground as another bolt struck one of the trees in the grove, splitting it with an almost deafening crack.

It fell to the ground next to them with a terrible crash, bringing their tarp down with it.

Eddy looked up, pulling his hands away from his ears. They were inside a half-tent made by the tarp and the collapsed tree.

Santi grunted and pointed. His horse had been struck and lay splayed out under the trees. It twitched a few times and then stilled.

Cassie was nowhere to be seen.

The rain slowed, though it kept up a steady pace.

Eddy tapped his loop.

Lex's voice spoke in his head. "Yes, Eddy?"

"Lex, there's a really bad storm coming through the Verge… it just killed one of our horses."

"I've been getting reports from across Darlith and the Verge. Something is messing with my biorhythms."

"Have you told Aaron? People in Micavery need to take cover."

"Yes, he's been notified. Are the two of you okay?"

"I think so. The worst of the storm seems to have passed."

"I'll let Aaron know."

"Can you get me Jendra?"

"One moment."

Eddy waited for his lieutenant to come on the line.

"Hi, Eddy. Bit busy at the moment."

"You heard about the storm?"

"Living it right now. We're getting everyone inside."

He nodded. "Thanks, Jendra. Knew I could count on you."

"Backatcha, boss."

LEX PROBED HER SYSTEMS, trying to figure out why things were going haywire. There was a wrench in the works somewhere, but her diagnostics were all coming up with nothing.

Something was drawing resources away from her core systems. She could see them flowing, disappearing into a black hole. She'd seen something like it once before, when Jackson had blocked himself off from the other Immortals. She'd been able to infer his presence from the system resources he was using, but his whereabouts were blocked from her.

*Do you think these things are all connected?* Ana's mind overlapped hers, making true speech unnecessary. More and more, she and her onetime nemesis were one and the same.

*I don't know. So many anomalies at once, though? It's likely.*

*The dead trees alarm me the most. Lightning?*

Lex expressed negation. *No storms big enough for that kind of damage, until now.*

They both remembered what had happened aboard the *Dressler*, when an almost microscopic fungus had brought down the whole ship.

Lex shuddered.

*We'll figure it out.* Ana sounded determined.

*We must.*

## 17

## SNOW

Eddy sat at the edge of the grove, watching the last bits of the storm recede toward the South Pole.

He'd decided to give Santi some space. He'd had no idea the man had been abused by someone. That had to be it, right? Not that Eddy had any interest in him in that way, in any case. But he hadn't meant to cross that line with Santi, even unintentionally.

Santi *was* a good-looking guy. Eddy had noticed.

In any case, it seemed best to put a little distance between the two of them, at least for a while.

The storm had done some serious damage. From where he stood, he could see dead trees stretching from the hill up along the curve of the world. There were a few larger black patches too... whether from lightning strikes or whatever had ailed those alifir trees, he couldn't be sure.

*So what now?* They didn't have a lot of options.

They'd lost both horses, one killed by a falling tree and the other gone during the storm. Cassie... he'd raised her from a foal. He could only hope she would find her way home eventually. Maybe she would be waiting for him when he returned.

He and Santi could make their way on foot across the Verge to see what Jayson was doing there. They could wait for reinforcements. Or they could start back toward home.

"Hey." Santi came to sit next to him. "*¿Cómo estás?*"

"Okay. Still a bit shaken up." He glanced at the grove behind them, where several of the trees had collapsed. "That was pretty intense."

He nodded. "I'm sorry for reacting the way I did."

"It's okay." Eddy rubbed his neck absentmindedly. "Must have been weird to wake up with me looming over you like that."

"Yeah." Santi grinned wryly.

There was a story there. Santi would tell him when he was ready, Eddy figured. "I'm sorry about your horse."

"Snowball. That was her name."

Eddy laughed in spite of himself.

"What?"

"That's something we'll probably never see again."

"Snow?"

"Sometimes I miss the cold." Eddy remembered a trip to Canada with his mother, when he was little. "And heat. Like when you used to get in a drone taxi in the summertime, and it had been sitting in the lot for hours waiting for a call…."

"And the heat felt sooo good. For a moment." Santi grinned.

"Yes, just like that." Eddy looked around the world, up to where the walls vanished in the distance above their heads. "I'm kind of used to this now. But it will never be like home."

Santi followed his gaze. "Yeah, I never thought I'd be so nostalgic for a blue sky." He hugged his knees to his chest. "My *familia* lived in Mexico City when my mother was a little girl. When one of the Burns killed almost a thousand people in the city, she and her sisters and parents fled to Little Mexico in Vancouver."

"I never made it to Vancouver."

"It was like the Wild West. So many people moving up from Mexico and the old United States after the Union." Santi smiled. It lit up his whole face. "It even snowed there when I was a kid, once."

"I grew up in Florida."

"Jesus."

"Yeah." He picked up a pebble and threw it down the hillside. It disappeared in a clump of glowing grass. "So… what do we do now?"

Santi shrugged. "You're the boss."

"We could go home. Start out again in a day or two." Eddy picked a blade of glowing grass. It faded in his hand.

"I thought this guy was important?"

"He is." Eddy wiped his hands on his pants.

"So maybe heading home isn't the best idea."

Eddy laughed ruefully. "Maybe not. So… we could stay here and call for reinforcements. Or we could walk the rest of the way."

"There's a fourth option."

"What's that?" Did Santi have wings he hadn't told Eddy about?

"We could go on horseback. If you don't mind me putting my arms around your waist."

"But we don't have a horse."

For an answer, Santi pointed sideways. "Will that one do?"

Eddy followed his gesture. "Cassie!" She was trotting over the next hill over, coming toward them, her light chestnut coat blending in neatly with the golden glow of the grass.

He was on his feet and running toward her before he realized he hadn't answered Santi.

"So, is that a yes?" Santi shouted after him.

"That's a *hell yes*!"


THE MAN SAT UP, rubbing his head. He was lying on a hay-stuffed mattress in a barn. His head was still fuzzy…. He couldn't seem to remember who he was or how he'd gotten here.

The nice people. They had taken him in.

Things flashed past his eyes—memories?

A big cavern underground. Women beneath him, with blank faces, as he expelled his need.

The Preacher. His Master.

Sometimes, if he sat still enough, if he closed his eyes and let the memories play out, he was rewarded with softer ones. Memories from a time before *here*. Before this place. When he'd had a mother and a father.

A brother.

A white house near the park, where he used to go to play.

Before the fog had come.

Sometimes there were more painful memories. Being prodded and poked by sharp things, both outside and in his head. Being strapped down and shown images that made him want to scream. Being *reprogrammed*. That was the word they had used.

Now, though, he sat with his back against the wooden wall of the barn, his freshly clean feet on the straw mattress, and a new memory came to him.

A dark cavern, kneeling next to his Master.

The man's eyes closed.

Cradling him in his arms.

Dipping into the ground below to connect with her. The goddess.

The ecstasy that had rampaged through him for a few brief moments, burning away the fog from his mind.

Then the utter darkness and loneliness as the fog crept back in.

Not so heavy as before, perhaps.

He nodded. Things were changing. One of these days, he would remember who he was and how he had gotten here.

For now, he lay back down, adrift in the fog like a warm blanket, speaking his Master's name.

"Davian."

MARISSA SLIPPED OUT OF BED, tiptoeing across the floorboards in the narrow space to Danny's bed. "Danny, wake up," she whispered, glancing at Delancy's sleeping form on the other side of the cabin.

"Whaaaaaat?" Danny groaned, turning over to look at her through bleary eyes. The night ivy cast a silver glow through the window, enough for her to make out the outlines of the room and to see Danny's face.

"Shhhhh. Move over."

He did as he was told in the small bed, and she crawled in next to him.

"I need your help." She spoke softly, directly into his ear.

"For what?"

Being this close to him, she was acutely aware of his beautiful body, of his scent. *Stay on topic, Marissa.* "They found our father."

"Gunner?"

She nodded. "Gunner, Jayson, whatever his name is."

"Mari… you don't want to go anywhere near him. Remember what he did to us. To our mothers."

She shook her head. "That's why I want to see him. I want to know *how* he did it." She bit her lip. "I want to know *why*."

He stared at her in the dim light. "Andy and Shandra will never let us go."

"I know. That's why I want to go now. Tonight. They found him at a farmhouse on the Verge. That's not far from here. We can be there in a day."

Danny frowned. He brushed his long brown hair away from his face and rubbed the back of his neck. "I don't know...."

"Look, we can say we're sorry later, but we may never have another chance like this." She glanced at Delancy. The girl was still fast asleep. "Remember that day we went into the canyons? There's one that goes straight down to the edge of the Verge. Andy told me about it. We can take a horse and just enough supplies for a few days." A lazy grin crossed her face. "And we'd be alone."

"We're not supposed to—"

She put a finger on his lips. "It's okay if we just fool around a little." If Andy and Shandra really didn't want any relations springing up among the Liminal kids, they would have brought some other kids here, right?

"Okay."

"Perfect. I packed our carry sacks when everyone was at dinner earlier." She pulled his from under the bed.

He whistled. "Damn, you *are* prepared."

She tried to shut him up, but she was too late.

"What are you two doing?" Delancy asked, sitting up in bed and rubbing her eyes.

The damage was done. "Nothing. Go back to bed."

"You're up to something...." She glanced at their carry sacks. "You're leaving, aren't you?"

"It's none of your business." Marissa fumed. Why did Delancy have to wake up, tonight of all nights? She usually slept like a log.

Delancy put her hands on her hips. "Tell me, or I'll go and get Andy and Shandra."

*What are you? Five?*

Danny shrugged. "Might as well tell her."

"All right." She slipped off the bed and back over to her own. No sense in shouting out their news to the whole schoolhouse. "We're going to find Gunner."

Delancey hissed. "They found him?"

Marissa nodded. "Yes. He's at a farmhouse on the Verge. *Please* don't tell Andy and Shandra. Not until we're gone."

"I won't. I swear."

"Thanks." Marissa heaved a sigh of relief.

"If I can come with you."

*Damn.* "It was just going to be Danny and me—"

"I'm *so sick* of this place. And I'm one of the oldest too. I want to see him." She looked down at her hands in her lap. "I want to ask him how he could do those things to us. To our mothers."

They *never* talked about their mothers. The women who had given them up and sent them *here*.

"Please?"

Marissa sighed. "Okay, but we have to go now. I want to have a few hours lead time before they come looking for us."

Danny frowned. "I don't want them to worry. They've been so good to us."

"I wrote a note." Marissa pulled out the folded piece of paper, opened it up, and used her charcoal pencil to append the name "Delancy" to it.

Danny glanced over her shoulder. "You were that sure I'd say yes, huh?"

Marissa blushed. "I'd hoped."

He laughed. "Okay, then, let's get going."

"I have to pack my things." Delancy got her carry sack out of the closet and started stuffing things into it.

When she was done, Marissa took one more look around the place she had called home for the last ten years.

She'd be back. It would only be a few days.

Nevertheless, a wave of sadness washed over her as she quietly closed the door behind them.


ANA AND LEX stood in Lex's valley. The stone tower, a fixture there since Lex had first created the sanctuary, was gone.

In its place was a wall that stretched up as far as they could see, and out to both sides of the valley. It was a vast mirror, reflecting the other side of the valley and the hillside where the forest took over from the grassy hills.

Ana reached out to touch it. It was lukewarm, maybe? Mostly it felt like nothing.

It flowed around her, threatening to engulf her fingers.

She jerked her hand back and looked at it. Her virtual skin was untouched.

A ripple extended from where she had been in contact with the wall, spreading up and out like she'd dropped a pebble in a perfectly reflective pond.

This was the third place they had found such a wall, the first being Ana's own private world, the Russian countryside of her youth. The second had been Jameson's world, where a bisected Frontier Station still floated above an unruined Earth.

*What is it?*

*I don't know. Something inside is using a lot of resources.*

*Can we get through it?*

*I don't know.*

Lex flashed a wave of distressed *red* at her.

They stared at the wall. Ana willed it to go away, to no avail.

*Your hand.*

Ana looked down. Her right hand, the one she had touched the wall with, was becoming transparent. She could still feel it, still flex it, but she could see right through it.

*That can't be good.*

# 18

## NIGHT

Marissa led her companions up out of the valley where the schoolhouse and their little community lay. It was dark out, more so away from the night ivy and luthiel lanterns that lit their home at night.

*Home.*

Marissa glanced back at the valley, fashioned from the wreckage of the mountain that had once held Agartha. In a way, she'd never lived anywhere else but this place—first as Agartha, and now at the schoolhouse. But certainly, Agartha hadn't been *home.*

She sighed.

"We'll be back soon." Danny put a hand on her shoulder.

Marissa nodded, rubbing her horse's neck. Mirabelle was a black mare Marissa had worked with since she had been a girl of six years old. They'd decided to walk the horses out of the valley to keep them as quiet as possible.

Marissa looked up. There were a couple of other patches of light in the arc of the world above, campers or other small settlements.

She imagined this was what it might have looked like at night from a valley on Old Earth, looking up to see the stars sparkling in the sky.

Other than when she had been rescued by Andy, Shandra, and the others, she'd never been far from the valley. She didn't really know what was out there. Well, she *knew.* Andy had shown them what it was like to visit Micavery and Darlith. But she'd never seen it with her own eyes.

Two broken slabs of rock formed an A shape over the lone exit to the valley. The countryside around the schoolhouse was ripped up and broken, a maze of dead-end passageways and canyons. It was a legacy of the destruction Andy had visited on Agartha. The rock was black and mostly unadorned, save by moss and the occasional creeper vines that had snaked their way into the mountains since they'd been constructed. "You guys ready?"

Delancy and Danny nodded.

Marissa led Mirabelle under the archway, shivering a little as she plunged them into darkness.

She'd come this way before, a few times when she and Danny had snuck out late at night. What they'd done had never amounted to more than a little groping in the dark. Neither of them really knew what they were supposed to do.

The others followed her out of the valley.

After a moment, her eyes adjusted to the dim light put off by the moss that grew wherever water typically ran.

In some places, the moss was green. In others it shaded more into blue.

The pathway had been flattened through the broken slabs of rock when the schoolhouse had been built. It twisted back and forth around the larger pieces of rubble, which rose above them in strange silhouettes, framed by the silver light from the spindle.

When Marissa judged that they'd come far enough from the schoolhouse, she mounted Miri and gestured for the others to do the same.

They continued on, the air around them still as death.

She hoped Andy wouldn't be too mad when she found out that they'd left. They'd taken some supplies, but only enough for a few days. It shouldn't cause a hardship for the rest of the kids.

She tried to remember what her father had looked like. Red hair, always serious, but the details of his features eluded her.

And what had happened to the other man, the Preacher? If there was any justice in the world, he lay dead in some dark, foul place in the pit of the world.

She resisted the urge to dip into the world mind. Andy and Shandra had said it was too dangerous right now. It was hard not to—touching the mind to see where she was or to check on the world outside, came as easily as breathing. Without it she felt like she'd lost a limb.

They reached a fork in the trail. There was a whole maze among the wreckage of broken rocks, meant to confuse intruders.

"To the right." Danny pointed.

She nodded and nudged Miri that way.

"How far until we reach the Verge?" Delancy's voice quaked a little, and she glanced around at the dark walls that hemmed them in, like little birds searching for an escape.

"It should only take a couple hours." Marissa grinned in the darkness. "As long as we don't take a wrong turn."

Delancy yelped.

Marissa laughed to herself. Delancy deserved that, for forcing her company on the two of them.

Danny snorted. "Don't mess with her. It'll take less than an hour, and we've been through here a couple times. We won't get you lost."

"I could just dip a little and find the way...." She trailed her hand across the rock wall on her left.

"Delancy, don't!" But Marissa was too late.

Delancy's body convulsed as she touched the rock, her whole frame shaking in violent movements as if she'd been shocked.

Cursing, Marissa slipped off Mirabelle and reached for the reins of Delancy's horse, Amaro, who was skittering back and forth nervously, trying to figure out what was wrong with his rider.

Danny followed suit and reached up to grab Delancy, pulling her out of her saddle to safety.

"Shhh, it's okay," Marissa whispered to Amaro, rubbing his neck.

He tossed his head back and forth and then settled, listening to her soothing voice. "Is she okay?"

Danny had set Delancy down with her back against the rock. "I think so? She's shivering."

"Here." Marissa pulled a blanket out of Amaro's saddlebag and handed it to him.

They covered her, kneeling next to her.

"Della... you okay?" Marissa pulled her chin up gently.

"Soooo coooooold." She shivered again. "Why was it so cold?" Her teeth chattered.

"When you dipped?"

She nodded. "I've never felt *cold* like that."

Marissa and Danny exchanged a glance. "Something's really wrong."

"No shit." Danny sat next to Delancy and pulled her close. "I'll warm you up."

Marissa nodded. Danny was right to do it, to put his warm body up next to hers. It was what Delancy needed.

She would *not* be jealous.


EDDY AND SANTI were up early the next morning. They'd shared a light breakfast of pastries and embrew. Sometimes Eddy really missed having real coffee.

They were ready to go when first light arrived.

The world around them flared to life, marred only where lightning had burned some of the trees and bushes or left a blackened, dark patch in the grasslands in between. Even those were starting to heal, as the fast-growing grasses took over the dead patches, returning them to a healthy greenish-golden glow.

They'd managed to pull the tarp out from under the fallen tree, though it was torn in several places. Santi's horse was another matter. A crew from Micavery would come out to retrieve Snowball, to carry its body off to one of the dissolution pits to be broken down into its component parts.

Santi knelt next to the horse, his hand on its neck, whispering something that Eddy couldn't hear.

When he climbed onto Cassie, sitting behind Eddie, his voice was rough. "Let's go."

"You okay?"

"Yeah. It's just hard letting him go. I've worked with him since he was a foal."

"I know. I feel the same about Cassie here." Santi's body was warm against his back. Eddy did his best to ignore that. Nothing could come of it. Besides the fact that Santi didn't want intimate contact, Eddy had no idea if the man was even attracted to guys. "Hold on."

Santi slipped his hands around Eddy's waist.

Eddy spurred Cassie down the hillside. "Ever been out to the edge of the Verge?"

"Not really. I went out a few times to mediate some land disputes, but only mid-Verge. It's a beautiful country."

Eddy nodded. "I'm told it resembles Tuscany... at least Tuscany before the Mediterranean hurricanes began and tore the countryside to shreds."

"If Tuscany glowed and spread upward into the sky, you mean?"

Eddy laughed. "Yeah. There is that."

They made it back to the Micavery Road. Out this far, it was still dirt, and the farmers preferred it that way. It made the whole place feel more rural.

Along the left side of the road, wood fencing marked one of the farmsteads and kept in the modified cattle that provided milk and meat to the colonists.

The original generation ship plans had called for the colonists to be largely vegetarian. But plans had changed after the Collapse, when Forever had to leave near-Earth space in haste.

A lot of plans were being rewritten.

On the way, they passed traffic heading into Micavery. Some of it was on horseback and some by traxx. The machines were simple enough that the colony had been able to keep most of them running, and they provided the workhorse operations for moving goods back and forth. But sooner or later, they were going to prove inadequate to the growing world's needs. And machines couldn't be repaired forever.

It was strange to see human society changing, evolving in a way that had little to do with technical advances and mechanized solutions to the world's problems. "Do you ever wonder about what the world will be like for our kids? For their kids?"

"You have kids?"

Eddy laughed. "No. I can barely take care of myself. I meant in general."

"It'll be different. None of them will have loops."

"Yeah, it's going to make communication harder."

"Slower, anyhow." He sighed. "Faster isn't always better. Look what technology brought us on Earth."

Eddy nodded. "You're right. It was a mess. Even before the Collapse. And yet...."

"What?"

"It wasn't all bad." He rarely told anyone about his past, but after what Santi had told him, it felt right. "Back on Earth, before I became a soldier, I was physically female."

"Holy shit, really?"

"Yeah."

Santi was quiet for a long time.

"Is that… I mean, does that bother you?"

"No. Oh, not at all." Santi grinned. "You're just so handsome now. I was trying to picture it."

Eddy grinned. *Score one for team gay.* "Well, thanks. I think." He waved at a passing farmer hauling a cart full of still-glowing corn husks. "Without technology, I'd still be female. Do you know, a hundred years ago, they were still doing transitions surgically?"

"I can't imagine." Santi squeezed him gently.

"I know. It was so invasive. I'm thankful I was able to have mine done genetically."

"Wow. Thanks for telling me."

"You're welcome. Can I ask you something?"

He felt Santi stiffen. "Um… sure."

"What happened to you?" He hoped Santi didn't mind the question.

"I'm not sure what you mean?"

Eddy bit his lip. "I mean… were you abused? You seemed… almost afraid? Were you…" He took a breath. "You know. Abused?"

Santi laughed. "No, nothing like that."

"Then what?" *Damn, I should have kept my mouth shut.*

"I'm asexual."

*Ahhhh.* "Oh, that makes sense." Ace. *Damn.* "How long have you known?"

"I'm so glad you didn't ask 'How long have you been.' That's what most people say. Or 'Why did you decide to be ace?' It's just something that's always been a part of me."

"Did you ever…? Never mind. That's rude of me to ask." He was doing a bang-up job of it.

"It's okay. And yeah. A couple times. With guys, if you want to know."

Eddy blushed. He *had* wanted to know. But he hadn't wanted Santi to *know* he wanted to know. "That's… nice."

"Ace doesn't mean aromantic. A lot of folks are both, but they're not the same thing."

"Gotcha." Now he felt like a complete idiot.

He'd *noticed* Santiago before. Who wouldn't? The man was ten years younger than he was and attractive in that tall, dark, and handsome way. They worked together in close quarters.

But Eddy had been with Mitchell until recently, when things had gone sour between them. He'd only reentered the market recently, and it was a small market.

To be honest, he wasn't sure quite what to make of the ace thing either. He'd always had a healthy sex drive. Then again, "healthy" was subjective, wasn't it?

He'd always been attracted to men, and many—most—men weren't. He understood what it was to be different.

Eddy was still working out what else to say when the world went dark.

COLIN KNELT over a virtual model of the world split in half like a geode. Well, a pipe-shaped geode.

He'd loved those when he was a kid. His father had bought one for him at a county fair, and when they'd cut it open, it had been full of purple crystals.

His new "geode" was far more intricate, stretching out for about fifteen meters, the world in cross-section.

He was looking at a spot out toward the end of the current build-out—past Darlith, past the open space that was starting to fill up with forest and estate homes—for a new settlement. "The Eire," he was calling it, a nod to his own and Jackson's roots in that beautiful green country.

They'd decided to keep most of the human population concentrated in cities, centralizing the burden on Forever's recycling systems and leaving wide swaths of the biosystem mostly untouched and self-regulating.

This town, as he envisioned it, would eventually stretch all the way around the world in a ring, allowing them to house thousands upon thousands of future colonists.

He supposed he should stop calling them colonists. The colonization period was long over. They were the natives now, or would be, once the next generation grew into their own.

Forever's first homegrown generation.

Andy's kids were being called Liminals, kids born here, on the cusp of the greatest change to ever befall the human race. He supposed it applied equally to the whole new generation.

Colin felt old, thinking about them, about how this would be their world in a way it could never be his. It wasn't the first time.

He could *look* young, here—he could remake himself in their image in vee space. But in the end, it was just another lie. He could refashion his body in vee, but not his soul.

"Colin, you need to come see this." Ana appeared, startling him.

"Damn, I hate when you do that." Ten years, and he still wasn't used to this virtual world. "What is it?"

Ana frowned. "Part of the mind—of vee space—seems to have been sectioned off."

"Show me." Everywhere he went, he seemed doomed to confront system failure of one type or another.

"It's—"

Then she was gone.

The walls of his office shimmered and seemed to rust away, dissolving as if eaten by a powerful fungus, leaving Colin trapped in a silver, reflective box. He could see his own distorted face, like he was looking into a pool of quicksilver.

Colin shuddered. "Ana, can you hear me?"

Nothing.

"Lex?"

There was no reply.

"Hello! Anyone?" His shouts didn't echo; rather, they seemed muffled, like they were being absorbed by something.

If he'd had a human heart, it would have been racing. This one time, he was glad he wasn't subject to human hormones and bodily responses.

He sat down and stared at the shimmering inside of the box where he was suddenly trapped, trying to figure out what to do next.

# 19

## CUT OFF

First light found Marissa and her friends at the edge of the mountains, making their way out of the broken stone labyrinth that surrounded the valley of the schoolhouse. They'd explored parts of it but had never actually left it before.

It was Marissa's first time out in the real world since she and the others had been rescued from Agartha. She'd spent hours as a child when she'd first come to the schoolhouse lying on her back in the tall grass. She would stare at the arc of the world as it wrapped itself above her. At the ring of mountains that girdled the world and at the lands on either side that lay beyond them.

It was hard to make out much detail, but on exceptionally clear days, sometimes she thought she could see rivers and roads up there. She even imagined she could see people on horseback or pulling carts or riding on the mechanical traxx vehicles.

Around the spindle, she also sometimes caught sight of people with wings —not their own, as Andy had explained—on their way from one end of the world to the other.

Now she was finally *here*. Outside the schoolhouse. Away from their beautiful little prison.

She spread her hands and took a deep breath, startling her horse. "It's okay, Miri." She rubbed the horse's neck reassuringly.

The world ahead of her sloped down toward Lake Jackson, with bands of color representing the regions. The Verge's grasses glowed golden with morning light, dotted here and there with farmsteads and fences. In the near distance, the orchards glowed a golden green. And beyond that, the shores of Lake Jackson were more variegated, a patchwork of buildings, roads, vineyards, factories, and areas set aside for other uses.

"It's beautiful," Delancy said breathlessly. Her chest heaved with the excitement, and Marissa frowned as she saw how that attracted Danny's attention.

"We should go."

"Where is it?" Danny asked, his eyes still transfixed on Delancy.

"About a quarter turn west of here. The house is right near the edge of the Verge." She spurred Miri forward, leaving the others behind.

She didn't have a body like Delancy. Maybe she would someday, but for now she was still as flat-chested as a boy. If that was all Danny cared about, he could have Delancy.

The line between the Verge and the mountains was strangely regular, a reminder that as natural as Forever looked, it was nothing of the sort. On her left, the grasses blew back and forth in the gentle breeze. On her right, the mountainous zone began, with sparse vegetation and gray rock walls.

A faint trail in the grass showed they weren't the first ones to ride here, along the margin.

"Hey, wait up!" Danny's horse galloped up next to hers. "What was that all about?"

Marissa glared at him. "I saw the way you looked at her." She glanced over her shoulder. Delancy was following them at a respectable distance. "I didn't even want her to come with us."

"Jealous much?"

"Should I be?" She glared at him.

"Sorry. I was just worried about her."

Marissa snorted. "About her breasts, you mean."

He sighed. "I can't talk with you when you're like this." He shook his reins and spurred his horse farther on down the trail.

"Danny, I'm sorry—" Her voice cut off as the world went dark around her. "Holy shit," she whispered, pulling Miri to a halt lest she stumble over something unseen.

Her horse nickered nervously.

"It's okay." Marissa slipped off the horse, taking the reins in her hand. "Danny! Delancy!"

"Stay where you are," Danny called. "I'm going to work my way back to you."

From behind her, Delancy called out, "I'm coming to you too."

Marissa had never seen such darkness before. There was no light, not even from the spindle. Holding her hand up to her face, she couldn't see a thing. Her heart was racing. "Danny?"

His voice replied immediately. "Keep talking."

"I'm right here. I'm standing next to Mirabelle." She looked around wildly. "It's so dark. Why is it so dark?" She tried to keep the tremble out of her voice.

"It's okay. I'm almost there." Danny's voice was trembling too.

Delancy reached her first. The nickering of her horse was comforting.

"Mari?"

"Right here, Della." She pulled the other girl to her, feelings of jealousy forgotten.

"What's happening?" Delancy squeezed her tight.

"I don't know. We'll figure it out."

"I'm here too."

Danny's voice, so close in the strange night, was immensely reassuring. "Take my hand." They fumbled in the darkness until they connected.

"Why did nightfall come so early?" Delancy asked, her voice sounding small.

"This isn't night. There's always some light at night. This is something else." She squeezed Delancy's hand in reassurance.

"Marissa's right. If only we had loops, like Andy and Shandra. We might be able to contact someone."

"Well, we don't. And I imagine normal communication channels are overwhelmed now." She bit her lip. "There's another way."

"It's not safe." Delancy's voice had an edge of madness to it.

"We can do it together. With all three of us, we're stronger."

The others were silent.

"Well?"

"I guess. Together." Danny sounded reluctant.

"Do you guys have a better idea?"

"No," Danny replied.

"No." Delancy was even softer.

"Is there somewhere we can tie up the horses?"

"There's a tree on the side of the path, just a little ahead." Danny laughed softly. "I ran smack into it on the way back."

"Sounds good. Lead us."

They went single file with their horses. Danny led them ahead until they found it, and one by one they felt their way to tie up their mounts.

Marissa rubbed Miri's neck to reassure her.

When they were done, they gathered in a circle a meter away and put their hands one upon another.

"Ready?"

"Yes."

"Yes."

Marissa braced herself for whatever might happen—snakes, cold—whatever. They knelt in a circle and put their hands on the ground.

They dipped.

Nothing. There was absolutely nothing there.

"What the hell?" Delancy's voice.

"Language."

"Sorry, what *in* the hell?"

The world lit up around them, banishing the darkness as if it had never been.

Marissa stood, looking around at the glowing grass and sky.

Everything seemed normal again, except that she couldn't dip. Couldn't touch the world mind.

It was like someone had thrown a bag over her head.


"Eddy, are you there?" Andy's voice crackled in his head. Eddy had never been happier to hear from another human being.

"Yeah, I'm here." The blackout, or whatever it was, had only lasted a few minutes. But it shouldn't have been possible at all. "What the hell is happening?"

"We don't know. I can't reach Colin, Ana, or Lex, and vee space is screwed up, but now I can't dip either."

"Holy shit." Something was badly amiss. "Is the world mind... broken?"

"I wish I knew. But we have another problem. Three of the kids have gone missing."

"Which ones?" He and Santi had dismounted when the world had gone black. Santi was calming the horse. "What happened?"

"It's Andy. She doesn't know."

"The three oldest—Marissa, Danny, and Delancy. They left a note saying they were going to find their father."

"Jayson."

"Yeah. How close are you?"

"We should be there in another couple hours, if nothing else happens." He looked around. The world looked peaceful, normal. If he hadn't just witnessed the blackout, he would have had no immediate reason to worry. "How are the other kids handling it?"

"They're scared." Andy was scared too. He could hear it in her voice. "Shandra's with them. Can you reach my father?"

"I can try. He won't answer you?"

"I think we're too far away. The world mind boosted the network signal. But now...."

He nodded. "Gotcha. I'll call him."

"Eddy?"

"Yeah?"

"Be careful."

"We will. I'll let you know when we get there." He cut the connection. "Lex, can you get Aaron for me?"

There was no answer. Shit, he'd forgotten. What could have gone wrong to block the world mind? Or worse, to damage or destroy it? If Lex was dead, they were living on borrowed time. "Andy said three of their kids have gone after Jayson. Misplaced father longing or something."

Santi nodded. "Understandable."

"No one can reach the world mind. I'm calling Aaron, and then we'll get on our way."

"Is the world ending?" Santi looked around and up at the arc of the sky.

"I hope not. I barely got my ass off Earth the last time." He tapped the loop three times, bringing up a list of recent access codes. It had been a long time since he'd had to place a call across the loop network manually.

*Busy* flashed across his retina. *Leave message?* He nodded. "Aaron, this is

Eddy. Things have gotten crazy, haven't they? Andy called. They're all right, but none of us can reach the world mind. We're pushing on to the Olaf estate. No need to call me unless you need me for something. We'll report from there." Eddy tapped his loop to cut the connection. "Okay, let's go."

They mounted up and set off down the dirt road at a good clip.

"These kids, they're Liminal ones, right? The ones with the abilities?"

Eddy nodded. All the sheriffs knew about the schoolhouse, though Aaron and the administration had tried to keep the information out of the public sphere. "Andy says the other kids are okay, just scared."

"Do you think they might have done this?"

Eddy frowned. "Not a chance. Why would you think that?"

"There have been a lot of rumors going around."

"At headquarters?"

"There… and in general. Some people are calling them witches."

Eddy laughed. "Hardly. They're good kids. I've been up there a couple times. Andy is teaching them how to use their abilities and how to fit in with society when the time comes."

Santi was silent.

"Do you have a problem with that?" Eddy asked.

"They *can* do things that the rest of us can't."

"Right."

"I'm not sure I want them mixed in with the rest of us." He sighed. "I know that's not the correct thing to say. But aren't we asking for trouble?"

Eddy glanced sideways at his deputy. Santi was a reasonable man. If *he* felt this way…. "I get that you're uneasy about them. But trust me, these are good kids."

"What if some of them aren't? Or if their children aren't?"

Eddy knew those kids. Not one of them would use their abilities to harm another human being. But Santi had a point. How could they know that someone else, at some point, wouldn't?

Eddy and Aaron were pretty certain that Jayson was the one who had destroyed Transfer Station and that he'd helped Davian enslave a whole village of people. Sure, maybe Jayson had been used, but even that would prove Santi's point. Eddy frowned. "So what, would you have them all executed? And Andy and Aaron and Sean too?" Aaron's youngest had just turned nine. Eddy was like an uncle to him, and the thought of someone doing him harm made Eddy's hair catch on fire.

Now Santi looked troubled. "No. I mean, of course not."

"Then what?"

"I don't know. Maybe find a way to neuter them."

"Their abilities, or for procreation?"

"Both."

Eddy growled. "Now you're sounding like those folks on Old Earth who wanted to keep the 'lesser races' from breeding. Did you know that people like me used to be sterilized in some countries in Europe and the Middle East?"

"That's insane. There's nothing wrong with you."

"My point exactly."

They rode on after that in silence.


ANA SAT on the ground staring at the reflective prison walls. They shimmered like the wall she and Lex had observed in vee space. She didn't dare touch them. Not yet. Not until she had exhausted all her other options.

Something or someone had invaded the world mind.

She had a pretty good idea who, but at the moment, that didn't really matter.

What *did* matter, to her at least, was that she'd been cut off from everything but the files that defined her core *self*. She had no way of reaching the others, let alone the outside world. For all she knew, there *was* no outside world anymore. Forever might be nothing but little bits of space debris.

Except... that would likely mean the world mind would be dying too, or already dead. It didn't feel like that was the case.

This felt too clean, too antiseptic to be the result of a catastrophic act of destruction.

One moment she'd been with Colin, and the next she'd been here.

So. Best to start with what she knew and with what she had.

She closed her eyes and ran a self-diagnostic. In this virtual world, she had access to herself in ways she'd never dreamed of when she'd had a corporeal form. Data flipped by, absorbed by her consciousness far more efficiently than her old human mind would have managed.

Files flagged in red represented Jackson's memories, gifted to her and Lex when Jackson had passed on, and then shared with Colin.

In her mind, she stood on a wide white field, and she panned out the files in batches across the sky. She might be trapped, but she could still create her own little world.

Ana's memories and thoughts were in blue on one side, and Jackson's memories in red on the other side.

And in the middle, everything else. Bits of research she'd done over the years, system files, projects she'd worked on with the other Immortals or with Keera and her crew.

There was a sizable chunk of files she'd shared with Lex as they'd grown closer over the years. While their conscious minds were still separate things, they had a lot of overlap, to the point which they would sometimes share thoughts or emotions. She marked those green.

That connection had been severed too.

*Think, Ana, think.* There had to be a way to get out of this box.

The shared files.

Excited, she cleared away the rest of her archive and concentrated on the green files.

If she really was cut off from Lex, why did she still have these files?

Maybe the entity that had done this to them wasn't aware of the connection they shared. Was there a way to use that against it?

She started searching through the files.

She set aside those that were older than a year. If they had had no activity in such a long time, they probably would be of no use to her.

Then she shuffled away any that were pure work-product. Files they had both linked to for things they were working on together.

Next, she sorted the remaining files by date, newest to oldest.

Something caught her eye. One of the files, and only one of them, had been updated in the last fifteen minutes.

She opened it excitedly.

It was an emotion expression… the shared moment when Jackson had taken his leave of them for the last time.

Why would that file have been updated?

As she parsed it, the wave of sadness passed over her again. She missed Jackson. He'd been a steadying influence, much more connected to the two of them than Colin was now.

She was missing something.

She ran through the file again, and it hit her.

It was a code.

Someone—Lex?—was using the emotion file to send her a message.

She pulled up Jackson's memories and searched for the one from that last moment. She found it.

JACKSON TURNED TO AARON. *"It's time." His hands were shaking.*

*Aaron nodded, looking brave.*

*Jackson was so proud of him. He hugged Aaron from one side and Glory from the other.*

*They held him tight. "Love you, Scout," Jackson whispered.*

*"Love you too."*

SHE LAYERED the emotion file over the memory, and as the two were joined, a message scrolled in the air in front of Ana.

*I KNEW you would figure it out.*

ANA WANTED TO DANCE, to sing, to shout to the sky above. Instead, she muttered softly to herself, "Lex, you're a fucking genius."

Then she set about figuring out how Lex had composed the message and how to write one of her own.

Ana was out of the box.

# 20

## ON THE VERGE

Marissa was numb.

It was one thing to know she *shouldn't* try to dip, shouldn't connect to the world mind. It was quite another to know she *couldn't*.

They were giving the horses a rest. Truth be told, she was having second thoughts about seeing Jayson. What would she say to the man who was, biologically at least, her father?

They were finally approaching the Olaf farmstead. She could see it a little way ahead, around the curve of the world. Like many of the newer structures on Forever, it was built in a style that would have been familiar to her forbearers two hundred years before—a white single-story house with two gables and a raised wooden porch that ran along the front of the house.

Next door was a bright red barn with white trim.

Beside her, Danny and Delancy rode in silence, seemingly lost in their own thoughts.

"That's it, I think." Marissa pointed at the farmhouse. It looked to be new, with only a small tilled field next to the main house so far and a smaller garden patch. Most people farmed their own vegetables to eat or to trade.

Danny looked up. "So, what are we going to do when we get there?"

"I don't know." The trip had been an impulse thing, an *if I don't do it now* plan that was seeming more and more foolish with each passing hour. "I was hoping…." She sighed. "It sounds stupid when I say it out loud."

"What?" Delancy's face was drawn. They were all tired, and whatever was blocking them from vee space and the world mind was demoralizing as well.

"He's Andy's uncle. He's our father... all of us. I wanted to see if there was any of *him*—the original Jayson—left in there."

"That's not stupid at all." Danny rubbed his chin, something he did whenever he wanted them to think he was giving something deep consideration. "I think about him a lot too."

"Do you ever hear from your mother?" Delancy's face was still pale.

Marissa shook her head. "Not really. I think she wanted to be rid of me. I reminded her of him."

"I heard from mine a few times. Sometimes she sends me letters." Danny's handsome face was solemn.

"Letters? Like real on-paper letters?" Marissa had seen them—Andy sometimes got them when they had visitors from Micavery. But she'd never gotten one herself.

He nodded. "Andy gives them to me in private. So the other kids don't feel jealous or sad about it, I guess."

"What do they say?" Marissa had long since given up hope of any contact from her own mother.

"She tells me about her family sometimes. She's married now and has a little daughter named Ivy. They live in Darlith."

Marissa tried to imagine it. A *real* family. "We have to be our own family."

Danny raised an eyebrow. "So, you're saying that Jayson's family too?"

"Right." The whole idea was crazy, to go to speak to the man who had raped all their mothers. But Marissa *had* to know if he could be what she needed him to be. "Come on. The horses should be rested enough. I want to get this over with." She shook the reins and dug in her heels, and Mirabelle took off down the dirt track toward the distant farmhouse, kicking up dust.

Danny and Delancy weren't far behind.

THE REST of the trip passed without incident.

Santi rode behind Eddy, his strong arms wrapped around Eddy's waist. His crossbow hung off the saddle.

Eddy kept his eyes straight ahead and tried not to think about Santi's proximity. Santi had no interest in being with him or with anyone.

He'd made that clear.

Eddy was still unable to reach the world mind. He checked in with both Andy and Aaron periodically—both reported that they were still disconnected from Lex and the world mind too.

Eddy tried to imagine what it would be like to be so in touch with the world around him one moment, then to lose that contact entirely the next.

"I'm sorry." Santi's voice startled him. They'd fallen into an antagonistic silence after their earlier argument about the Liminals.

"Sorry for what?"

"I know you're close with a lot of those kids."

Eddy nodded. "I've known them since we rescued them from Agartha. They really are good kids."

"Maybe."

"You need to meet them. You'll see."

Santi grunted. "Maybe that's part of the problem. You keep them all locked up in that schoolhouse of theirs. No one sees them. The unknown is always a hell of a lot more frightening than the things we can see."

"They're not things."

"Hey, sorry. I didn't mean it that way. But maybe if more people knew what they were really like and what they could do…."

"I get what you're saying." Eddy rubbed his chin. "Maybe we've been too careful."

They rode on for a few moments in a silence that was much more companionable than before.

The dirt road was mostly empty this far out into the Verge. They'd passed the most densely inhabited part—out here, there were only a handful of households. They were an interesting mix of traditional and modern and reflected the diverse array of cultures that had been thrown into Forever's melting pot.

They'd passed a couple more clusters of dead trees, though it was hard to tell if they had been burned by lightning or whatever had killed the alifirs.

He called Brad Evers.


*Hey, boss.*

*Any update on those dead alifirs?*

*Yeah. It's weird. The lab checked it out, and it looks like they were killed by some kind of toxin.*

*Someone sprayed something on them?*
*No… they think it came from the inside out.*
*Gotcha. Thanks, Brad.*
*You guys doing okay out there?*
*Yeah. We should be at the Olaf farmstead shortly. Thanks, Brad.*
*No problem, boss.*

"Brad says some kind of toxin killed those alifirs."

"No shit?"

Eddy nodded. "Came from inside, they think."

Santi's arms tightened around his waist.

"Um…."

"Sorry. Just a gut reaction." Santi loosened his grip.

"I'm the one who should be sorry. I'm not handling this whole ace thing all that well, am I?" Eddy remembered all the awkward questions he used to get about being trans. People felt like they had a right to his private life, to all his deepest secrets. Whether he still had girl parts. How he had sex.

"It's all right. You're trying. That means a lot." He squeezed Eddy gently in reassurance.

Eddy squirmed in the saddle, trying not to show the effect that touch had on him.

"I knew I liked guys a long time ago. When I was five, I think—I loved that old Buck Rogers serial on the tri dee. But not because of the whole *spaceman* thing. More the space*man* thing."

"Yeah, me too." Eddy laughed. "I miss tri dee." *Settling in with a guy on the couch to catch an episode of* Fargo Law. *Cheering for the contestants on* NAU Talent.

"Tell me about it."

"So…?"

"When I was in high school, there was this other gay kid who was the captain of the soccer team. His name was Aasim Nour, and he was the most beautiful boy I'd ever seen. One night, after a game, I waited for him outside the locker room."

"Damn, that's hot."

"Yeah. You'd think so, right? He invited me to his place. We drank a few beers—I was a real lightweight back then—and we screwed." He was quiet for a long moment.

"Was it... did you like it?"

"Not really. I mean, it wasn't horrible or anything. It just... there was no emotion. No connection. It was like... like watching tri dee without the color."

"If that's what it was like, you might have been doing it wrong." Eddy's joke fell flat, and he knew it.

"That's what everyone tells me." Santi's voice was tight.

Eddy flushed. "That's not... I'm sorry. I didn't mean that. Go on."

"I had a couple boyfriends in college, but I was always just going through the motions with them sexually." He sighed. "Neither one stayed with me long once they realized I didn't enjoy having sex with them."

"Did you ever try to get help?" Eddy could have kicked himself as soon as the words came out of his mouth.

"Get help for what? I don't have a problem."

*Fuck.* "I'm sorry. I don't know how to talk about this." What was he supposed to say?

Santi laughed, but it was an ugly sound. "No one does. I thought maybe you were different."

Eddy cringed. "Look, you're right. I'm sorry. I'm a huge ass." He tried to imagine a life without sex and failed. "It's just hard for me to wrap my head around it."

Santi laughed again, and this time it was more rueful. "You *are* an ass. But at least you're trying. You asked when I realized? It was more of a gradual sort of thing. I've just learned that sex isn't something I want or need in a relationship. You can imagine how popular that makes me."

"Yeah, I suppose so." Something stirred inside Eddy, elicited by the wide-open honesty with which Santi had just shared his thoughts. "So... do you ever date?"

"I haven't for a few years. I've been waiting for the right guy to come along."

Eddy didn't respond to that, not right away. He *liked* Santi. He did. But the whole ace thing was something he had to give some thought to.

A gentle squeeze told him Santi understood.

A few moments later, they arrived at the Olaf homestead. A new wooden fence led up the driveway to the barn and farmhouse.

A blonde woman was waiting for them in front of the barn. "Sheriff Tremaine?" She was trembling.

Eddy and Santi dismounted. "Yes, and this is my deputy, Santiago Ortiz." He shook her hand.

"I'm Sandra Olaf."

"Nice to meet you. Is everything okay? You look worried."

She shook her head. "Ever since the blackout—whatever that was—our visitor has been… disturbed."

A loud wail arose from the barn.

"My husband Sven is with him. Come on. You can tie up your horse there." She pointed to a wooden post along the side of the barn.

"Go. I'll take care of it." Santi led Cassiopeia to the post.

Sandra took Eddy inside. It was a beautiful barn, probably built by hand with one of the kids from Micavery. Spindle light shone through cutouts just under the roof.

A tall blond man knelt next to a figure curled up against the wall, his bare feet covered with dust. It was Jayson Hammond, all right.

The blond looked up at him. "He's been like this for a couple hours." He stood and stepped away from Jayson. "This started after the world went dark. Any idea what the hell that was about?"

Eddy frowned. "No, sorry. We're working on it. Will he talk to me?"

"I don't know. All he does is rock back and forth and moan."

"Okay. Let me see what I can do." He knelt next to the man and put a hand on his shoulder. "Jayson, can you hear me?"

The man continued to mumble and rock on the balls of his feet.

Eddy touched his cheek. Maybe he'd respond to his other name, the one Davian had used with him. "Gunner—"

The man looked up, his eyes darting wildly back and forth. Then they focused on Eddy, and he let out a heart-wrenching moan as his eyes lit up in recognition.

He pushed Eddy away as if he were made of paper, sending Eddy sprawling on the ground.

Eddy jumped up, but the man was out of the barn before he could catch him. Cursing, he ran after Jayson, praying the man wouldn't do any damage or escape before they could calm him down and talk to him.

He emerged into the light. Three other horses waited in the courtyard.

Marissa had dismounted from her horse and held a shovel.

Jayson ran toward her.

She lifted the shovel and slammed it down on his head.

The man fell in a heap, with a grunt.

"So glad you could make it," Eddy quipped.

"Hey, Uncle Eddy!" She dropped the shovel and ran to give him a hug. "It looked like you could use the help."


COLIN LOOKED UP.

Nothing had changed. He was still trapped in a mirrored box.

This was starting to feel hopeless. There was nowhere for him to go. Nothing for him to do.

What would Aaron do?

He knelt, splaying out his hands on the white surface.

It was strange. The ground was neither warm nor cold. It wasn't hard or soft either. In fact, his virtual senses didn't register anything when he touched it. Only that it stopped his movements.

Now that he looked at it more closely, it wasn't really silver either. Instead it was… it was hard to describe, is what it was. Like the film of a soap bubble, full of subtle colors that eluded cataloging by human senses.

Colin had always envied Aaron's ability to dip beneath the surface of things, to connect the hidden with what was visible.

An idea struck him, as absurd as it was inspired.

He had Jackson's memories, the essence of the man before he'd been absorbed into the world mind. Those were still left to him although the rest of the world mind was cut off.

Could he gift himself those same abilities, in vee space?

He sat down and closed his eyes, pulling up Jackson's memories, searching for a key that might set him free.

# 21

## SHAPES, DIMLY SEEN

MARISSA KNELT next to her father to check his pulse. He was breathing shallowly, and his heart beat steadily. "He's okay." She smiled at Eddy. "I'm so glad to see you here."

Eddy nodded. "Andy let us know you'd flown the coop."

"The coop?"

"Old idiom. Never mind. Just a sec." He tapped his loop, and his eyes went unfocused for a moment. When they focused again, he grimaced. "She had some… choice words for you three, but she's happy you're okay."

"So the loops are still working?"

"The range is reduced, but yes."

The farmer looked down at Jayson. "Is he dangerous?"

"He can be." Eddy wondered where the man had been all this time. "I'm Eddy Tremaine, sheriff for this side of the mountains, and this is Santiago Ortiz, my deputy."

"I'm Sven Olaf, and this is my wife, Sandra."

"Nice to officially meet you."

"I'm Marissa, and these are my schoolmates, Danny and Delancy." Sven and Sandra shook their hands.

"Schoolmates?" Sandra looked back and forth from one to the other.

"Yes, we're from the schoolhouse, up there in the mountains."

"Ah."

"Can we get this man secured somewhere?" Eddy asked, looking around the property.

"Matthew!" Sven called.

A young kid, maybe sixteen or seventeen, with dark hair and brown eyes, appeared from behind the barn. "Yeah?"

He was cute. And those muscles.... Marissa didn't like to think that she cared about such things, but still....

"Matt here is staying with us on an internship, learning all about farming. Of course, we're learning too." Sven smiled. "Back on Earth, I was a professor of physics in Stockholm, and Sandra ran an NGO helping resettle displaced climate refugees."

Marissa whistled and upped her opinion of the woman substantially.

"Matt, help me carry this man inside, and then grab some rope from the barn."

They took the man into the house and soon had him lying comfortably on a bed in Matt's room. Sven tied his arms and legs securely to the four posts. "These last few days, he's been out in the barn." Sven shook his head. "We had no idea he was dangerous. What did he do?"

Marissa and Eddy exchanged a glance.

"He hurt many people," Eddy said after a moment.

Marissa nodded. No need for them to know all the gory details. "He wasn't really himself."

*That* earned her a sharp look from Eddy. "We can't do much with him until he wakes up."

"Why don't you all join us for dinner?" Sandra offered. "You must be hungry after so much time on the road."

Marissa grinned. "Yes, we're hungry." A little bit of normalcy would be really welcome now.

Danny and Delancy grinned. "Starving. Thanks."

They stabled their horses in the barn, and Sandra led them inside the farmhouse. The Olafs had a small place, built by hand from one of the farmhouse kits out of Micavery, Sven told them proudly.

It was sparsely furnished, decorated with handmade crafts.

Their table was too small to accommodate all five of the new arrivals, so Eddy and Santiago stood while they ate. Dinner was simple—some cooked grains and vegetables, a hearty bread, and a small slice of meat.

"This is good." Marissa savored the protein. "What is it?"

"It's a new variety of chicken, bred for our unique circumstances here. They're hardy and produce a lot of eggs."

"We're a little sick of eggs, honestly." Sandra grinned. "So you kids are from the schoolhouse?"

Marissa looked back at Eddy, who nodded. "Yeah. We… decided to take a break from our classes."

Sven nodded. "It's important to see the real world too, not just be shut up in the classroom all day long."

"Yeah." They had no idea what things were really like in the valley.

"You seem like good kids. I don't know why folks are so afraid of you." Sven stared off into the distance, chewing on a bite of his bread. "I suppose people are always afraid of things that are new and different."

"People are afraid of us?" Marissa had heard that before, but it had always seemed like something distant and irrelevant, far from their lives at the schoolhouse.

"Don't worry about it." Sandra put a hand on hers reassuringly. "You're safe here with us."

Marissa nodded, but she suddenly felt a whole lot less safe in general. The less time they spent out here, away from Andy and Shandra and their friends, the better.

"Are we all ready for dessert?" Sven stood, picking up his plate.

"That sounds nice." Marissa looked toward the hallway, which led to the room where Jayson was being held.

"I made a red berry pie earlier. I'm happy to share it with you." Sven picked up her plate and those of the others who were finished with their meals.

"I'd love a piece." She *needed* to see him. "Excuse me. Where's your bathroom?"

"Down the hall to the right." Sandra pointed the way.

"Thanks. Be right back." She smiled reassuringly at Eddy, then turned down the hallway. A single luthiel lamp provided a golden pool of light.

When she was sure no one had followed her, she turned to the left and pushed open the door.

Jayson lay there on a cot, bound to the corners hand and foot. His eyes were closed.

He looked so sad, his long hair lying flat against his scalp, his face pale and slack. Very different from Andy, and from Aaron, his brother.

She pulled up a stool and sat next to him. So this was the monster. The rapist. The man who had made her.

She reached up to his forehead. Her hand touched his cool skin, and her world exploded.

It was like Alice's fall down the rabbit hole that Andy had simmed for them once in vee—spinning and spinning as flickers of someone else's life passed her by.

She screamed, but no sound came out, only a thin stream of something that looked like smoke. She shut her mouth and tried to close her eyes, but she couldn't *not* see the swirl of images that surrounded her.

Then as abruptly as it had started, the manic slide show ended, and she slammed into a dark place.

She lay there for a while, wondering what had happened to her.

She couldn't remember. She'd been in a dimly lit room with... someone. She had reached out to touch them, and the rest was a blur.

Dazed, she pushed herself up to her knees.

It was dark. Really dark.

Her heart raced. *Not again.*

It had been dark... before. With Danny and Delancy.

They had been on their way to find Jayson. Their father. The memories flooded back.

It wasn't pitch-black *here*. She could make out dim shapes in the darkness, though it was hard to determine what they were or even how far away they were.

She got up on wobbly knees. The ground at her feet, if she could call it that, was soft and uneven, like sand.

She closed her eyes and tried dipping.

Nothing.

"Hello?" Her voice was strangely muffled by the darkness.

She'd been at dinner with her friends. With Eddy and Santiago and the Olafs.

Then she'd gone in to see Jayson on her own, like an idiot. She was paying for that mistake now.

She sighed.

There was nothing to do but explore the strange place in which she found herself.

She picked one of the dim undefined objects and set off to find out what it was.

"SHE'S IN HERE!" Eddy called to the others.

Marissa was slumped over Jayson's body, her hand laid across his forehead.

Eddy knelt and lifted her up, hoping she would wake when he broke her contact with Jayson. She was so light, so small in his arms. "Marissa," he said softly, shaking her gently.

"Is she okay?" Danny and Delancy crowded into the small room.

"I don't know. She was lying on top of Jayson. I think she tried to reach into him." He brushed past the two worried kids to the hallway. "I need somewhere to lay her down."

"Bring her to our bedroom." Sandra led the way to the back of the house, where a larger room boasted a chest of drawers, a rocking chair, and a big bed. "You can lay her down here. What else do you need?" Her brow was furrowed, and Eddy could hear the worry in her voice as he lay the girl down on top of the Olafs' homespun comforter.

He touched Marissa's forehead. "A cloth with some cool water? She's burning up."

Sandra nodded.

Delancy and Danny had followed them into the room, along with Santi. "Has she ever done anything like this? Tried to reach into someone else, mind to mind? Someone human?"

Danny looked away.

"Look, you're not going to get in trouble, but we need to know what we're dealing with here." Eddy signaled for Santi to check the girl out. He had some medical training.

"I… some of us, we've tried it. Andy told us once about how she freed us in Agartha."

Eddy frowned. "I was there. It was a terrible place. So you tried it… how?"

"We would sit in front of one another and reach out our hands on the other's head, with our thumbs on their temples like this." He demonstrated on Delancy. "We could sense each other's thoughts, at least the surface ones. We never tried anything too dangerous."

Santi touched her forehead. "She's warm, you're right. Her breathing is really shallow, especially for someone who is unconscious, and her heart is racing. And look at her eyes."

Eddy turned to look at the girl. If anything happened to her, Andy would kill him. These were her kids, well, hers and Shandra's, as much as they were anyone's. Marissa's eyes were moving behind her eyelids, and her eyelashes were fluttering. "She looks like she's in REM sleep."

"Did you guys ever experience anything like this?" Santi asked.

Delancy shook her head. "No. Nothing like that at all."

Sandra returned. "Here's a cool cloth." She handed it over, looking at the girl with an expression of deep concern. "Is she okay?"

"I don't know." Eddy sat next to Marissa and wiped her head with the cloth. She was so young. With her eyes closed like this, she looked no more than ten.

Sandra sat next to him and took Marissa's hand in hers. "What's going on? First the stranger—"

"Jayson."

"Jayson. Then the blackout, and now this. They're all connected, aren't they?"

Eddy frowned. "I think so." He was afraid to panic them, but one glance at the farm holders showed him they were already well on their way to abject fear. "We should talk. Someone needs to stay here with Marissa, though, to keep an eye on her."

"I will." Delancy nodded.

"Sorry, we need you and Danny with us."

"I'll do it." The farmhand, Matt, edged into the room. "I can watch her."

"I'd appreciate that."

"What do I have to do?" The boy was young, but he seemed to have a good head on his shoulders.

"Just wipe her forehead down with this and keep an eye on her. If anything else happens, come get us."

"Okay." Matt took Santi's place on the far side of the bed, pulling up a wooden chair. He took Marissa's hand tenderly and reached up to wipe her forehead gently.

Eddy reached across the bed and squeezed his shoulder in encouragement.

The rest of them filed out of the room to the small living room at the front of the house.

Sandra brought a few chairs in from the dining table and sank down on one of them. It was dark outside, but a couple of luthiel lamps lit the room. "So tell us."

Eddy sat on one of the living room chairs. "We think there's something wrong with the world mind." He was afraid that news would cause additional alarm.

Instead, Sandra looked at Sven and nodded. "We'd figured that much. It's not taking our requests."

"There's more." They listened calmly as he recited the incidents he was aware of, starting with the dead stand of alifir trees, the attack on Andy in vee space, the big storm, and what everyone had taken to calling the "blackout."

When he was done, Sandra glanced back at the hallway. "Who is *he*?" Her voice trembled but only a little.

Eddy gave her a lot of credit for that. "He's Aaron Hammond's brother, Jayson. We think he was responsible for the destruction of Terminal Station."

"Holy shit." Santi was staring at him, his mouth open.

"Yeah, I guess we left that part out of the briefings." Too late to worry about it now. "He's also the father of these three kids, and the others at the schoolhouse."

"So he's—"

"The reason they can do what they do. It's a family trait—stronger in some than others, but it seems to be dominant." Eddy closed his eyes, remembering for a moment that dark night in Agartha ten years before. *Has it really been a decade?*

"So you think he's behind all of this?" Now Sandra did look pale, having realized the potential danger she'd let into her house.

Eddy sighed. "We don't know. I don't think so, at least not directly. In Agartha, the place under the mountain where these kids were born, there was another man, the one who ran things there. They called him the Preacher. I knew him as Davian."

"Where is he now?"

Eddy shook his head. "No one knows. But Jayson might."

ANA OPENED THE LATEST MESSAGE, excited. They had found a way to communicate, despite whatever was going on outside that had locked them in these prisons.

With each message that passed through the barrier, their connection grew stronger.

This one, however, startled her.

*WE NEED TO MERGE.*

SHE STARED AT IT, considering the implications of such a suggestion. Though they had become closer over the years, emotionally and in the overlapping of their bits and bites, Ana had always maintained her own unique awareness, her *self*. She was still the little girl who had witnessed the falling of a satellite into the river in the Caucasus Mountains. She was still the young woman who had survived her father's death at the hands of terrorists, and who later had continued his work to create the seedling and ultimately this world.

And she was still the flawed, prideful *bitch* who had framed Jackson Hammond, and whose poor decisions had created a cascade of events that had led to that poor man's death.

Maybe she really wasn't worthy of saving.

She sent a simple reply.

*WHY?*

THE RESPONSE WAS ALMOST INSTANT.

*WE ARE STRONGER TOGETHER.*

LEX TOO HAD her own life, her own story and history of events, good and bad.

Ana had come to admire her, to look upon her as every bit as real and amazing and flawed as any human being. One who fought to protect those in her care, even if she wasn't always blameless in the course of events.

On the balance, it was a match that could only improve her own questionable character.

She'd already lived a long life, longer than she'd hoped for.

And if things went wrong, then who was to say Jackson wasn't right? Maybe there was something better waiting.

At worst, the sweet oblivion of death would cradle her in its arms, and she would need worry no more.

It was enough.

*How do we do it?*

# 22

# STORM CLOUDS

Marissa stood before the first of the dim shapes she'd seen in the distance, down in the depths of Jayson's mind. It was a towering thing, though what sort of thing was not readily apparent. It resembled a storm—a tightly contained storm—full of billowing clouds made of something gray that seemed thicker and more coherent than water vapor but less so than a solid surface.

It *emanated* pain.

Andy had told them all, more than once, about the storms that had clouded their minds in Agartha. How she had drained them like pus from a wound, freeing up the minds of those entrapped by the poison from Jayson's mind.

This was one of the sources of that poison; she was sure of it.

She was strong, maybe the strongest of her generation. Certainly of the three of them who had come to the farm together.

Maybe she could do something about it. Maybe that was why she was there.

She held her hands out, palms first, and touched the storm.

Incredible pain lanced through her hands and into her arms. Her skin was being flayed off, being melted from her bones. She screamed and let go, jerking her arms away.

She looked at her virtual skin. It was still whole.

*It's only pain.*

She tried again, plunging her hands into the seething gray mass, and once again was forced to pull them out as the pain built quickly to a burning crescendo.

Breathing heavily now, she glared at the cloud. How could she let the inanimate mass of nothing get the better of her?

Then it hit her. She shook her head, laughing at herself for missing the obvious.

None of this was real.

She was only constrained to a human body because she believed it to be so.

She closed her eyes and imagined herself drifting apart like a mist, growing to encompass the storm like a cool spray of water.

She felt it when she made contact. It hurt, but not like before. Instead, it was like a hundred small aches, spread out over her whole body.

She concentrated on smothering the cloud, opening her awareness to it. The dim light faded to a uniform gray.

The storm was all around her now, was a part of her. It seemed to be growing stronger, though, not weakening. She started to panic, clawing at the oily gray air, but she couldn't get hold of anything. It slipped out of her grasp, and she was drowning in it, sucking it in like black bile.

Was this how Jayson had succumbed to whatever had been done to him?

She tried to draw herself back together, but she was too dispersed.

She tried to scream, but she had no lungs. If she had, they would have been drowning in pain.

There was nothing she could do.

Marissa let go.

*JAYSON LAY ON THE RACK, stretched to his limit. It was a fiendish, ancient form of torture, combined with a hypnotic flow of images on the screen above created to break him down. To rip his self, the core of his being, off its moorings.*

*Pain flared through his body, from his feet up along all the muscles of his legs, along his spine and up to his bound hands.*

*Who were these bastards? What did they want from him?*

*There was no one to tell him. Only pain, endless pain.*

*Then something cool spread across his body, starting at his core and making its way up and down his form like a chill mist. Wherever it touched, the pain abated.*

*He sighed, tears running down his face as his calves stopped aching, as the mist covered the screen above, darkening it and muting its sound.*

*His bonds dissolved too, and he drifted down onto something soft, something that gave underneath his weight.*

*Something warm touched his cheek, and he opened his eyes to see a young girl, her face blue like the sky, smiling down at him.*

*He closed his eyes again, finally at peace.*


MARISSA OPENED HER EYES, finding her body laid out flat on the ground.

The cloud was gone, and in its place was a golden glow. She stood up, back in her human form, and looked around.

The light shone on a white plane that extended a few meters in each direction, a bright spot in the otherwise dim world of Jayson's mind.

In the distance, there were other storms.

She understood now why she'd felt compelled to come in search of her father.

She wasn't there for answers, though she would likely find them, anyway.

She was there to save him.


EDDY LOOKED IN ON JAYSON. He was still unconscious and still tied down firmly to the cot. "Are you two ready?"

Danny and Delancy nodded. They'd spent the better part of an hour talking with Aaron and Andy through Eddy's loop, getting advice on how to proceed. Andy thought Jayson was still in there somewhere. Aaron wasn't so sure.

It had been decades since Jackson's younger son, Jayson, had been abducted, apparently by Chinese intelligence, forcibly recruited to their cause. Aaron thought Jayson's mind was irreparably broken.

He hadn't seen firsthand what Andy had done to help these kids and everyone else who had been imprisoned in Agartha.

There was a dull rumble and the whole room shook. "Kids, come here!" Eddy shouted, pulling them under the doorframe into his arms.

The noise roared to a crescendo, and something crashed in the living room.

Then it was over.

"Everyone all right?" His old earthquake training paid off. *Foreverquake?*

Danny and Delancy nodded.

"What was that?" Danny asked, his eyes wide.

"I don't know. Go check on Marissa and Matthew." Since when did Forever have earthquakes? Or were they *Ariadnequakes?* Eddy peeked out of the hallway to find Sven and Sandra lifting a bookshelf that had fallen during the shaking.

"What was that?" Sven asked. The poor man looked spooked.

Eddy scowled. "I don't know. Nothing good."

Sandra laughed darkly. "That's an understatement."

Whatever was happening out there, it was quickly getting worse.

Danny returned from the master bedroom. "Marissa's still sleeping, and Matt's fine."

"Okay, let's do this, then. The sooner we can help Jayson, the sooner we'll get answers." He *hoped* Jayson had the answers.

Delancy sat on one side of the cot in the small room, and Danny on the other.

Dust floated in the air from the quake, lit by the single luthiel lantern on a small wooden table next to the cot. Miraculously it hadn't broken.

Eddy sneezed, trying to knock the dust out of the air with his hand.

Danny and Delancy looked at each other across Jayson's unconscious body, a spark of understanding passing between them.

Eddy wondered what it was like to be able to do the things these kids could do. To be both blessed and marked as different at the same time.

Santi watched over his shoulder. "You're right," he said softly.

"What?"

"They're good kids."

He nodded. That didn't mean Santi's earlier argument was wrong. But there had to be a better way to deal with potential problems between Homo Sapiens and Homo Liminal.

Danny and Delancy took each other's hands on one side and put their other hands on Jayson's forehead.

They both slumped forward onto his chest.

"Is that... normal?" Santi's brow was creased.

Eddy laughed ruefully. "None of this is normal." Eddy took two blankets Sandra had brought in and laid one over each of their forms.

"What do we do now?"

"We wait." He led Santi through the living room, where the Olafs were cleaning up after the quake, and onto the porch outside.

It was the normal darkness of night, but Eddy couldn't help but compare it to the suffocating blackness they'd experienced earlier in the day. Maybe the world *was* ending. Or worse. Maybe there was nothing they could do about it.

They sat next to one another, looking out into the darkness, little pinpoints of light here and there like stars marking other farmholds along the Verge.

He was sick of being alone.

"Santi?" Eddy said after a long moment.

"Yeah?"

"Do you... do you want to be with someone?"

"You know I don't want to—"

"Not like that. I mean, just *be* with them."

"Ah."

Eddy wondered if he'd said something wrong. He'd never spent this much time with Santiago before, and he was starting to feel something... good. The whole ace thing was new for him. But the potential impending end of the world was having a wonderfully clarifying effect on his perspective.

Santi took his hand. "I think I'd like that."

Eddy smiled in the darkness. They sat in companionable silence for a long time.


COLIN SAT BACK in the silver box he was trapped in.

He'd completed his survey of Jackson's memories, integrating them with his own. There was nothing there to help him.

Maybe his abilities had been a physical byproduct of whatever wetware update he'd applied to himself all those years before.

Maybe they were a part of his soul, the thing that had departed with him from Forever ten years earlier, or from his physical body when he'd died.

Perhaps no one could bottle lightning.

Colin opened his eyes and looked around. He was still trapped in his box.

He sighed. While he was stuck in here, who knew what the hell was going on out there? Was Trip okay? Were his friends in danger? Aaron, the plucky Andy and her charges?

If only he had some way to reach them.

He beat at the ground in frustration. He. Felt. So. Fucking. Impotent.

There was a *crack*.

He looked down at the ground, startled.

The place where he'd aimed his blows had split open, and a small green vine was questing its way through the opening from below.

As it grew, it spread the crack wider.

It extended into the sky, growing rapidly larger, until it had the girth of an oak tree and then a redwood.

*It's Jack and the fucking beanstalk*, Colin thought in amazement. He reached out his hand, and the tip of the vine bent down from the top of his box to touch the tips of his fingers, sending a little shock down his arm.

"I did it. I damn well did it!" He jumped up and down like a ten-year-old, waving his arms. Somehow he had figured out Jackson's abilities, after all.

When he calmed himself down, he stared at the vine, which waited patiently for him.

Not up, then, like the storied Jack, but down.

He wrapped his arms around it, feeling its cool touch.

The vine responded immediately, pulling itself into the crack at a breakneck pace, carrying a screaming immortal with it.

# 23

## CAGES

Marissa lay on her back, watching the third cloud dissipate. This one had been worse than the others, a memory of Jayson's, seeing his own brother Aaron across the bay at Transfer Station just hours before the station's destruction.

Not being able to speak to him, to reach out to him in any way. Forced by the imperatives laid upon him to destroy the station and everyone inside.

The guilt of that one had almost killed him and had helped to burn out the little remaining bits of Jayson Hammond that had existed in his head.

Marissa wept for him, for what he'd been put through because of what he could do. His grief reverberated through her, leaving its mark on her heart.

Never before had she so clearly understood what a threat people like her could be to the world. How she might one day be used against the people she loved. How those not like her might come to really hate her and her kind.

The pain Jayson had endured was beyond comprehension, forcing him to shut down almost entirely to escape it.

She began to understand, too, how he had been capable of the awful things he'd done to her peers and their mothers in Agartha.

Jayson Hammond was a hollow shell.

And yet....

There were still bits of himself locked inside. Pieces that might be freed by taking away his pain.

Marissa sighed. She didn't know if she could do this.

She sat up, wiping her eyes, and tried again to wake herself, to search for an escape hatch from this dark place.

Nothing.

"Hello?" she called, as if a search party might be right over the next bend in the strange landscape of Jayson's mind. She laughed ruefully at her own stupidity.

"Marissa?" a voice called back.

"Delancy?" It had to be wishful thinking—her friend couldn't be here, could she? "Over here!" She stood in a white patch in the general gloom of Jayson's mind, staring out into the darkness.

When Delancy's face appeared, Marissa grinned, and her smile stretched even broader when she saw Danny right behind her. Delancy hurtled into her arms. "We were so worried about you."

"How did you know I was here?"

"Eddy found you slumped over Gunner. Jayson. Our father." Danny frowned. "I don't know what to call him." He looked around. "Quite the place you have here."

"Jayson's been through some terrible things. He's so shut down I don't think he has the slightest idea any more of who he was." Marissa pointed at the dim shapes. "Each of those is a terrible memory that holds him captive in some way. I've cleared three of them so far, but there are too many...."

"Cleared them?" Delancy frowned, staring at the closest one.

Marissa nodded. "I embraced each one, and... I don't know how to explain it. Became one with it. Felt it. Found the bit of Jayson at its core and freed him from it." The experience had left her raw, but it was worth it.

"Like Andy did for each of us." Danny rubbed his chin.

"Yes. But there are so many." Marissa sighed.

"Maybe we can disperse them together." Delancy marched off toward the closest cloud.

"It's not easy." Marissa ran after her, and Danny followed.

Delancy reached the cloud and put her hand out to touch it. She jerked it back as if she'd been scalded. "Ouch, that hurt."

"It's fifteen or twenty years of pain, building on itself. I can't imagine how he survived."

"So how do we do this?" Delancy walked around the perimeter of the cloud, glaring at it.

"I reimagined myself as a cloud of soothing water. Here, take my hand." She grasped their hands and surrounded the cloud. "Now imagine you're water vapor, and… *flow*." Her body expanded, like it had the first time.

Her friends followed her lead.

*It's going to hurt, like a thousand bee stings.*

She was right. It *did* hurt, but this time the pain was shared among the three of them. They entered the cloud, and everything shifted.

JAYSON KNELT BEHIND A GARBAGE DRONE, panting heavily, trying his best to be quiet.

He was being *hunted*.

He'd noticed them trailing him on the way out of the Asteroid Strike, a dive bar in the grimy heart of Old Seattle.

Few folks lived there anymore, preferring the megarises up on Capitol Hill and Queen Anne. Sea-level rises had swamped parts of the lower city, but higher up the hill had become a refuge for those who couldn't afford the high prices in the megas, with their three hundred plus stories.

He'd made the mistake of showing off his skills in the bar to impress a guy. A couple of guys, actually. He'd shown them how he could hack into the bar mind and procure the three of them free drinks.

It had been looking good for a bit, like he might be in for quite the night with Jacques and Flick. But Flick had gotten sick… rather fabulously… and Jacques… well, Jayson hadn't been the hottest guy in the bar that night.

He lifted himself up to look over the curved top of the drone.

The streets were empty.

He stood, letting out a soft sigh of relief, and turned to head back to base. He had training at 6:00 a.m. sharp the next morning.

Something whipped around his neck and pulled tight, giving him a white-hot shock that slammed through his body and sent him falling to the hard pavement. As one of his teeth broke off, someone above him laughed and said, "Got him."

Then his world dissolved into pain.

He floated in it for an eon or two. It became a part of him, permeating his soul, comfortable as an old coat. An old coat full of pins.

Then as quickly as it had begun, the pain dropped away.

He opened his eyes, looking up at the three children who had laid their hands upon him.

No, not kids. Young adults. Fourteen? Fifteen?

They looked so solemn.

He smiled at them, and one by one they smiled back.

Then they were gone, and he was at peace.

"Wow." DANNY sat on his ass, his hands splayed out on the ground behind him. "They hunted him. Roped him like an animal."

Marissa sat up and wrapped her hands around her knees. She closed her eyes and took a deep breath. "Earth was a dark place by then."

"Could they...." Delancy's voice broke. "Could they do that to us?"

Marissa shook her head. "I don't know." She'd been thinking the same thing. She was starting to realize how sheltered they'd all been at the schoolhouse. It was time for that to end. For better or worse. "Are you guys okay?"

Her friends nodded.

"It's easier with three." Unspoken went the thought that there was too much pain for just one of them to handle. Or for Jayson. How had he survived it all these years? "Ready?"

"Sure." Danny looked exhausted.

Together, the three of them got up and trudged off toward the next cloud.

EDDY RUBBED HIS EYES, checking his loop. It was about one in the morning.

He considered streaming a *Terraterza* trigsynth tune he had stored in his loop. They always calmed him down. It was a shame no one made music like that anymore. Another thing lost to the Collapse.

Sven had brought in piles of homemade blankets, sewn together from panels of old clothing and stuffed with Forever cotton grown on a nearby farmhold. The farmers traded for almost everything, Sven had told him, and had a good barter economy going.

Marissa had been brought in to lie on the floor with the other two kids, and Eddy and Santi were watching over them.

All three appeared peaceful, as if they were just taking a nap.

Santi *was* asleep. It had been a long day, and Eddy figured the poor guy needed a little rest. He got a warm feeling in his gut when he looked over at his sleeping deputy.

Nothing much was happening at the moment, and he figured a little walk would help him stay awake. He picked up one of the extra blankets—it had the logo of some long-dead Earth football team on it—and laid it gently over Santi's slumped form.

The man was beautiful in repose, so peaceful. Almost angelic, with his dusky skin and the thin beard that ran down his jawline.

Eddy shook his head. *This is no time for daydreaming.*

He went out into the hallway. The walls were bare and white—in another age, they might have held faded photographs of parents and grandparents, of children hard at work out on the farm. *So many lost memories.*

He found Sven in the living room. The man was lighting a candle on a small shelf beneath a wooden cross. It was one of the few decorations in the house, something that made it stand out immediately.

"Sorry to disturb you," Eddy said softly. "Trying to keep myself awake."

Sven turned and gave him a friendly smile. "I couldn't sleep." He glanced back at the cross and candle. "You probably think I'm old-fashioned."

Eddy shook his head. "Not at all. There's a lot of comfort in religion, and we could all use a bit of that now."

Sven nodded. "How are the children?"

"Hard to tell. They seem peaceful."

"Here, take a seat." Sven gestured toward the couch and then sat down in one of the hand-carved chairs. "They are amazing, aren't they?"

"The kids?"

"Yes." He picked up a pipe and dropped in a small handful of crushed leaves. "Medicinal."

Eddy grinned. Some things never changed.

"It's a new hybrid. Someone has been growing it about half the circle from here."

"Is it good?" Eddy had smoked his share of weed and tobacco before.

"Very. Wanna give it a try?" He held out the pipe. "Mellow. No nicotine. It's almost healthy."

Eddy accepted it and took a toke. It spread through his lungs and gave him a delightful feeling of warmth throughout his body. "Very nice." He handed it back. "Have you always been religious?"

"Yes. Well, the Church of Sweden is… used to be one of the most progressive churches in the world. So I'm not a religious nut, if that's what you meant."

Eddy laughed. "Not at all. I've always been more of an agnostic, myself. But I have great respect for those of the faith." He grinned lopsidedly. "Usually."

"Touché." Sven set down his pipe. "Sandra and I were talking about these children of yours. People fear them, you know."

Eddy nodded. "Do you?"

"No." Sven crossed his hands in his lap. "They're God's children, like any other." He reached up and scratched the back of his head. "Or maybe not like any other. They're our salvation, I think."

"How so?" He leaned forward, putting his chin on his hands. This was fascinating to him.

"We're at an evolutionary dead end. Look what we did to the Earth. To each other. Maybe these kids will find a different path."

"Do you think that's likely?"

Sven shook his head. "I really don't know. We made such a mess of things, our generations and the ones that came before. It's time to try something new. It's their turn, in any case."

"Yes, it is." He sat back in the chair, lost in thought. These kids really *were* something new. Maybe mankind did have hope, if they could get through the current crisis. Eddy pointed at the cross. "Did you carve that?"

Sven shook his head. "It's the only thing we brought with us. My grandfather made it and gave it to me when I was ten years old."

"It's beautiful." He smiled. "So how did you two meet?"

"Sandra and I? She was in Sweden on a scholarship from the NAU. I was a college student with dreams of revolutionizing the world of physics." He grinned. "Do you know Stockholm used to get snow in the winter?"

"What's snow?" Eddy grinned.

"Yeah, I know. Right?" He leaned forward, his face animated. "One time, when I was about seven, it snowed in Sergel's Square, right in the heart of Stockholm. It only lasted for a few hours—"

"Eddy?" Santi popped out of the hallway.

"What happened? Sorry, Sven—"

"It's all right. We can talk more later."

Santi was shaking. "You need to come see this." He led them down the hallway.

Eddy peered into the room. "Oh shit."

Jayson's whole body was shaking, and he was covered in sweat.

"What do we do now?" Santi looked at him, and there was fear in his gaze.

"What else can we do? We wait."


ANA OPENED HER EYES.

She was momentarily disoriented—the reflective cube where she'd been imprisoned was gone. Instead, she was floating in a huge white, nearly featureless sphere. Somehow shadows from her own body cast themselves around the space, shifting back and forth as she moved and giving it definition.

She felt… different.

She was Ana. She was Lex. She was him and her, and neither.

And both, and everything along the spectrum in between.

Ana held out their arms in wonder, reached up to touch their virtual face.

She'd been deathly afraid of losing her own identity, but that didn't begin to describe what had happened.

They weren't less together. They were more.

We *are more.*

She was entwined with Lex. No, fused was a better word. Their lives and experiences were one now. Growing up in the Russian countryside was every bit as valid a piece of her life experience as awakening in the heart of a spaceship.

*Who are we? It doesn't matter. I'll figure that out later.* We'll *figure that out later. Right now we need to find a way to break free.*

## 24

# FOUND

Marissa looked around.

The landscape of Jayson's mind had changed. Instead of the dark, dank place full of threatening clouds that it had been on her arrival, it was bright and clean and clear, a grassy park bordering a lake where the water was the clearest blue. It was transparent, like someone had traced it out with the barest of necessary colors.

One more cloud remained.

She was exhausted. She imagined how Andy must have felt when she'd freed all those people in Agartha, one by one. *At least* I *have help.* "You guys ready?"

Danny nodded. "What happens when we finish?"

"I have no idea." Maybe nothing. Maybe Jayson was too badly damaged for anything else. Maybe they were just giving him some peace. *That has to be enough, right?*

Danny took one of her hands, and Delancy the other. Funny how she didn't feel that spark any more when she touched Danny's hand. She closed her eyes, and they repeated the thing they'd done at least thirty times, for one last time.

As the pain swelled around her, she took it in, became one with it, and passed it on.

When she opened her eyes, the three of them were standing in a circle inside a small cavern. It was a replica of Agartha, only on a vastly reduced scale.

His Master, the Preacher, lay on a raised platform, staring up at Jayson eagerly. "It's time."

Marissa shivered at the sound of his voice. Suddenly she was four years old again, trapped in her own head.

The Preacher seemed unaware of the three teenagers who watched the scene.

Jayson's face was gray. He shook, as if he were fighting some unseen binding.

"Now. Do it *now!*" The Preacher's voice was grating. He was not used to being disobeyed.

Marissa shivered too. She would have peed her pants if she'd been flesh and blood.

As it were, she wished she could be any place but here.

The Preacher grabbed Jayson's hand and pulled it down, inch by inch, to touch his face. "Do it *now* or I will kill them all."

He meant the children of Agartha. He meant *her*.

Jayson grunted and closed his eyes.

Marissa knew what she was watching. Andy had told them all about it. This was a *transfer. Holy Ariadne, the Preacher is in the world mind.* Suddenly it all made sense, the snake, the blackout, all the other strange things that had been happening.

As Jayson's other hand touched the ground, he stiffened as though he was being electrocuted, his body jerking as his Master's mind and memories passed through him.

Marissa wanted to stop him, wanted to throw herself at him and knock him away from the Preacher. But she remained rooted in place. It didn't matter. This was all in the past.

"It's only a memory." Delancy squeezed her hand.

It went on for an eternity.

When at last it was over, Jayson slumped over the Preacher's lifeless body, sobbing softly.

Suddenly Marissa was free to move. She ran forward and threw her arms around him. As she hugged him, he grew brighter and brighter, until she had to squeeze her eyes shut lest the light blind her.

An explosion sent her flying, and she lost consciousness as she hit the ground.

When she awoke, moments or hours later, Danny and Delancy were staring down at her worriedly.

"Are we still—"

"Inside?" Delancy nodded.

Marissa sat up and looked around. The park was fully sketched out now, its colors bold, brighter than real life.

The lake was a deep, almost disturbing blue. A man stood at the lakeside, dressed all in white, his back to them. Next to him was a closed door that seemingly led to nothing.

Marissa stood, feeling a little wobbly, which was weird since she was walking on virtual legs. She laughed—in the grand scheme of weirdness the last few days, that was pretty tame. "Come on. He's waiting for us."

They crossed the grass-filled space between them and the man in white. As they approached, he turned to face them.

Marissa gasped. He was *so* young. "Jayson?"

The man frowned. "I think so? I don't really remember."

"How do you feel?"

"I feel peaceful. Clear."

Marissa nodded. "That's good."

"Who are you?" He frowned again. "I think I *should* remember. But there's nothing there. I'm sorry."

She squeezed his shoulder. "It's all right. You've been through a lot." Much of which she and the others had seen, as close to firsthand as possible.

"There was a man." His brow furrowed. "He made me... do things."

Marissa smiled encouragingly. "You resisted, though. I saw it."

"I resisted."

"Yes."

"What's behind the door, Jayson?"

Jayson looked at her, and then at the door that stood alone in the middle of the grass. "I don't know." He looked dejected, like a puppy who'd been scolded.

She reached for the doorknob.

"Don't! It's not safe to open it."

She stared at him and then nodded. Maybe he had something locked up in there that he wasn't ready to deal with, or that he didn't want anyone to see. "Okay, I'll leave it alone."

He visibly relaxed.

"But in return, we need your help." She put a hand on his shoulder.

"Who are you, again?" He frowned, his brow creased.

Marissa bit her lip. "We're your children."

He stared at her for a moment and then looked at the others each in turn. Then a big smile spread across his face, and he laughed, a warm, beautiful sound. "Of course you are." He pulled them all in for a hug. "My three beautiful children."

Marissa refrained from telling him about the other thirty-five. Time enough for that later. "So, you'll help us?"

"Of course I will." He let them go. "What do you need me to do?"

"You need to let us go."


EDDY STIRRED.

He found himself seated on the ground between Santi's legs, with his back to Santi's chair. His head lay on the man's warm thigh. Damn, he must have been tired.

*Something* had awoken him. He looked around.

Morning light flooded the room through the open window. Marissa and the other kids were awake.

Eddy sat up and shook Santi's leg. "They're back!"

Santi rubbed his eyes groggily and looked around the room. He was adorable when he was only half-awake. "What?"

"Marissa, Danny, and Delancy."

"How long were we gone?" Marissa sat up and rubbed her temples.

"You? About seven hours. The others about five. Are you okay?" Eddy knelt next to her.

She nodded. "We found him."

"Who?"

"Jayson. Our father." She pointed to the supine form on the cot. "You can untie him now."

Eddy shook his head. "He's too dangerous."

"Not anymore. He was... really broken inside. Now he's better, I think. It's hard to explain. He has a lot of catching up to do."

The man's eyes were open.

Marissa reached over and squeezed his hand. She started to untie the first knot.

Eddy stopped her. "Are you *sure?*"

She looked him in the eye, and there was fire there. The same fire he'd seen in her aunt Andy's eyes. "The people who hurt him, who used him… they tied him up like this and tortured him for weeks. Untie him. *Now.*"

Eddy knew better than to argue with that glare. He started in on the next knot.

Soon they had him free.

Jayson sat up, his eyes sharp and clear. *He looks human again. Younger, even.*

"Where are we? I need to get home. My parents will be missing me." He tried to get up, but Marissa pushed him gently down on the cot.

"Your parents are gone," she said softly, putting a hand on his cheek.

She looked like an angel in the golden light.

"What?" He looked back and forth between them, a confused expression on his face. "When?" His voice sounded small, for all the world like a five-year-old boy's.

"He really doesn't remember anything since he was a teenager?" Eddy looked up at Marissa.

"No. But he needs to." Marissa glanced at Danny and Delancy.

They nodded.

The three of them gathered around Jayson, laying their hands on his head. They closed their eyes.

"What are you going to do?" Eddy asked, alarmed.

"Give him his memories back. Without the pain." Then she was lost in concentration.

Eddy sat back, wondering what she was talking about. What memories? The pain he could imagine, based on what he knew of Jayson's life.

There was a loud boom outside.

Eddy rushed to the window to see what was happening.

A storm had gathered in the night, more massive than he'd ever seen on Forever. It made the tempest that had almost killed them seem like a mere fog bank.

The monster hung above them twirling around the spindle, electrical charges racing along and through it, and the light in the room dimmed.

Santi came to stand next to him and looked up at the sky. "Holy shit." He took Eddy's hand and squeezed it tightly.


DAVIAN EXULTED in his new form. He'd planned this for a long time, locked in his secret retreat, away from the prying eyes of the world mind.

Gunner had proven invaluable, hiding them both and providing for them as he laid the groundwork for his plan.

He'd watched as that horrid woman had transferred Colin McAvery's consciousness into the world mind. In that moment, he'd finally understood why destiny had brought him to Forever—so he'd be able to achieve his ultimate destiny and never be trapped again.

It had been surprisingly easy. Gunner had fashioned a place for him, and he'd bided his time, building his defenses, planning for his enemies' defeat. Even then, they hadn't seen it coming.

Now the so-called "Immortals" were all locked away in boxes, just like he'd been. Only he'd been kind enough to omit the torture. *Fools.*

The keys to the kingdom were his.

He'd bring the world to its knees in short order, and then it would be his to do with as he liked.

He wondered if this was how his captors had felt, when they'd held ultimate power over his life.

He finally understood why they'd enjoyed it so much.

Now it was his time to play.

## 25

## OPENING DOORS

MARISSA OPENED her eyes. She looked down at Jayson nervously, biting her lip.

She had shown him the memories they'd cleared from his mind, sheared of all the pain. She could only hope they helped to bring him back to himself.

*The Preacher. Davian.* She had to tell Eddy who was behind all of this.

She kissed her father's forehead. Strange, how she was starting to form a bond with him after all these years. Maybe it was just concern for someone who had been lost for so long.

Maybe it was something more. Maybe he really *could* be her father. Someday. "You two keep an eye on him?"

Danny nodded. "We've got this."

The room was darkening. Was there another storm? Marissa waved her thanks and ran into the hallway.

Eddy and Santiago were staring out the open window.

Marissa's steps slowed as she saw what they were looking at. "It's... that can't be...."

They turned to look at her. "We have to get everyone to safety."

Marissa shook her head. "It's Davian. We have to find a way to fight him."

"Davian?" Eddy looked confused.

"He's inside the world mind. I saw it, in Jayson's head." She turned away from the window, searching her memory. They had to do *something*, and they had to do it *now*.

She tried to dip into the world mind, but she couldn't find it. She was as cut off as she'd been before, and the ache of it pulsed through her anew. She wanted to scream in frustration.

Still, there had to be some way to get in. A back door they hadn't thought of....

*A door.*

"I think I know how to get to him."


ANALEX WANTED TO SCREAM.

They'd pushed as hard as they could against the walls of their prison, to no avail. They'd searched every virtual inch of it for a flaw or crack, any place where they could gain leverage.

They were trapped like a firefly in a mason jar.

*Interesting... I don't know that one.*

The part of them that had been Ana frowned. They had no time for indulgence.

Maybe there was an answer in one of Jackson's files.

*He was really good in vee space—*

The floor split open, and AnaLex scrambled out of the way of the bright green vine that grew up through the crack. Its color was all the more remarkable in contrast to the mirrored background that framed it and reflected it a hundred times.

*What is it?*

*Jack and the Beanstalk?*

*Explain.*

*Later.*

A gray-haired head appeared through the crack and then a face, a curiously grinning face.

"Colin?" They ran forward to embrace him.

"Ana?" He squinted. "Lex?"

They nodded. "Yes. It's a long story. How did you do that?"

"A little trick I picked up from Jackson. I broke out. I've been sizing up the enemy. I don't think he realizes I'm free."

"The enemy?"

"Our old friend, the former Lord of Agartha." He winked. "Are you two… um… are you ready to get out of here?"

They nodded. "We've been trying for a long time."

"Climb aboard. I'll show you what I found."

EDDY CUT his connection to Andy and Aaron. "I'm not sure this is such a good idea." They'd all moved into the storage room that sat in the middle of the house, but even in there he could hear the wind howling outside like a wounded coyote. "The last time you three went in, we barely got you back."

"What did Andy say?"

Eddy sighed. "She said we had to do whatever we could to stop the storm. To stop Davian."

Jayson shivered. "I don't know if it's a good idea either." His face was ashen white. He'd woken up screaming, and it had taken three of them to calm him down. The man had looked like he was sixty years old when they'd first arrived at the farmhold, worn and tired. Now he seemed to shine with new energy, and if Eddy hadn't known better, he would have put the man's age at no more than forty.

"We have to do *something*." Marissa was the calm voice of reason, staring pointedly at each of them in turn.

Jayson shook his head. "*He's* in there. I don't want to see him again."

Marissa knelt next to him. He was seated on the floor between two shelves full of storage bottles, his knees drawn up to his chest. "I know how he hurt you." Marissa put her hands on his knees. "But if we don't stop him, he will hurt many more." She reached out and touched his cheek. "Is that what you want?"

Jayson stared at her, his lower lip trembling.

*Geez, what did Davian do to you?* Eddy wished he'd left Davian Earthside. He would have stayed there himself if he'd had any idea of the evil that lurked under Davian's handsome face.

"It's okay. We'll be there with you." Marissa indicated Danny and Delancy.

"I haven't approved that yet," Eddy warned.

Marissa shot him a look that said his approval wasn't required. "So what do you say, Jayson? Father?"

His head whipped around, and he stared at her again. "You're beautiful and amazing." He tucked a stray strand of blonde hair behind her ear. "I don't deserve to be your father."

"Yes, you do. Help us now. We need you." The last bit came out strained, and Eddy remembered how young she really was. These kids were only fifteen, and they'd been tasked with a burden he wasn't sure he would have been able to bear *now*.

At last, Jayson nodded. "What do I do?"

"Come sit with us." Marissa pulled him up into the middle of the storage room, and he sat in a circle with the three kids.

Thunder rumbled ominously outside.

Eddy knelt next to Marissa. "Are you sure?"

"There's no other choice."

Eddy hugged her. "Stay safe. Andy will kill me if I lose any of you." He didn't mention that he'd likely kill himself instead.

He stepped back, and Santi, leaning against one of the shelves, pulled him close, wrapping his arms around Eddy's chest.

*He trusts me.*

The other four grasped hands, and a moment later they slumped over.

"What do we do now?" Sandra asked.

Eddy rearranged them in more comfortable positions on the floor. "We keep them safe."


DAVIAN SAT in his throne on top of the stone tower he'd found in one of the world mind's vee spaces. They were a bit of a bore, these virtual worlds—far too realistic and tame. He'd conjure up a suitable menagerie of creatures to populate them when he'd secured things. Then he could take his time with some of the kids who had escaped his grasp at Agartha. Fashion them into sadistic little soldiers to enforce his will on the general populace.

He grinned.

He couldn't see the world himself, something he considered a shortcoming of the overall system. But he could hijack the eyes of many of the colonists through their loops.

Davian amused himself flipping from place to place, seeing the scenes of terror that were playing out as his storm destroyed buildings and trees and rained electric terror down on the populace.

When he found Eddy, he'd have to thank the man for bringing him up here. This was turning out to be better than his wildest dreams.

No hotbox for him, not anymore.

COLIN AND ANALEX stood on the rim of a wide valley. Colin looked around. He knew this place. It had been Lex's playground, the same one Jackson had described to him all those years before. He'd been there many times since he'd become one of the Immortals.

It was Lex's no more.

The stone tower was now a castle, built of rock as dark as the heart of the void. It was surrounded by a tangle of thorny brambles and then by a wide moat full of rancid water.

The green hills had yellowed and blackened, too, as if a vast fire had swept through the valley.

AnaLex frowned. "How did he get in?"

Colin shrugged. "I'd guess the same way I did. The same way Ana and Jackson got here."

"Someone transferred him in." They looked off into the distance, their brow furrowed.

Colin found it hard to look at her. Or at them. One moment she had Ana's angular, sharp features, and then the next she had softened to Lex's beautiful, younger face. Sometimes they were both present at the same time.

At times they looked feminine, but then they shifted into a more masculine appearance, or something in between.

The effect was creepy.

"How do we get in?"

"We just—" AnaLex frowned. "That's weird."

"Can't get there?" Colin wasn't surprised. He'd tried it earlier.

"No. There's some kind of block." AnaLex became Ana for a moment, her scientist's gaze trying to work it out.

"I tried Jackson's tricks earlier and couldn't get past the moat." He glared at the black castle.

"Can you reach the outside world?"

Colin frowned. "I don't know." He closed his eyes. *Aaron.*

Nothing.

"I don't think so." It was strange to be so limited. He'd gotten used to being an Immortal with all the powers the name implied.

AnaLex grinned, particularly eerie when they flashed two sets of overlapping teeth. "Maybe if we can't get in, we can force him out."

MARISSA OPENED HER EYES. She was standing with Danny and Delancy by the peaceful lakeside, in front of the door Jayson had shooed them away from earlier. "Where's Jayson?"

"Here." He was standing behind them, sweating profusely.

"Best to get this over with." Marissa reached for the handle. As she grasped it, a surge of electricity rushed through her hand, knocking her backward through the air. "Damn." She got up and dusted off her virtual self. "That would have hurt in-body."

"I think he has to do it." Delancy looked at Jayson.

He looked at each of them in turn. "You'll protect me?"

Marissa nodded as she rejoined the group. "We're right here with you." She wondered how things were going out in *meat space*. She grinned to herself —using the term Andy had taught them for the real world.

"Okay, here it goes." Jayson opened the door.

The world went dark, and they were all sucked through into the other side.

THE HOUSE HAD TAKEN a direct lightning bolt hit in the storm, and Eddy suspected that only the heavy rain had kept the whole place from going up in flames.

Nevertheless, the blow had almost deafened him and had sent jars and boxes and other items careening off the shelves.

The sleepers seemed undisturbed.

The rest of them worked to clear debris to the side of the room. They had one remaining working lantern, which cast a jumpy golden glow across the cluttered space.

Sandra and Sven knelt next to the children, whispering prayers over them.

Santi looked at Eddy, and he shrugged. "Whatever helps."

Eddy started taking the remaining items off the shelves and stacking them as neatly as possible in corners of the room, hoping to remove any additional potential missiles.

The house shook again, and the movement was followed by another peal of thunder.

"That was close." Had it struck one of the trees near the house? Eddy found Santi suddenly in his arms. "Hey, it's okay."

Santi nodded. "Just startled me." He leaned down and kissed Eddy.

Eddy savored the kiss and then pulled away, staring at his deputy in the flickering light. "I thought you said…."

"Doesn't mean I don't like a little romance."

Eddy grinned. "I can work with that."

Marissa woke in utter darkness.

She sat up, breathing quickly, trying to calm her fear. Her heart would be racing, if she had one in vee space.

She felt all around her. There was nothing. She was floating in an inky blackness. "Oh no, oh no, oh no…." She closed her eyes, but there was no difference.

Where was she? What had happened when she'd opened that door?

A white slit appeared, widening until it revealed a giant cartoonish eye. "I remember you." The voice rumbled through the darkness.

"What… who are you?" She tried to scramble away from its gaze, but there was nowhere to go.

"Oh, pardon me." The eye closed.

Suddenly there was light, a diffuse white glow, and she was gently lowered to the floor. She was in a box, a silver, shimmery box. She looked up to find a man standing there before her. He offered her a hand up.

She declined, rising awkwardly on her own. "You're the Preacher."

He laughed. "Yes, that's what the folks in Agartha called me. You've probably heard a lot about me."

"What is this place?" She frowned. Aside from the whole black-as-night thing, Davian didn't seem sufficiently evil.

"You and your friends stumbled into my new domain." He waved his hand and the world changed, revealing a stone-floored room lit by flickering candlelight. He extended a glass of red wine to her.

"No, thank you. It's always a bad idea to eat or drink in the nether realms."

He laughed again. "They've been teaching you well. What have they told you about me?"

"That you're evil?"

Davian shook his head. "We often vilify that which we don't understand."

"I don't—"

He snapped his fingers, and two chairs appeared. He sat down and gestured for her to do the same.

She frowned. She didn't remember any fairy tales where someone got herself in trouble just for sitting.

"Back on Old Earth, they let everyone do whatever they wanted. It worked for a while, but eventually there were too many people who wanted too many different things." He leaned back and spread his arms out on the back of the chair. "They started fighting over what they had and what there was—food, water, land. The fighting got worse and worse over time, not better. They used it all up, and in the end, they destroyed whatever was left, and each other."

Marissa frowned. That wasn't exactly what she'd been taught. "The nation states did it, not the individual people, and often they were brutal and repressive to their own people."

He grinned. "You're very intelligent, aren't you?"

She blushed. "I don't know—"

"Was there ever any crime in Agartha?"

"I don't think so—"

"Did you ever lack for anything? Food? Water? A place to sleep?"

"No." He made it seem so simple.

"We're in a generation ship, one that's going to take hundreds of years to reach its destination." He waved his hand, and an image of the ship appeared.

She stared at it, fascinated. Andy had shown her what the world looked like before, but it still amazed her to see it.

"If mankind does the same thing all over again, we'll strip this world of its resources long before we get there. Forever is a closed system. Once we use it up, there's no more."

Marissa frowned. It made sense.

"I want your help." He looked pained. "It's not going to be easy, bringing order to chaos. You're the oldest of your peers, right?"

She nodded. "One of them."

"They listen to you. I can tell." He grinned, and she was warm all over. She *wanted* to like him.

She shrugged. "Maybe."

"I'm going to need people I can trust in the real world. People who can help me ensure that order persists."

"What about freedom? Individual will?"

Davian swatted away the idea. "Freedom is an illusion. We're all trapped, controlled by society." He put a hand on her shoulder. "We need to think about the greater good."

She *remembered.*

*His hand was on her shoulder, as he stared into her eyes and told her what to do.*

*Trapped in a web of gray static, the world around her wrapped in film.*

*Dull days and dull nights, mechanically eating, sleeping. Even working when her tiny fingers were nimble enough to weave.*

*Pain. Endless pain.*

She pushed him away. "Leave me the fuck alone! I don't want anything to do with you or your plans."

Davian gaped at her, and then a lazy smile crossed his face. "I'd hoped you'd make this easy on me. On yourself too. But there are other ways." He waved his hand theatrically, and she was plunged back into her box.

This time she wasn't afraid. She laughed at him, at his theatrical flourishes, at his veiled threats. "Fucking asshole."

Then she started poking around, looking for a way out of her prison.

## 26

## BOXED IN

COLIN PASSED the skills he'd learned from Jackson on to AnaLex. It was strange, seeing them as one person, but he supposed he would get used to it. He'd gotten accustomed to much stranger things before this.

Would he ever want to be so intimately linked to anyone?

*Maybe to Trip. No one else.*

AnaLex nodded. "It passes outside the normal subroutines. We always wondered how Jackson and his progeny managed to tap into us without us knowing."

"Yeah, kinda like the limbic system bypasses the normal veins and arteries in the body." He reached down and coaxed up a green vine. It rose to chest height, questing around in the air. "It would be amazing to do this out in meat space."

"Like a super power." AnaLex experimented with a vine of their own. "So what do we do?"

Colin grinned. "When strategy and finesse fails, try brute force."

THE WALLS of the storage room rattled in the wind.

"How strong is this house?" Eddy asked, casting a worried glance at the ceiling.

Sven shrugged. "Strong enough to survive a regular storm. We never considered the need to worry about hurricane-force winds."

"I don't suppose there's a basement?"

Sven shook his head.

There was a loud crash.

Eddy shuddered. "That didn't sound good."


COLIN AND ANALEX wove a cage of vines over the stone castle, intertwining them to make a nearly impenetrable cage. They worked side by side, combining their strength to hem Davian in.

With the cage completed, they squeezed it tighter, encountering the invisible barrier Davian had erected to protect himself, the one they couldn't cross.

Though they pushed with all their might, it held.

He was strong, or else his barrier was proof even against Jackson's abilities.

Colin dropped to his knees, exhausted. "It's too difficult. We'll never get past it."

"Perhaps we're going about this wrong." AnaLex cupped their chin in their hand, staring at the cage.

"How so?"

"Look at the shape."

Colin looked up at the cage of vines. "It's a dome. So?"

"So, what happens when you compress the entire surface of a dome equally?"

"It... gets stronger." He stood up, staring at it.

"Up to a point. With infinite force, we could break through like this. But we don't have infinite force."

He nodded. "But we can apply the force more strategically."

AnaLex were becoming more cohesive, more of a single entity. "Apply enough force at one point—"

"And we might break through. Where?"

"There, at the very top."

He nodded, and together they pushed.


DAVIAN VIEWED scenes of destruction through the eyes of people from Darlith to Micavery. The Rhyl, the river that ran through Darlith, was swollen with rain and threatening to overflow its banks. Winds whipped at the buildings, ineffectual where they encountered bricks but devastating when they contacted wooden structures and roofs.

In Micavery, the waters of Lake Jackson were in turmoil, and at least one tornado had swept through the town, leaving a path of devastation.

In the farmsteads along the Verge, he at last caught a glimpse of Eddy, his ex and nemesis. Interesting. He shifted to see things from Eddy's point of view.

There were three of Gunner's kids—the kids from Agartha—lying unconscious on the floor. The three he'd captured trying to catch him by surprise, he'd guess. And the fourth....

He gasped. It was Gunner. So *that* was how they'd gotten to him. But Gunner hadn't been there with the others.

"Hello, Preacher Man."

Davian spun around to find Gunner standing behind him. He was different. Taller. Stronger. Younger? "Gunner. I'm so glad to see you."

"Where. Are. They?"

"Who?" He had a pretty good idea who Gunner was looking for. He could trap the man like he'd trapped the others. "It's just me here." Davian played for time as he constructed another virtual cell.

"The kids. *My* kids." Gunner advanced on him, seeming to grow larger with each step. "And my name's Jayson, not Gunner."

Davian sighed. "Gunner, Jayson, what does it matter?" He reached to ensnare the man, whatever his name was, to banish him from sight until he could deal with him at his leisure.

Nothing happened.

The man grinned. "I taught you all those tricks, remember? And I'm better at them than you are." Gunner leapt at him.

Davian reached again, and then he had the girl, Marissa, struggling in his grasp.

Gunner stopped short. "You can't hurt her. She's not real here."

"Oh but I can. I can burn her out. Enough power, applied in the right place, and her mind will be reduced to a cinder in her head."

Jayson growled. "Let her go."

"I don't think so." He stared warily at the man, his former servant. "Time for you to back up." He held Marissa's virtual form by the neck.

Jayson snarled but took two steps back.

"Farther."

He backed up against the wall. His angry glare could have disemboweled an elephant.

"Now you're going to let me put you in a safe place—"

There was a huge crack and a chunk of the ceiling fell in, slamming him with rubble.


A PIECE of the farmhouse's roof came off, showering Eddy with water and debris. He threw himself across Marissa and the others, trying to shield them with his body.

Rain poured in through the opening, and the rest of the structure shook ominously.

"Everyone okay?" Eddy shouted. The howling of the wind made it difficult for him to hear his own voice.

"We're over here!" Eddy looked over to see Sven and Sandra huddled in one corner.

They crawled toward him, putting their bodies between the kids and harm's way too.

"Santi?"

No response.

"Santi!" Eddy sat up and looked around the ruined storeroom in the dim light. "Keep an eye on these four!"

Sven nodded. "Go."

Eddy made his way toward the wall where they'd been sitting. It had partially collapsed. Bits of the ceiling were falling down around him.

"Santi!" he called again, before spotting a dark-haired head partly covered in rubble. "No, no, no, no." He scrambled over to where Santi lay on his stomach and started pulling debris off the body. "Please be okay. Please be okay."

Sven came over to help, and they removed the remains of the ceiling and wall that covered Santi. He threw the last of the boards away.

Eddy slipped his hand under Santi's neck, looking for his carotid artery. Nothing for a second, two, three.... "There it is. Oh thank God." He knelt. "Santi, can you hear me?"

For his answer, he got a long, drawn-out groan. He kissed Santi's head. "You're gonna be all right." Eddy stared up at the dark storm, willing it to go away.

They couldn't take much more of this.


THERE WAS A SHARP CRACK.

Marissa looked up to see a green vine winding its way into the room. More followed, ripping the roof off piece by piece, peeling it back to reveal the sky.

She took advantage of her captor's moment of distraction to shift her form, becoming mist just as she'd done to help clear Jayson's nightmares.

She slipped out of his grasp and flew to Jayson, taking his hand. "Can you block him?"

He nodded. "But he's very strong."

"Use my strength." She probed her surroundings.

Whatever had happened had weakened Davian's blocks. She found Danny and Delancy and let them out of their cages.

They ran to join her, taking her hand on one side and Jayson's on the other.

Davian snarled at them. "You think that's going to make a difference against *me*? I *live* here now. The world mind is a part of me. You're just visitors."

"Maybe so, but we've been here a lot longer than you."

Davian spun around to see Colin and another person. She? He? They were a stranger to Marissa, though they looked strangely familiar.

Davian cursed. He began to grow, stretching upward and outward like a nightmare.

Maybe they could reach the real world once more. Marissa called out in her head. *Andy!*

*I'm here.* The voice filled Marissa with hope.

Davian towered over them now, and he laughed.

*I need you. All of you.* Geez, Davian was strong.

*We're here. All the Liminal kids are with me.*

The strength of Andy and the others passed into Marissa, and she passed it on to Jayson. She expected him to grow to challenge Davian, but instead he became calmer. More solid. Stronger.

They formed a circle around Davian, who reached down to try to scatter them with the back of his hand.

Jayson shouted, and a shock went around the circle.

Marissa held on tight as energy coursed through her.

Davian froze.

Jayson squeezed her hand. "Hold on."

He lifted his arms, and the rest of them did the same.

Davian came back to life, thrashing around inside the circle. He couldn't reach them. He snarled. He was trapped. "What the hell are you doing to me?"

"Putting you back in the box."

Davian began to shrink, his face turning white, then burning red with anger. "Oh hell no!"

Jayson pulled them closer. "That's right," he said calmly. "I saw your darkest fear when I put you in here."

Davian shook, his face turning almost black. "You can't do this to me! I'll fucking kill you. I'll kill you all!"

Marissa's arms were burning, the power coursing through her making her sweat. She trembled but held firm. She glanced over at Danny. He was sweating too. She nodded at him.

Davian had shrunk to his original size. He lunged out and slashed Delancy across the throat.

She clutched at her neck, breaking the circle, and disappeared.


EDDY HELD Santi in his arms, sheltered under the protection of a half-collapsed wall where they'd dragged the teens. Sven and Sandra protected them with their own bodies, blocking some of the rain.

Delancy sat up, taking a huge, gasping breath, clutching at her throat.

"Hey!" Eddy put a hand out on her shoulder. "It's okay. You're back in the land of the living."

She was breathing heavily, her eyes darting back and forth. She struggled to take in air.

"Deep breaths." He rubbed her back.

She calmed herself, putting her head down between her knees and slowing her breathing.

At last she looked up, the crazed look gone from her face.

"What happened?" Eddy asked when she was able to look at him.

"The Preacher. He... cut my throat." She reached up to feel her neck again. "It felt so real."

Sandra put her arms around the girl. "It's gonna be okay." She rocked Delancy back and forth.

Eddy ran his fingers through Santi's hair. "You're gonna be okay, handsome," he whispered.

Was it his imagination, or was the rain finally slowing?

"DELANCY!" MARISSA shouted.

Davian snarled like a cornered animal.

"Complete the circle!" Jayson shouted in her ear. "She'll be okay!"

Marissa reached out to grasp Colin's arm. Power surged through the circle once more.

Davian started to shrink again, and a glowing box appeared around his feet. He tried to strike out at them again, but this time the circle held.

The box grew up around him. "You can't fucking do this to me." He tried to pull his feet out of the box, but they moved like he was standing in molasses. "Don't do this," he pleaded. "Please don't do this to me. Don't put me in the box." Davian was crying now.

Marissa turned away.

The box closed over his head, and the screams stopped.

She started to let go of Jayson's hand.

"Not yet." He squeezed her hand.

The box shrank.

"What's going to happen to him?" She wasn't sure why she cared. He'd looked so sad, so forlorn. So broken.

The box shrank in half, and then in half again, and eventually down to nothing.

It disappeared with a small pop.

"He's trapped, hopefully for good."

The world around them shimmered and changed.

Marissa looked around. They were standing in a clean round room at the top of the tower. The debris was gone, and so was Davian.

Jayson pulled Marissa and Danny to his chest and hugged them. "I'm so sorry for what I did to you, to your mothers."

Marissa hugged him back. It was strange, but at the same time, it felt like completion.

He was her father.

She'd always wondered what that would feel like. He had fought for her, for them. That had to be enough for now.

They'd figure out the rest, in time.

THE RAIN STOPPED.

Eddy peered out at the sky. The clouds were dissipating, and what was left of the local vegetation reasserted its glow, leaving them in a dim, wrecked gloom.

He looked down to see Santi staring up at him. "Hey." He cradled Santi's head with his hand.

Santi flinched at his touch, but only a little. "Hey. What happened?"

"I don't know. I think it's over." Eddy leaned down and kissed Santi's forehead. "You got hit in the head by some falling debris."

"Ah. That explains the splitting headache." Santi reached up to touch his temple. "That's weird. I think my loop's broken."

"We can have it checked out back in Micavery." Not that there was much they could do about it if it was truly shorted out.

"Is the storm over?" Santi sat up, wincing.

"I think so." Eddy gave Santi another quick kiss, this one on the lips, and got up to look around.

The farmhouse was destroyed, but most of the barn was still standing, though it had taken a beating. Cassie had survived her second great storm. She nickered at him, and he rubbed her neck affectionately.

Trees were burned or knocked down all around the property, but some remained. Forever plants grew back quickly.

The people of Forever would survive and rebuild. They would make it past this.

Santi stumbled up to him. "What a shitstorm."

"You're telling me." Eddy put his arm around Santi's waist.

"So, do we have a shot?"

Eddy nodded. "We can rebuild. It will take time, but—"

"No, you idiot." He grinned. "You and me."

Eddy looked at Santi and laughed. "I hope so. I think I'm kind of falling for you."

For his response, Santi kissed him, hard.

Behind them, Marissa and the others cheered.

# 27

## CHANGES

MARISSA PACKED up the last of her meager belongings. She was going to live with the Olafs on their farmhold to help them rebuild. She had talked with them over the network via their loops and the world mind, and they seemed like genuinely nice people.

And Matt was there.

After the Dark Day, she and the others had returned with Jayson to the schoolhouse to make the point that it was time for the Liminal kids to live in the real world. Being locked away at the schoolhouse only perpetuated the fears and stereotypes about her kind and what they could do. The youngest would remain with Andy and Shandra for another year or two, but even they would make trips out to see what life on Forever was about.

Still, it didn't make the actual doing of it any easier.

"Hey, got a minute?" Andy popped her head in the cabin door, looking around. "Where are Danny and Delancy?"

"They went to say goodbye to some of the other kids."

"Got it." Andy sat down on her bed and patted the mattress.

Marissa sat down next to her. "What's up?"

"I just wanted to tell you how proud I am of you. Even if—" She poked Marissa in the ribs. "—you disobeyed me and ran off into the wilds."

Marissa snorted. "The Verge is *hardly* the wilds."

"Maybe not, but I was worried to death for you." Andy sighed. "Just like I'm worried now."

"I'll be okay—"

"Oh, I know you will." She put an arm around Marissa's shoulder and pulled her close. "I realize I'm not your mother, but you kids are as dear to me as if you were my own." She kissed Marissa's cheek. "You be careful out there, and do us proud."

Marissa was surprised to feel tears at the corners of her eyes. "I will." She gave Andy a hug.

When they separated, Andy started to leave.

At the door, she turned and gave Marissa a smile. It was as full of sadness as it was of cheer. "You come back and see me, okay?"

"I will."

Then she was gone.

Marissa finished packing her things in her carry sack and went to the door.

She too turned, taking one last look at the place that had been her home for almost ten years.

It was simple. And small.

It had been hers.

Then she turned to look at the magnificent sweep of the world awaiting her, the Anatov Mountains arrayed around and above her, the glow of the Verge, where the grasses had already grown back after the violence of the storm, and in the distance, Micavery.

"Adventure awaits," she said softly and took the first step toward her new home.

EDDY HAULED YET another log up onto the wagon. They'd almost cleared the Thatch Hill district now, reclaiming the larger pieces of wood to be prepped for new construction. The rest would be thrown into the dissolution pits to be broken down by the world mind.

Half of Micavery had been destroyed in the storm. Thirty had died, by the latest count, far fewer than Eddy had feared. Still, that meant funerals up and down the length of Forever, with the bodies ceremoniously lowered into the pits. Everything on Forever was a cycle, as he had learned over the last fifteen years.

"That's about it for this run." He eyed the wagon.

"Gonna keep the mill busy for weeks," Santi agreed, pulling off his work gloves and giving Eddy a kiss.

It would be a year or two before things got back to normal again, by Eddy's best guess.

The two of them had settled into an easy rhythm with each other, and they'd even gotten physical a couple times.

They'd had long talks about it, and Santi had assured Eddy that, while he had no desire to have sex, sometimes he enjoyed bringing his partner pleasure. Eddy still wasn't sure about it all, but he'd decided they would figure it out. He was quickly learning what an amazing guy Santi was and how relatively unimportant sex was in the grand scheme of things.

They hopped onto the wagon and Santi took the reins, setting the horse off toward the mill. People waved at them as they passed.

The story of the Dark Day had gotten around, and Eddy found his public profile had gone up quite a bit.

There was talk about organizing an official local government to deal with disasters and disputes and all the things that happened when a bunch of humans rubbed elbows.

"What do you think about me running for mayor?" he asked Santi.

"I think that you'd make a great one." Santi gave him the *look*.

"What?"

"It's just that you have your hands full as it is. Could you really take on being the mayor too?"

Eddy thought about it for a moment. "With you at my side, I think I can do anything."


LANYA WAS hard at work at her station when Colin found her there. She was feeling something approximating female—it was strange to remember a time when a precise gender had seemed so important.

Those were Ana's memories.

She'd chosen the new name as the best of a number of questionable alternatives—Lexana, AnaLex, Lexsta—that had all made her groan.

She was surprised how quickly her two perspectives had merged into one.

"What are you working on?" Colin asked, looking over her shoulder.

"A better way for people to get around." She showed him her three-dimensional sketches, complete with genetic coding.

"Wings?" He arched an eyebrow.

"Well, when you say it that way…."

"No, I mean it's kind of brilliant. I'm just not sure our colonists are ready for that level of genetic manipulation."

"You're probably right. It's so easy to play God."

He nodded. "Maybe it's something we could introduce gradually. A tweak here, a pinch there…."

"It was just an idea." She turned to give him her full attention. "How goes the cleanup?"

"It's coming along. I'm working with the authorities, such as they are, in both Darlith and Micavery to set up more of an official government."

"Good idea."

"We're not just a little colony anymore. Speaking of…." He made a grand gesture and a model appeared.

"What is it?"

"The next city for Forever, halfway between Darlith and the sea you've been planning."

She got up and examined it. Two walls, each running 360 degrees around the world. "It looks like it could hold thousands."

"Tens of thousands, comfortably."

"What's it called?"

He grinned. "The Eire. After my old Irish roots. And Jackson's."

"I like it." She sat back down at her workstation. "We need to find a way to prevent what happened from ever happening again."

"How?" He pulled up a chair.

"I don't know. It could have destroyed the whole world."

"Or worse."

She shuddered. "Or worse."

He put a hand on hers. "We'll figure it out. We always do."

She nodded. She had enough data to back that up with him, in both her incarnations. "We always do."

# PART III

## FLIGHT

2188 AD

# 28

# IT BEGINS

Jayson poled the kayak into the shallows of the Rhyl with one of his oars, sliding it up into the mud along the riverbank.

He closed his eyes, breathing in the fresh air—the humid loamy smell of the earth next to the water, the spicy scent of the alifirs that lined the eastern bank. This far north from Darlith, the land was mostly uninhabited, and Mother Nature, aided by sprayings of the bioagent that broke down the rocky surface of the world, was taking the lead in filling out Forever with fast-growing Forever plants.

Jayson loved floating down the river. It was one of his favorite times—peace and quiet away from the clatter and clamor of humankind. Since Marissa and the others had cleared the storm from his mind, he'd come to appreciate true peace and quiet. Out on the river, it was just himself and his companion, the boat, and the elements.

It also reminded him of the time he used to spend with his father, Jackson, fishing the Red River in Fargo.

He sighed. Those days were long gone.

He clambered out of the boat and into the river with his walking stick, soaking his socks and shoes. They'd dry overnight. "You coming?"

Sean nodded. Andy's seventeen-year-old brother had opted to come with him to see his sister and Shandra, up at the schoolhouse. They'd made the upriver trip by hot air balloon, with the lightweight kayak strapped to the side of the gondola.

Andy and Shandra were lonely up there now that the Liminal kids—Jayson's kids—were all gone. They'd received him warmly, as they always did. Part of him still thought he was undeserving of such treatment, after all he'd done.

They hauled the boat up onto the bank where it would be safe for the night. Jayson pulled out his carry sack, full of new purchases from Darlith. The city was bigger every time he visited, with new stories and restaurants. And action.

Jayson was fifty-eight—too old and set in his ways to think about settling down with someone. But a man did have his *needs*, and Darlith had its share of younger guys who appreciated the whole bear thing he seemed to have going.

Sean had gone off for the night with friends of his own, and Jayson—well, he'd sated his appetite in the meantime.

Jayson chuckled to himself. In many ways, he was still a young man himself, his fifty-eight-year-old body notwithstanding. He'd missed so much, living in the fog as he called it now. He was blessed to have a life at all. He set aside the stick, pulled off his wet shoes and socks, and hung them to dry.

Together they set up camp. Jayson rolled out his sleep sack, and they sat down to enjoy dinner.

"It's beautiful out here." Sean looked around appreciatively as he chewed on some dried jerky. "So quiet."

Jayson nodded. "I was just thinking how much I enjoy these times away from everything."

"Is that why you came out to the Eire?"

"Kind of? Your father asked me to come. Said he could use my help getting the colony started." He bit into an apple. The juice was sweet on his tongue. "Truth be told, I think he saw how unhappy I was in Micavery. Too many people there."

Sean snorted. "Not compared to Earth, from what I've heard."

"You're right about that." He closed his eyes and thought about his youth —before he'd been captured by Chinese-African agents. Living on the edge, not a care in the world, a new boy in his bed every night. And the vee worlds he'd explored, full of sex and debauchery the likes of which Forever would never achieve. Not to mention his lost weekend.

"What are you thinking about?"

He opened his eyes. "Oh, just the good old days. Stars. Yeah, looking up at the sky at night and seeing stars. Pass me some water?"

Sean handed over the canteen.

Jayson touched the ground, closing his eyes to sense what was afoot in the world around him.

He could feel the trees growing nearby and sense the flow of waters past the reeds at the bottom of the river. The weather was calm. There would be no rain that night. Jayson looked up into the sky-that-was-not-a-sky. "Here it comes." He lit the luthiel lantern on the front end of the boat.

Sean looked over his shoulder.

The curved expanse of the world north of them had gone dark, and nighttime was hurtling toward them. Jayson smiled. He loved this time of day. "We should be back home tomorrow afternoon. I'm looking forward to sleeping in a real bed again."

"Yeah, me too. Though it gets a bit... lonely out there in the Eire." Jayson's face was bathed in the luthiel's golden glow.

"Did you see Cherin in Darlith?"

"Yeah. We had dinner. I think she's getting tired of seeing me only once a month."

"You should invite her out to the Eire sometime."

"You think Mom and Dad would allow it?"

"Yeah." Jayson grinned slyly. "I can sit them down and tell them how much you need a little more *human contact*."

Sean laughed. "That would be great. I could show her the North Pole, and the shuttle, and the new sea...."

The boy's enthusiasm made Jayson happy. He had become jaded, worn out by life. Sean reminded him of what he'd been like, what Aaron had been like at that age.

This new generation gave him hope.


THE NEXT MORNING, Santiago woke to first light as it swept through the bedroom. The potted plants Eddy had artfully arranged on a series of shelves framing their second-floor window lit up, bathing their bedroom in light.

Santi was up early almost every day to make his mail runs out to Darlith and back. It was his dream job, letting him be up in the air every day, floating high above the amazing world they found themselves in.

Here on Forever, he was free, unlike the cramped, limited life he'd lived with his mother and three brothers in a squalid flat in the heart of Vancouver's Little Mexico. Food had been scarce and water scarcer, and he still remembered his mother waiting in line for hours under the hot sun just to bring them something to drink.

Santi closed his eyes, whispering a prayer *a Dios* for his mother's soul.

He reached over to find Eddy. His husband usually slept through first light. The poor guy was old… fifty-five this year. Santi laughed at himself. He would be fifty in a few more years—he was no spring chicken himself.

Eddy wasn't there.

Santi frowned, looking around the room. Maybe Eddy had gotten up to go to the bathroom.

Things were so much better now that the Liminal kids had started working to improve their living situations, plumbing their waste pipes right into the world systems to be recycled, among many other contributions.

Santi got up and pulled on his underwear. He padded over to the bathroom, but Eddy wasn't there.

*Maybe he has an early day.* Now that Eddy was the mayor of Micavery—and the city had a functioning government that grew every year—he was in demand all the time.

The city population had swollen to several thousand, many of them children needing an education, clothing, and food. There was a lot for Eddy to administer on a daily basis, even with a city council, a full-time staff, and the world mind's help.

The new jail was usually empty but had seen its share of revelers drunken on home brew.

Thank God they'd started building the Eire to take off some of the pressure. He'd heard Darlith was bursting at the seams as well.

He went to the window to look out at the new day.

The weather in Forever was almost always good. Even the rains were usually light, warm enough to walk around in. It reminded him of winter in Vancouver and his first rainstorm with his brothers. They'd danced in the warm rain until they'd been soaked through, and he'd opened his mouth and laughed as the water fell from the sky in big warm drops on his tongue.

One of his friends from the sheriff's office was walking by.

He waved. "Hey, Brad… how's it going?"

The man stopped and looked up at him, stared for a moment, and then went on his way without a word.

*That's weird.* Had he said something to piss Brad off? They hadn't seen each other for a few months, so that seemed unlikely.

He clambered down the wide mallowood stairs to the first floor. The house was officially the mayor's residence, but as the first mayor of Micavery, Eddy had insisted that it be kept small. So it had two bedrooms upstairs with a living room, kitchen, and an office-library downstairs.

It was funny how quickly the printed word had come back into vogue, even if the printing process was fairly archaic by present-day standards. Someone had figured out how to make a printing press, with a few improvements, and now they cranked out a new book each month, ranging from nonfiction how-to books to sci-fi, fantasy, lit fic, and romance.

He found Eddy in the living room, seated on one of the wooden chairs Andy had made for them.

Something was wrong.

Eddy was naked, and he sat up on the chair with his back straight.

His gaze was vacant, though his head twitched every now and then.

"Hey… you okay?" Santi knelt next to Eddy, putting his hand on Eddy's knee.

Eddy didn't respond.

Santi put a hand on Eddy's forehead in an age-old gesture. It was cool, except for his left temple, which was really hot.

*His loop?* Eddy had mentioned having trouble with it a few days before— little glitches connecting to the network, bursts of static inside his head. But nothing like this.

Santi's own loop had burned out seven years before on the Dark Day. Nothing he'd tried had been able to bring it back up, and he'd gotten used to life without it.

He missed being able to query the world mind, or send messages from his head to someone else's. Hell, the Liminal kids didn't have loops, but they had their own separate connection to the world mind. What he wouldn't have given for one or the other.

The hardest part was no longer having his pictures of his mother in his head. Though he could still remember her like it was yesterday, her winsome smile, her ability to make so much out of the little that life had handed her.

It was one of the reasons he liked being a mailman. It was an old-school way of communicating that didn't rely on networks or electrons or other things that could so easily fail.

"Eddy, look at me." Santi took Eddy's chin in his hand, trying to turn his head.

Eddy turned, and his eyes focused on Santi for a moment. His fist came up, hard, and knocked Santi onto the ground.

His head spinning, Santi tried to get up, but Eddy was on top of him in an instant, his hands reaching around Santi's throat.

"Eddy... whaaaaat the heggggh...." He grabbed Eddy's arms, trying to pull them away from his neck. *What the fuck?*

Desperate, he used his body weight to throw Eddy sideways. They tumbled across the living room, slamming into a bookcase that showered them with books, knocking Eddy off him for a second.

Santi struggled to get to his feet and lurched out of the way as Eddy came at him again.

Eddy's eyes were blank.

Santi shivered.

They circled each other warily, and Santi used his sheriff's training to size up Eddy's moves. They'd fought each other years before when Eddy had trained Santi to be a deputy, but it had been a long time ago.

Santi had let himself get rusty.

Yet Eddy wasn't using any tactics at all, simply attacking him with brute force.

Santi grabbed a ceramic vase off one of the shelves, glancing at it regretfully. It had been a wedding present from Trip, a beautiful blue-glazed piece of art. *When in need, anything is a hammer.*

Eddy lunged at him, and Santi jumped to the side, smashing him across the back of the head and bringing him down. "Sorry, I had to do it, *mi amor.*" He knelt to check that Eddy was really out and went to get some clothes and some rope to tie his hands and wrists.

When he had Eddy dressed and secured on the sofa, he threw on some clothes himself and ran outside to find help. *Having a working loop would be really helpful.*

More people were walking by, all heading in the same direction. No one so much as glanced at him.

Some had children in tow, children who fidgeted and pleaded, but none of the adults were listening.

It was like some shit out of a zombie movie.

Then someone noticed him.

One of the zombies pointed at him and murmured something under her breath.

Then another did, and another, and soon twenty people were standing there, staring at him with vacant gazes, pointing.

*This is some seriously fucked-up shit.* Santi had to get out of there. He knew when he'd been *made*.

Santi closed and locked the front door and grabbed a carry sack from the closet. He shoved as much food from the kitchen as he could manage inside—dried meats, bread, cheese, fruit—and threw it over his shoulder. Then he strapped on his throwing knives.

He turned to see three of the zombies at the window, staring at him.

Santi pulled the curtains closed.

After throwing a blanket over an unconscious Eddy and lifting him into his arms, Santi ran out the back door, brushing past three more of the zombies, on his way to the only place he could think of that *might* be safe.

The post office.

It was a harried slog across the city, carrying Eddy over his shoulder and dodging the seemingly enthralled citizens.

Micavery had grown over the last seven years since the Dark Day, spreading up into the hills. The Mayor's House was in town, in one of the original dorms that had been rehabbed as individual housing units, but the post office was closer to the edge of town.

As Santi crouched behind a jerrywood bush, out of breath, he peered through its dense branches to see a mother walking by with a crying child. She knelt next to him and put her hands on either side of his head and whispered something to him.

He immediately stopped crying and his arms drooped to his sides, his gaze going vacant like hers. She took his hand and led him onward toward Lake Hammond.

It was the creepiest thing Santi had seen since he'd left Earth.

As he made his way from cover to cover, he got glimpses of the whole town gathering down by the docks of Lake Jackson.

He decided he wanted to be anywhere but there.

As he approached the gate to the post office, he had to break through three men who saw him crossing the street, two blonds and a dark-haired man. They all had the same strange vacant look in their eyes. Santi didn't recognize any of them.

He didn't want to fight them. Didn't want to use his knives. But they were between him and his escape path.

Santi laid Eddy's bound body down and grabbed a branch to knock them out of the way.

The first blond went down with a grunt. The second evaded his swing but slowly, like he was moving underwater.

Santi took him down on the next pass.

The brunet grabbed the end of the branch as Santi swung it at him.

Santi shoved hard, forcing the man to the ground.

The man let go of the branch.

Santi picked Eddy up in his arms to make a run for it. He knocked the man down again with a sharp elbow on his way past. He got through the gates and made his way around the two-story gray block building to the landing pad behind.

Thank God, he'd left his striker in the balloon basket the night before. Santi set Eddy down inside the gondola and climbed in himself, glancing at the man he'd bowled over. He was standing again and staggering toward the balloon.

Santi got the burner lit and fired it up, and the balloon's envelope began to lift into the air.

Santi used his stick to keep the man at bay, though it took a few hard pokes to make his point.

There was a groan from the bottom of the basket. Eddy was awake and struggling against his bonds. Santi didn't dare release him.

The brunet lunged at him in that moment of distraction.

Santi held the stick out in defense.

The blood drained from his face as the man impaled himself on the sharp stick, still clawing at him as blood poured out of his chest. Santi held on firmly until the man's motions slowed and ceased, his face turning white, and then slumped against the stick.

Santi threw it and the man aside, nausea rising in his stomach. He leaned over the edge of the gondola to vomit his guts out. "Oh God, oh God, oh God." *I killed a man.*

When at last he was done, he wiped his mouth with the back of his hand. He stayed there for a moment, panting. He didn't want to look at Eddy after what he had just done.

Santi glanced up. The envelope was almost full, and the balloon was straining against the rope that held it to the ground.

Santi untied the rope, sickened by the smell of his own breath, and the balloon started to rise above Micavery. The post office roof dropped below the gondola, and soon the whole business district of the city spread out before them.

Santi took out his canteen and swished some water around his mouth, spitting it out over the edge of the basket. Then he looked back toward the lake.

There were thousands of people there, all standing in perfect order, each a couple feet from the next one. All of them were staring out at the lake. Like toy soldiers set out for play. *What the hell is happening?*

Santi shuddered and turned away. He knelt to check on Eddy. The bindings were holding, but Eddy stared up at him with malice in his eyes. He'd never seen that expression on Eddy's face before.

For some reason, he thought it was best if Eddy couldn't see him. He tied a blindfold over Eddy's eyes, whispering, "I'm sorry."

Then he concentrated on nudging the craft toward the spindle, into the slipstream above that would take them out to the Verge.

Below, Micavery was laid out like a patchwork quilt, the downtown district blending into Thatch Hill and the old Embassy quarter, where visiting dignitaries from Earth had once stayed. The air was fresh and warm, as if the world didn't know or care what was happening in the city below.

Santi prayed Marissa and Matt were unaffected by whatever was going on in Micavery.

MARISSA WAS GROWING A BARN.

They'd finished their farmhouse a few months earlier—a small single-story structure that was much stronger than the Olaf's old house.

The structures Marissa grew were anchored into the ground by the roots that made them and were far more fire- and storm-resistant than homes made from alifir wood.

They *looked* different too. Where the old farmhouses, most of which had been destroyed by the storm, were near-replicas of their Old Earth counterparts, these were made of living wood, giving them a much more curvaceous, natural appearance. Their lines were more organic too.

"How's it coming?" Matt wiped his brow, pushing back the flop of dark hair that constantly tried to obscure his eyes. He carried an armful of wood shavings to the dissolution pit behind the barn and tossed them in.

He was working on a new bed for them, building it out of wood they'd traded for from the forests on the north side of the Anatovs, between the Verge and Darlith. Andy and a group of the Liminals had constructed a paved road along the old railway line a couple years before, connecting the two cities by land and replacing the now defunct train service.

Colin had laughed about that. Something about her grandfather Aaron and how he'd finally been proven wrong.

Marissa sighed. She didn't understand old people.

"Good." She focused on getting the living wood to grow straight up, thickening it out along the base. As it reached a height of about three meters, she curved the branch, guiding it into the shape she wanted. That was the first of six main posts she'd put in place before she worked on the walls. "Think I'll get this side done today."

Matt grinned. "It'll be nice to have a barn to work in. But don't push yourself too hard. Don't want to upset the little one."

As if in response, there was a little kick inside. *Hush, Colin. Sleep.* A warm glow filled her stomach at that thought. They'd chosen the name to honor the man who had died helping to save them.

Marissa wasn't the first of the Liminals to get pregnant, but the connection she had established with her child at about eight weeks still amazed her. "He's happy."

"Yeah?" Matt put down the saw and came over to touch her belly. "Is he kicking?"

She shook her head. "He was, but now he's gone back to sleep."

"You told him to."

She blushed. "Maybe."

He kissed her. "You're going to be a wonderful mother, but I'm jealous. I wish I could talk to him like you do."

"Maybe you can." She pulled Matt close to her, laying her hands on either side of his face. "Close your eyes."

He obeyed.

*Can you hear me?*

He nodded.

She had gotten more adept at this over time, but she only used her ability with him. She'd learned how frightened others could get at things they didn't understand, especially when they thought she could read their minds.

She found her baby's voice. *Colin, your daddy wants to talk to you.*

A surge of curiosity came through their bond. She passed it on to Matt.

His eyes flew open, shining with wonder. "Holy Ariadne, I felt that!" He kissed her. "I felt our baby!"

She laughed. "He wants to know what all the fuss is."

"Tell him to go back to sleep. And that I love him."

She did and got a warm *gurgle* in return.

Matt took a step backward, looking into the sky over her shoulder. "That's weird."

She turned to see a hot air balloon in the distance. "It's awfully early for the mail."

"It's the wrong day too. Doesn't it usually come on Monday, Wednesday, and Friday?"

She nodded. "From Micavery, yes."

"I hope it's not bad news. Wish I had a loop."

"Let me see if I can find out." She closed her eyes and dipped into the world mind. "Lanya, can you find Aaron for me?"

There was no response.

She tried again. "Colin? Are you there?" One of the Immortals had to be available.

Again, no response.

She opened her eyes. "There's something wrong. No one is answering."

The balloon was growing steadily larger. It was striped orange and gold, definitely the postal balloon. But Santi should be landing closer to the highway, at the waystation where everyone went to send and receive their mail.

This was starting to feel eerily familiar.

Matt put his arms around her, and they awaited their visitor.

SANTI FIRED the side thrusters on his balloon, steering it as close as he could to the Dale-Callas household. The balloons had been modified to navigate Forever's unique weather system, with luthiel-oil-powered air thrusters that could nudge the craft back and forth. It wasn't a perfect system, but it did allow people like him to travel long distances with cargo in relatively short amounts of time, and as an experienced balloonist, he was good about bringing her down close to target.

There were currently at least fifteen balloons in service in Forever, mostly for cargo runs and dispersal of the bioagent over newer parts of the world. He was the only mailman, and he took pride in his vocation and skill.

This time, he was about fifty meters off. This wasn't his usual landing location, and these certainly weren't normal circumstances.

He came down in the couple's cornfields, crushing a square section of the plants.

Marissa ran up to the gondola from the house, Matt not far behind her. "Hey, Santi, what is this? Special delivery?" She said it lightly, but her eyes narrowed. "You took out a nice section of our corn field."

"Sorry, but this is an emergency." The envelope was starting to deflate. "Mind if I leave this here?" He lifted Eddy into his arms and climbed over the edge of the gondola using the foot hole.

"Of course." Matt was staring at Eddy. "What the hell happened? You guys aren't in some kind of—"

Santi shook his head. "Can we go inside? I'll explain it there."

"Sure. This way." Marissa led them through the rows of corn toward the farmhouse. "Is he okay?" She glanced back at Eddy, concern naked on her face.

"No, he's not. Something's happened in Micavery."

She nodded. "I figured something was going on. I can't reach Colin or Lanya."

They approached the house, and Matt held the door open for them.

Santi smiled gratefully, climbing the steps of the porch to enter their home.

Light shone in from outside, and some beautiful potted plants gave off a radiance of their own, making the space glow with warmth.

Doorways led off in two directions from the main room. "Nice place."

"Thanks. Here, bring him into the bedroom." Matt gestured toward the door on the right.

Eddy had stopped struggling in his arms and now lay still.

*He's listening.* For some reason that creeped Santi out more than his husband's earlier violent attack.

He lay Eddy down on the bed, covered him with an off-white hand-sewn quilt, and mimed silence to Marissa and Matt. He signaled for rope to tie Eddy down.

Matt reappeared with a length of handwoven rope and handed it over to Santi. "We get it from—"

"Shhh." He tied Eddy down, firmly but loosely enough that he wouldn't cut off his husband's circulation. Then he gestured for them to follow him outside.

When they were twenty meters from the house, he pulled them aside behind the barn. "I'm so sorry to barge in on you like this, but I didn't know where else to go."

"You're always welcome here." Marissa hugged her belly. "What the heck is going on?"

He shook his head. "I don't know. I woke up this morning and he was... I don't know... blank. Gone. Lost."

"What do you mean?" Matt glanced at the house, his brow furrowed.

"Just that. I woke up and he wasn't in bed. I found him sitting in a chair downstairs, naked and just staring into space. I tried to get his attention, and he attacked me. Tried to strangle me." He rubbed his neck. It was still sore.

"Holy shit. What did you do?" Matt put a hand on his shoulder.

"I was able to overpower him." He looked around at the farm—the bones of the new barn, the farmhouse, and the neat rows of the fields.

The world looked so normal, like nothing at all was amiss. But he knew what he'd seen in Micavery. "It's not *him*. He wouldn't do that to me."

"Of course he wouldn't." Marissa pulled him in for a hug. "Eddy's a good guy."

"So why come here? Couldn't someone in Micavery help?" Matt swallowed hard. "I mean, we're glad you came to us, but it seems like a long way to go for assistance."

"Because the rest of Micavery has gone crazy too." He told them what he'd seen on his mad dash to escape with Eddy. The zombie populace, the gathering down by the dock.

Matt whistled. "Holy shit."

"I know." He closed his eyes. "I killed someone."

"Oh, Santi." Marissa's eyes were wet at the corners.

"He came at me, just rammed himself onto the stick I was using to defend the gondola." When he closed his eyes, he could see the expression on the man's face. Had it been a momentary look of horror? Had the man become himself again as he'd died?

"It's not your fault." Matt slapped his back. "You were defending yourself, and Eddy."

"I want to believe that. I really do."

"We've been here before." Marissa's eyes were narrowed. "You know what I'm thinking?"

Santi nodded. "It sounds like Agartha."

"Yes." She bit her lip. "It can't be. We *trapped* Davian. I was there—I saw it."

Santi shrugged. "I don't know what to tell you." He glanced at the house nervously. "The worst thing is, I think someone else is watching me *through* him. Or listening. I don't know… I just got the strangest feeling from the way he looked at me."

"If so… they could be sending someone here."

Santi nodded miserably. "I covered his eyes once we left Micavery, so they won't know where we are, not exactly. But he heard your voices… I may have gotten you into something awful."

"Nonsense." Marissa shook her head decisively. "From the sound of it, we'd have been plunged into it soon enough. At least you gave us fair warning."

"I guess." Still, he was miserable, about the man he'd killed and about this.

"So… we need to figure out what's wrong with him and fix it if we can." She pushed a stray lock of blonde hair back behind her ear, her eyes unfocused, and rubbed her stomach.

"Are you… pregnant?" Santi didn't know a delicate way to ask.

"Yes. About two and a half months now." She smiled, and her face lit up the world.

"Are you sure it's safe for you to do this?" God, he didn't want to be responsible for harm to an unborn child too. He already had one death on his conscience.

"I don't think we have a choice." She closed her eyes for a moment. When she opened them, she smiled again brilliantly. "Colin says hello."

"Are you serious? You can… talk to him like that?" Even now, the Liminal kids still surprised Santi.

"Well, not so much talk yet. But he knows you're here." She squeezed his shoulder. "Don't worry. We'll be careful."

# 29

# OUT OF THE LOOP

JAYSON RODE up the elevator shaft of the Seattle megarise, lifted on a stream of antigravity. As he rose, he stared out the plas at the city below. The view from the building on the top of Queen Anne Hill was nothing short of spectacular. The whole city was spread out at his feet.

His pulse raced. He'd been chatting on his loop with this man for weeks, arranging the terms of the evening. Now it was here, and he was scared shitless for what was about to happen to him. After this, he swore he'd never gamble again.

He'd stepped into the elevator shaft. It was too late to turn back now.

His ascent slowed as he approached the three hundredth floor. He held out his hand, flexing his fingers. It would be the one of the last things he controlled until the weekend was over.

The elevator doors opened, and he stepped into the entryway and looked around. It was a round wood-paneled room—cherrywood, he guessed. Expensive, if it was *real* wood. The floor was cold white marble.

There was a soft chime.

"Take off your clothes." The voice was male, firm but kind.

Jayson did as he was told, pulling off his shoes, then his shirt and pants, and folding them to lay them on the floor. He took off his underwear and socks, and soon he stood there naked on the cool floor. "All done." His heart beat faster.

The doors in front of him slid open soundlessly. The man he'd been talking to over his loop, Stave, stepped into the room. He was likely in his sixties, though it was hard to tell. He was a strong-looking man, his hair black with silver at the temples.

Stave walked all the way around him, taking in his unclothed form. He whistled. "Nice. You're everything the tri dee promised." He put a hand on Jayson's cheek. "Are you sure you're ready for this?"

Jayson shuddered at the man's strong touch. "Yes. Yes, Sir."

Stave nodded. He pulled out a silver disk. "You know what this is?"

Jayson nodded. "It's a *'slaver.'*

"Once I put this on you, you will have no more control over your body or your bodily functions. For the next forty-eight hours, you will be mine to do with as I please."

"Yes, Sir." On Monday, he'd have $100,000 NAU deposited in his account, enough to pay off his recent gambling debts and save his legs from being shattered with a sonic hammer.

Was there a small sliver of him that actually… maybe… wanted this? Regardless of the promised payment?

"Are you ready?" Stave looked down, and a grin crossed his face. "I see you are." Calmly, almost gently, he slipped the 'slaver over Jayson's left temple.

Jayson felt his whole body stiffen and then go limp.

"Follow me." Stave retreated into the penthouse. "There are so many things I want to do to you."

Jayson's fear blossomed in his mind, but he no longer had any choice in the matter. His body followed dutifully behind his new Master.

JAYSON WOKE UP WITH A START. It was morning, and he was on Forever, millions of miles away from that apartment in space and decades in time. He'd been experiencing these cognitive aberrations—resurfacing memories, really—ever since Marissa and the others had helped him put his mind back together. They weren't usually so long or so vivid.

It had been a long time since he'd remembered that part of his life. He'd been so young, so lost, so in need of someone else to take the reins.

And yet… had his relationship with Davian in Agartha really been all that different?

It hadn't been sexual. But the man *had* been a sadist. Was there some part of Jayson that had enjoyed Davian's power over him? The things he'd made Jayson do?

He sat up and found Sean staring at him. "You okay? You were mumbling in your sleep."

"Yeah. Just some old demons." He got up and stretched.

"Demons?"

He shook his head. "Nothing you need to worry about."

Sean let it go, but he continued to stare at him, his brow furrowed.

They had a quick breakfast and then packed their few belongings away in the kayak.

Jayson went through the centering exercise he'd learned from Andy, the one he did every morning to keep himself on track.

There were days when he actually missed his old mindless, brain-fogged state. Missed being controlled, being told what to do and when. Missed not *having* to make his own decisions.

It had been horrible, a corruption of his soul, but it had also meant he hadn't needed to think for himself. Hadn't been forced to think for himself.

Hadn't needed to come face-to-face with his actions every single day.

He sat on the riverbank, his legs crossed, his hands resting on his knees. *Breathe in.* Deeply through the nose, puffing out his stomach.

*Hold it.* Under his bare ankles, he could feel the grass that lined the riverside. Though his eyes were closed, he could almost see the river, hear the babbling of the water as it flowed down to the recently created sea.

*Breathe out through your mouth.*

Next to him, he could hear Sean pacing restlessly, eager to get on his way.

*Repeat.*

When he was driven to near despair by the thoughts that hounded him, by the allure of the fog, he had learned to take the time to center himself and to clear his mind. The trick, Andy had told him, was to detach himself from the thoughts. To realize they were just that—thoughts—and nothing more. Just let them float by.

And she'd told him one more thing—that he needed to find a way to forgive himself.

He opened his eyes. "Ready to go, *sprout*?"

Sean glared at him.

"What? You used to love that name." He levered himself to his feet using his walking stick. Getting up was a lot harder than it used to be.

"When I was nine, maybe."

"Well, *I* still like it." He pulled on his now dry socks and shoes—new ones he'd picked up in Darlith—and sniffed the air. "There's a storm coming."

Sean frowned. "How can you tell? I don't feel anything."

Jayson scanned the curved horizon. "Decades of experience. Come on. Let's get going." Something was *off*. If pressed, he would have had a hard time explaining it, but he suddenly needed to be back *home*. As much as it was his home now.

They climbed into the kayak, and he used one of the oars to push the boat off into the river.

In no time, they were drifting down the Rhyl's course toward the Eire.

THE WEATHER WAS CLEAR, the spindle unobstructed by clouds. Marissa stared up at the sky, wondering what new hell was upon them this time.

Matt put his arm around her shoulder. She kissed his cheek.

"You okay, Ris?"

"I don't know." She'd thought they were done with the Preacher, with Agartha. With all of it. She sighed. "I suppose we'd better get this over with. If someone's coming, we'll need to find a safe place to hide."

She led the men back inside, stopping in her kitchen to get her poppy seed extract. Her aunt Keera had helped engineer a variety of poppy flower that would grow in Forever's unique environment, and Marissa had created an opium extract from it that was perfect for banishing pain. Heavy-duty pain. She planned to use it only in dire circumstances, and then sparingly. Keera had warned her the stuff could be dangerously addictive.

The current situation seemed to qualify despite the drawbacks.

"I'll need you to hold his mouth open," she said softly to Santi, "while I apply this. It should make him a bit loopy."

Santi nodded. They followed her into the bedroom.

Eddy lay there silently, but when he heard them, he thrashed about on the bed, grunting and straining at his bonds.

Santi looked pained but stayed silent.

They sat on either side of the bed, and at Marissa's signal, Santi pried open Eddy's mouth, holding it as Eddy tried to bite his fingers.

Marissa managed to get a few drops of the opiate liquid inside.

They stepped back, and she gestured them out of the room. "Let's give it about half an hour to take effect," she whispered when they had reached the front porch. "Then he'll be flying high."

They sat on the porch in silence, lost in their own thoughts.

Marissa stared out at the Anatov Mountains, wondering what was happening *this time*. It bothered her that she couldn't reach Colin or Lanya. It worried her even more that Andy and Aaron weren't answering her calls. Andy and Shandra were still living up at the schoolhouse. Keera, Aaron, and Sean were out at the Eire, starting up a new settlement there.

Marissa scanned the sky for any sign of a rogue storm. For anything at all out of the ordinary, really. It was, from all appearances, a completely normal day. Deceptively normal, in fact. "Have you been able to reach anyone?"

Santi shook his head. "No, nothing. Total radio silence."

"Radio?" That was a new one.

Santi smiled. "Long story." He got up and strolled the length of the porch. "Sorry, just feeling antsy." He glanced back at the house.

"We'll figure this out." She touched his arm. "Whatever *this* is."

"I know." He looked around at the yard. "You guys have done a lot since the last time we made it to your place." He looked over at the just-begun barn. "I wanted to apologize to you. I never found the right time, before."

"For what?" She stared up at him, wondering what he could possibly have to apologize for. He'd been a good friend these last seven years since the Mind War and a regular guest since they'd started the farm.

"Before we met, I had a different opinion of you Liminal kids. I thought you were dangerous—"

She nodded. "We can be."

He growled. "Let me finish. I *used* to think like that. But what you did, the way all of you put yourselves in the path of danger to save the rest of us.... I just wanted to tell you I was wrong."

She held on to the railing, staring out at the farm. The glowing corn plants, the empty space where she planned to raise the barn, the deflated balloon in the distance. "Thank you," she said at last, softly.

"You're welcome." He glanced back at Matt, who was staring off into the distance. "And thank you for taking such great care of Marissa, here."

Matt smiled weakly. "Mostly she takes care of *me*." He got up and kissed Marissa on the cheek.

Her cheeks were warm. "It's time." She looked up at Santi, reading the fear and worry in the lines of his forehead and his tightly pulled lips. "You ready?"

"Ready as I'm gonna be. Will he understand us if we talk?"

"I doubt it. That stuff's pretty strong." She led them inside.

Eddy was singing under his breath.

Santi leaned over and listened, and a smile crossed his face. "I think it's 'Ninety-Nine Bottles of Beer on the Wall.'"

Matt laughed. "How old is that song? We used to sing it in Micavery."

Santi shook his head. "Older than any of us."

"So *he's* still in there." Marissa sighed with relief. "That's good." She pulled up her bedside chair and felt his forehead. "He feels hot... here on the left side."

"That's where his loop is."

"Interesting." If she pressed down on his left temple, she could feel it under the skin, a spiral shape. "Okay, I'm going to see how he's feeling."

"You sure it'll be okay?" Matt hovered over her like a protective father.

She pulled him down for a kiss. "I'll be fine. Now give me a little space." She put her hands on either side of Eddy's face, closed her eyes, and reached into his head.

It was empty.

She jumped back in surprise.

"What happened?" Santi asked.

At the same time, Matt asked, "Are you okay?"

"Yeah, I'm fine." Marissa frowned. "It's just... it's like there's nothing there."

Santi turned white as a sheet. "He's gone?"

"No, I mean, his personality.... Look, we don't know anything yet for sure." She squeezed his hand. "Don't freak out on me."

Santi's mouth snapped shut. "Sorry," he managed.

"Hey, I'm just saying don't worry until we have something to worry about."

"This isn't enough to worry about?"

She sighed. "I mean until we know something for certain. Let me try again." She touched Eddy's face again, staring down at the man who had been a mentor to her since she was four. He had to be in there somewhere.

She closed her eyes and reached again.

She was in a vast empty space. There were no colors, no black, no white. Just... space. She turned around, looking in every direction, but with no point of reference, it was hard to tell if she'd moved at all.

And yet… there was *something*.

She closed her eyes and concentrated on it.

*There.*

She couldn't see it. But there was a ripple. A wave that moved through this place that was no place inside Eddy's head.

Or rather, spiraled.

She could feel it, passing through her, a spinning wave.

It blanketed the emptiness. Maybe the strange wave created it—dampening Eddy's thoughts, his personality. His whole mind.

She let go.

"What did you find?" Santi stared at her from across the bed, his eyes pleading for an answer.

"Something is shutting down his mind. There's this wave—I couldn't see it, but I could *feel* it. I think it's flatlining his brain activity. Maybe interfering with his natural brain waves?"

"Where's it coming from?"

"It's weird. It's a spiral. Like…." Her fingers traced the spiral of Eddy's loop, under the skin. "It's coming from his loop."

"Holy shit." Santi sat down on the bed, feeling his own temple.

"If that's right…." Matt scratched his neck. "Santi, you have a loop, right? Most of the Earth-born have them."

Santi nodded. "Yeah, but mine's been broken since the Mind War."

"I've always been able to reach people through their loops." Marissa touched Eddy's forehead thoughtfully. "Now someone else has found a way."

"One of the other Liminals?"

Marissa closed her eyes. "Damn, I hope not." It was one of the things she'd feared ever since the Mind War. "I don't think any of us is strong enough for this, though. Not without the help of the world mind. Was *everyone* in Micavery affected?"

Santi nodded. "As far as I could tell. Wait, there was something." His mouth fell open. "Oh crap."

"What?"

"There was a woman with a little boy who was crying. As I watched, she knelt beside him and… she *did* something to him." He played it back in his head. "She touched his face with both hands and… after that, he didn't cry anymore."

Her hand went to her mouth. "It's Agartha all over again."

"Sounds like it to me." Santi caressed Eddy's face with his hand. "How do we help him?"

"We have to break the connection." She frowned. "We have to take out the loop."

"Isn't that dangerous?"

She nodded. "We can cut the feed nerve first. That will minimize the backlash. But he could still end up... damaged."

Santi stared at her and then at his husband. "There's no other way?"

"Not that I can think of." She looked down at Eddy, resting her hand on his head and threading her fingers through his hair. What if she hurt him? What if things went terribly wrong?

"Give me a minute with him?" Santi rubbed Eddy's shoulder absently.

"Come on, Matt." She pulled him out of the room.

They left him alone with Eddy.

Outside the closed door to their bedroom, Matt pulled her close. "I'm not sure what I'd do if something like that happened to you," he whispered.

"I know." She hugged him hard. "It's happening to everyone else, though. We have to fight this."

"Just be careful. I need you. And him." Matt touched her belly.

The bedroom door opened. Santi's eyes were red. "Okay, let's do it."


SANTI WATCHED as Marissa prepped her patient. It was easier for him if he thought of Eddy like that.

She'd covered his face with a clean cloth after dosing him with more of the opiate.

Some home spirits served to clean the incision site, and a salve she swore would help numb the pain—something she'd used on cattle, apparently, at need.

The surgical knife she'd produced from somewhere had been boiled first on the stove, which he took as a good sign.

She'd mentioned the basic training she'd had with Ana on surgical techniques, in vee, but he wasn't sure about letting her operate on his husband.

"Okay, I'm going to need you to hold down his arms and legs, Santi. He's drugged, but he's still going to feel this." She sanitized the knife with some more home brew. "And Matt, you need to hold his head steady when I make the incision. Damn, I wish I had something to use as a topical anesthetic."

Santi lay down over Eddy's midsection, grasping his arms firmly.

Matt took up a place near Eddy's head and held it between his strong hands.

"Okay, if you're squeamish, you might want to look away."

Santi *had* to watch. He owed Eddy that.

"I'm cutting the artificial nerve that connects the loop to his brain." She rubbed her finger back and forth over the upper part of his left temple. "I can feel it… right here." She made a quick incision, and blood welled up in the cut. She blotted it up with a clean cloth.

Eddy growled.

"Hold him!" Marissa stepped back with the blade.

"Oh God." Santi did as she said.

Slowly, Eddy's screams faded into anguished cries. Each sob ripped into Santi like a dagger. "Isn't that enough? Can't we just leave it at that?"

"I wish we could." Marissa looked pained. "As long as it's in there, it can broadcast those waves."

Santi looked up to see tears at the corner of Marissa's eyes too.

"It *has* to come out. The nerve is just the direct connection. It can also transmit into his brain through the skull. It has to come out."

Santi gritted his teeth and nodded.

Eddy's cries had subsided to dull sobs.

Marissa squeezed his arm. "I'm going to make two quick incisions and pull it out. When I'm done, I'll douse the wound with spirits to clean it." She washed off the knife again with the bottle. "The faster we do it, the sooner this is over. Matt, I'm going to need you to put this cloth over the wounds when I am done and hold it to slow the bleeding."

Santi stared at it, concerned. They were so far from a hospital setting here. "Is it sterile?"

"Like the others. I boiled them all long enough to kill any germs."

Santi closed his eyes. When he reopened them, he met Marissa's eyes. "Do it."

She sat down next to Eddy. "It's okay," she said softly, caressing his face. Slowly he calmed down.

When his breathing had slowed to something closer to normal and his sobs were coming only every half a minute, she looked at Santi.

He nodded.

She leaned over Eddy as Santi and Matt held him down and made two quick incisions. As he started to scream again, she fished out the loop and dropped it into her bowl. "Pressure."

Matt did as he was told.

"There, it's done." She sat back in her chair.

Santi held on to Eddy, trying to ignore his husband's anguished cries. "Holy fuck, this is hard."

She rubbed his back. "The worst is over. Now we let him calm down, and then we bandage him up.

"Will he be okay?"

"I hope so. We'll know when he wakes up."


EDDY FLOATED IN A RED HAZE, his whole being throbbing. He was all alone, lying on a broken stretch of pavement, covered with bits of debris and blood. It was hot and muggy.

In the distance, bombs were going off, and burned air—the result of laser cannon fire—filled his nostrils.

He stared up at one of the wrecked Hong King megascrapers, seeing the sun filter down through a haze of smoke and dust.

A whistling sound sent him scrambling out of the way as a heat seeker came in, smashing against the wall where he'd just been lying. It showered him with cement and pieces of pavement, but he got clear without major injury.

His temple ached. He reached up and touched it, and his hand came away red with blood....


EDDY OPENED HIS EYES.

It was comfortable and dim here. Wherever *here* was. The building was gone, as were the smoke and debris and the horrible smell in the air.

He was lying on something soft.

"Hey," someone said quietly.

Eddy turned to see Santi sitting next to his bedside. The movement sent a shot of pain through his head.

"Hey."

Santi came to sit beside him on the bed. "Do you know who I am?"

He snorted, which hurt. "Of course. You're my Santi." He reached up to touch his husband's face. Santi looked ten years older than the last time he'd seen him.

"Oh thank God." Santi kissed him gently. "Marissa, Matt, he's awake!"

"Marissa's here?" Eddy sat up and was rewarded by another spike of pain. He reached up to his left temple and encountered something padded. He looked around, confused. "Where are we? This isn't home."

"We're at Marissa's place. I brought you here this morning. Do you remember anything?"

Eddy thought back. "I had this massive headache. Last night. I think it was last night. I got up to get a glass of water…." Then what? Had he gone back to bed? He couldn't remember. He tried to check his loop for the time. It wasn't there. Eddy's heartbeat started to race. "Santi, I can't feel my loop… it's not working!" He reached up again for his temple. "Why isn't it working?" He clawed at the soft thing and pain blossomed across his forehead.

"Hey, it's okay." Santi pulled him close. "We had to take it out. I'll explain it all. But it's going to be okay."

Eddy fought back his tears. He looked up to see Marissa and Matt standing above them.

Marissa smiled, but it gave Eddy a chill. It was the smile you gave to a cancer patient who had just a couple months to live.

"What's happening to me?" he whimpered.

"You're okay," Santi whispered again, rocking him gently.

"What's wrong with me?"

# 30

## ON THE RUN

"I can't reach anyone." Sean frowned.

"That's odd." Jayson tried to dip into the world mind, but there was nothing there. It was like a blank wall.

They shared a concerned look. "We'll be back home soon, right?"

Jayson nodded. "Come on. Let's get there a little faster." He picked up his oars, and Sean picked up the others.

They heaved on the oars, and the kayak sped along on top of the Rhyl's current.

The banks on either side slipped by, lit only by the sky glow. They'd passed out of the civilized and planted parts of Forever into the wilderness, where the rocky plane hadn't yet been broken down, let alone planted with grasses and trees and flowers. This part of the world was stark and lifeless except for the flow of the river and the naked forms of rock that suggested future hills and valleys.

After another half an hour, the Eire came into sight ahead, a green oasis in the heart of the black shale landscape. The river curved up around the world about a quarter turn, swinging this way and that in oxbow bends, charting a greenish blue course ahead of them.

From this distance, nothing looked amiss.

Jayson tried dipping again, but the wall was still there.

He ground his teeth.

The Eire was still a modest project—two homes, a barn, and a couple outbuildings. Off to one side was the concrete pad where the relics of the space program awaited the building of the future "Earth Museum."

The four of them—Aaron, Keera, Sean, and Jayson—had gone out there the year before to lay the groundwork for Forever's next city, and they'd spent much of the intervening time preparing the ground and planting the trees—bushes and grasses that would provide light and food to the colonists when they began to arrive.

"What do you think happened?" Sean's voice quavered, just a little. "Why can't we reach anyone?"

Jayson shook his head, his eyes fixed on the rapidly growing green patch ahead. "I wish I knew. Nothing good." All his life, he'd had the ability to dip into the devices in the world around him. To mess with the servitor bot at a restaurant and get his meal free. Or to change his grades in vee space. To spin the wheels on a tri dee slot machine the way he'd wanted, until he'd gotten caught.

On Earth, sometimes that connection had come a little too easily, the world intruding on him instead of the other way around. So he'd learned to push it back, to limit its connection to him.

That ability had made him invaluable to Davian, and in his damaged state, he'd allowed the man to use his abilities to fashion a perverted kingdom under the mountain.

Opening himself up again, after all those years, had been a difficult process, one he still wasn't sure he'd mastered.

This lack of connection to the world mind should have been comforting. He'd gotten used to it, after all. Instead, it filled him with a growing sense of dread.

"We'll find out when we get home," he said at last, and set himself to paddling all the harder.

The black shores passed steadily by, monotonous in their sameness.

He'd done his best to teach Sean what he knew. The boy was gifted, like his father, like all the other Liminal kids. *His* kids.

Jayson felt a great debt of responsibility to them. He would protect them from whatever came, no matter the cost.

. . .

"How much can you carry in that balloon of yours?" Marissa was rummaging through her stores in her pantry, deciding what to take.

The house wasn't safe, if what Santi had suggested was true. Whoever or whatever was behind all this knew Santi had come here. Marissa had strong suspicions about who it was.

"I can carry a fair amount. The balloon gondola is made of superlight material. I can take up to eight passengers, and I've also loaded in cargo, in addition to the mail I bring on each run."

"Good. I want to pack enough to get us out to the Eire, if need be."

"Have you heard from your aunt and uncle?"

She shook her head. "It has me worried." Aaron and Keera had retired from public life and now were out on the edge of civilization, starting the construction of the most ambitious project yet, a new city to hold more of the ever-growing population of Forever.

Both had loops.

"Hey."

She turned to find Eddy, holding on to the doorframe to keep himself upright. She glared at him. "You should be sleeping."

He grinned weakly. "We're in danger here, aren't we?"

She nodded. "Santi thinks so."

"Because of me?" He looked pale.

"No. Because of whatever is happening." She packed a bunch of dried food supplies into a basket—cheese, meat, bread—some of which she'd made herself, some of which she had traded for.

She wanted to plant some red berries like they'd had up at the schoolhouse, but she hadn't gotten around to it. Andy had brought them a couple jars of preserves the last time she was here, though.

She considered the weight. Santi had said they should have plenty of room.

Into the basket they went.

"If we need to get out of here, let me help." Eddy was staring at the basket.

"You *should* be resting." She threw a few more things in the basket, then covered it with a dishcloth.

"It hurts too much to sleep." He touched the place where his loop used to be. "And it feels awful to be cut off from the network."

She nodded. "I'm so sorry, Eddy." She hugged him, being careful not to graze his bandage.

"I had these photos in the loop of my mother. They were the only ones I had of her." He closed his eyes. "I know you had to do it. But it's hard to let that go."

She kissed his cheek.

"Why don't you come help me get the balloon ready?" Santi picked up the basket. "We should be on our way as soon as possible."

Marissa nodded. "That sounds good."

Eddy allowed himself to be led off.

Matt climbed down the ladder from the attic with another basket. "Here are the emergency supplies."

"Thanks, handsome." She pecked him on the cheek and took the basket, setting it down on the floor of the living room.

"The horses have been let out. We can round them up when we get back."

"Perfect." She was glad he'd taken care of that. She'd had Mirabelle since she was a little girl, and it would kill her if the mare came to any harm.

Eddy burst through the door. "Guys, we gotta go. Now."

"What's happening?" Marissa threw a couple more things, including a phostorch and a couple of hand-carved bamboo knives, into the basket.

"We have company coming down the road. Whatever you don't have, leave it. Santi's getting the balloon ready. Come on!"

Marissa said a brief goodbye to their home, kissing her hand and touching it to the wood. As they left the front door, she dipped and called the wood to grow across the entrance, effectively locking out anyone who didn't have an ax or a torch.

She sighed. Who knew if the house would still be standing when they returned?

As soon as the door was blocked, she ran after the others, toward the orange and gold stripes of the balloon's envelope that was starting to rise again above the cornfield. She carried the supplies basket.

She glanced back to see two horses coming down the road that ended at the entrance to their farmhold.

They looked like Jo and Elsa's horses from the next farm over.

She reached the balloon and threw her basket inside. "Wait. They might need our help."

Santi shook his head. "We can't take the risk."

"I have to know for sure." She ran back toward the house as the horses came to a halt, kicking up a cloud of dust.

She stopped at the edge of the cornfield, watching.

Jo and Elsa dismounted, walking over to the house and staring for a moment at the blocked doorway. They moved methodically, almost robotically.

Then Jo stepped up onto the porch and started to pry at the branches that blocked the entry.

Elsa turned to survey the yard, and their eyes met.

Marissa gasped.

Elsa's eyes were utterly blank, not a flicker of recognition. She ran toward Marissa without a word.

"Oh damn." Marissa turned and ran back into the cornfield toward the balloon.

Santi had let up on the burner. He turned to see her running toward them, and cranked it up full blast.

The envelope filled quickly, and the balloon started to pull the gondola off the ground.

Marissa glanced over her shoulder and was terrified to find Elsa right behind her.

She leapt at the gondola, catching it with her hands but knocking the breath out of her lungs with the impact.

The balloon lifted her off the ground as Matt and Santi pulled her arms.

Hands grabbed her leg, and she glanced down to see Elsa holding on, staring up at her with that implacable gaze.

"Get off me!" She shook her legs, connecting with Elsa's face in a sickening smack with her other foot.

Elsa lost her grip and fell to the ground with a grunt.

The woman got up, and Marissa breathed a sigh of relief. *Thank Forever she's okay.* Jo came to stand next to Elsa, watching them soar into the air.

They were such a lovely couple. They'd been over to the house a few times. But there was no trace of humanity left in their dead eyes now.

Marissa breathed a sigh of relief as the balloon sped skyward, leaving their home and almost everything they owned behind.

. . .

SANTI GUIDED them up toward the spindle, its glowing, sparkling thread a beacon for his course. It was a clear day, but darkness threatened in the distance. He stared at the clouds that were gathered near the North Pole. There was something odd about them, something that didn't quite make sense.

He snorted. Nothing about this day made sense. "I'm sorry I brought this down on you," he said to Marissa, who was looking out at the world below and above them.

She turned to glare at him. "If you hadn't, we'd likely be zombies now like the rest of them."

"Maybe so." He fired one of the lateral jets, scooting the craft toward the jetstream that would take them toward the North Pole. He didn't want to get all the way into it or they would overshoot the mark.

The schoolhouse wasn't far from the Verge. Plus the zero-gee zone around the spindle played havoc with hot air balloons, which relied on a clear sense of up and down. "You okay down there?"

Matt was huddled on the floor of the gondola, where he couldn't see the ground below them. He looked up and nodded, and then looked back down at his feet.

"He's always had a thing about heights." Marissa knelt to kiss her husband's cheek.

"That's all right. Very brave of him to come along, anyhow."

*There.* The wind picked them up and started moving them north. He closed the luthiel valve and let the balloon float in the wind. He also let out a little of the hot air from the parachute valve at the top of the envelope. He'd been flying these things for five years now and was adept at the process.

Eddy smiled.

"Feeling better?"

Eddy nodded. "I've never actually seen you fly one of these things before."

"I invited you lots of times." Santi looked over the edge of the basket, judging how soon they'd need to make their descent.

"I know." Eddy put his arms around Santi's waist. "I was always too busy. Guess I should have made time."

"So, what do we know?" Marissa cut in, pushing the topic they were all avoiding to center stage.

Eddy leaned forward. "Lay it out for us."

"One, something has taken over the world mind, again. Two, something, probably the same something, has found a way to take over people this time, too, via their loops."

Eddy's hand went unconsciously to his temple. "Right. Damn, that still hurts. Literally and emotionally."

Marissa flashed him a sympathetic look. "Three, whoever or whatever it is seems to have the ability to pass on the mind control thing."

"Like a virus, maybe?" Matt looked a little less green than when they'd first launched.

"Maybe." Marissa bit her lip. "Jayson did something similar to us in Agartha."

Eddy rubbed his chin. "So... who do we think is behind it and how?"

"It's Davian. It has to be." Marissa looked a little sick herself now. "Oh, sorry!" She leaned over the edge of the gondola and threw up.

Matt managed to get to his knees. He rubbed her back. "Morning sickness."

"She's pregnant?" Eddy asked.

"Yes, she's pregnant." Marissa sank down in the gondola next to Matt. "Maybe I'll just stay here with you for a bit."

"Good idea. Did I tell you that you've never looked prettier?" He handed her one of the towels from the basket to wipe her mouth and chin.

She took it gratefully. "Sorry, that kinda comes with the territory."

Santi frowned. "I have to ask this again. Are we sure it couldn't be one of the Liminal kids?"

"Santi!" Eddy glared at him.

"Sorry. But we have to consider all possibilities." He loved those kids, especially Marissa, but he didn't know all of them, not really.

"No, he's right." Marissa looked troubled. "I don't think any of them is capable of something like this. But the Liminals *could* do it. Maybe."

"I think we have to assume that anyone with a loop has been compromised." Eddy frowned at Santi. "That means Aaron and Keera. Does Jayson have a loop?"

Marissa shook her head. "It burned out before he came to Transfer Station, I think."

"Andy and Shandra have loops, don't they?" Matt's question hung in the air between them.

"Yes," Marissa said softly. "Yes, they do."

"So what do we do?" Santi looked down at the terrain below. "It's about time for us to make our descent."

"How long until nightfall?" Marissa asked.

Eddy cursed. "Dammit, I keep forgetting I don't have my loop anymore."

"Probably an hour. Why? What are you thinking?" Santi had gotten used to estimating the time.

They listened intently as Marissa explained her plan.

SEAN AND JASON leapt out of the boat, pulling it out of the water and tying it to the wooden dock on the edge of the colony.

There was something wrong in the Eire. Jayson could sense it. He stood in the middle of the pier, looking all around, trying to tell what was making him so uncomfortable.

Again, he met the wall.

The air was warm, comfortable, the sky glow casting an even golden light over the small colony.

A well-worn path led through the dirt to the edge of the compound.

Sean started toward the buildings, but Jayson pulled him back, shaking his head.

Sean stared at him, his eyes narrowing. *What?* he mouthed.

*Wrong.* Jayson shook his head. It was too quiet.

At this time of day, Keera and his brother, Aaron, should have been out working on the compound or tending the fields. It was well past lunchtime, if his time sense didn't lead him wrong.

He gestured for Sean to fall in behind him and approached the compound.

A hand-painted sign hung above the metal gateway, proclaiming this place to be "The Eire." It swung gently in the breeze. Beyond it, an open courtyard was surrounded by the barn on one side, grown by Aaron and Jayson, and the housing units on the other, prefabs brought in from Micavery piece by piece by balloon. At the far side, the storage building loomed, built out of gray rock strong enough to withstand a storm like the one that Davian had unleashed upon them seven years before.

As he stepped under the gateway, a distinct chill ran up Jayson's spine. He'd learned to trust his instincts. *Wait here*, he mouthed to Sean.

The boy shook his head, jabbing his finger toward the house where he and his parents lived.

Jayson sighed. The boy had a right to come, but he didn't have to like it.

He put a finger in front of his lips and then mimed for Sean to follow him.

The prefabs were made of a lightweight but sturdy material extruded by the world mind in approximately square sheets. These could be cut to shape and fastened together, and could have windows cut out of them.

With the temperate climate inside the world, few had need of windows, and there was no universal power grid for things like air-conditioning.

Jayson had built these with his own hands, along with his family. He knew them inside and out.

He crept along the side of Aaron and Keera's house to the kitchen window. Carefully, quietly, he peered inside.

Everything looked normal. The dishes were washed and left to dry, and the mallowood countertop was spotless.

Sean peered inside too. He looked at Jayson and shrugged.

*Come on.* They snuck past the window toward the back of the rectangular structure. Jayson trailed his hand across the wall's surface. It was bumpy under his fingertips, like braille.

They reached the bedroom window. Jayson looked through the window, expecting it to be empty.

Instead, he found his brother and his wife, both lying on their beds in their nightclothes, staring wide-eyed at the ceiling.

At first he feared he'd stumbled on a postcoital scene.

And yet when he peeked back in again after thirty seconds, neither of them had moved.

"What is it?" Sean whispered in his ear.

He pushed Sean back away from the window gently. "They're both asleep on the bed, but I think there's something wrong with them." He had a bad feeling about this. The sight of Keera and Aaron laid out like that brought back a whole lotta bad memories. "Listen, I need you to go back to the boat and get my carry sack."

"Why?"

"Don't argue. Just do it." He pointed back the way they'd come.

Sean tried to stare him down.

Jayson held firm, and after a moment the boy's shoulders dropped, and he turned and ran back into the courtyard.

Jayson sighed. *Kids today.* He returned to the window, peering inside to plan his next move, and hissed.

Aaron was gone.


EDDY STARED down at the small valley that sat improbably at the center of the rocky wreckage left by the fall of Agartha. Andy and Shandra had carved this little piece of safety and beauty out of the collapsed mountain, and they'd raised a group of truly exceptional young adults there.

Only Andy and Shandra lived there now, and neither one was anywhere to be seen.

He missed his crossbow. He felt naked without it, especially going into danger.

He glanced over at Marissa. She was calm and collected, even in the midst of whatever craziness was enveloping them. "What's it like? Being back here?" he whispered.

She shook her head. "I don't know. Strange. It's weird to be coming home like this."

*Home.* Well, he supposed it had been, more than anywhere else she'd lived until now.

The valley was dark, lit only by night ivy that covered many of the cottages where the students had once lived. The famous schoolhouse vineyards were hidden by darkness.

Since the children had left, Andy and Shandra had converted the schoolhouse into a first-rate winery, using grape stock provided by Keera's team down in Micavery. While the vines were still young, the Schoolhouse Red was exceptional.

"*If* this is anything like Agartha, and that's still a big if, they'll be in their cabin… there." Eddy pointed, mostly for Santi and Matt's sake.

Marissa pushed a lock of hair back behind her ear, barely visible in the darkness. "I hardly remember that time at all. We were always either working, eating, or resting." Her shadowy form turned toward him. "Do we have to cover Andy and Shandra's eyes? It feels so… invasive."

"Yes. They can't be allowed to see who we are."

They'd brought the balloon down on the back side of the schoolhouse vineyard to try to avoid detection. They'd waited for nighttime and the cover of darkness.

"I've been giving it some thought." Santi's voice floated out of the darkness. "I think I know how to disable their loops without cutting them out."

"How?" Eddy rubbed the bandage on the side of his head. He was certain to have a scar there. "That would be nice."

"Remember how I burned mine out?"

Eddy nodded. "Electrical shock from the lightning strike, wasn't it?"

"Yeah. If we can find something here that can deliver an electric shock…. Marissa?"

She shook her head. "Sorry, nothing like that here. But maybe… never mind."

"What?" Something nonintrusive would be ideal.

"I might be able to burn it out myself."

Eddy shook his head. "Absolutely not. It's too dangerous. If you lost control…." He shuddered. "We might lose you, or you might lose the baby. Or both."

Matt seconded him.

"What if I could jam the signal?" Marissa whispered.

"Jam it? How?" Eddy was getting impatient. They needed to act before something tripped up their plans. But if there was a way to free Andy and Shandra that was less painful and debilitating than cutting out their loops….

"I can find the loop signal from Micavery and block it from reaching the loop, I think."

"Without reaching in?"

She nodded. "Then Andy and Shandra can disable their own loops, internally."

Eddy scratched his chin. "I don't see why not. We can try it. So, are we ready?"

"I am."

"Matt? Santi?"

"Let's go." Santi squeezed his hand.

"Remember, no talking. We get in, grab them, cover their eyes, and separate them. Then Marissa tries her thing."

Everyone agreed.

The little band left their hiding place in the gondola and descended into the darkness without another word.

· · ·

MARISSA CREPT UP to the porch of the cabin that Andy and Shandra shared. The night ivy illuminated the porch with its silver glow, and a cool breeze caressed her skin as she climbed the steps.

She felt like an interloper, intruding on her mentors like this. Never mind that they were probably lost to whatever was holding most of the people on Forever hostage. This had been her home once. Now she was sneaking in like a thief in the night.

It was necessary, but she hated it.

One of the floorboards on the porch creaked.

She lifted her foot and indicated the offending board to Matt, who was just behind her.

Eddy opened the door and gestured for her to enter.

She passed through the living area, pausing for just a second to look around. Nothing had changed. Delancy's chair sat next to the writing desk, and dishes were stacked neatly on the kitchen counter.

She reached the door to the bedroom. That space had always been by invitation only, a little bit of privacy for the two women who had been like mothers to her.

With just a little hesitation, she pushed inside.

There was only one woman lying on the bed. *Shandra.* She lay perfectly still, her arms at her sides.

Marissa looked around for Andy, peering quietly into the bathroom. Nothing.

*Where is she?* Eddy mouthed to her.

*I don't know.* She gestured at Shandra with a shrug.

Eddy nodded.

Santi readied himself on one side, and Matt on the other.

*Go!*

Matt and Santi sat on the bed, pinning Shandra's arms, while Eddy lay the blindfold over her eyes and tied it behind her head.

Shandra struggled, getting in a good kick on Santi's side, but they had her outnumbered and soon they had her subdued.

Marissa slipped in and laid her hands on either side of Shandra's head.

"Who are you?" Shandra's voice was flat. Weird.

Marissa ignored it. She reached, feeling for the place where Shandra's loop was connected to the network.

"You're a clever one. Ones. How many of you are there?" The voice was deeper than Shandra's, and it sounded bizarre as it tried to match its own usual timbre with her vocal cords.

There. Marissa visualized it, a green thread running into the side of Shandra's head.

"Won't talk to me, huh? Let's see what you do if I add a little pain. Like this."

Shandra's body twisted and contorted, and she let out a scream.

"Hold her down!" Marissa shouted. She was so close.

Shandra's body relaxed. "Ah, yes, I know that voice. Marissa. So nice to—"

Marissa slammed a mental block between Shandra and the signal. "Got it."

Eddy shot her a look. *Are you sure?*

Marissa nodded. She pulled off the blindfold, maintaining the block. "Shandra, can you hear me?"

Shandra's eyes opened, and she looked around wildly and started to struggle.

She took her mentor's face in her hands again and forced Shandra to look her in the eyes. "Shandra, it's me, Marissa!"

Shandra *saw* her.

"It's okay. It's Marissa. Do you understand?"

Shandra nodded.

"You're going to be okay, but I need you to—"

Something crashed behind her, and Santi fell away from the bed.

"It's Andy! I'll take care of her. Stay with Shandra—get her free." Eddy left her side.

Marissa concentrated on maintaining the block, ignoring the sounds of fighting. "Shandra, I need you to turn off your loop. All the way." She squeezed Shandra's hand. "Something has been controlling you, and it's coming through your loop. Can you do that?"

Shandra stared at her wild-eyed, but she nodded. "I can." She closed her eyes, and in a moment she reopened them. "It's done."

Something else crashed behind them, and Marissa let go of the block. "You still okay?"

Shandra nodded. "Andy—"

"—is our other problem at the moment." She turned to find Andy being held by Matt and Eddy.

Santi was rubbing his head, and shards from a vase littered the floor.

Andy grinned at her, a gesture that distorted her features. "I see my old friends have planned a bit of a reunion for me. Didn't expect to see me again, did you?"

"Davian."

"Or at least a really good copy." His grin subsided. "You're causing me a bit of trouble, when I'd rather be working to bring everyone together."

"Turning everyone into zombies, more like." Marissa reached for Andy's face.

"Did you know I could reach inside this one and literally stop her heart?" He laughed, and she hesitated. "I'll see you all soon."

Andy's eyes closed, and then she started to shake.

"Damn." Marissa placed her hands on Andy's face and cut Davian's connection. It was much easier this time, now that she knew what she was doing.

Andy's eyes opened, but they were filled with fear. She was clutching her chest. "Help… me…."

"Quickly, lay her down!" Eddy pulled the blanket off the bed and laid it on the floor. "She needs CPR." He knelt beside her and started to administer it, five compressions on her chest, one breath.

Marissa kept Davian blocked as she watched with fearful fascination.

Five compressions, one breath. Five compressions, one breath.

After thirty seconds—or was it an eternity?—Andy's eyes flickered open, and she took a deep ragged breath.

"She's alive!" Marissa knelt over Andy's prone form. "Andy, you have to shut off your loop." She took Andy's hand and looked into her eyes. "Can you do that?"

"What?"

"Shut off your loop!"

She nodded. "It's done."

Marissa let go of the block on Davian and the world mind and collapsed on Andy, wrapping her arms around her and sobbing.

She had almost lost the woman who would be the grandmother—one of them—to her unborn child.

Andy put her hand on Marissa's head. "It's okay, Rissa. I'm still here."

Marissa closed her eyes and lay still, feeling safe for the moment.

Feeling *home*.

# 31

# TWO HOMES

JAYSON CREPT back to the kitchen window. He peered inside, but Aaron was nowhere to be seen.

A *crack* brought him around to find his brother standing there barefoot in the space between the two prefab houses, staring at him strangely. "Hello, Gunner." His voice was stretched, as if someone or something else was using it and didn't quite have the hang of it yet.

"Master." The word slipped from his lips before he realized what he was saying.

Aaron/Davian nodded. "Good. You remember." He reached his hand out, a little jerkily, and put it on Jayson's head. Almost gently, he pushed Jayson down to his knees.

Jayson sighed. It felt so natural. He'd submitted to this man's will for so many years, subsuming himself to Davian's commands, becoming his servant, his vassal.

Never mind that the man was dead and gone. Or should have been.

"I'm happy to see you, Gunner. I have plans for you. Now that I've taken over the other Immortals, I have this whole word at my feet."

"The other...?"

Aaron/Davian grinned. "Yes. I made a mistake last time, trying to imprison them. When I finally found my way out of the little trap you set for me, I bided my time. This time, there's no one left in the world mind to fight back." The grin became a twisted parody of a smile, showing too many teeth. "And I owe it all to you."

Jayson's face burned with shame. His Master was right. Jayson was the one who had opened the door for Davian, given him the keys to the kingdom.

Jayson flashed back to that lost weekend in Seattle, when he'd done things, and had things done to him, that had forever altered his soul. He was meant to serve. He could feel it in his bones. Meant to be at this man's feet. The intervening time had just been a colorful dream.

"Uncle Jayson? Dad?"

Jayson's head snapped up. Davian's spell was broken as quickly as it had been cast.

*I have children now. A nephew. Family.* He wasn't the man he'd been in his twenties. He was almost sixty now. He had come through the cauldron a changed man. A stronger man. He didn't need to submit to this monster any more. "Sean, stay back," he growled.


HE LOOKED UP AT AARON/DAVIAN and saw him for what he was. Not an all-powerful Master, Preacher, but a scared, pathetic husk of a man, always hounded by his demons, trying desperately to build a wall between himself and their ripping, grasping claws.

Aaron's body was just his puppet.

He stood, his eyes locked on Aaron/Davian's. Fear filled those eyes.

"Don't you dare disobey me—"

Jayson's hand shot out to touch Aaron's cheek. He reached into his brother's head, and quick as a snake he struck, severing the link Davian had to Aaron through his loop.

Aaron collapsed in a heap.

"Watch over him!" he called to Sean as he ran toward the bedroom window. He'd seen the mad anger that had crossed Aaron's face as Davian had been thwarted. Keera was in mortal danger.

Jayson pulled himself up through the window frame, thanking the stars there was no glass on these windows, and dropped into the bedroom. He looked around wildly.

Keera was gone.

*The kitchen.* He knew how Davian's mind worked. His former Master would try to punish Jayson for his intransigence, take away something he cared for.

Jayson dashed into the front room, but he was too late. Keera had grabbed a knife, and she held it against her own neck. "I'll do it. I'll kill her." Davian's command over her vocal cords was better. He was learning quickly.

Jayson estimated the distance between them. He was too far to reach her in time. "Don't do it. What do you want?"

"That's more like it." She grinned one of those unearthly grins of the possessed, and her hand relaxed on the knife. "I want you to—"

Then she yelped and tumbled to the ground, the knife skittering across the floor to stop at his feet. *What the hell?*

Sean stood there outside the window, a branch in hand. "I didn't hit her too hard, did I?"

Jayson knelt next to Keera, skipping his hand across her temple and cutting the loop link to the world mind. "I don't think so. She's breathing."

"What the hell was that?"

"I'll tell you later, after we bring your father inside—"

A deep rumbling shook the house, knocking dishes out of the cabinet and onto the ground.

Roots exploded through the floorboards, questing about for him, for Sean, for anything they could destroy. Davian wasn't so easily denied.

Jayson reached inside and pushed, sending his spark outward, creating an expanding null space like the one he'd made in Agartha. As it passed, the writhing roots within its influence stilled. Soon the whole complex was silent.

Keera moaned in his arms.

"It's okay now." He kissed her forehead and then got up to survey the damage. The house had held together, barely, but it would be safer if they were all outside in the courtyard.

So Davian was back. *Round one to me.*

It wouldn't be the last.


NIGHT HAD FALLEN. Marissa sat on the porch of the schoolhouse, staring out at the dark world beyond.

Here and there, patches of silver light marked homesteads where night ivy and other night-shining plants gave off their reassuring glow. The world was peaceful and quiet. She could almost imagine there was nothing wrong.

How many times had she sat on this same porch at night with Delancy and Danny, staring out at this same view? Wondering what was going on in the wider world?

She rested a hand on her belly. Her son sent her a spark of recognition.

She smiled, then frowned. What kind of world would he grow up in? Would it be any less terrible than the one she'd been born to in Agartha?

Behind her, she could hear the others preparing a quick dinner in the schoolhouse kitchen. They needed to strategize, but as Andy had pointed out, they had to eat too.

The building had always served as both a classroom and a dining hall for the Liminal kids and their teachers. Another bit of the past to relive.

She was about to get up and go inside to help when Andy came out. "Hey there." She sat down next to Marissa on the steps. Andy put an arm around her and pulled her close. "How are you doing?"

Marissa pulled her hair back behind her ears. "I'm okay. I was just remembering all the time we spent here with the other kids, looking out there." She sighed. "Do you think we're safe?"

Andy shrugged. "For the moment, yes? As safe as anywhere. There's no easy way to get here on foot, and we're far enough away from Micavery and Darlith to make other methods of transportation inconvenient. But we can't stay here long." She crossed her arms and leaned forward, looking out into the darkness. "Hard to believe Jayson and Sean were just here."

"I hope they're okay."

"I was thinking the same thing."

Andy glanced down at her stomach. "So—you're expecting?"

Marissa nodded. "In about six and a half months."

"That's amazing!" Andy hugged her. "Your father will be so proud."

"I hope so. I can't reach him. I'm worried." *That* was an understatement. What was the word for when the world was ending?

Andy rubbed Marissa's back. "He'll be fine. He's strong. He had to be to last through all those years inside the storm."

Marissa nodded, looking down at her feet. "I hope so."

"Come on inside. We'll figure all of this out after we have some food in us." Andy helped her up. "I'm really proud of you, Marissa."

Marissa blushed. "I just do my best. It's not much."

"That's all any of us can do."

. . .

THEY SAT down to a full meal, courtesy of the schoolhouse stores. Andy looked around the table and smiled. However terrible the circumstances, it was good to have them all here.

It was all vegetarian—a bean salad, mashed squash, grilled mushrooms as big as Andy's fist, and a red berry pie for dessert.

They sat inside the walls of the schoolhouse, and while they ate they talked about everything except their current situation.

Andy and Shandra filled Marissa in on changes to the schoolhouse since she'd been there last, including some new plantings and the latest wine grape harvest. They had high hopes for a white wine they were debuting the following year.

Marissa told them about the barn she and Matt were building and their plans for the nursery when the baby came.

Santi and Eddy talked about the latest news from Micavery, which had become a bustling metropolis bursting at the seams. "We've got to get some of these people moved out to the Eire… once we figure out what's happening, that is."

Andy nodded. "Do we think it's Davian, then?"

"Yes. He outed himself when he used you. It's Agartha all over again."

Shandra frowned. "But Agartha was controlled by Jayson's abilities." Marissa shuddered. "Do we think Davian has those powers now? How did he even return?"

Andy set down her fork and stared out the window. *After all these years….* She got up and started to pace around the room. "Could one of the Liminal kids be helping him?"

Marissa frowned. "I don't know. I hope not."

"The Liminals *could* do something like this. Maybe. If Davian controls the world mind again…." Andy reached out through the open window, lightning-fast, to grab something and threw it on the ground, crushing it under her heel. "Biodrone." She looked outside for others.

Eddy whistled. "Oh shit."

"Biodrone?" Matt looked confused.

"Colin used them occasionally as his eyes and ears out in the world." Andy sighed. "Looks like Davian's found his stash. We've been made."

Eddy nodded. "Santi, maybe you should fire up the balloon and bring it a little closer?"

"Will do." He got up and kissed Eddy on the cheek. "Back in a few."

"Does it make a difference?" Marissa was frowning. "You said earlier it would take a while for anyone to reach us."

"Any*one*, yes. Shandra, we need to gather—" Andy went rigid and then fell to the hard wooden floor.

*IMAGES FLASHED BEFORE HER EYES.*

*The North Pole station, where the world mind was. Bodies slumped over consoles.*

*A crowd of people in Micavery, their hands lifted up toward a man who spoke to them from a raised platform made of world wood, their mouths hanging open and their eyes blank.*

*A raging storm that hid the North Pole.*

*The world mind itself, looming above her in its cavern.*

*And a message, meant for her eyes only.*

*She gasped.*

SHE WOKE WITH A START, finding Shandra staring down at her, her eyes filled with concern.

"Andy, is it you?"

For her answer, she pulled Shandra down and kissed her. Warmth flowed into her, taking away the fear of what she had seen.

"What happened?" Shandra asked when they parted. She helped Andy up.

Andy brushed herself off, none the worse for wear after her fall. "The Immortals. They found a way to send me a message. It's all true. Davian has taken over, and he's planning…. We have to find a way to get to the North Pole, and soon."

"We're not safe here?" Marissa's hand went unconsciously to her belly.

She shuddered. "Nowhere is safe from what's coming."

EDDY FROWNED. "What did they tell you?" Either Andy was being purposely obtuse, or there was something here he wasn't understanding.

"They need us to come to the North Pole. It's the only way to end this thing decisively."

"So it's Davian alone?"

She nodded as she gathered things from her kitchen and bedroom, throwing them into a carry sack. "Apparently he saved a piece of himself somewhere in the world mind or the network."

"So, what exactly will we be doing at the North Pole?"

"They were vague on that point." She eased around between him and the bed, pulling out a couple changes of clothing from the chest of drawers. "We'll have to figure it out when we get there."

"But there's a huge storm at the North Pole. We've seen it. You said you saw it." He tried not to sound exasperated. "How are we going to get in?"

"We'll find a way."

"Are we going to try to land and hike in?" He scratched the stubble on his chin. "That's a huge climb. Straight up almost five miles."

Andy shook her head. "I don't know, and asking me ten more times isn't going to make me magically come up with an answer." She sighed. "It's not like it's just floating around in my head."

He snorted. "They kind of are…." Floating. Flying.

She shot him a black look. "Okay, I think that's everything."

"Holy shit." Eddy sank down on her bed, stunned at the pure daring of the idea he'd just had.

"Yeah, I know. You ready?"

"No, I mean, I think I know how we can do it." *Jesus, I've gone stone fucking crazy.*

"Do what?"

"Get to the North Pole." It was *insane*. But it just might work.

Andy sat next to him. "I'm listening."

"Out in the Eire. They're planning that new museum, right? Things from Earth for future generations to see?"

She nodded. "I don't get how that helps—"

"The Moonjumper! I flew it out there a couple years ago for the museum. It's being stored there."

"Won't work. Davian can take control of it."

"No, he can't." Eddy grinned. "It's very 'low tech' high tech. No ship-mind, no automated controls. All manual."

Andy's eyes widened. "Holy shit."

He nodded. "And I know how to fly it."

"But it still won't work."

"Why not?"

"It's too small. We need something to carry at least four of us. You, me, Marissa, and Shandra—"

"Why Shandra?"

She closed her eyes. "I can't tell you. You just have to trust me."

So she *was* hiding something. He stared at her for a long time.

What if she were compromised? How could he know for sure?

At last, he nodded. He trusted her. If she wasn't telling him something, she had a good reason. "You've never steered me wrong before. But really, you can tell me anything."

"I can't tell you *this*. Not yet." Her eyes pleaded with him to understand.

"Okay." He cast about for a solution. The Moonjumper could carry two. Maybe three, over a short distance. They'd managed four with the escape pod in tow. He smacked his forehead. "That's it. The escape pod is there too. We can tow it with us, and it's also manual only."

Andy nodded. "It could work."

"You have a better plan?"

"I—"

The ground started to shake.

"What the hell is that?"

Andy's face was white with fear. "Come on!" She grabbed his hand and dragged him through the living room and out the front door of the little cabin.

"What is it?" Eddy looked around as the whole valley shook.

"Davian! I hope Santi's back with that balloon!"


THE BALLOON FLOATED through the still night air just above the vines of the vineyard, nudged along by Santi's careful hand across the schoolhouse valley. He was almost to the building that gave it its name.

A deep rumbling reached him, emanating from the ground.

"That can't be good." He stared ahead into the darkness, looking for any sign of his friends and Eddy.

Roots shot out of the ground, questing about like the tentacles of an octopus. Dust filtered into the air, obscuring the scene below, and an awful crunching sound floated up to him as cabins were crushed one by one by the flailing roots.

The gondola floated just above chaos.

Santi gritted his teeth and flew on.

At last he spotted them. They had gathered on the roof of the school-house, so far unmolested, but it wouldn't be long before the destruction reached them.

Santi cursed under his breath and sent the balloon flying toward the roof. "Eddy!" he shouted. "I'm coming!"

He dipped as low as he dared, and as he pulled closer, he used the thrust from his lateral jets to slow the craft down.

Still, it was going to be close. He had one shot at this.

As he approached the roof, Marissa stood at the edge, ready to climb aboard.

He reached out and grabbed her arms, rocking the gondola, and pulled her in.

Andy and Shandra were next, with a helping hand from Matt and Eddy.

"Go!" Eddy shouted at Matt.

Matt leapt at the gondola and grasped it with both hands.

Andy and Shandra hauled him in, but they were past the roof now.

"Eddy!" Shanti shouted, frantically slamming the lever for one of the lateral jets to slow their forward progress.

It wasn't going to be enough. Santi stared in disbelief.

"Take this." Matt found the anchor rope and fed it into his hands.

Santi took it gratefully. "Eddy! Get ready to jump! Grab the rope!" he shouted.

Eddy ran to the far end of the roof and then turned and ran back.

Santi threw out the rope.

Eddy leapt off the end of the roof into the air, as one of the great wooden tentacles reached up and slammed down across it, leveling the schoolhouse behind him.

Eddy's hands reached....

Time slowed down.

Eddy grasped the rope.

He swung down along its length like tri dee Tarzan, rocking the gondola.

"Pull him up!" Santi fired the main burner, and the balloon jerked upward, lifting Eddy along with it.

Below them, one of the roots reached up toward Eddy blindly, then fell down to the ground.

Santi let loose his breath. He helped the others pull his husband up over the edge of the gondola.

Eddy collapsed on the floor, his chest heaving. "Holy... crap... that was... close," he managed between breaths.

Santi knelt and pulled Eddy into his arms, hugging him tightly. "Don't you ever put someone else first again. I could have lost you."

Eddy flashed his lopsided grin, the one that had made Santi fall for him. "It's kinda my job to save others." He looked up at Matt. "You overcame your fear for me?"

Matt nodded. "I couldn't let you die. Santi would have killed me."

Santi glared at Eddy "*You're* gonna kill *me*, one of these days, pulling stunts like that." He looked up at the others. "Everyone okay?"

Andy nodded, though her face was grim.

"Where are we going?"

She almost spat it out. "The Eire. And then the North Pole."

# 32

# AT WHAT COST

NIGHT HAD come, and Jayson and his family huddled in the middle of the courtyard around a small fire, roasting one of the colony's chickens over a spit.

Sean kept casting wary glances at the darkness outside the small fire's circle of light.

"He can't get in. Without one of us as his eyes, he can't even see what we're up to." Thank the stars they were so far away from civilization, away from other people who might be turned into Davian's spies.

And what had he meant when he said he'd said *there's no one left in the world mind to fight back?*

Jayson threw another piece of broken root on the fire. He'd chopped one of them into pieces. At least they'd get some good out of Davian's attack.

"How did he survive?" Keera looked haunted by the possession of her body. Her cheeks were hollow, and the skin under her eyes was gray.

"I don't know." Jayson had been trying to work that out himself. His old Master's reappearance had him all jangled up inside, resurfacing emotions and urges and conflicts he thought he'd long before put to rest. "We thought we extinguished him the last time, in vee."

Aaron squeezed his shoulder. "You did what you could. And if you hadn't come back when you did...." He shuddered. "What about Colin? Lanya?"

Jayson shook his head. "Gone. Dead? Enslaved? I don't know." Jason pulled the spit off the fire. "I think she's ready." He put it down on one of the platters they'd retrieved from the shattered kitchen and carved off a few pieces, handing them around the fire.

"What do we do next?" Sean attacked his chicken leg. Poor kid was probably starving.

"I'm going after him." Jayson had no choice in the matter. He and Davian had a destiny to fulfill. It would probably kill him, but he wouldn't shirk this duty. He had to do this, for the sake of his kids if nothing else.

"I'll come with you." Aaron's eyes met his. "We can leave at first light—"

"I'm going alone."

"I can't let you do that—"

"*You* need to take care of your family. Of your son." The boy was a good kid. Maybe he and his kind would find a way to fix all the things Jayson's generation had screwed up. "I've already packed the things I'll need."

"Keera and Sean can take care of themselves." Aaron's voice was just above a growl. "I'm coming with you. You're going to need me." He looked up at Jayson, his face hard, but his lower lip trembled.

"I don't want you to get hurt." Jayson couldn't bear any more deaths on his conscience.

"Staying here's no guarantee of that. Look around."

Jayson laughed harshly.

"You're my brother. We look out for each another." Aaron offered his hand. "Deal?"

Jayson took a deep breath, looking around at the broken buildings. Davian was strong. And after all these years, after all the time piled up between them, his big brother was still looking out for him. Maybe they did need each other. He nodded at last. "Deal."

They shook hands, and Jayson was hopeful for the first time since this whole thing had started.

"You really think Keera and Sean will be safe here?" Aaron's eyes narrowed.

"Yes, as long as they stay in the circle." It would remain until he removed it.

"I want to go too." Sean put on his best pleading look. Jayson knew. He'd seen it before.

"No!" Jayson and Aaron said in unison.

Keera laughed. "It's good to see you two united like that."

Aaron shrugged. "He's my brother. And things are pretty dire."

Jayson grabbed his arm, pulling him in for a hug. "Thanks."

"What else is family for?"

They would fight Davian, and somehow they would find a way to defeat him.

But at what cost?


EDDY LEANED against the inside of the gondola, his chest heaving. He'd scraped it scrambling up over the metal edge of the basket, but he'd never been more grateful to be in pain.

He thought he'd left war behind back on Earth, but they were engaged in a new kind of violence, fighting with the mind that controlled their world.

How could they ever be sure Davian was gone, after this? The whole system was infected, apparently. He'd come back from the dead now twice. Eddy prayed the man didn't have a cat's nine lives.

"What's in the Eire?" Santi asked as the balloon ascended in the darkness toward the spindle.

"The Moonjumper. The ship I came here on, during the Collapse." Eddy closed his eyes and remembered that harrowing flight in the little tin can, sweating and fearful for their lives.

"Ah. So… what's the plan?" Santi sounded doubtful.

Andy was staring out into the darkness. "We land, grab the Moonjumper and the escape pod Eddy flew in with, and fly them through the storm to the world mind."

"Do you think you can navigate it through high winds and lightning, while keeping the escape pod attached?"

Eddy frowned. "I hope so." The whole thing was sounding more and more crazy under the silver light of the spindle.

What were they going to do if they broke through? Set fire to the world mind? They needed it to keep the world in balance. To manage the atmosphere. To keep adding to the space they would need to survive the centuries. If the world mind died, so would what was left of mankind. Wouldn't it?

He didn't know what the right move was. It was a heavy burden to shoulder.

Eddy had another crazy thought. Maybe they *should* let Davian win. Maybe he was the one who could get them safely across the stark divide between stars—keep humanity from tearing itself apart again.

But at what cost?


FOR HER PART, Andy was thinking ahead.

What Lanya and Colin had asked of her was almost unthinkable. She was still trying to wrap her head around it.

She was out of sorts, which was no great surprise. She was quite literally rootless, her home for the last seventeen years torn to pieces under her feet. She floated unmoored from her old life, and a new one beckoned.

She stared out at the dark world all around them and wondered where she was headed. The spindle provided a silver light, but the ground was shrouded in darkness.

Shandra slipped her arms around Andy's waist. "It's all gone," she whispered.

Andy nodded. "I know."

Shandra sighed. "Sometimes I wonder if it's worth it. We build our lives—homes, gardens, friends, livelihoods—and then something comes along and knocks them out from under us."

"I know." She turned to face Shandra, pulling her close. "What if we could find another way?" she whispered into Shandra's ear.

Shandra frowned. "What do you mean?"

"I'll tell you later. Just don't lose hope." She kissed Shandra, realizing in that moment that she had what she needed. How little everything else mattered, if Shandra was still there with her.

"Okay."

They parted, and Andy laid a hand on Shandra's cheek. "It's all been worth it, to be with you."

Shandra's eyes narrowed. "You're scaring me."

"Don't be." She would tell Shandra, once they could find a little time alone. "All we need is each another."

"I know." Shandra turned to look out at the world. "I've never been up in the air like this." She closed her eyes, and a smile slipped across her lips.

"You're not scared?"

Shandra shook her head. "We'll figure it all out."

No matter what, things were going to change. She could accept that for herself.

Shandra would have to make up her own mind. Either way, things would change for her too.

But at what cost?

MARISSA LEANED against Matt's chest, feeling his warmth through his shirt.

She was tired—the crazy events of the last twelve hours had taken more out of her than she cared to acknowledge.

Just this morning, their future had looked bright—a new beginning on a plot of land all their own. A new life coming into the world that was a little bit of each of them, and a little bit of something more.

Something *divine*?

She'd never known her great-grandmother, Glory. Andy had told them that Glory had been devout, believing in God. In a higher power.

Sometimes Marissa longed for that kind of faith, for the feeling that something greater was out there, looking out for her family. For Matt. For the little baby they'd soon bring into the world.

Knowing that would make everything easier.

Religion had taken a beating in the Collapse and in humankind's forcible separation from Earth. Who could believe in a God that would allow something like that?

And yet, Glory had. Marissa's grandmother had exemplified a simple faith, an unquestioning belief in good in the world.

Maybe others would find a way to believe in it too.

Marissa reached down into her stomach to touch the little miracle growing there.

He reacted with joy and light, an effervescent sparkle that made her smile, despite the terrible things going on in the greater world outside. *Here* was life, existence-affirming life. *This* was what she needed.

She opened her eyes and sat up, stretching her arms.

"You doin' okay, babe?" Matt asked, putting a warm hand on her shoulder.

She nodded. "Just thinking."

"Yeah, me too." Having Matt there with her made all the difference.

"What happens if we fail? I don't want our baby growing up like I did in Agartha."

"Then we won't fail."

She glared at him, but he looked serious. "You can't guarantee that."

"Maybe not. But I know it in my gut. We can't afford to fail. Therefore we won't."

She laughed. "I wish it were that easy." *I wish I had your faith.* Her hand strayed down to her belly.

Matt reached forward to take her hands. "Look, I've known you now for, what, seven years?"

"More or less."

"And never once have I seen you tackle something that you didn't end up overcoming."

She shook her head. "This is different. We have a child to think about. What if—"

"*Don't* say it."

"What if he comes to harm?"

Matt grimaced. "He won't. You're doing this for him, right?"

"Yes. But—"

"No *buts*. You're his mother. You'll protect him. End of story."

She stared at him for a long moment, then nodded. "I guess I will." She lay back down on his chest. "Thank you for believing in me."

"Of course. It's in the 'spouse' job description."

She laughed. "Maybe so." They would find a way through all this—she had to believe that.

But at what cost?

THE ENTITY that had been Davian watched the balloon ascend into the sky through the eyes of one of its surrogates, a woman once called Maris who had been camping not far from the schoolhouse.

The balloon's flame lifted it through the darkness toward the spindle, up and away from his reach for now.

No matter. They would have to come down eventually. Meanwhile, he had bigger fish to fry.

After his last defeat, he'd spent years sealed off in the box they'd built for him. They'd thought they'd banished him forever. Instead, they'd just put him in the hot box again.

He'd screamed for days, for weeks, railing against its confining walls. He'd battered his virtual fists bloody.

Then he'd lain inside, broken, for a year, while his mind gradually learned to accept his new condition.

And then he'd begun to plan. To figure out what he would do if he ever got free.

A long time had passed, and it had twisted him, reshaped him into something new. Something stronger. Freed of his human flesh, freed of even the semblance of humanity, he was a force of nature now. This world was his, and soon he'd squeeze the last little bits of resistance out of the so-called Immortals who shared the world mind with him.

This time, he'd come prepared.

They were building gallows at his command in Micavery and Darlith. When they were ready, he would hang those who had opposed him as an example to all the rest.

He would permit them a small kindness, letting them have their free will back for an instant as they died.

Then he would commence his new world order, shaping humanity into something better. Something that would know its place at his feet.

Yes, he'd been planning this for a long time, and it was all finally coming to fruition. All he'd needed had been a small crack in his prison, his box.

He laughed, an ugly sound even to his own virtual ears.

It had been well worth the cost.

# 33

## THE EIRE

JAYSON STARED at his brother's back as they paddled down the Rhyl in the golden morning light. A storm was gathering at the end of the spindle ahead, close to the North Pole. It looked like it would be a monster.

The river had broadened out into a wide delta—artificial, of course, but meant to mimic a natural one on Old Earth. Someday this would all be marshland, filled with mud and boggy things.

The thought made Jayson smile.

He hadn't spent much time with his brother alone, even out at the edge of current human civilization where there were only four people.

Part of it was shame over what he'd done, of who he'd allowed himself to become. Even if some of it wasn't his fault.

"We don't talk enough, you and I." It was as if Aaron were reading his thoughts. His brother glanced at him over his shoulder.

Jayson frowned, looking up at the storm again. "My fault, probably."

"You're not the only one in this relationship." Aaron sighed. "This might be a one-way trip, you know. We need to bury the hatchet between us."

Jayson nodded. "I'd thought the same thing."

Silence filled the space between them for a couple moments as they paddled down toward the nascent sea.

"Why did you leave?" Aaron asked at last.

"Home?"

"Yeah."

Jayson frowned. It had seemed so clear back then, but the events of intervening years had muddied his reasons. "I think I just needed to be out on my own, to be far away from home. I never was religious—not like Mom and Dad." He hugged himself, looking down at the ground. "It was a little stifling, sometimes."

Aaron nodded. "Yeah."

"And *you* left too."

Aaron whistled. "Yeah, I suppose I did."

Jayson took in a deep breath of the morning air. "It was weird when you left. Suddenly it was just me and Mom in that little house."

"I suppose it was." Aaron sighed. "So, did you ever find what you were looking for? Before...."

"Before the Chafs took me?"

"Yeah. Sorry."

Aaron considered the question. "I thought so, at the time. It ended up being a mirage, and a mountain of gambling debt." His Master, placing his hand on Jayson's head. *Then* and *now* blurred together for a moment, and he shuddered.

"And now?"

"Now I know there are other things that matter." He was eager to get off the topic. "Look, it's the sea at last."

The "sea" was really more of a large lake. It spread about a quarter of the way around the curve of Forever on either side and ended at the North Pole ahead.

It was hard to make out much detail. The black rock at the end of the world seemed to drink in the light. Later it would extend all the way around the curve of Forever, when the world mind had extracted enough ice from Iris, the latest asteroid captured just seven years before. If there was a later.

Somewhere below ground, special tunnels recycled the water from the growing sea, extracting nutrients and redirecting the clean liquid upstream to the mountains or back to the guts of the world for clouds.

"Think the sea will be finished in our lifetimes?"

Jayson laughed harshly. "Probably not, and our lifetimes may be measured in mere hours."

Aaron shrugged. "I've lived a good life. Do you have a plan for getting up the wall to the Far Hold without alerting Davian?"

Jayson shook his head. "Not yet."

He turned and grinned at Jayson. "I think I know how we can do it."

SOMEWHERE AROUND MIDNIGHT, the hot air balloon passed over Darlith. The city's streets were dark, but a glow lit up the central plaza, where Andy had built her sculpture of Old Earth so many years before.

She shuddered to think what might be happening down there and wondered if the McHenrys—the family with whom she'd stayed with when she'd been creating the sculpture—were okay.

The others were asleep in the gondola, all except for Santi, who was manning the balloon. He looked exhausted.

"You should get some rest," she said softly.

He shook his head, blinking blearily. "Someone's got to fly this thing."

"I can do it. Show me how, and you can at least get a nap."

"It's a lot to learn—"

"I'm a quick study." She climbed over Shandra's sleeping form to stand next to him. "Besides, for now I just have to keep us from dropping too far or climbing too high, right?"

He grinned. "I suppose so."

"How long until we reach the Eire?" She'd been out there a few times but never by balloon.

"Not until after first light."

She nodded. "Any idea what time it is now?"

"If I had to guess, I'd say about 2:00 a.m.? We just passed over Darlith, so that would be about right."

"So, it takes, what… about sixteen hours, Micavery to the Eire?"

"More or less." The burn of the flare lit his face in gold for a moment, and then it faded back to black. "That's why I make the run once a week. You know, back on Earth packages could be delivered to the other side of the globe in less time."

Andy shook her head. "I have a hard time conceiving of it. Of how big it really was."

"Too big. I like Forever—it's a good size."

"So what do I do?"

"It's simple. Just keep us in the flow. Open this valve to heat up the air in the envelope—that's the big bag overhead." He pointed up. "At the top, there's a release valve—that lets out some of the hot air."

"How do I know which to use?"

"Easy. If the balloon starts to slow, we're dropping out of the current. Heat up the air, just a little, until we're moving again. If we get too close to the spindle, you'll know it, because the ropes holding the envelope will start to slacken as we approach the zero-gee point."

"And that would be bad."

He laughed softly. "Yes. Because we all might go floating out into midair."

"Got it. So open the envelope valve up top and let out a little hot air."

"You got it." He grinned. "As you said, you're a fast study."

She practiced with each valve until Santi seemed certain she had it down. "You sure you want to do this?" He yawned.

Andy nodded. "Yeah. I can't sleep, anyhow."

"Thanks, angel." He kissed her cheek and went to lay down with Eddy, pulling his carry sack under his head to use as a pillow.

Andy took a deep breath. She'd secured herself a little quiet space from which to reflect on the insane events of the day.

She'd gotten a taste of what the people in Agartha had endured for years on end. Like being imprisoned in a cloud of ash, where every action and every turn was muffled by the stuff.

She shuddered. She still had ash on her soul.

So much of what this world was, for better and worse, was because of her family and what they could do. Without Jackson, there might have been no Forever. He'd taken the steps to save the world mind because of his unique gift and ability to connect with her.

Aaron, her father, had used his gift to help Colin transition into the world mind. And she herself had used it to free the people of Agartha from Davian's grasp.

And yet....

Those same abilities had been used to destroy Transfer Station, and her beloved Ronan, the station mind.

Those same powers had allowed Agartha to exist in the first place. And they had allowed Davian to infiltrate the world mind.

Those things were all because of her family too.

The balloon was slowing down. Andy fired the burner for three seconds and it lifted back up into the current, which pushed it along toward the Eire.

Her parents were there, along with her uncle, Jayson, and her brother, Sean. He was seventeen now, on the cusp of adulthood. What kind of world had he been born into?

What could she do to atone for the woes she and her family had brought upon the world?

Maybe her father would have some idea.

She needed to see him, anyhow, before... before the end.

Her thoughts continued to tumble through her head unchecked. Her old life was gone, wiped off the face of Forever as completely as if Davian had used a giant eraser.

Her new one terrified her. There was no chance of sleeping, not while she was in such turmoil.

She glanced down at the dark forms in the basket, lit by the silver glow of the spindle above.

These people were her family too.

She would do whatever it took to protect them.


THE MAN'S *motions slowed and ceased, his face turning white, and then he slumped against the stick that had impaled him.*

Santi shook himself awake, scrambling to get away from the man's horrified eyes, scrambling backward up against the inside of the gondola.

Eddy was next to him in a second. "Hey... you okay?"

Santi looked up at him, Eddy's face framed by the golden light from the spindle. Daylight had returned. "Um... yeah. I think." It took Santi a moment to realize where he was.

"You were dreaming."

He shook his head. "It was real. I mean... it really happened. When I was trying to get you away from Micavery. I stabbed a man in the gut with a sharp branch." He squeezed his eyes shut. "I can still see it. I killed him. No one could have survived that. Not without surgery."

The others were gathered around them. No one gasped.

"We're in a war." Eddy pulled him close and held him. "It's not your fault." Eddy's face held nothing but compassion.

"Maybe so. But it haunts me."

Eddy touched Santi's cheek. It didn't matter that ten years separated them, or that Eddy was the older one. They were a perfect match.

Andy nodded. "If you hadn't done it, we might all be dead now. Or worse." She shuddered visibly.

Santi closed his eyes. "I just keep seeing it."

"Maybe getting us the ground will take your mind off it." Andy reached down to help him up.

"No problems last night?" Santi stretched. He'd developed a crick in his neck in the awkward sleeping position.

"A few. I figured them out." She gestured to the world before them.

Forever was bright with daylight. In the distance, the black storm clouds loomed, but the morning had come once again. Somehow, that made him feel better.

He looked down. They were well past the estates that had popped up between Darlith and the Eire over the last two decades. Most of the ground below was still raw and black, lit only by the sky glow and the spindle.

A little ahead and off to the right was the green spot that would one day be Forever's third city.

"You did good, kiddo." Santi gave Andy an impromptu hug. "But yeah, looks like it's time to take her down." He reached up to open the envelope valve a little, and they dropped down out of the jet stream, losing speed in the process.

He fired one of the lateral jets and sent them off toward the Eire.

As long as he kept his eyes open, he could pretend he didn't see the man's last terrible gasp of recognition. Or at least not think about it so much.

He had a job to do.

MARISSA WAS the first to see there was something wrong. "Oh no." She covered her mouth with her hand.

"What?" Matt came up next to her and slipped his arm reassuringly around her waist.

She pointed.

The Eire had been attacked. The small buildings that had sprung up along the earthen road were in partial ruin, the ground all around them churned up into chaos as if a giant pickax had torn up the dirt. "Davian," she whispered.

Andy, Shandra, and Matt came to look, and the gondola tilted.

"Hey, not everyone on the same side of the balloon at once," Santi called. "We'll be down there soon enough to see what happened."

Marissa *knew* what had happened. It was the schoolhouse all over again.

Andy turned away. "They're gone, aren't they? My parents. Jayson. Sean. They're gone." Her voice was hollow, and it tore at Marissa's heart.

"We don't know that." Marissa stared at devastation below. "Maybe they got out before it happened."

"How?" Andy turned to look at her, her eyes red. "Tell me how."

"Maybe someone warned them. Like Santi warned us."

"Maybe." Andy paused to consider it. "Maybe you're right."

"We don't know *anything* yet." Shandra pulled Andy close and reached out to touch Marissa's shoulder. "We have to believe they're okay."

Andy nodded.

They waited as the ground came up to meet them. Marissa said a little prayer to whomever or whatever might be out there. Maybe Glory would hear her.

"Where was the Moonjumper?" she asked to distract herself.

Eddy pointed. "On the concrete pad over there, along with the escape pod and one of the shuttles." He pointed away from the destruction. There were several shapes covered in tarps. "It looks like it survived."

"Small favors." Marissa squeezed his arm.

"Indeed."


THE BALLOON DESCENDED toward the ground. Andy waited, anxious. The rough square where the five or six buildings of the outpost had once stood was demolished. Strangely, the corners of the square still had live, glowing plants, while a perfect circle contained most of the debris and a ring of dead grass. Outside the square, the ground was still black and new, roughed up in places but otherwise untouched by the colony.

Santi brought them down about a hundred meters from the scene of the attack, onto the balloon landing pad next to the tarmac with the covered ships. He tied the balloon down to its post, and they all climbed out.

Andy ran ahead of the rest of them into the compound. "Dad? Mom? Sean!" The buildings were in shambles.

"Andy? Is that you?"

"Sean?" Andy looked around for the source of the voice.

"Over here!" Sean popped out of the storage building at the back of the compound, the structure that had sustained the least damage.

She ran to him and threw her arms around the boy. "You're alive, sprout!"

"Again with the *sprout*?"

"Live with it. Where are the others?"

Keera appeared at the door to her house with an armful of plates. "Andy!" She stopped. "It is really you, isn't it?"

"Yes. Marissa cut me free of Davian's hold on me." In two long steps she had her arms around her mother. "Where are Dad and Jayson?" She looked around, confused.

"They're gone." Sean took the dishes from his mother and carried them off into the storage building.

Marissa and the others arrived, and the girl threw her arms around her grandmother.

"Gone?" Andy's heart dropped.

"No, not like that." Her mother frowned. "They went down the river. They're going after the world mind."

"How long ago?"

"This morning."

Andy tested her connection to the world mind. It was blocked, but it felt different than before. "Jayson made a dead zone, didn't he?"

Keera nodded. "To keep Davian out. But he did some damage... before."

Sean returned and greeted all the newcomers.

"What happened here?" Eddy asked the boy.

"Jayson and I came home from Darlith, and we found them asleep. Or something."

"It was like we were in a fog." Keera looked distant. "Jayson and Sean managed to break Davian's hold on us too. Then the ground started to shake."

Sean nodded. "They decided someone had to go after Davian. But they wouldn't let me go."

She hugged him again fiercely. "They were right."

Soon she was surrounded by her mother and niece too, and for a moment she felt safe and warm.

When they let go of one another at last, Andy looked up at the storm in the distance, frowning. "So what do we do now?"

## 34

## REGROUP

"So how do we get to the top?" Jayson stood at the base of the North Pole, looking up the rough black rock face. It was a long way up. This close, it seemed like it really did go on forever.

Aaron was looking back and forth along the length of the wall. "There's an old escape shaft somewhere. It was built when the Far Hold was first constructed."

Jayson looked back the way they'd come. It was dark underneath the storm clouds that boiled above their heads. Jayson shivered, thinking of the chaos the storm would unleash.

They'd rowed across the lake that would one day be a sea and had pulled the kayak up onto the broken black shale. A short hike across the intervening space had brought them there. "A shaft?"

"Yes. It's fitted with a manual cargo elevator that has no links to the world mind. Colin was a bit... paranoid on that point."

"Apparently with good reason." The *Dressler*, and then his own misadventure with Transfer Station, had proven that.

Aaron sighed. "Apparently."

"Where's the entrance?"

"It's hard to get my bearings in this darkness. But if memory serves, it was a bit to the east of the Rhyl." He rubbed his temple. "Times like this, I really miss my loop. But maybe I can dip...." Aaron touched the wall. "Old trick," he explained to Jayson's confused look. "This was the first way I learned to interact with the world mind."

"How? The world mind's blocking access to vee space."

"I can… feel its autonomic processes. Things even Davian wouldn't be aware of. They guide me where I need to go." He pointed east. "It's that way."

Jayson grinned. "You'll need to teach me that trick someday."

"Deal." They set off along the wall.


EDDY PULLED off the tarp and poked his head inside the old Moonjumper. The cramped space smelled stale after having been closed up for so long.

An almost overwhelming wave of nostalgia flowed through him—not for the frantic flight up from Earth, but for everything else it represented. His mother. His military buddies. His home. The skies of Earth.

He closed his eyes and steadied himself against the frame of the little craft. Those things were dead and gone. Most times he no longer thought about them, at least not more than five or ten times a day.

Now that his loop had been cut out, he'd taken another step away from that time—and from who he used to be.

He sighed and climbed inside.

Matt poked his head in behind him. "I've never seen one of these before."

Eddy patted the console. "Shame we have to use it. I don't suppose it's coming back in one piece."

Matt shot him an alarmed look. "That's not reassuring."

He grinned ruefully. "Sorry. I hope all of us will come out of this alive. I certainly want to. But this is bigger than any of us. If this is the hill I die on, so be it." He fired up the control panel. "Everything looks good. We're low on fuel."

"Can we use luthiel?"

Eddy shook his head. "Won't work. It's not pure enough."

"I thought this thing ran on some special kind of drive?" Matt raised an eyebrow.

"It does. But it works off antigravity, and you have to boost it into the air first with liquid fuel. And in this case, we'll be using the x-drive to haul the escape pod."

"What about the shuttle?"

"Good thinking. There may still be a little of the purified luthiel Ana and

Keera created in there. We had to fly it out here, after all. 'Scuse me." He climbed out of the Moonjumper.

The shuttle was covered by a much larger tarp. It loomed over the other small craft—the Moonjumper and the escape pod—that occupied the small tarmac.

Eddy lifted the tarp and ducked underneath. He opened the hatch and went inside to find one of the spare fuel containers, a screwdriver, and a hammer.

He hauled them out and looked for the external tanks.

Matt was right behind him. "We'll probably need some pipe to siphon off the fuel—"

"No need." He chose a spot, high enough up on the tank, and used the hammer to drive the screwdriver through.

It took five blows, but on the last one, a fountain of ship fuel spouted out. Eddy captured the stream of fuel in the can. "Do me a favor?"

"Sure."

"Under the seat in the Moonjumper you'll find an old pack of gum. Grab it for me?"

"Gum?" Matt looked confused.

"Just go look." The spare fuel container was about halfway full.

Matt came back a moment later holding his old pack of Snap gum. "Unwrap a stick for me?"

Matt did as Eddy asked. "What is it?"

"Chewy flavor. Mostly sugar."

The fuel can was almost full. "Okay, pop the gum into your mouth and chew, but don't swallow."

Matt started chewing the gum. "Wow... geez, that's sweet. What's that flavor?"

Eddy scratched his head with his free hand. "I think it starts with watermelon, moves into cherry, then finishes with banana."

Matt laughed. "I don't know what any of those things are."

"Let's see... cherry is like red berry. The others? It's hard to explain." Eddy checked the container. *Just about there.* "Okay, spit it out." He held out his hand.

Matt spit the wad of gum into his waiting palm.

Eddy took it and wedged it into the hole he'd made in the tank, sealing it shut. "There, all fixed." That brought back a few memories too.

Matt eyed it warily. "Is that spaceworthy?"

Eddy shrugged. "Hope so. I plugged a hole in the Moonjumper that way twenty-two years ago. But give me the rest of the pack. Just in case."

ANDY PACED the edge of what she was calling the dead zone.

It was a circle about two hundred meters wide, centered on the destroyed outpost. She urgently needed to know how Jayson had done what he had done. It could be useful when the time came to fight Davian.

She stared off at the North Pole. How was he going to get into the Far Hold? Would he and her father find a way to beat them there? Frowning, she turned her attention back to his handiwork.

The dead zone was a sphere inside which she couldn't reach the world mind, and apparently it couldn't reach her either. Jayson had done something similar in Agartha, cutting off that little chunk of the world.

She'd never learned how.

"Can you feel the difference?" She stepped over the line they'd drawn in the dirt.

On the one side, she could feel that the world mind was there. Her abilities were blocked from it, but she could tell it existed.

She stepped back across. It was as if her senses were wrapped in cotton.

Marissa and Sean tried it too. "Yeah, I can feel it," her former pupil said. "It's like when the blackout hit."

Andy nodded. "It's like Agartha, too, but you weren't old enough to know what you were missing. How did he do it?"

"I can show you." Sean was staring at the line thoughtfully.

"How?" Andy hadn't spent much time with her brother, as far apart as they were, except for the few times he'd come to visit, like the last week, and three years before when he'd come to live with them at the schoolhouse for three months. But they'd formed a deep bond then. They'd also seen each other regularly in vee space ever since.

"He showed me how to do it. He called it *null space*."

*This is good.* "So how did he do it?"

Sean took both of their hands and pulled them out of the null space zone.

Sean knelt. "You know how when you dip, you can feel what's beneath you?" He put a hand to the ground. "And you can dip into vee space?"

"Yes."

Marissa nodded.

"Okay, and you know how it feels when you reach into someone? Through vee space, or the network, or one on one?"

"Yes." Where was this going?

"Null space is like the opposite of those. You must find the place inside you where the reaching and dipping comes from. Here, feel mine." He took their hands and placed them on his chest. "Close your eyes and look for the spark."

"Your spark?" Marissa frowned.

"The place inside where I'm connected to the world. It's not really in my chest. This just makes it easier."

Andy reached inside him, and there it was. The source of his abilities. It was simultaneously hard as crystal and soft as mud. It shone a golden light, and threads extended out from it into the world.

"Feel it?"

"Yeah. I've never visualized it like that before." Marissa's eyes were wide.

"Me neither." Andy was surprised that there were still things for her to learn about her ability.

"Okay, now reach inside and find your own." Sean looked inordinately proud of himself.

Andy grinned to herself. How often, after all, did he get to teach the adults something? She reached inside. There it was. It didn't glow as strongly in her as it did in Sean.

She wondered about that. Would this ability be watered down in time, as the Liminal kids merged with the general population?

Or was it dominant? All the Liminal kids had it.

"I found it."

Marissa nodded. "Me too."

"Okay, now take it and push it out of you." He demonstrated. The little spark exited his chest, and a translucent sphere appeared around him. As he pushed the spark farther away, it rode the surface of the sphere, which got bigger and bigger.

"How large can it go?"

Sean shrugged. "I think it depends on the strength of the Liminal. Uncle Jayson can push his really far."

That made sense. "He's strong."

Sean grinned. "He is. Go ahead—give it a try."

She took her spark and pushed. Her spark left her chest, but when it was about a meter away, the pain started. "Ooooh."

"I know. It hits you when you near your limit."

Andy stared at him. "My limit's a meter, but Jayson pushed his out a hundred?"

"He had a lot more practice."

Marissa's expanded to encompass all three of them before she faltered.

"You're strong too, girl." Andy made an appreciative whistle. "Just like Jayson."

Marissa sighed. "I'm worried about him and Uncle Aaron."

Andy turned to find her brother trying not to cry.

"I'm sorry. I should be stronger." Sean's face was drawn and his eyes wet.

"Nonsense. Come here." She pulled him close. "You too, Marissa." Andy enfolded both of them in her arms. "I don't want to hear any of this nonsense about being *strong*. Far better to be *human*. Do you understand me?"

"Yes," they both said in unison.

"We're all going to be okay."


SANTI STARED at Andy and the Liminal kids. What was it like to have been born in a generation that had never lived on Earth? To be the first true space-faring humans?

What was it like to be so connected to the world around them? Although at times like this, he wanted to disconnect—from the events that were moving to engulf them and from his own painful memory of the day before.

He shook his head to try to dispel the look in the man's eyes as he died.

"Brave new world, huh?" Keera caught his gaze.

Santi sighed. "Yeah, it sure is. Do you ever wonder—"

"How things will be different for them?"

Santi sighed. "I do. So many things you and I had in common, they're just gone." He turned back toward the house. They were trying to secure every-thing that had survived the attack, taking it inside the storage building. "Philly cheesesteak sandwiches."

"Philadelphia." Keera grinned.

"Tri dee. Oreos. Destra Vanity."

Keera laughed. "Oh my God, that woman could sing. Augmented voice or not."

"She always swore it wasn't." Santi managed a slight smile. "The grid. You could find *anything* on the grid."

"Oh… chocolate. Dark *fricking* chocolate."

"Yes!" Santi laughed. "So do you think the Liminal kids will fit in?"

"They already have." Keera nodded in the direction of the shuttle pad. "Matt over there… it doesn't matter to him what Marissa can do. The new generation doesn't see them as weird or different. It's just us stuck-in-the-mud adults."

"Maybe so." Santi let down his latest load inside the darkness of the storage building—a box of clothing from Jayson's home. "Still, Davian couldn't have gotten into the world mind without help from those abilities."

"True. But men have always taken advantage of those around them and of technology. Name me one piece of tech that someone didn't put to an evil use." Keera put down her armful of pots and pans.

"Um… sonograms?"

Keera laughed. "Easy. Some people used them to abort fetuses that were differently-abled."

"Yeah, I suppose so." He concentrated on the work, tying off the knot just right.

"Are you scared? For Eddy, for what he's about to do?"

"How could I not be?" Santi looked at her. "But I'm proud of him, too. He never walks away from a fight."

Keera nodded. "From what I can see, you don't either."

They crossed the courtyard and went back into Jayson's cottage. "Eddy has always taken the lead."

"Don't sell yourself short. If you hadn't done what you did, we'd probably all be under Davian's sway right now. Because of you, we have a shot."

Santi sighed. He hadn't confessed his crime to Keera yet. "I killed a man."

She stared at him. "In cold blood?"

"When we were fleeing Micavery. He came at me, his eyes dead. I didn't know what else to do. I tried to fend him off with a stick and he got impaled on it."

She put a hand on his shoulder. "Santi, listen to me. You're a good man. I've watched you and Eddy, and I don't see how he could have chosen any better." She looked him in the eye. "We're at war. You did what you had to, and because of that, we may all come through this thing alive, and free."

"I guess—"

"No, no guessing. You saved my little girl." She pulled Santi in for a hug. "For that, I'll be forever grateful."

Santi's eyes welled up, and he hugged Keera back. "I miss my mom. But you've been so good to me. If I could have chosen a replacement, I couldn't have done any better than you."

Keera laughed. "Hey, I'm only fifteen years older than you."

Santi smiled through his tears. "Nevertheless."

"So Eddy will take Shandra and Andy and Marissa in the Moonjumper and the escape capsule to fight Davian, and you'll take Sean, Matt, and me to Micavery to pick up the pieces if they win?"

"That's the plan."

Keera squeezed his arm. "Then they'd better win."

# 35

# GOODBYES

It was late afternoon when Jayson and Aaron finally found the entrance to the emergency escape shaft. The storm still raged overhead, but it hadn't yet moved or let loose its fury.

Jayson had used his walking stick to navigate the landscape of dust and broken rock.

The entrance was covered in rock debris. If Aaron's dipping hadn't led them to it, they would have passed it by.

Jayson stared at the pile of black rock. Taking the main elevator would have been so much easier, but it was certain to be a death trap. Davian would know they were coming and would stop them. This way, they had a chance. "You sure about this?"

Aaron shrugged and then grinned. "It's all we've got."

"Fair enough. Let's get to it, then."

One by one, they hauled away the rocks that had covered the door. As they worked, a corner of the door and then the top few inches emerged.

It was a thick steel door set into the rock, looking like nothing so much as an old bank vault.

They worked in the dim light under the clouds, and Jayson glanced up at the storm every now and then as he tossed rocks down the hillside behind them.

At last, they removed the last of the pile.

The door had a round metal "spindle" handle that looked like it had once been painted red but now had only flakes of paint left.

"Here goes nothing." Aaron grasped the handle and turned it. Or tried to. "Holy crap." He grunted as he tried to get it to move. "Damn, I'm getting old."

"It's probably jammed with dirt and water after all this time. Here, let me help you." Together, they grasped the spindle and tried to turn it.

It wouldn't move.

"Here, let me try this." Jayson picked up his walking stick and wedged it into the wheel. The wood was strong, formed from one of the world roots. He took a deep breath and put his whole weight on it, and the wheel turned. Just a little, but it turned. "Want to help me?"

Aaron stepped up next to him, and they managed to move it a quarter turn, and then halfway around.

They stopped, their breaths coming in ragged spurts. "Saving the world is a lot harder than I imagined it would be." Aaron grinned.

Jayson burst out laughing. It felt really good, a releasing of the tension that had held him tighter than a bowstring since the day before, when he'd had the premonition that something bad was coming. "It is. It really is." He slapped Aaron on the back affectionately. "Shall we try again?"

They reset the walking stick, and this time, the spindle moved a little easier. One more hard push, and it spun freely.

Aaron turned it until the latch clicked and then pulled open the door with a loud groan of protest.

Jayson peered at the vacant space inside. There was a cable that extended up into the darkness "I thought there was an elevator?"

Aaron stepped into the dark room. "I thought so too. I don't see any controls."

Jayson looked around in the dimly lit space. "There *are* stairs. An awful lot of stairs."

Aaron frowned. "Yeah, about four kilometers of them, straight up."

Nighttime arrived as they explored the small space, plunging them into darkness.

Aaron's voice carried through the inky blackness. "I hope one of us brought a phostorch."

. . .

NIGHT PASSED over their small patch of the world, thrusting them into darkness.

It was time.

Andy looked back at the broken compound. Her life had been a series of leaps from one thing to the next—from the overrated "safety" of Transfer Station to Forever. From a hoped-for life as an artist and sculptor to the teacher and protector of a remarkable set of children.

And now this.

Jayson's life, too, had been remarkable, but in ways that were so much worse and more painful than hers.

All that missed time, when he had been *here*, on Forever, when no one but Davian had known.

"It's time." Keera's eyes were wet.

"I suppose it is."

Her mother hugged her. When she finally let go, her eyes were red, and her cheeks were puffy. "I'm so proud of you, Andrissa."

"I love you too, Mom."

She squeezed Keera's hand.

"If you find your Dad and Jayson… you guys take care of each other, okay?"

"We will." Andy turned to her brother, determined not to let him see her cry.

Andy hugged Sean fiercely, which was a little awkward through the bulk of the space suit. "You take care of Mom and Dad, okay?"

He nodded. "I will. Love you, sis."


SANTI FIRED up the hot air balloon, preparing it for takeoff. He'd have three passengers this time—Keera, Matt, and Sean.

It was time for their little party to split up, with some of them carrying on the fight, and the rest of them going back to Micavery in the balloon. Maybe they could do something to help there, while the others were off trying to save the world.

Poor Matt was beside himself at the thought that Marissa was going on without him, but there was no way to squeeze another body into either of the two spacecraft, and Andy had been strangely insistent that Shandra had to come.

She was hiding something, but what it was, Santi couldn't decide. He trusted her implicitly, but it made him uneasy to forge ahead without all the information at his disposal.

Eddy approached him, his face grim. "I wish you were coming with me."

"I do too. Are you sure about this plan of yours?"

Eddy laughed ruefully. "Sure? No. Not even close. But it's the best we can come up with. Going through the storm… that's just crazy. This is marginally better."

"What are you going to do once you get there?" Santi refused to say *if*.

"I'm leaving that up to the Liminals. I'm just the bus driver."

"Bus… another word destined for the dustbin of history."

"Yeah, probably so." Eddy put his hands on the side of Santi's face and kissed him, and Santi melted. When they separated, Eddy wagged a finger at him. "Be careful. Take care of yourself and our friends."

"Hey, I'm not the crazy one, taking a century-old spacecraft out for a test spin. I'm just taking a sedate balloon ride through friendly skies."

Eddy glanced at the storm clouds. "Maybe not so friendly. And hell, the Moonjumper might only be *ninety* years old."

"Oh yeah, that's so much better." Santi pulled Eddy close again. "You be careful too." He kissed his man.

"I'll see you on the other side."


STANDING ON the tarmac next to the Moonjumper, Matt took Marissa's hand. "Can I feel him?"

Marissa nodded and put his hand on her belly, over her suit. She reached into her little boy's mind, and Matt squealed in delight. "I *can*! I mean, really touch him, inside of you."

Marissa nodded. "He's so pure."

"Can I talk to him?" Matt's face was radiant.

"Sure. He won't understand your words, but the emotions will come through."

Matt knelt, still touching her belly. "You're going to be an amazing person when you grow up, because you have an amazing mother." He kissed her belly. "But I need you to do something for me. I need you to look out for her while I'm gone."

A burst of warmth came through Marissa's bond with her son. "He will."

"I'll see you soon, little guy." Matt stood and pushed a loose strand of blonde hair behind her ear, and then he kissed her. "We still have so many things to do, you and me."

She looked down at her feet. "I'll be back. I have to do this."

Matt kissed her forehead. "I know. I'll be with you all the way."

Eddy came back from his own farewell with Santi. "We gotta go."

"Okay." She looked at Matt and ran her hand through his hair. "Love you, tiger."

"Love you too, Ris."

"ALL STRAPPED IN?"

Marissa shot Eddy a nervous glance. "Yes."

Matt had disappeared into the darkness in the direction of the balloon.

Eddy closed the Moonjumper's door.

"Yes."

He squeezed her shoulder in reassurance, and she flashed him a weak smile. "It's gonna be okay."

"How can you know?"

Eddy shrugged. "I don't. But it's what you're supposed to say."

He opened the radio channel, dialing down the signal power to transmit in a short radius. He didn't know if the world mind could pick up radio transmissions, but it didn't hurt to be careful. "You two ready to go?"

"Yes, Captain."

"Okay, initiating liftoff." He'd decided not to use the main jet. The auxiliaries would run less risk of toasting the escape capsule while they had it in tow and would use less fuel too. "Here we go."

Eddy fired the jets, and the craft lifted off the ground. "Maneuvering over your position." He eased the Moonjumper over the other craft. "Engaging the x-drive."

There was a solid thunk as the drive pulled the Moonjumper down and the escape pod up.

"Gotcha. Okay, here we go." He lifted the two craft up off the ground about thirty feet and then shifted two of the jets to send them off in the direction they'd come from in the balloon, south toward Micavery.

Andy and Marissa were 90 percent sure they could open the massive air lock at the South Pole. He prayed they were right.

Then again, maybe he should have taken his chances running the storm.

But once they were out, they would be free from Davian's grasp.

The little ship raced through the darkness toward the South Pole. He guessed they'd get there in about two hours at their current speed.

"So," he asked over the radio, "what are we going to do once we finally get to the operations center at the North Pole?"

Andy's reply shook him to the core. "We're going to kill the world mind."

DAVIAN FUMED. He'd lost track of his most important quarry.

He had been thwarted by Gunner—the one they called "Jayson" now. He was dead, along with his family at the outpost called the Eire.

But the others had vanished.

Ghosts of the other Immortals haunted him, their thoughts shooting through his with alarming frequency. That religious freak Jackson was reciting something or other from the bible, and Lanya was waxing eloquent about her little valley, or some river in Russia. It was hard to tell.

He tuned them out.

He had no more bug drones to send out. Colin had managed to destroy most of them before he'd locked things down, and it would take time to make more.

His quarry had been in Agartha—the schoolhouse, they called it now—and then they were gone.

Maybe they were all dead.

Somehow, he didn't think his luck was that good.

He particularly wanted to find Eddy, Andy, Shandra, and Marissa to make them pay for what they had done to him, both in Agartha and ten years later in vee space. He owed them a blood debt, and he intended to pay it in full.

Well, if he couldn't find them himself, maybe the storm could.

He unspooled it, loosing the winds to push it along.

It started extending tendrils of itself out along the spindle. Soon it would grow and make life difficult for anyone who still lived in the physical world.

With any luck, he'd take out the remaining resistance in one tempestuous blow.

Then he could get on with raising his new society from the ashes of the old.

# 36

## FLAMES AND THUNDER

"I THINK I need to sit down for a minute." Jayson looked up the stairway and the open shaft and then back down the way they had come. "I'm too old for all this."

Aaron laughed ruefully. "You and me both. I'm two years older, you know. Sixty this year."

Jayson sank down to the ground, grateful for a moment of not climbing. "They say up here on Forever that sixty is the new seventy."

"Sounds about right." Jayson leaned over the shaft, shining his phostorch down into the blackness. "What do you think is going on out there?"

"I don't know. Nothing good, I'd suppose." He closed his eyes, remembering a time, not so far past, when things had been easier.

"I don't understand."

JAYSON STARED at the pandemonium on the schoolhouse grounds. There were kids everywhere, of all sizes and shapes and colors. "How can all these be mine?"

Andy put an arm round his shoulders. "You were... busy back in Agartha. You don't remember any of it?"

He shook his head. "Women have never been... um... my type."

Andy laughed. "Yeah, sorry, can't really sympathize with that part."

Andy, Shandra, and the schoolhouse kids had welcomed him to their home after the Dark Day. He'd had no place to go. He didn't know anyone, and most people—especially the ones here—had ample reason to hate him.

And yet here he was.

Andy must have seen the pain on his face. She squeezed his hand. "You can stay with Shandra and me until we can build you your own place. Come on. I'll show you around." She kissed him on the cheek.

"Jayson, look over here!" One of the kids—Timothy?—was doing a handstand.

"Very nice!" Jayson flashed Timothy a thumbs-up.

"See? You're a natural daddy." Andy led him by the hand toward her cabin. "I think you'll fit right in."

And he had, for four years, until the kids had all gone away to other homes.

JAYSON OPENED HIS EYES.

"Hey, I think I see something up there." Aaron was shining the light up the shaft.

"Yeah?"

"Take a look." He handed the phostorch to Jayson and stepped back.

Jayson peered upward. "Yeah, looks like there's something there. Come on!"

They clambered up the stairs three more flights. Sure enough, the elevator was suspended in the shaft, caught on a piece of railing that had bent outward, stopping its downward movement.

Jayson and Aaron exchanged a look. "Do you think there's anyone inside?"

Aaron shrugged. "Let's have a look." He handed the phostorch to Jayson and climbed farther up the stairway until he was above the roof of the elevator. Levering himself over the railing, he reached out, grasped the cable, and pulled himself onto the top of the metal box. It swayed a little, then steadied.

"Careful." Jayson watched his brother nervously.

"Got it." Aaron knelt. "A little light please?"

Jayson complied.

Aaron found the latch and opened it with a loud *screech*. "Hand me the torch?"

Jayson handed it over carefully. They didn't want to lose their one source of light.

Aaron peered inside. "Oh crap."

"WHAT DO YOU MEAN, we're going to kill the world mind?" Eddy was sure he must have heard it wrong.

"I know. It *sounds* insane." Andy's voice was ragged. "But it's the only way to root Davian out. Otherwise he'll enslave or kill us all."

"But we can't *live* without the world mind," Marissa protested. "Forever would die."

"There's a plan" was all Andy would say.

Eddy whistled. It better be a *goddamned good* plan.

The little Moonjumper ran ahead of the storm, buffeted by the oncoming winds. Eddy glanced backward. He couldn't see directly behind them, but what he *could* see worried him. "Davian's gotten tired of waiting."

Marissa nodded. Her face was white.

"You okay?"

"Not really." She gritted her teeth.

"First time flying?"

"Yeah." She gripped the seat arms tightly.

"You're gonna be fine."

A gust of wind slammed the little craft, knocking it sideways.

Marissa yelped.

"I'm going to take us up, get closer to the spindle. It should be calmer there."

"Sounds good to me."

He nudged the little craft upward. The first tendrils of cloud were starting to envelop them now. He looked down and got one last glimpse of the ground before the storm closed off the view. They were almost over the Anatovs.

It suddenly went dark all around, and the craft bucked and rattled as the winds increased. Lightning flashed in the darkness, and Eddy grimaced.

"Are we okay?" If Marissa had been white before, she was positively green now.

"Give me a sec." Up, up, up….

He could feel his weight dropping as they soared away from the ground, and he started to float up in his seat, but his seat belt held him down.

Then they burst through the cloud top into the clear. The spindle shone brightly just above them.

Eddy flicked on the radio. "Things are gonna feel weird for a bit. We're in close to zero gee."

"Got it," Andy replied over the radio.

He left the connection open and stared out at the tunnel of clear air, surrounded by angry clouds. They were in the eye of the storm, only this eye extended for miles and miles in front of and behind them. It was one of the most amazing things he had ever seen. If it was anything like Davian's last temper tantrum, he feared for everyone on the ground.

He could see the South Pole ahead in the distance. "You guys said you had a way to get us through that wall, right?"

"We think so." Andy's voice sounded tinny and hollow over the radio connection.

"Could you figure it out soon, please? Otherwise we're gonna be stuck inside this beastie or worse, and she seems to have a bad case of indigestion."

"Marissa, can you reach to me?"

"I'll try." She had a little more color in her face now.

"Quickly."


Marissa closed her eyes and reached.

Normally she was in physical contact with the other person when she did this, or at least within eyesight. Having access to the loop network or the world mind and vee space made it easier.

She tried to picture Andy, sitting in the escape pod beneath her.

There was something. A spark of light.

Marissa dove toward it, and it expanded into a tiny star.

She reached out to touch it, and Andy was there.

"Hey, kiddo. You ready?"

Marissa nodded. "What do we need to do?"

"We have to gather as many of the others as we can find. Then when it's time, we'll try to break through Davian's control to open the air lock."

"Got it."

"You're strong. Even stronger than you were the last time I saw you."

Marissa would have blushed, if she could. "How do we do this?"

"Look for the sparks."

Marissa looked around.

There. In the distance, a silver one shone in the darkness. She shot off toward it, her form becoming a lightning bolt. As she drew close, she could *feel* it. She *knew* that feeling. It was Danny.

They connected.

"Marissa!" He hugged her virtually. "What is this place?" He looked around at the darkness.

"No time to explain." It was so good to see him. "Where are you?"

"Hiding out somewhere outside of Darlith."

"We're taking the fight to him."

"Davian?"

"Yes."

"I'd guessed. What do I have to do?"

Marissa was flooded with warmth. She'd always been able to count on him. "Help me find the others. Look for the sparks." She pointed at two in the darkness.

"Gotcha. Stay strong, little sister." He kissed her forehead.

He zipped off, and she did too.

In the end, they gathered twenty of the Liminals, plus Andy.

It would be enough. It had to be.

She didn't want to think about what had happened to the others.

ANDY LOOKED out of the small porthole of the escape capsule. It was déjà vu. This same little vessel had saved her life—and her father's—once before, when Transfer Station had been under attack.

Now they were engaged in another desperate flight, albeit one with more of a purpose and a plan.

She shifted to view things through Marissa's eyes. She'd never ridden with so many others before. The South Pole was coming up quickly, though they probably still had twenty minutes before they arrived.

She hoped the others on the balloon were faring all right.

It was a strange feeling to ride through the tunnel of the storm. It reminded her of the tornado from the old *Wizard of Oz* tri dee, or maybe surfing a giant wave.

Would they crush the Wicked Warlock when they crashed down to earth?

Sometimes she missed tri dee.

The others in the link were all trapped by the storm in various places. They were with her through the bond, twenty-three minds ready to fight the rising tide of Davian's madness.

Shandra squeezed her hand. "You okay?"

"Yeah. Too much to handle for one person. Fortunately, I have you and a couple dozen friends." She kissed Shandra, marveling that this woman had stuck with her through so much.

"Y'all ready with that door key over there?" Eddy's voice came through in stereo, through the radio and via the link with Marissa.

"As ready as we're gonna be." She squeezed Shandra's hand. "Here we go."

Andy closed her eyes and found her father and her Liminal kids. In her mind, they all stood in a circle, taking one another's hands. Andy took Marissa's. "You're the strongest. You take the lead."

Marissa nodded, though she looked a little pale.

"You can do this." She squeezed Marissa's hand in encouragement, just as Shandra had squeezed hers. They had come so far. They would pass this test too.

POWER FLOWED into Marissa from the others, until she was almost bursting. Still, she had to wait.

It filled her like adrenaline, triggering her fight-or-flight response. As her anxiety mounted, she breathed in and out deeply, slowly, trying to calm her mind and corral her scattered thoughts.

Too soon, and they might risk Davian overpowering them. Too late, and they might smash into the South Pole wall and all would be for naught.

Eddy took her hand. "You guys can do this. I believe in you." He glanced over at her and smiled encouragingly, though his voice cracked a little. He was under incredible strain. They all were.

She *would* do it. They *all* would. She had to. Her unborn child and husband were counting on her.

They had to be passing over the edge of Micavery by now, judging by how close the wall was. The clouds were churning as they collided with the South Pole, kicking up banks of fog to obscure their way.

*Ready?*

A chorus of *Yes!*

She gathered herself and reached.

A barrier lay between her and the lock, strong and invisible, but with the power of twenty-two other minds behind her, she smashed right through it. The world mind might be strong enough to stop her, but she had the element of surprise on her side.

The way into the air lock opened, ponderously slow.

Then something pushed back.

"Is it clear?" Eddy's voice reached her.

"Yes… I think so." She gathered herself and pushed back, but everything was obscured.

"You *think so?*" Eddy sounded panicked. "I can't see a thing through the clouds."

The clouds were suddenly in her own head.

She fought them back, trying to keep them at bay.

They were like the fog that had once trapped her and everyone in Agartha. Davian was trying to take control of her mind.

"Get the fuck away from me!" Marissa hated cursing, but Davian warranted it. She pushed back hard, drawing on the full force behind her. Gasps of pain came through the link, but she couldn't stop. Didn't *dare* stop. "Get the fuck out of my head!"

Suddenly her head was clear. "It's open!" she shouted out loud. "Go!"

She opened her eyes to see Eddy punch it, sending the Moonjumper practically screaming through the clouds.

They cleared out of the way at the last second, revealing a gaping hole in the wall.

Eddy adjusted their course, and they sailed through it, just missing the edge. "Close it!"

Marissa reached again, and the massive rock walls closed like the mouth of a monster, sealing them in.

She threw open the outer gates as soon as the first ones had closed, and the whoosh of atmosphere pushed the little ship out through the gap with meters to spare.

Marissa collapsed in her seat, exhausted.

"Holy crap, you did it! We did it!" Eddy reversed the thrust of the little craft, slowing it down and then sending it back in the direction from which they had come.

Marissa sat up and looked out through the window of the Moonjumper at the stars. "Oh Ariadne, they're beautiful."

Eddy stared at her, his mouth open. "You've never seen stars." It made total sense, but it was still a stunning thought.

"No. It's... kind of overwhelming."

He nodded. "Even when you've looked at them all your life from Earth, it's different to see them from up here."

She relayed the view to the others in her link, and then turned her attention to the world they had just left.

It was a long, grand spinning tube lit by veins of glowing yellow light. "That's home?"

Eddy nodded. "It is *now*."


SANTI FIRED UP THE BALLOON.

As it lifted off the ground, the Moonjumper did too. Eddy maneuvered it over the escape pod and picked it up.

Santi held his breath.

The jumper ascended, passing the balloon, and rocketed toward the spindle.

Their own climb was slower.

Santi glanced at the onrushing storm clouds. He handed out lengths of rope. "Everyone lash yourself to the gondola. It's going to get rough in a couple minutes."

They had one chance—to get high enough to avoid the worst of the storm.

Matt, Keera, and Sean followed his instructions, and soon they were all tied to the gondola.

"What about you?" Keera asked, her brow furrowed with concern.

"I have to stay here with the burner. I'll be all right." He hoped he was right. Just in case, he gave them a crash course in hot air balloon control.

They were high above the ground now. The shuttle they'd left behind was shrinking to just a small gray dot below.

The first gusts hit them. Thankfully he'd been able to refuel before they'd left. He poured on the flame, taking it as high as it would go as fast as he could, as the wind started to knock them around.

Soon they were enveloped in clouds, and bits of moisture slapped him in the face as the wind pushed them along toward Micavery.

The envelope started to distort, and a few times he had to ratchet back on the flame lest he melt the material, but they rose steadily toward the spindle. "Everyone okay?" he shouted over the rain and thunder.

"So far. We can't take much more of this!" Matt's face was grim.

"We shouldn't have to!"

A particularly nasty gust slammed the gondola, knocking Santi to the side. The world spun by as he flew over the edge. *I'm gonna die.*

Then strong hands caught him, and Sean hauled him back down, anchored by his rope, pulling him back into the gondola.

"Thanks!" Santi tried to slow his breathing. *I almost died.*

Then the darkness lifted as the balloon rose toward the spindle.

"Made it." He turned off the flame.

"I feel a little… weird." Sean put his free hand over his stomach.

"It's zero gee. Or near enough." He grabbed hold of the edge of the gondola and lashed himself down with enough rope to reach the burner. "We've almost reached the spindle, where the centrifugal force is the least."

The balloon's envelope was distorting again. Up was no longer up.

Marissa's baskets started to rise out of the gondola.

Santi pointed. "Grab those!"

Keera got one and Matt the other.

"What do we do now?" Matt asked.

"We wait out the storm."

# 37

# FREEFALL

THERE WERE two bodies.

Jayson tried not to stare at them as the elevator climbed slowly toward the Far Hold. They'd been moving upward for at least half an hour.

A faint stench arose from the man and woman who had died there, making his stomach twist in his gut.

As far as they could tell from the uniforms, the two had been technicians. They had been mortally wounded before stumbling into the elevator, with holes punched in their guts.

He dreaded the scene that would meet them when they reached the top of the climb.

The elevator moved slowly up the cable. It was really old-school—mechanical and slow, but it looked sturdy as hell. Colin had apparently had a thing about biominds—understandable, after the *Dressler* and what Jayson himself had done to Transfer Station when he'd been under the control of the Chafs. Only a minor miracle had prevented major loss of life there. He had that to be thankful for. "Why is this thing going so slow?" He glared at the ceiling.

"When it slammed into the stair railing, I think the shock mangled the pulley system. We're lucky it can move at all."

Jayson growled. "I wonder what happened up there?"

Aaron glanced at the two bodies, then looked up at the ceiling. "Nothing good."

"I'd guess you're right—" The elevator lurched to a halt. "What the hell?"

There was a snapping sound.

Jayson stared at the ceiling, his brow furrowed. "What was that?"

"*That* was the sound of a cable breaking. We need to get out of here." Aaron looked around wildly.

"I don't think I can reach the ceiling hatch."

"No need. Give me your walking stick."

Jayson handed it over.

The elevator dropped two feet, and Jayson's stomach did the same.

Aaron stuck the stick between the doors. "Quickly, help me pry these open."

An ominous groan came from somewhere up above. "Come on!"

They threw their weight against the stick, forcing the door open.

The elevator shuddered.

"Go!" Aaron pushed him toward the opening.

"No, you go first. Keera and Sean need you."

"Don't argue. Go!" Aaron all but shoved him out the door.

"All right!" Jayson grabbed the rail and scrambled over it.

As he fell hard onto the staircase, the elevator dropped another ten feet.

"Aaron!" He scrambled down the staircase three steps at a time, wincing at the pain in his tired legs. *I won't lose you again.*

He reached the still open doors.

Aaron had fallen to the floor inside. He scrambled up, and Jayson reached out his arms. "Give me your hands!"

Aaron reached out for him and their hands connected. "Pull!"

Jayson did so, and Aaron's body came out halfway before getting stuck on one of the doors.

"Harder!"

Jayson heaved, but Aaron was jammed. "Can you turn sideways?"

"I'll try." Aaron squirmed around, managing to twist his torso, and all at once he came free.

They tumbled back against the wall just as the cable snapped, the broken part slamming into the rock just inches from Jayson's face and sending the elevator plunging down the shaft.

Jayson breathed a heavy sigh of relief. "Fuck, that was close."

Aaron laughed nervously. "I owe you one, little brother." He looked up. "At least we got a bit closer to the top."

THE MOONJUMPER CRUISED along the edge of Forever, out of reach of Davian and the world mind. Marissa and Andy had dissolved the link, fearful that Davian might be able to use it to get at the others or find out where they were.

Marissa stared at the world in wonder. It was long and cylindrical, with a great round sail fanning out from one end.

She knew, intellectually, that she lived inside a living ship that was headed out to the stars. But until now, those had been just words in her head. Even the simulations Andy and Shandra had shown them as kids paled next to the reality of the starry void.

Out here, she really could see Forever. There was nothing but a thin wall of plasform between her and eternity.

Off in the distance, one star was larger than all the rest. "Is that the sun?"

Eddy nodded. "The star that gave birth to us all."

"It must be so far away. It feels strange to think I'll never see it up close."

Eddy laughed. "You'd get quite a sunburn."

"Sunburn?" She wasn't familiar with the concept.

"The UV rays. Even through Earth's atmosphere, they could burn your skin if you were out under the sun too long without protection."

"Ah." Life had been so strange on Earth.

"So… how are we going to get through that?" Eddy pointed at the glowing translucent sail that extended for a hundred kilometers in each direction from the "north" end of Forever.

"Better ask Andy." The sails captured space dust and funneled it into the world, expelling it on the other side to build up velocity. They were also propelled by solar winds. They'd spent weeks studying the world's propulsion systems at the schoolhouse.

She sat back to enjoy this once-in-a-lifetime flight through the heavens.

"ANDY?" EDDY opened the radio connection. "Everything cozy over there?"

"Good so far. Gorgeous view you have up here."

He grinned. "Thanks. Hey, listen, see that big sail up ahead?"

"Yeah."

"So...."

"How do we get through it?"

"Um, yeah." They were going to need a solution sooner than later.

"I'd say just punch through."

Eddy stared at the radio. "Punch through?"

"Yes. It'll heal."

"You sure about that?"

"Pretty much? Let's say 95 percent. It's made to self-repair in the event of meteor strikes. Do we have enough fuel to go around it?"

He checked the gauge. "Not even close. Nor the time, judging from the storm we left behind."

"Then *through* it is."

"Okay." It was good to be out in space again, free of the confines of Forever for just a few moments. To remember there was something outside the walls of the world. To remember there actually *were* stars.

He hoped Santi was okay, down there on the inside. That was a nasty storm, and his husband's brilliant piloting skills aside, a hot air balloon was no match for it. He closed his eyes and said a quick prayer to whatever deity might be watching over their little world in the depths of the void.

In five more minutes, they were approaching the sail. "Okay, folks, we're getting close. Gonna be punching through in five, four, three, two, one...."

The ships impacted the sail. It slowed their forward momentum with a gut-wrenching jerk but then ripped apart, letting them pass through.

"So far so—"

Eddy was wrenched sideways in his seat. "What the hell?"

Something caught his attention out of the corner of his eye. The escape pod had separated from the Moonjumper and was spiraling away into space.

Eddy had a frightening moment of déjà vu. This was too much like his last journey to space.

"Not gonna happen." He wasn't going to lose Andy and Shandra to the void.

Glancing warily at his fuel gauge, he blasted off after them.

. . .

ONE MOMENT the escape pod they were in was attached to the Moonjumper via the x-drive's attractive power, and the next they were spiraling off into the void all alone.

"Oh shit…." Shandra's face was white. "We're gonna die."

Andy took her hand. "Shhhhhh. Close your eyes." Inside her heart was hammering her chest. *Not again.* The last time, *she'd* been sure she would die. This time she was scared to death, but she had to have faith. "Eddy will catch us."

Shandra stared at her, wide-eyed in the dim light of the pod's running lights. "Are you sure?"

She gulped and nodded. "And if not… you're the one I want to be with when the end comes." She hugged Shandra to her.

When they separated, Shandra looked her in the eye. "What aren't you telling me about this plan of yours? You're holding something back."

Andy sighed. Shandra always could see through her. "Truth?"

"Truth."

Andy took a deep breath. "I didn't want you to worry…."

It all came tumbling out.


"OKAY, I need you to reengage the x-drive when I tell you to."

Marissa nodded. "How do I do that?"

"Just push the button here." He indicated the drive button.

"Got it."

Eddy slung the Moonjumper out past the tumbling escape pod, masterfully intercepting its course as Forever shrunk behind them.

It occurred to her that they might all die out here, far from the warmth of the world. *Little one.* She basked in his love for her and cast her doubts side.

Eddy would get them home. She *knew* it, and yet she stared at the fuel gauge nervously as it inched downward.

Eddy opened the radio link. "We're coming for you."

"We're here." Shandra's voice sounded shaken. No big surprise there.

Eddy was matching course and speed with the escape pod now. "They have a little more spin than we do. Nothing I can do about that in the time we have."

Marissa looked down. The little pod was approaching slowly. She could see Andy's face through one of the view ports as it spun by. *We'll catch you.*

"Ready?"

"Ready." Marissa's hand hovered above the x-drive.

"Do it… now!"

Marissa punched the drive and the pod slammed into them, grinding and knocking them sideways as the jumper absorbed the rotation of the other craft.

Eddy fought the spin, firing off the jets to bring them back to stability. At last, he breathed an audible sigh of relief. "Everyone okay over there?"

There was silence. "Yeah, we're okay," Andy said at last over the radio. "Just a little banged up. We have enough fuel to get back?"

Marissa let go of her held breath and the edge of her seat.

Eddy checked the gauge. "Roger, if we're careful."

"Define careful." Andy sounded worried. Andy *hardly ever* sounded worried.

"I'll get us there. Gonna cut the connection. I need to concentrate."

"Roger."

He spun the craft around in a wide arc.

*Smart.* Less fuel waste than trying to brake and change direction.

Forever came back into view. It seemed so far away.

Slowly they headed toward home.


EDDY WATCHED the fuel gauge nervously. They were running dangerously low. The impromptu chase and rescue had used up most of their reserves.

He nudged the little craft and its payload back toward Forever, gauging each thrust and using it to maximum effect.

Bit by bit he nudged them across the space before the great sail, back toward the world itself.

Forever was quite different when seen from this angle. The last asteroid they'd picked up, Isis, had only been partially consumed over the last seven years. Its rocky bulk, along with the sail, made the world look like some great fantastic, gnarly mushroom.

The sail funneled particles down into the sides of Forever, just behind where Isis was attached to the long cylinder that was the body of the world.

"They're like gills," Andy had told him of the intake ports that lined the side of the world. "They lead into the guts of the world—the stomachs that digest the material, and the lungs that sift out the incoming material and also provide the world's breath."

*The world's breath.* There was something wondrous about that thought. *As long as she breathes, we breathe.*

Then another thought hit him. *We're going to kill the world mind. Holy crap, I hope you know what you're doing.*

Eddy surveyed the scene ahead of them. The tear they'd created in the glowing sail was already healing, sewing itself closed as he watched. She was an amazing beast, the world they lived in.

That gave him an idea.

"I want to try something," he said over the radio. "But it's gonna be a bit rough."

"Will it get us inside?" Andy's voice sounded tired and a little forlorn.

"Yes, I think so. I want to use the sail as a ski slope and slide down inside the world. That should leave us enough fuel to maneuver once we're inside. There may be a little bouncing, though."

"Ah."

"I'd like everyone to put their suit helmets on now, please." He pulled his on and made sure it was properly attached.

Then he nudged the ships down toward the sail at a shallow angle and fired two of the jets to send them into a slight roll. "Everyone hold on."

The fuel gauge hovered just a smidge above empty.

The connected craft glided down toward the sail, ever so slowly. As they spun, it would come into view, wrap around the window, and then disappear again behind them in a stately cosmic dance.

The next rotation, the glowing white sail kissed the ships, and they pushed down and then bounced up off the resilient material like a pair of giant rubber balls.

The rotation was making Eddy dizzy. He closed his eyes as they arced up and then back down, bounding closer to the edge of the world. "Everyone okay?"

"A little queasy, but it'll pass." Andy's voice sounded strangely distant. Maybe the connection was bad.

They came down again and bounced once more toward the bottom of the sail, this time a little lower.

Three more times, and they were sliding instead of bouncing.

Eddy opened his eyes to see one of the "gills" looming ahead of them.

Most of the particles captured by the sails were microscopic, but occasionally something a little larger would fall into the lungs for processing.

Andy had described the process in depth. Once they were inside, he'd need to push through the mucus that guarded the interior of the world, dissolving the various bits of space debris it encountered, absorbing them as world-building fodder.

The gills were long, dark slits in the side of the world that ran along the base of the sails, each one about fifty meters wide and maybe twenty high. They were dark inside, the ominous blackness of a monster's maw.

They passed under the edge and the dim light from the sail faded. A gelatinous membrane captured the craft, halting their forward momentum.

Prepared for this, Eddy powered through it, burning the last of their fuel to push the two ships to the other side.

"Everyone out! Don't touch the goo!" Eddy grabbed the last three sticks of gum from under the seat.

They cracked the hatches and climbed out quickly but carefully, avoiding the sticky stuff that covered the two ships.

The lights from inside the two vessels lit up only the rocky space around them and nothing else, but he had the sense that he stood in a wide-open space.

He flicked on the helmet light and shone it over the Moonjumper.

The ship's skin was pitted, a white vapor rising into the air as the world began to digest it.

Andy patted him on the shoulder. "She's not gonna make the museum now."

The sturdy little ship had saved him once, and now maybe twice. It was sad to see her being reduced to her component molecules.

He raised his hand in salute. "Farewell, old friend."

# 38

# BELLY OF THE BEAST

MARISSA SWEPT her helmet lamp up into the air and gasped.

The others followed her gaze.

Something *massive* loomed overhead. It was hard to make it out—a collection of gray ridges and folds something like a crumpled towel. The whole thing expanded and contracted in a slow, rhythmic motion.

"What is it?" she asked over her suit radio.

Andy smiled. "The lungs of the world."

The room lit up, seams of golden light lining the ridges of the lungs. The light illuminated the huge space they were in too. It was formed of rough rock and ran around the full circle of the world. The lungs filled the space, stretching off into the distance, huge beyond belief.

Marissa knew the world was about twenty-six kilometers around, but knowing it and seeing the size of the lungs that filled it were two different things.

Thick roots like tree trunks crossed the intervening space at regular intervals, plunging into the rock on the other side of the gap.

"They're beautiful." What an amazing world she lived in. How *alive* it was. "How can we kill this?"

"And what will happen if we do?" Eddy was frowning up at the lungs.

Shandra looked worried.

"Let's get there first." Andy turned away and headed back in the direction of the rest of Forever.

The others followed her under the overhanging lungs.

Marissa stared up at them, as she approached close enough to touch them. She reached out, wishing she weren't wearing the suit. "Is the air here breathable?"

Andy shook her head. "I don't know. My guess is that it's pretty stale. The suit's rebreather makes it passable, but I wouldn't take a chance without it."

The ground rose up around them into parallel channels. In the middle of each channel, a deeper rut led down the center of the floor.

Liquid from the sticky barrier flowed down the channel, carrying half-dissolved bits of the ships.

There was no way back now.

Andy touched the ground and pointed to one of the channels. "This way."

They entered the U-shaped pathway, and soon the walls rose overhead to meet above them, creating a tunnel.

Marissa wondered how the world mind had built all these structures. The scale of this place, the intricate detail of Forever… it was stunning. "Can he… sense us here?"

Andy, walking just ahead of her, shook her helmet. "We're in the belly of the beast now. Unless we do something active, he'll have no idea we're here."

"What about when we *need* to do something active?"

"Then we'll test out your father's little dead zone trick."

The tunnel was straight. There was enough space on either side of the smaller channel for them to walk. There was nothing flowing through their passageway now.

"Are these tunnels ever full?" Eddy asked, sounding as in awe as she was.

"Only when the world needs to process a lot of debris." Andy's voice sounded tinny over the com. "Out here in the void between the stars, it's unlikely."

After a ten-minute hike, they came to the end of the tunnel. Their helmet lights showed a man-sized closed three-part valve, like a pie chart but a little twisted.

Andy put her hand against it, and in a moment, it spiraled open, revealing a large space beyond that shone with a golden glow. "These valves open all the time." Andy answered the question Marissa hadn't asked. "He won't notice."

They stepped through.

Marissa gasped at the sight.

The room was a huge cavern, maybe a hundred meters wide and twice as long. Other valves lined the wall along the near side, and one of them was open, dumping the remnants of their transportation into the golden lake.

Where the two met, the glowing liquid churned and steamed.

"It's one of the stomachs." It was huge, and it was one of probably hundreds.

Andy nodded. "Very good. Follow me along the outer edge, and try not to fall in. The liquid's not as corrosive as the barrier, but it can still peel your skin off with a bit of time."

Marissa shivered. *Belly of the beast indeed.*

They followed the rim of the cavern. This was the kind of place where Ana had died, when Andy's own father had transferred her into the world mind.

There was a deep rumbling and an explosion loud enough to be heard through the helmet.

Marissa spun around to see a huge bubble rise to the surface and burst about fifty meters away. She lost her balance and started to slip down the short slope toward the golden liquid.

"No you don't." Andy grabbed her by the arm and hauled her back up to the pathway, pulling her back hard against the rock face of the cavern.

*Geez, that was close.* Marissa was breathing heavily. "Thanks," she managed.

"Looks like our ships gave her a bit of indigestion."

"Do you think Ana and the others…. Did they survive?"

Andy frowned. "I don't know. We'll find out once we get there. You okay to keep going?"

Marissa could see the concern on Andy's face. "Yeah. I'm fine." She reached for Colin, and a reassuring wave of warmth and love came back in return. "Yeah, I'm good."


EDDY WATCHED Andy and Marissa as they made their way around the strange cavern.

There was something beautiful in the way Andy cared for the girl—well, young woman now—something maternal. Andy and Shandra had never had kids, but the Liminals *were* their children, in every way that mattered.

It was bizarre to be wandering around in the guts of the world. Intellectually he'd known they were here, but he'd never thought to actually find himself inside them. How different this place was from Old Earth. Humans were like bacteria—or maybe parasites—in the belly of this great world.

As they reached the far side of the stomach cavern, Andy touched the wall again. There were valves there, too, but they were both fewer and larger than the one they had entered through.

"How are we going to get up to the world mind? That's got to be a good four kilometers above us, give or take."

Andy nodded. "We're going to fly."

"Seriously?" He looked around at the four of them. "We have no wings. Unless you're hiding a pair under that suit of yours."

She turned to stare at him through her visor and grinned, something that sent chills through him.

"I'm not going to like what you have planned, am I?"

She turned away. "Probably not."

ANDY CHOSE one of the valves and opened it. She was going on feel alone, but it hadn't guided her wrong yet.

Her father had taught her how to do this, tapping into the low-level neural systems without alerting the world mind. It was a controlled form of dipping.

The other side held another tunnel, but these ones were made of an organic material, intended to shuttle the digested stomach fluid to various parts of the world's body. "We need to hurry."

"Why?" Shandra asked.

"Because once these valves open, the stomach contracts and pumps the fluid through them. I'm guessing we have about two minutes before we're part of the stomach stew." She led the way inside, and they ran about thirty feet before she stopped them.

She pulled out a knife from her pack and started to hack at the lining of the tunnel.

Behind them, an ominous rumbling commenced.

The tunnel wall was thicker than she'd anticipated. They had to cut their way out to get to the air tubes and to escape Forever's digestive system, and if she couldn't make a big enough exit in time, this whole mission was for naught.

The rumbling increased behind them.

"Andy…." Shandra's voice sounded worried.

"Almost there." She strained at it with both hands, and at last she broke through muscle and sinew. She worked the knife downward to enlarge the opening, and the skin peeled away, leaving a gash that she purposefully extended toward the ground.

Behind them, fluid started to gush into the tunnel.

"Got it. Marissa, go!" She all but pushed the girl through the hole, glancing back at the onrushing fluid. "Shandra, go!"

Shandra dove through, followed by Eddy, who struggled but then squeezed through the gash.

Andy was last to go. She was halfway out when the wave hit her.

Panicked, she managed to slosh her way through, slipping out onto the hard ground on the other side, covered in the digestive fluid.

She ripped off her helmet and threw it, stepping clear of the growing puddle of fluid. "Stay away!" She held out her hand in warning.

She peeled off the suit and jumped out of it, turning to see the gash she'd cut in the tube closing up, shutting off the flow of fluid.

The suit lay in the puddle of intestinal fluid, slowly sagging. It did take time for the stomach juices to break things down. Her father had stood in them for ten minutes, but of course they'd been diluted then by water inflow.

Her carry sack was a total loss.

Eddy levered off his own helmet. He sniffed the air curiously. "Is it safe to breathe in here?"

"Should be."

Eddy nodded. "Are you okay?"

"Close call. But I'll live." Andy had experienced too many of those on this journey. One of them was bound to be a little too close. And then….

She cut off that line of thought. She looked around at the narrow cavern. They'd come out on the other side of the lungs, which glowed above them with lines of golden light.

The feeder tubes branched out and extended along the floor and up into the darkness above. Another set of parallel tubes climbed the far wall.

She pointed at them. "Those are the air pipes. They will carry us up to the world mind." She looked back at her things, dissolving in the golden puddle. "Anyone have another knife?"

. . .

THE STORM HAD FINALLY BLOWN itself out.

As first light flared past them, Santi let the hot air balloon drift down toward the ground.

Darlith lay below them. The town was in tatters. The stronger buildings, built out of rock, had survived, though many had their roofs ripped off.

The wooden buildings were destroyed.

As they drifted down, the extent of the damage became clearer. The Rhyl River had overrun its banks, and the streets were flooded.

"Where are all the people?" Matt stared down at the disaster scene beneath them.

"Did he kill them all?" Keera's hand went to her mouth, and her eyes were wide.

"No, look." Aaron pointed at the town hall, a sturdy brick building on a hill above the rest of the town. A door had opened, and people the apparent size of ants were coming out.

They walked in perfect lines like an army.

"He still owns them." Keera frowned. "Probably didn't want his army of slaves harmed."

"We should steer clear of them. I'll take us on toward Micavery." Santi fired up the balloon, and they lifted higher in the air.

"Shouldn't they have gotten there by now?" Matt asked, looking toward the North Pole.

"Maybe they were delayed." Santi didn't want to say what they were all thinking. *Maybe they failed.*

As they watched, the people below started moving out in teams of six, still perfectly aligned, toward the piles of rubble nearest to the town hall.

"They're like toys to him." Keera glared at the scene below.

"What if...?" Sean asked.

"Don't even think that. They'll find a way." Santi too looked back toward the North Pole. *Where are you, Eddy?*


DAVIAN STARED out at the ruins of Darlith through the eyes of one of his vassals. The city had taken quite a beating. The Rhyl had flooded, washing away the buildings closest to the shore, and the winds and lightning had destroyed about half the remaining structures.

It didn't matter. Soon, his people would have the streets cleaned, and he could set them to building a more appropriate city suited to his new rule.

He'd sacrificed a lot, giving up his corporeal form, but he'd discovered he could still enjoy the pleasures of the flesh through these puppets he now controlled. He planned to take full advantage of that, now that his enemies had been vanquished by the cleansing power of the hurricane.

And if they came back?

He smiled. It was too late to stop him. They would become more cogs in his great machine.

Life had never been sweeter for him. Even after death.

## 39

## SEEDLING

Marissa produced a knife from her sack. "Will this do?"

Andy took it and looked it over. "Nicely, I think."

Marissa stared at the breathing tubes. There were hundreds of them, running up the wall as far as she could see around the curve of the world. Each of them vibrated slightly. She tried to imagine the huge volumes of air they were capable of moving. "So we're going to ride the air... up there?" She pointed up into the darkness.

The tubes let off a faint glow, but it wasn't enough to illuminate the space above them for more than a few hundred meters.

Andy nodded. "Come on! The longer we wait, the more he consolidates his control." She led them over to the row of tubes. Each was about two meters wide.

Marissa touched one of them. It was soft, like leather, but tough. "What's to stop us from being blown out four thousand meters above the ground?"

Andy laughed. "Were you paying attention in your Ariadne anatomy course?"

"I guess not. Was there a part where we talked about flying up its air tubes?"

"It'll be fine. Trust me."

Marissa glanced over at Eddy. Even he looked a little green at the prospect, and he flew spacecraft. She swallowed hard.

"Okay, stand back. There's going to be a bit of air pressure when I cut this thing open." She made a neat slice and air gushed out in a steady, strong breeze. "Okay, Eddy, you first. Climb in, and I'll seal it behind you. Keep your arms at your sides, but be ready to catch yourself when you reach the top."

Eddy shook his head. "I don't know. Are you sure about this? Ever tried it before?"

"Ridden up to the North Pole control center on a puff of air inside one of the world's air pipes? Nope. First time." She pointed at the gap. "Keep your arms flat at your sides and pretend you're a superhero. Now go!"

He shrugged and forced his way inside, through the air stream. The wind pushed his hair back, but he grabbed the sides of the tube and managed to climb inside.

Andy pushed the gap closed, and it began to heal immediately.

Eddy's shoes shot up out of sight as the gap closed. There was a slight bulge in the tube as he rose.

"Okay, your turn." Andy pointed the knife at Marissa.

Marissa smiled, trying to cover up her fear. "You don't have to threaten me."

Andy hugged her. "It will be all right. I promise." She moved to the next tube and sliced it open.

Marissa pushed her way inside, and immediately the pressure started to lift her up. As Andy sealed the tube, she ascended, and the walls of the tube passed her by at a rapid pace. She kept her hands at her sides, as instructed.

Every ten or twenty meters—it was hard to tell exactly at the speed she was moving—a dark ring constricted the tube, and she counted these as she ascended. Her fear gave way to a sense of wonder as she reached fifty, then a hundred, and then lost count altogether.

It was like flying.

She wondered if Andy and Shandra were on the way up too yet, and what they would all find at the top.

In what was probably less than ten minutes but felt like an hour, the tube walls suddenly brightened, and in seconds she was thrust up and out of the air tube and into a vast white cavern.

As she fell helplessly toward one of the walls, she windmilled her arms, trying madly to break her fall.

. . .

EDDY TRIED TO STAND. Gravity was weak to nonexistent up here, and the soft surface he found himself on was really difficult to navigate on foot. The irregular white wall extended in a large sphere from where he stood out around him, and it expanded and contracted steadily. With each contraction, a gust of air was pushed out through its membranes, forcing air up through his clothes.

It was a disconcerting sensation. Eddy felt like Marilyn standing over the Manhattan subway grate, an image that had endured long past the city that had fostered it.

The open space encircled a thick rock column in the center.

As he tried to stand for the third time, Marissa came flying out of one of the tubes and then soared toward him, shouting, her arms flailing.

She slammed into the white surface, and the shouting stopped.

"Hey there… you okay?"

"I… think so?" She sat up. "What is this?" She looked around.

"The top of the lungs, I think. So… the throat?" It seemed as good an analogy as any.

Shandra came flying out, but she took it like a pro, pivoting end over end to land easily a short distance away. "So this is what the top of the world looks like, huh?"

Eddy grinned. Then he remembered what was going on outside. How many of his friends were injured? "Where's Andy?"

As if in response, she flew out of another tube and landed close by. "Everyone okay?" She got up and dusted herself off.

"Yeah, I think so?" Marissa looked around. "This is… so strange."

"Kinda *Journey to the Center of the Earth*."

"Huh?" Marissa looked confused.

"Before your time." Eddy laughed. "So?"

"Now we go up there." Andy pointed to the rock cylinder above. She started climbing, pulling her way up hand over hand across the material of the lungs.

Eddy and the others followed.


AS SHE CLIMBED, Andy's heart beat faster. It was all coming to a head—soon it would be over.

If all went to plan.

She had to admire the simple beauty of Lanya's idea and the poetic justice of it.

Shandra had been frightened at first, but she'd come around.

Andy glanced back at her. Shandra gave her a reassuring smile. Her expression said *it has to be done.*

The lungs beneath Andy contracted and expanded, reminding her of the great life-form she lived inside. Compared to its massive scale, she was just a gnat crawling on an elephant's back.

They approached the rock column that housed the control center and the world mind. The roughly cylindrical chunk of black rock was pierced in numerous places by thick nerve cables that connected the mind to the rest of its systems and sank down into the material of the throat and lungs.

Andy arrived at the closest of them and reached out to grab it. Here it really was zero gee, and she was able to pull herself along it with ease.

The others followed.

She approached the rock face. A bundle of nerves came together ahead of her, and there was enough room to crawl through the space between them.

She reached the narrow entrance and turned around to face the others. "Marissa, can you make us a null space?"

Marissa nodded. She closed her eyes and concentrated.

The world around Andy went dull.

She gritted her teeth at the annoying sensation and started into the narrow tunnel.

JAYSON AND AARON reached the top of the stairs. They had diverged from the shaft about fifty steps before, and the stairway had ended on a landing. Now they were at the entrance to the Far Hold, and he stopped to catch his breath.

What would they find on the other side of the door?

*Nothing good.*

"Ready?" He looked over at Aaron.

Aaron grasped his arm. Their eyes met. "Whatever happens."

Jayson nodded. "Whatever happens."

He took one last deep breath and opened the door.

. . .

MARISSA CRAWLED out of the end of the tunnel after Andy, letting go of the null space she had created. The time for secrecy had passed.

She stood up and looked around the wide-open space. It was maybe a hundred meters tall, and the walls were beautifully sculpted in a dizzying array of swirls and fanciful lines that shone with a golden glow as they wound up toward the ceiling.

And high above…

The world mind hung over them, the bundles of nerves running up to find their termination there.

Andy and Eddy stood beside her, staring up at the wonder that had kept their world humming along for half a century and that now threatened everything they had built.

The room shimmered and changed.

"I was wondering what had happened to you all."

Marissa turned to find Davian, dressed all in black and seated on a throne made of skulls.

"Very theatrical." Andy laughed harshly. "I would have expected more from you, though. No heads on spikes?"

He climbed down from the throne, crunching bone underfoot on the way. "How did you get here? I have to admit, you three managed to surprise me."

"You left your back door open."

"Well, thank you for that. I'll have to close that little loophole."

He reached out and touched Andy's face, and electricity raced through his arm. Andy stiffened, her face tightening into a rictus of pain.

"Let her go." Marissa was done with being intimidated by this man. He'd stolen her childhood. He'd attacked her and her family twice.

Davian turned to look at her, still holding on to Andy.

Andy's eyes were bulging now.

"I remember you. You've really grown into quite the young woman." He let go of Andy, and she collapsed on the ground, gasping and holding her throat. "I gave up a lot to become mankind's savior." He shrugged, looking her up and down. "The pleasures of the flesh, for instance."

Marissa snarled. "We don't need your help."

He smiled, an expression that set her teeth on edge. "It's for the greater good. Who else could guide us to our new home *and* ensure we don't all kill ourselves before we get there?"

"We were doing just fine without you."

"For now, maybe. But look what men did to Earth." He took her hand. "You have to admit they made quite a mess of things."

He had a point.

She shook her head, casting out his words. He was working his charm on her. "It's not—"

He reached out and caressed her cheek, and his virtual touch sent a shiver through her very real body. "There are *ways* for me to still enjoy the flesh. You could join me. We could run this world *together*."

She recoiled from him. He meant he would *use* some poor soul's body. "There's not a chance in hell I'd ever be with *you*." She pushed him, and he fell backward, crashing into his throne of skulls and shattering it into dust.

Andy stood and took her hand. They looked at each other, and Marissa nodded.

Their minds united. As Davian stood, they reached into vee space, seeking out Aaron and Sean and all the others.

As they connected, one by one, Marissa swelled with power.

Davian dusted himself off. He glared at her and advanced toward two of them, sparks flying from his hands.

She took her own spark and pushed it outward, creating a space around herself that he couldn't penetrate.

Davian slammed into it hard, making it shake, but he couldn't break through. He pushed against it, but Marissa pushed back, knocking him against the wall of the throne room once again.

He jumped up and his face darkened. His entire body turned as black as the void, and he ran forward, rage in his eyes, to batter the bubble she'd created around herself.

He slammed into it, and the shock waves sent her and Andy flying backward.


THE DOOR OPENED onto a small room cut out of the rock, next to the elevator doors. Flashing lights revealed streaks of blood on the walls. Jayson glanced at Aaron. His brother's mouth was set in a grim line.

Aaron hissed. "These poor people. They didn't deserve this."

They followed the access tunnel up to the main control room. Jayson had been there years before, on a visit with Aaron.

The place was a slaughterhouse. The equipment, all irreplaceable from Old

Earth and painstakingly cared for, was smashed to bits. But worse was the human toll. Bodies had been punctured and ripped limb from limb, some almost unrecognizable.

Jayson covered his mouth to stifle a sob.

The people hadn't had a chance. Davian had come after them with no apparent warning, striking with surgical precision.

Someone else entered the room from another passageway.

"Shandra?" Jayson couldn't believe his eyes.

"Jayson! Aaron!" The relief on her face was palpable. She rushed to Jayson and gave him a hug. "How... how did you two get up here?"

"I could ask you the same. Who else is here?"

"Andy, Marissa, and Eddy. Andy sent me to find something Lanya left behind."

Aaron gave her a brief hug. "Where are they?"

"Down there, with the world mind." She pointed down the hallway from where they had come.

Jayson nodded. "Let's go."

He and Aaron hurried down the tunnel, stepping over the bodies of the dead.

They came out into the vast room that held the world mind. It was curiously untouched.

Andy and Marissa stood in the middle of the room holding hands, transfixed by something.

Eddy was there too. He turned toward them, and his face broke out into a wide grin. "Oh Lordy, you guys have no idea how glad I am to see you."

"They're in vee?"

He nodded. "With Davian."

Jayson took his brother's hand. "Let's go get him."

He dipped—the way to the world mind was open there. They stepped through.


MARISSA SQUEEZED Andy's hand and they leaned forward, pushing back against Davian.

He hit her shield again, his eyes blazing, and forced them back once more.

"Geez, he's strong." She drew on the power from her bonds and pushed back, slamming into him just as he powered forward again, into her null space shield.

The world exploded in light.

The walls of the throne room shattered outward, crashing to the ground and revealing a dark sky above.

The three of them stood facing each other across a black plain as lightning and thunder crashed in the background.

It was time to take this fight to him.

Marissa dropped her shield and let go of Andy's hand. She no longer needed the physical contact to maintain the link. They were fully inside vee space now.

She stepped forward and put out her hand, and pure blue lines of force extended toward Davian, writhing like living things.

He stood and met her force with his own, his power blazing red and gold.

She drew more from her bond. The beginnings of pain flared through the connection, but she ignored it.

This was too important. They could lick their wounds when they were done.

She pushed hard, and Davian staggered back a step.

Then he dug in, pushing the virtual ground into a hill behind his feet, and pushed back with such strength that he forced her back, step by step, across the dark plain.

Now the pain burned through the link more acutely.

The Liminals were nearing their limits. It wasn't going to be enough. Davian was too strong, too entrenched in the world mind, and they were human, whatever else they might be.

She dropped the lines of power and sought to shield herself. She cut the bond and threw Andy out of vee space, leaving herself alone to face Davian's wrath. She threw up a zone of null space.

Davian grinned, continuing his assault, forcing her null space shield back toward her as he squeezed it smaller and smaller. She crouched, defying him.

She held on, but now the pain ripped across her own mind.

Inside her, her unborn child protested too, his mental wail seared through her mind.

It couldn't end this way.

. . .

"Why don't you pick on someone a little older?" Jayson taunted his old Master.

Davian turned his attention away from Marissa, whom he had trapped in a ball of coruscating red-and-gold energy.

*Damn, he's strong.*

Davian stared at him. "I hoped you would come." A leer stretched across his face. Then Davian's face changed, becoming Lanya's. "Yes, we're all here," the apparition said in Lanya's voice. "I *own* them all now, their thoughts, their memories, their very *souls*." He shifted again, this time appearing as Colin, but a twisted version of the man who'd given everything for this world. Colin had never sneered like that. "There's no one here left to oppose me this time. I learned a little something from our last round." His face shifted once more, and he was Davian again. "One last chance. Serve me, and I'll let you rule this world at my side."

"We can fight him," Aaron whispered at his side. "We have to fight him."

Jayson stared at the man who had owned *him* for so long. It was all coming back to him now. This was the moment he'd been waiting for, his last chance.

Jayson pushed Aaron backward and went to kneel before Davian, bowing his head. "I accept." He was clear, calm. This was the thing he needed to do.

"What the hell are you doing?" He felt Aaron reach for him, but it was too late. Since the day he'd agreed to that fateful weekend that had changed everything.

Davian put his hand on Jayson's head, and that familiar rush of submission flowed over him.

"Welcome home." Davian gloated. "I knew you would come back to your place."

Jayson closed his eyes. It was time. "I did too." He reached up to grasp Davian's arm, and *pulled*.

Davian's face went red with rage. "What the hell are you doing? Let me go!"

Jayson got up and continued to *pull*. He would take it all inside of him. All of the world mind. What would happen next, he had no idea, but he doubted he could hold so much raw power.

Davian shrieked as his very substance started to melt, his *essence* breaking apart and flowing toward Jayson. "We could do so much together."

Jayson shook his head. "You've suffered too long. It's time to end this."

Davian's essence flooded into him, and along with it those of Lanya and Colin. "My mother and father believed in God. I never really took to their religion. But they believed in something else too. Redemption."

Davian stuttered, trying to respond, and then his face started to split into a hundred pieces, golden light shining through the cracks. His hands reached up to his face, and his mouth opened in a silent scream.

His fingers clawed at his cheeks, peeling off the skin to reveal a shimmering light beneath. Then he started to collapse, his fingers falling off, his shoulders slumping, his entire body falling down in a thousand pieces that formed a sparkling dust. Then that too was swept up into the tide that flowed into Jayson.

Jayson fell to his knees, glowing with the light of a sun, his skin almost translucent.

"What did you do?" Aaron knelt before him, putting a hand on his cheek, lifting his face gently.

Jayson was filled with lightness and dark, and his whole body thrummed with energy. It was too much. He stared into Aaron's eyes, pleading for understanding. "I freed him. For my kids."

Aaron nodded. "I know." His eyes were wet. "What now?"

Marissa had been freed from her imprisonment. She knelt next to him too and threw her arms around him. "You're going away, aren't you?"

"It's too much." He was five people. No, six. A part of Jackson was there too. And... Glory? "Mom? Dad?" He started to shake. All of a sudden he was six years old again, lost in the park, and his parents were there to find him. To take him home.

He looked at Marissa through the blinding brightness. "I can see them. Mom and Dad."

"Of course you can." Marissa kissed his cheek.

"Tell the others... I loved them." He touched her belly in wonder. "Your child... he's going to be something extraordinary."

She smiled, but it didn't reach her eyes. "You think so?"

"Glory told me."

Aaron hugged him, and so did Marissa.

"I'm going home," he whispered in Aaron's ear, and his brother squeezed him harder.

Then he let go. With one last lopsided grin, he followed his parents into the light.

. . .

JAYSON GREW BRIGHTER AND BRIGHTER. Then his body vanished in a flash of light that would have blinded her in the real world.

When the light faded, he was gone.

She hugged her uncle, and they both cried. "He's gone," she managed through sobs.

"Yes." He looked back at the space where Jayson had been. "He did this for us. For you. Hold on to that."

She nodded and looked up. The dark world around her shimmered and melted, the sky withdrawing like a receding fog. Then they were standing in the real world once more, in the middle of the room that held the world mind.

Eddy sat against the wall, holding Andy's head in his lap. He looked up at her.

"Is she okay?" She knelt next to Andy.

"I think so. Check on Jayson and Shandra." He pointed across the room.

"Jayson's gone." Marissa knelt by her father's body. His eyes were closed, and he looked like he was finally fully at peace. She knelt and gave him a quick kiss on the forehead. "I love you."

Then she went to Shandra, who lay with her leg at an odd angle. Marissa knelt next to her. She was still breathing. "I think she's going to be okay." There was a dark patch on her left temple. Marissa touched it. It was warm. "It looks like her loop burned out. What was she doing?"

Eddy pointed toward the ceiling.

Marissa looked up. The world mind was dead. It was gray, sagging between its supports.

"She killed it." Andy sat up, rubbing her temple.

"How?" The full impact of that statement hit her. The world mind was *dead*.

Which meant they were all dead too. It was only a matter of time. Jayson's sacrifice had been for nothing.

"An altered fungus, like the one that killed the *Dressler*. This one was engineered by Lanya to kill the world mind, before it took her over entirely." Andy stood and staggered over to Shandra. She turned her lover over gently and caressed her forehead. "Shandra, it's time."

Shandra's eyes flickered open. "Okay. I'm ready."

Marissa's eyes narrowed. "Time for what?"

"Time for the end."


SANTI FLEW the balloon low over Micavery. It was the same as in Darlith, people in groups of six working to clear the debris in a robotic fashion. He watched the antlike hordes in despair.

It was over. Eddy and the others must have lost. Or been lost.

"I don't know what to do." He looked at the others. "There's nowhere else to go. If—"

"Look." Sean pointed down at the city.

Santi looked back down, and one by one, the people started clutching their heads and collapsing.

Keera grabbed her skull and screamed. She dropped to the bottom of the gondola, writhing in pain, and then went still.

"What in Forever is happening?" Sean knelt next to his mother, checking her pulse. "She's knocked out."

"It's the loop." Matt knelt next to him. "Look."

The skin over her loop had darkened.

"Holy shit, something burned it out!" Santi looked north. "I think Eddy and the others did it. They made it!"

Matt looked up at him, his eyes filled with hope. "They made it?"

Santi nodded. "I'm taking us down."


"WHAT DO YOU MEAN THE END?" Marissa was frowning at Andy. "The end came when we killed the world mind."

Andy closed her eyes. Sending Shandra for the fungus that Lanya had left for them in the replicator in the Far Hold control center had been easy enough. Though with the dead bodies there, it had likely been a grisly task.

Marissa had kept Davian distracted while Shandra climbed the walls to deliver the death blow via a syringe. Now came the hard part.

Andy lifted Shandra up off the ground carefully and stood, unsteady on her feet. "This way."

"What's going on?" Eddy looked confused.

"I'll show you." She left the room, following the hallway that led up toward the command center.

The others followed.

Partway there, she turned down a different passageway.

At the end of the short hall, there was another room, about the same size as the one that had held the world mind.

In its center, on the ground, was a seed. Andy laid a hand on it. "Thank you, Lanya." Then she lay Shandra down next to it. "You okay?"

Shandra looked up at her and smiled. "Yes."

*God, I love you.* Andy stood and ran her hands over its rough surface. *This* was what Lanya had shown her. Her destiny. Hers and Shandra's.

Marissa followed them into the room, and her hand flew to her mouth. "Is that...."

Andy nodded. "I need you to help me." She was calm, collected.

"No. No, I can't do it." She turned to Eddy. "Don't make me do it."

Eddy looked confused. "Do what?"

Andy smiled sadly. "Transfer Shandra and me into the new world mind." There was no more time to hide, to delay, to equivocate.

"I can't...."

Andy took Marissa into her arms. "Yeah you can, baby." She brushed Marissa's long hair away from her face. "It's okay. It's what has to happen next."

"You *knew*." Marissa's voice was raw. It was an accusation.

Andy didn't take offense. "Yes."

Marissa shook her head. "It's not right. There *must* be someone else—"

"Who? You? You have a baby. Eddy? He can't do it alone." She squeezed Marissa's hands. "There isn't anyone else. It has to be us. And it has to be you. It has to be you who does it. I wouldn't want anyone else to shepherd my soul."

Marissa took a deep breath and sighed.

Andy squeezed her tightly.

Eddy's cheeks were wet. "Are you sure?"

Andy turned to him. "I wasn't before. But I am now."

He nodded and hugged her. "Gonna miss you, kiddo."

"You too." She sat down, next to Shandra. "Let's get this over with."

MARISSA KNELT NEXT to the two women who were the closest thing she had to parents. "I love you both." She kissed their cheeks.

They both took her hand. "We love you too." Shandra's eyes met hers, and they were full of love.

There was nothing else to say. Marissa touched the seed and closed her eyes.

She could do this. She *had* to do this.

And then it came to her. Maybe, just maybe, there was another way.

She reached into Shandra and Eddy, and then into the seed, and opened herself up as a conduit. She braced herself for the tidal wave, but instead, it was like a cool stream current.

Andy and Shandra's memories flowed through her:

*The day they first met on their way to Agartha.*

*The founding of the schoolhouse.*

*A thousand small moments with the children.*

*Andy creating her sculptural art.*

*Shandra walking along the beach with her mother as a child on Earth.*

*Andy holding Marissa in her arms.*

It lasted for an eternity, and for a single moment. Still, it wrung her out and left her drained.

When it was over, when the last memory passed through her, she closed her eyes. *It's done.*

She collapsed into unconsciousness.


ANDY OPENED HER EYES.

She was in a dark place, but then it lit up. It was formless, a gray netherworld, waiting for shape and substance.

Shandra lay next to her.

"Hey." She nudged Shandra.

"What?" Shandra opened her eyes and sat up. "Where are we?"

"I think we're inside the seed." As she looked around, the gray started to take on some kind of structure. She stretched, grew, extended out. If she concentrated, she could feel her body enlarging, sinking roots into the rock floor and walls.

*Their body.*

She and Shandra were in this together.

"We did it!" Shandra laughed, and the sound dispelled all of Andy's sadness.

"Yes, we did!" She wrapped her arms around Shandra, and they dissolved into the seed mind, merging and becoming one. Their energy swirled around inside the seed as it grew and flew along its roots as it dug into and became a part of Forever. They sprouted lungs and veins and breathed in, taking up the fresh sweet air and expelling it into the world. They found their stomachs and appropriated them, adding them to their growing self.

And then they found something unexpected. A gift left behind, inside the seed, by the previous Immortals. Who, as it turned out, hadn't been so immortal after all. A memory.

Lanya's serene face stared at the two of them. They were neither male nor female but something different. "The time has come. We have all been given far more than we hoped, more time in this life than is offered to most of humankind."

Colin nodded. "I don't know if Jackson is right about the whole afterlife thing. I suppose we're about to find out. Davian is back, but you, my dear Andy, have no doubt found the way to defeat him."

"We are content. Now it's your turn to carry the torch for a little while." Lanya held out a spark.

They took it. Then Lanya's and Colin's ghosts were gone.

Andy and Shandra looked closely at the spark, and it expanded and unfolded in their mind. Encoded in it were all the memories of Lanya and Ana and Colin and Lex, and of Jackson, Andy's grandfather.

They held them up to look at them all—glorious gossamer things.

Although the other Immortals had passed on, a piece of them remained behind.

SANTI BROUGHT the balloon down as close as he could to the center of Micavery. As soon as they were down, he sprang out and tied the balloon to the closest post, along the front of the general store.

Keera groaned.

"Mom? Are you okay?" Sean helped his mother sit up.

"Yeah, except I have the worst headache of my life." Her hand went up to her temple.

"Your loop is burned out. I think it happened to everyone." Santi knew what it was like to lose that connection to what had been.

Sean's eyes went wide. "The world mind. It's... gone. I can't feel it."

Santi frowned. "Maybe Andy, Eddy, and the others have Davian occupied."

Sean shook his head. "No, it's gone. There's... nothing there, not even that weird numb feeling." He looked up at Santi, the color draining from his face. "I think it's dead."

"If that's true...." Santi stared off toward the North Pole. Without the world mind to regulate things, they were all doomed to a long, slow death as the air and water slowly grew stale.

Sean helped his mother to her feet.

"Nothing we can do about it right now." She gazed out across the wreckage that had been Forever's first city. "People are going to wake up, and they'll need someone to lead them, to tell them it's okay."

Sean nodded. "You're right. We can deal with what comes later... later."

Santi helped them out of the gondola. "It looks like the old mess hall survived." He pointed to the low-slung building that sat between the town square and the lake. "Let's set up camp there. We can see about getting this recovery jump-started."

"Good idea. Deal with what we can." Keera started off.

Sean lagged behind. "Do you think she's okay? *They're* okay?"

Santi bit his lip. "I do," he said at last. "Andy and Eddy will find a way to get through this and get back home to us."

Sean hugged him. "Thanks. I needed to hear that."

Santi had needed to say it too.

Half an hour later, Santi and the others were getting the old mess hall into shape to serve as an emergency center.

He and Sean picked up a table to move it into the middle of the room.

Sean stopped in midlift and set his end down.

"What happened?" Santi set his end down too.

Sean didn't respond at first. "Can you feel that?" he asked finally.

"What is it?" Santi asked.

"It's the world mind." Sean frowned. "Or... no, it's not."

"Is it Davian?" Santi feared the answer. After all they had gone through....

"No. It's.... Andy. Andy and Shandra." He looked at his father with a mixture of wonder and fear. "They're in the world mind. Does that mean...?"

Keera crossed the space between them in an instant. "We don't know what it means yet." She pulled her son into his arms. "It means for sure that they're still with us."

Santi nodded. What the hell had happened out there? And what about Eddy and Marissa? And Aaron and Jayson?

ANDY OPENED HER EYES.

"Hey there, you okay?" Eddy was kneeling in front of her. Marissa was next to him, along with Aaron.

"What happened?" She looked around wildly at the chamber. "Did we fail?"

She was propped up against the wall, staring at the burgeoning seed. It was growing rapidly.

Shandra sat next to her, her head on Andy's shoulder.

*What the hell?* "How are we still alive?"

Marissa grinned. "I found another way."

Shandra mumbled something.

"Hey, gorgeous." Andy caressed her face.

Shandra's eyes opened. "What happened?" she asked groggily. She sat up and winced, touching her broken leg.

They both turned to Marissa.

Marissa looked back at the seed, and then at the two women. "When the time came, I realized I didn't have to transfer you. So I copied you instead—your memories, emotions, thoughts, all of it."

Andy's mouth dropped open. "A copy?"

"You were right. You two are the ones we needed to guide the world mind. But some of us needed you here too."

Andy started to cry. She'd been sure her life with her friends, her family, was over. Sure she would never hold these beautiful people in her arms again. She'd been ready to pay that price, for the good of the world.

Now... now she could see her Liminal kids grow up. Hold their children in her arms. Finish out her life among the living.

She reached out and touched Marissa's belly, feeling the new life within, and a spark of understanding passed between them. Marissa lunged forward and hugged her, and there wasn't a dry eye in the room.

Aaron knelt beside her, cupping her chin in his hands. "You'll always be my little girl." His eyes were wet, but he wiped them with the back of his hand.

"I love you, Daddy."

He kissed her forehead. "After your Uncle Jayson passed... I couldn't have borne it if you had gone too." He reached up and pulled the silver chain from around his neck. "This belonged to your grandfather. A priest gave it to him on the day of my confirmation."

"Confirmation?"

He nodded. "It was a religious ceremony in the church. He lost it when he... when he died. But Ana gave it back to me." He put the chain over her head.

She put her hand over it. "It's beautiful. But I'm not religious—"

He nodded. "I know. But it was your grandfather's. It belongs with you." He squeezed her hand. "We're part of a long, proud line, you and me. I am so proud of you." He put his arms around her, and she felt safe and warm and five years old again.

As she hugged her father, she stared at the seed.

Having a doppelgänger in the world mind was going to take getting used to. She wondered if other-her knew yet?

Still, it was a small price to pay for life.

SANTI WAS LADLING out soup to yet another refugee. They were coming in as fast as they could be fed, and Keera was organizing those who were in decent shape to start caring for the others—finding suitable temporary housing, treating wounds, making meals, and getting the city back up and running.

It would take time—a lot of time. But now that Davian was gone, it would get done. And they'd find new ways to do things, better ways.

He'd been right. All the loops had been burned out in the final battle between Davian and the others. While it still wasn't clear what had happened, he knew all their lives would have to change now. One of the last bits of Old Earth was gone.

Sean touched his shoulder. "Can I talk to you?"

"Sure." Santi pulled Olly Forbes over to serve in his place. "I'll be right back."

Olly nodded.

Sean took him outside.

"What's up?"

Sean put his hands on Santi's cheeks, and for a moment, he thought the boy was going to kiss him. Instead, Sean closed his eyes.

"Santi?"

Santi closed his eyes and heard Eddy's voice in his head. "Oh my God, is that really you?"

"Yeah. We're okay. They did it! They destroyed Davian and the old world mind."

"*Old* world mind?"

"I'll explain later. There are two Andys now, and two Shandras. And a new world mind."

"What does that even mean?"

"We're all okay. That's all you need to know. How are things there?"

"The town is a mess, but most everyone survived. We think Davian was keeping them safe to use them later as slaves."

"Thank God."

Santi could almost *see* Eddy's look of relief.

"Shandra broke her leg. Andy and Marissa set it, but she's gonna need some medical care when we get home. And Aaron's here."

"What about Jayson?"

"No. He... he didn't make it."

"I'm sorry."

"He gave himself to save the rest of us."

Santi whistled. "You'll have to tell me all about it when you come home. We're getting things organized on this end. I'll find someone to look after Shandra when she arrives."

"Marissa says hi, by the way."

Santi laughed. "So does Sean." *I could get used to this kind of communication.*

"So how *are* you getting home? We *need* you here. You *are* the mayor, after all. This place is going to take a lot of work to get back into shape."

This time Santi could feel Eddy's grin. "I was kind of hoping you'd come give us a ride?"

# EPILOGUE

ANDY RODE up the pathway to the McAvery-Trip estate. Shandra had offered to come with her, but she had wanted to make this journey alone, in memory of the dear man who had brought her out there so many years before.

They'd settled into an apartment in Darlith. After so many years in the middle of nowhere at the schoolhouse, it was nice to be in the heart of things once again. And it was a good place to raise their daughter.

Andy rubbed her stomach. In another five months, she would welcome a new life into the world, with Eddy's help. A little girl who would be surrounded by people who loved and adored her. They had decided to name her Bella.

Six months after the Great Storm, the city was starting to get back to normal. Somehow, her sculpture of Old Earth had survived the tempest, and now the town square teemed with life every day as an open-air market provided a place for the city's once-again thriving trade.

Her Liminals were having to find their way in the new world too. Their abilities had been mostly proscribed under the new order. It was Lanya's doing. They had tinkered with the new seed's genetics and had locked out many of the Liminal kids' abilities in the process. For now. Who knew what course their evolution would take?

They could still use vee space and reach one another through the world mind, no small thing. But no more could they call upon the world roots or transfer human minds into it.

That was way too dangerous.

Andy dismounted and tied Dandi up to a post outside of Trip's house.

So strange to think of it as Trip's and not Colin's, though it had been years and years since Colin had left the mortal life. Andy would always remember Colin waiting for her on that porch, wearing a robe and bunny slippers.

Which brought her to the reason she was there.

*Andy?* Her own voice spoke in her head.

*Hey, Andy*, she replied. She could hear the laughter behind her own voice.

That had been a shock for both of them, but she was getting used to it. *Are we ready?*

*Ready as we'll ever be.*

The flesh and blood Andy knocked on the door.

There was a shuffling inside, and then the door opened.

Trip was much older now but still handsome, his white hair and beard trimmed neatly. He had to be in his eighties. "Andy!" A grin spread across his face. "What a surprise. Come on in!"

Andy followed him inside. "How are you, Trip?"

"Doing okay. I have a couple farmhands now to help me with the place. They're off at the Market in Darlith today." He gestured to her to take a seat. "Can I get you something to drink?"

"Just some red berry juice, if you have it."

"I do. No ice, though."

She laughed. It was an old joke between them. "No ice is fine."

He came back with an old glass cup. "Brought these up from Earth, back in the day. Only three of them left now."

"Thanks." She took a sip. "Ooooh, that's marvelous." She did miss ice, but her palate had gotten used to it by now. "I brought you something."

"Really? That was kind of you."

She came to sit next to him and put her hands on the sides of his face. "Close your eyes."

He did. "What kind of present is it?"

"A little message from Colin." She showed him.

. . .

"Hey, Trip. I never got to say a proper goodbye. I know this is a poor substitute, but I wanted you to know that I never forgot you." Colin paused to wipe his eyes. "I know Andy will find a way to get this to you. You were the love of my life, and I'm proud to have called you husband, partner, and friend. You were always the one."

Andy let go.

Trip's face was wet with tears. "Thank you. How did you—"

"It's something the new world mind found and asked me to bring to you."

He accepted that without question and squeezed her hand. "It means so much to me to hear his voice one more time."

Andy spent the afternoon with him. They talked about Colin, about the estate, and about Earth.

When it was time to go, she accepted a batch of red berries to take back home to Shandra.

They stood on the porch in the late-afternoon glow.

"He loved you like a daughter, you know."

Andy nodded. "I miss him. He would have been a grandfather soon." She rubbed her belly.

"I wondered, but I didn't want to ask." He smiled in delight. "That's wonderful!"

She gave Trip a hug and then untied Dandi and climbed onto her saddle.

Trip put a hand on her knee. "You're always welcome, if you feel like keeping an old man company."

"I'd like that. I'll come to see you again soon." Andy blew him a kiss and started back on the road to Darlith, Shandra, and home.

# ABOUT THE AUTHOR

I live with my husband of 28 years in a Sacramento, California suburb, in a little yellow house with a brick fireplace and a couple pink flamingoes.

As a writer, I've always lived between *here and now* and *what could be*. Indoctrinated into fantasy-sci fi by my mother at the tender age of nine, I devoured her library. But as I grew up and read the golden age classics and modern works, I began to wonder where the people like me were.

After I came out at twenty three, I decided it was time to create stories I couldn't find at Waldenbooks. If there weren't many gay characters in my favorite genres, I would reimagine them myself, populating them with men who loved men. I would subvert them and remake them to my own ends. And if I was lucky enough, someone else would want to read them.

My friends say my brain works a little differently - I sees relationships between things that others miss, and get more done in a day than most folks manage in a week. Although I was born an introvert, I learned to reach outside himself and connect with others like me.

I write stories that subvert expectations, and transform sci fi, fantasy, and contemporary worlds into something new and unexpected. I run both Queer Sci Fi and QueeRomance Ink with Mark, sites that bring people like us together to promote and celebrate fiction that reflects us.

I was recognized as one of the top new gay authors in the 2017 Rainbow Awards, and my debut novel "Skythane" received two awards. In 2019, I won Rainbow Awards for three other books, and became full member of the Science Fiction and Fantasy Writers of America in 2020.

My writing, whether queer romance or genre fiction (or a little bit of both) brings LGBTQ+ energy to my stories, infusing them with love, beauty and power and making them soar. I imagine a world that *could be*, and in the process, maybe changes the world that is just a little.

# GLOSSARY

**43 Ariadne:** Asteroid used to start Forever

**Aaron Hammond:** Jackson and Glory's oldest; Director of Forever Project

**Agartha:** The world under the mountain that Davian and Gunner built

**Alberto:** One of the Liminal kids

**Alifir Trees:** "Native" Forever trees, piney scent

**Allied African States:** Union of African nations

**AmSplor:** The space arm of the NAU

**AnaLex:** The combined minds of Ana and Lex; see also Lanya

**Anastasia Anatov:** Crew on the *Dressler*, doctor/geneticist

**Anatov Mountains:** between Darlith and Micavery, formerly Dragon's Reach

**Andrissa "Andy" Hammond:** Daughter of Aaron Hammond

**Bella:** Andy and Shandra's daughter

**Biodrones:** Small drones created by the world mind

**Biomind:** Artificially grown minds

**Brad Evers:** Community ambassador at the refugee camp, later a deputy

**Candra:** Part owner of the cleaners where Andy stays when in Darlith

**Captain Trip Tanner:** Captain of the Herald; Colin's lover, later husband

**Cassiopeia aka Cassie:** Eddy's horse

**Cave Cheese:** Cheese grown using the fungus found in Forever's caves

**Chafs:** Derogatory name for the Cino-African Syndicate troops

**Chris:** One of the Liminal kids

**Cino-African Syndicate (CAS):** China / African nation alliance

**Clearing:** Removing the mind fog from those afflicted by Gunner's control

**Colin Dale:** Son of Marissa and Matt (Matthew)

**Colin McAvery:** Captain of the Dressler, later Transfer Station director

**Collapse, The:** The end of the Earth

**Crons:** Currency/coin on Forever/Ariadne

**Dania Thorpe:** Personnel manager at McAvery Port, Micavry city manager

**Danny:** One of the oldest of the Liminal kids

**Dark Day:** The day Davian first tried to take over the world

**Darlith:** Second town built within Forever

**Davian "Dav" Forrester:** Eddy's ex and a systems specialist

**Delancy:** One of the oldest Liminal kids who also has a gift for woodworking

**Delia:** Andy's ex-girlfriend

**Devon Powell:** Member of the McAvery Port team

**Dimensionals:** 3-D entertainment shows

**Dipping:** Interfacing with Forever's mind, more intense than Transfer

**Dissolution Pit:** Where bodies are dissolved into component parts upon death

**Dressler:** Mission-class ship

**East:** Facing North, to the right

**Eddy Tremaine:** Former military (NAU Marine Corps), formerly Evalyne

**Embassy District:** Part of McAvery Port

**Estate:** Colin and Trip's retreat

**Fabrication Center:** Factory where the world mind crafts needed supplies in conjunction with the colonists

**Far Hold (aka North Pole):** The station that controls the building of Forever

**Fargo Port:** Launch port for AmSplor

**Fargo:** Capitol of the NAU

**First District:** The land from the South Pole to the Anatov Mountains, including Micavery

**First Light:** Advance of light in the morning on Forever

**Forever:** Common name for Ariadne, the seedling world

**Frontier:** Earth's primary space station

**Ghosts:** Supposed supernatural beings held responsible for petty theft and other issues on Forever

**Gia Rand:** Rancher on the Verge
**Giorgio:** One of the Liminal kids
**Gloria "Glory" Hammond:** Jackson's wife, Aaron's mother
**Gordy:** Kid who worked for the Red Badge in New York City
**Groundfowl:** Flightless birds engineered for Forever
**Gunner:** Another empath who has similar powers over the world as Andy and her family
**Harris:** One of the Liminal kids
**Home Spirits:** Home-brewed liquor of various types
**Immortals:** Lex and the humans who have transitioned into the world mind
**Jackson Hammond:** Engineer aboard the Dressler, later part of the world mind
**Jayson Hammond:** Younger son of Glory and Jackson Hammond
**Jendra Khan:** Lieutenant Officer in Micavery
**Jerrywood Bush:** A thick shrub bred for Forever, fill of dense branches
**John:** Part owner of the cleaners where Andy stays when in Darlith
**Keera Kelly:** Aaron's wife
**Knife's Edge:** Weapons store in Micavery
**Lake Jackson:** Lake on the "Southern" end of Forever, named after Jackson Hammond
**Lanya:** Ana's and Lex's combined personalities in the world mind
**Lex:** Ship-mind of the Dressler, later the World mind of Forever
**Lilith Lott:** Head of the Red Badge in New York, later was transferred into a bio mind
**Liminals (aka Liminal kids):** The first native-born generation on Forever—descendants of Jackson Hammond, who have a special ability to connect to the world mind and manipulate the world
**Long Interval:** The time between departing Earth and arriving at the other end
**Loop:** Communication device and personal assistant
**Luna Base:** The NAU base on Earth's moon
**Mallow Tree:** Tree on Forever similar to mahogany
**Mallowood:** Wood from the mallow tree; a hardwood, it is known for its red color
**Margene:** Dania Althorpe's girlfriend
**Marissa:** One of the oldest of the Liminal kids

**Matthew (Matt) Dale:** Marissa's husband

**McAvery Port:** The initial colony, later called Micavery

**Mega/Megarise:** Skyscrapers 300 stories tall or taller

**Mestra Vaughn:** Nurse who takes charge of refugee camp

**Micavery:** First town built on Forever, previously McAvery Port

**Mind War:** Another name for the Dark Sky day

**Moonjumper:** Cheap vehicle made for quick hops to and from the moon, retired around 2125

**Morning Brew (aka Embrew):** The Forever equivalent of coffee

**Night Ivy:** One of the few Forever plants that retains a slight glow at night

**North American Union (NAU):** The combined countries of Canada, USA, and Mexico

**North Pole:** Far end of Forever

**North:** In the direction of the North Pole (the far endcap)

**Null Space:** A zone where the world mind is blocked within Forever

**Nutrisynth Bar:** Nutritional bars

**Ovango Cookies:** An Earth brand of cookie

**Pantir:** Musical instrument like a violin, with an earthier sound, created by Rolly

**Phostorch:** Flashlight that uses phosphorescent materials.

**Photoplas:** Picture frame for digital photos, made from clear plas

**Plasform (Plas):** Advanced polymer used for many applications, usually clear

**Preacher:** What the residents of Agartha call Davian

**Pull:** Forcibly pulling a mind out of the world mind

**Pulse Weapon:** EMP device

**Push:** The act of creating null space by pushing a Liminal's spark out of their body

**Rafe:** Devon's on-and-off boyfriend, later his life partner

**Reach:** The act of reaching into someone else's mind by one of the Liminals

**Red Badge:** Lawless group of technophiles involved in domestic espionage and wetware arts

**Red Berries:** The Forever equivalent of raspberries

**Red Ferns:** Forever plants that glow at night, giving off a pinkish glow

**Rhyl River:** River that runs through Darlith

**Riding:** Sharing someone else's senses

**Rolly:** One of the Liminal kids, invented the pantir

**Ronan:** Transfer Station mind

**Santiago Ortiz (aka Santi):** Sheriff's deputy in Micavery, son of Dana Ortiz

**Sara Finch:** One of the women in Xanadu

**Schoolhouse Red:** Famous wine from the Schoolhouse vineyard

**Schoolhouse:** The place where Andy and Shanna teach the gifted

**Sean Hammond:** Aaron and Keera's second child and Andy's brother

**Second District:** The land from the Anatov Mountains past Darlith

**Seed Ships:** Three generation ships grown from seedlings

**Seedling:** The starter for one of the seed ships

**Shandra Clarke:** Traxx driver, later Andy's girlfriend

**Ship-Mind:** Biological mind grown to run AmSplor ships

**Skyrises:** Supertall towers in NYC

**Solos:** People who don't have the "Liminal" talent of the descendants of Jackson Hammond

**South Pole:** Transfer Station end/starting end of Forever

**South:** In the direction of the South Pole (the near endcap)

**Spindle:** Aggregation of energy and glowing pollen in the sky that stretches from pole to pole

**Superscraper:** Two-hundred-plus-story towers

**Tanner Ridge:** Ridgeline near Micavery

**Terfies:** Hallucinogenic smokes made from a dried fungus

**Terraterza:** A musical group on Earth that played trigsynth

**Thatch Hill:** Residential district on the outskirts of Micavery

**Tim:** Ex of Eddy's

**Timothy:** One of the Liminal kids

**Toby:** One of the Liminal kids

**Transfer Station:** The space station that accompanied Forever until the Collapse

**Traxx:** Ground transportation on Forever that hauls produce

**Tri dee:** The 22nd-century equivalent of TV

**Trigsynth:** a style of synth music that is heavily mathematically based

**Vee space:** the generic term for the virtual worlds within the world mind

**Verge:** The edge of human occupation before the Anatov Mountains

**Warehouse District:** Part of McAvery Port

**West:** Facing north, to the left

**World Wood:** The "root" material Forever uses as its spine, nutrient transport mechanism, and more.

**X-drive:** Small, powerful antigravity drive that allowed rapid expansion to the moon colonies

**Xanadu:** Nickname for Agartha

**York Street:** A street in Darlith

**Zach:** Owner of the Knife's Edge in Micavery

# ALSO BY J. SCOTT COATSWORTH

**Liminal Sky: Ariadne Cycle:**

The Stark Divide | The Rising Tide | The Shoreless Sea

**Liminal Sky: Oberon Cycle:**

Skythane | Lander | Ithani

**Liminal Sky: Redemption Cycle:**

Dropnauts

**Other Sci Fi/Fantasy:**

The Autumn Lands | Cailleadhama | The Great North | Homecoming | The Last Run
| Spells & Stardust Anthology | Wonderland

**Contemporary/Magical Realism:**

Between the Lines | I Only Want to Be With You | Flames (June 2021) | The River
City Chronicles | Slow Thaw

**99¢ Shorts:**

Across the Transom | The Emp Test

**Audio:**

Cailleadhama | The Stark Divide (Summer 2021) | The River City Chronicles
(Summer/Fall 2021)